NOT ALL USERS OF MAGESTONES ARE APPROVED BY THE ORDER.

Holding the bowl in one hand and the pendant in the other, Borthen stood motionless for a long moment, wrapped in deep concentration. Then he beckoned Gythe and Gwynmira to join him. "We three must be in physical contact if you are to participate in my vision," he said. "My lord, place your hand on my right shoulder, and you, milady, place yours on my left."

Gythe did as Borthen had instructed. "What are we going to see?"

"Your brother and his confederates, as they are at this very moment in time."

After a short time, Gythe became aware of a tingling in the fingers that rested on the dark mage's arm. Borthen uttered a single guttural syllable of command, and a plume of murky green smoke boiled up hissing from the bottom of the bowl. At once the walls of the surrounding room began to fade from view. For a moment, all was cloudy. Then a new scene began to take shape.

Two robed figures were sitting side by side on a large flat boulder several feet to the right of the firepit. Even as Gythe stared at them, the smaller and slighter of the pair stretched, turning his head so that his face was visible in profile. Gythe bit his tongue hard to keep from crying out in shocked disbelief.

For the face belonged to his brother, Evelake.

Also by Deborah Turner Harris
published by Tor Books
   THE MAGES OF GARILLON
   Book I *The Burning Stone*
   Book II *The Gauntlet of Malice*

SPIRAL OF FIRE

DEBORAH TURNER HARRIS

A TOM DOHERTY ASSOCIATES BOOK
NEW YORK

SPIRAL OF FIRE

Copyright © 1989 by Deborah Turner Harris

A TOR Book
Published by Tom Doherty Associates, Inc.
49 West 24 Street
New York, NY 10010

ISBN: 0-812-53954-0   Can. ISBN: 0-812-53955-9

First edition: April 1989

Printed in the United States of America

0 9 8 7 6 5 4 3 2 1

Spiral of Fire is affectionately dedicated
to Bonnie Holloway, Elaine Bradley,
Marion Fuller, and Gayla Riedley,
who have been cheering me on
from the start

With special thanks again
to Betty Ballantine for her guidance,
encouragement, and above all, patience!

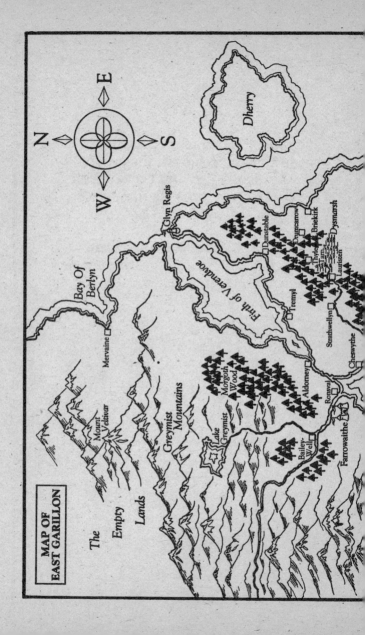

Cast of Characters

Gandian Loyalists
Devon Du Penfallon: Seneschal of Gand
Kherryn Du Penfallon: Devon's sister
Jorvald Ekhanghar: Marshall of Gand
Tessa Ekhanghar: Jorvald's daughter; commander of the
    Free Company of Gand
Owain Arillan: Tessa's esquire
Duncan Drulaine: Tessa's second-in-command
Vult Hemmling: a farmer from Rhylnie, turned outlaw
    captain
Ulbrecht Rathmuir: Kherryn's teacher, a magister from
    Ambrothen
Corwyn Ap Culross: a magister of Gand
Lliam Brynmorgan: Grand Master of Gand

Whitfauconer Alliance
Evelake Whitfauconer: rightful Lord Warden of East
    Garillon
Caradoc Penlluathe: a mage from Ambrothen
Margoth Penlluathe: Caradoc's sister
Serdor Sulamith: a minstrel from Ambrothen
Gudmar Ap Gorvald: a guild-master with the League of
    Merchant-Adventurers, captain of the *White Mer-
    maid*
Harlech Hardrada: Gudmar's good friend and fellow
    mariner, captain of the *Yusufa*
Lady Fayah: a widow living in Telphar
Mackai: Fayah's bodyguard
Jamie Greenham: pilot aboard the *White Mermaid*
Rhodri Blantyn: the *Mermaid*'s carpenter
Giles Penrith: the *Mermaid*'s sailing master
Geordi Glendowr: the *Mermaid*'s founder
Houssein: the pilot of the *Yusufa*
Aengus: a seaman aboard the *Yusufa*
Geston Du Maris: a Farrowaithe Guardsman

The Du Bors Adherents

Gythe Du Bors: Evelake's half brother, usurping Lord Warden of East Garillon

Gwynmira Du Bors: Gythe's ambitious mother

Borthen Berigeld: a renegade mage

Earlis Ap Eadric: Prior of Kirkwell; an ally of Borthen's

Muirtagh: Borthen's lieutenant

Khevyn Ap Khorrasel: Commander of the occupation army of Gand

Gervaise Du Lacque: the Du Bors ambassador to Pernatha

PROLOGUE

THE SQUAT SQUARE BUILDING THAT served the town of Abercroft for a gaol had once been a butcher's icehouse. Stone without and stone within, its grey walls, especially in summer, exuded a dank chill that was tainted with the ghostly lingering stench of spilt blood. In late October, the four bare cubicles underground were punishingly cold. Even upstairs in the guardroom, and despite the redolent presence of two charcoal braziers, the sergeant had good reason to be glad of his cloak. Technically he was in charge of the interrogation presently being carried out in one of the icy cells below.

Three of his subordinates, sitting at a dilapidated table on the north side of the room, were playing tarocco with their collars drawn up. The sergeant turned his back on them and sauntered across the room to stand over one of the braziers with hands outspread to gather the inadequate warmth rising off the embers. He was still there when the desultory conversation among the card-players was interrupted by a hollow knocking from underneath the trapdoor in the opposite corner.

At a curt gesture from the sergeant, one of the gamers at the table laid down his cards and went to raise the trap. The soldier who clambered up from below wore, like his companions, the livery of the mercenary Brotherhood of the Red Gauntlet. In response to his superior's dourly elevated eyebrow, the newcomer stiffened to attention and said, "Sir, the prisoner—he's passed out again."

The sergeant glowered at him. "So wake the rebel bastard up."

The guard squared his shoulders more firmly. "We've been trying to, sir. He isn't responding."

"Isn't he?" The sergeant surveyed his subaltern with some suspicion. "You haven't accidentally killed him, have you?"

The younger man bristled. "No, sir. We've been taking things slowly—just like you told us to."

"That's good," said his superior tartly, "because the esteemed Territorial Governor of Gand is going to demand our fundaments for fishbait if we let this one give up the ghost without first spewing out the name of his leader. Have you gotten anything out of him so far?"

"Not much, sir—beyond the admission that the rebels were directly responsible for making off with those supply wagons last week."

"As if we didn't know that already." The sergeant scowled into the middle distance, then exhaled on a note of irritable sufferance. "All right. I'll go see what—if anything—I can do with this bloody would-be martyr. You may as well stay here. Barth can give me whatever assistance I need."

Left alone with his peers, the young guardsman first warmed himself, then strolled over to the table where a new game was just beginning. The senior member of the group, an ensign with a ginger mustache, indicated a vacant stool off to one side. "Don't just stand there, take a seat. You want us to deal you in?"

The young guardsman shook his head. His eyes were hot. "Stiff-necked son of a bitch," he muttered resentfully, with a darkling glance in the general direction of the trapdoor to the cell holding the prisoner they had captured earlier that day. When his companions looked up from their cards, he continued angrily, "We're never going to get anywhere at this rate. Why doesn't Berrick stop playing around and put the fire to the rogue? Offer to singe his manhood for him, and I bet he'll sing like a canary in a cage."

"Don't be too sure about that," said the ensign. "These Gandian rebels are a fanatical lot, and fanatics are a queer breed. Too much pain all at once, and they just clam up and die on you. Take your time, and eventually you can bring 'em to their senses."

"Tell that to Lord Khevyn," grumbled one of the other men-at-arms. "His High-and-Mightiness is getting just a bit impatient over all these hit-and-run raids."

The ensign shrugged. "Fortunes of war. You don't march in with an army and seize control of a city the size of Gand without making some enemies. Pity his own lads couldn't have taken the castle as well the same night."

He blew air gustily through his nose. "I'm damned glad I wasn't there. By all accounts Black Khevyn was mad enough to chew nails and spit rust. He didn't come prepared for a siege campaign, and now he's having to wait around for ordnance and reinforcements with this mongrel pack of self-appointed watchdogs nipping at his tail every chance they get. Thank your lucky stars, boys, that we're out chasing rebels, instead of squatting on our hurdies outside the walls of Gand Castle."

The guardsman sitting opposite him scratched his chin through his beard. "Do we know anything at all about the man who's supposed to be directing the activities of these outlaws?"

The ensign grimaced. "Not much—apart from the fact that he's said to be tall and lean, and probably fair-haired. It would certainly make our job a whole lot easier if we could come by a name to hang the description on—"

A knock at the outside door set all four men groping reflexively for their sword hilts. "Daffyd! Go see who that is," snapped the ensign.

The guardsman with the beard leaped up and went to unlatch the peephole panel in the upper half of the heavy slab-oak portal. He peered out warily, then relaxed. "It's all right," he called over his shoulder. "It's only the innkeeper's wench with our supper."

The ensign glanced obliquely around at his companions. "Is she alone?"

Daffyd took a second look. "No, there's an old geezer with her—fusty old bird with only one leg."

The clean-shaven young guard curled a lip. "Most likely her father, coming along to make sure we don't tamper with his daughter's virtue."

His colleague by the door pulled a face. "He could easily have saved himself the trouble. You'd get more satisfaction cuddling a garden rake than you would taking a tumble with this one."

"Plain, is she? Just our luck," said the ensign with mordant resignation. "All right. Unbar the door and let 'em come in before the grub gets cold."

The innkeeper's daughter was first into the room, balancing a covered tray from which steam and the smell of stew was rising. Conspicuously taller than average, she wore her ill-fitting homespun gown with the stilted angularity of a stick-insect, and the short slatternly wisps of hair escaping from under her kerchief were an indeterminate shade of pale. Once across the threshold, she lurched to an awkward standstill, gazing dully about her in slack-jawed stupidity. Hobbling in behind her on his wooden peg leg, the grey-bearded companion clucked his tongue in exasperation and gave her elbow an admonitory tap. "Don't just stand there gawking, lass," he chided. "You go set your tray down on that table over there, and mind you don't tread on anyone's feet while you're about it."

The girl blinked slowly, almost like a sleepwalker, then shambled obediently into motion again. Seeing the expressions on the faces of the four men-at-arms, the old man gave a dry cackle of laughter. "Bit slow in her wits is our Tassie," he explained, "but she's strong and she's biddable, eh?"

The three men still seated hastily edged their stools aside as the tall girl with the vacant blue eyes lumbered past them and set down her burden on the tabletop with a dull chink of crockery. "That's a good girl," said her mentor approvingly, coming up behind her. "Now you go wait over there out of the way until I'm finished serving these gentlemen—"

"Thank you, but we'll serve ourselves," said the ensign curtly, thrusting aside the old man's outstretched arm. "You take that half-witted doxy of yours and go home."

The old man blinked. "Yes, sir. But what about my crockery?"

"You can call back for it in the morning," said the ensign caustically. "Now do yourself a favor and take yourself off."

The old man nervously knuckled an eyebrow and backed away. The girl shuffled docilely after him. The guardsman with the beard grinned at them from the threshold. "Don't worry. We'll call you if there's anything else we want," he said, and took hold of the door handle.

In the same instant, someone on the outside drove the door open with a kick like a mule's.

Figures, armed and masked, lunged for the gap. The old man gave a bleat of fright and dived out of their way as they charged into the room. One of them caught the girl by the elbows and spun her into the arms of the bearded guardsman as he leaped to intercept them. Her flying skirts fouled his legs, and he pitched to the floor with her screaming weight on top of him.

Booted feet hammered past him. Weapons clashed harshly amid panted surprise and profanity. Cursing vehemently, the bearded guard tried to hurl the woman off him, but she was thrashing about in a brute frenzy of dull-witted panic. Even as he struggled to free one of his arms long enough to deliver a knock-out punch, an elbow sharp as an adze cracked him in the mouth. The impact of his head against flagstone was the last thing he remembered.

Down below in the interrogation cell, Sergeant Berrick started up at the sudden muffled crash of furniture being overturned. "Barth! Stay here with

the prisoner!" he ordered sharply, and bolted from
the cubicle, leaving his subordinate fumbling for his
weapon.

Outside in the narrow passageway the sounds of a
brawl were clearly audible. The sergeant drew his sword
and raced for the steps leading up to the ground floor. In
the same instant, someone wrenched open the trapdoor
in the ceiling, and a shape that was more or less female
clumbered down through the gap in an untidy flurry of
skirts.

Two masked men plunged after her. The girl gave a
hoarse squawk of alarm and dived off the steps in a
clumsy attempt to elude her pursuers. Berrick caught a
fleeting impression of wide blue eyes and a gaping O of a
mouth before she lost her balance on impact and tumbled to the floor in front of him, arms flailing like the
wings of a plucked hen.

The masked men following hard on her heels had
steel in their hands. Dismissing for the moment the
question of who the girl might be, Berrick plucked
her out of his path with his free hand and strode
grimly forward to meet the invaders. Blue sparks flew
as three blades clanged off one another in a flurry of
ripostes.

Leaving the mercenary sergeant to the offices of her
two henchmen, Lady Tessa Ekhanghar, commander of
the Free Company of Gandia, rolled out of harm's way
and picked herself smartly up off the floor. Pausing only
long enough to pluck a long dagger from the sheath
concealed beneath her petticoat, she made a feline
bound for the half-open door at the end of the passage,
and came face to face with three feet of naked broadsword.

The guardsman holding the weapon was not expecting a woman. Tessa caught the underside of his blade on
the cross-guard of her poniard and whipped the sword
aside so that its edge bit into the wood of the doorframe.
A kick in the abdomen drove the man back in a clangor

of chain mail, but he kept his grip on his sword hilt. Even as Tessa dropped warily into a fencer's crouch, there was a loud twang from the open doorway behind her, and a crossbow bolt, fired at point-blank range, sent her prospective adversary crashing into the opposite wall in a thin spatter of blood.

Tessa didn't bother to look back. Leaving her peg-legged associate to deal with his victim as he saw fit, she sprang for the left-hand wall where a sandy-haired young man hung limp from one shackled wrist.

The other hand, dangling helpless at his side, was a contorted knot of broken fingers. Using her own shoulder as a prop, Tessa carefully eased him upright. "Owain!" she called with quiet urgency. "Owain, can you hear me?"

Her squire's shadowed eyelids flickered, and she caught a feverish glint of blue between his short, thick lashes. His sweat-soaked forehead contracted in a frown. "M-milady?" he faltered.

"I'm glad you still know me, in spite of this idiotic wimple." Tessa slipped a gentle supporting hand under the young man's drooping chin. "Go ahead and lean on me. I promise you I won't break."

Instead of obeying, Owain made a move as if to stand unaided, then caught his breath sharply as his injured hand brushed the wall. After two hoarse gulps of air, he said raggedly, "There were a dozen soldiers lying in wait for us when we got to the rendezvous point. Lorian—"

"Got away safely. She's the one who brought us the news that you'd been arrested and were being held for questioning." Tessa kept her voice steady, despite the effort she was making not to be sick.

The injured man shuddered under the spur of physical pain. He said haltingly, "I've got news for you: the hostages Black Khevyn demanded from the burghers of Gand are going to be taken under guard to Farrowaithe, there to be turned over to the Dowager-

Regent. The party . . . leaves tomorrow. By the Cheswythe road . . ."

He slumped against her, unable to say any more. But he had already told Tessa enough. "You've done well," she said quietly. "The rest of us can take it from here."

Something jangled next to her ear. She turned to find that her peg-legged counterpart had finished searching his victim. "Here's the key to those gyves," said Duncan Drulaine, flourishing the implement before her eyes. "We'd better hurry up and get out of here. Seth reports there's another detachment of soldiers approaching the town along the east road."

They freed the prisoner swiftly. Between them they half dragged, half carried him to the ladder where some of his fellow foresters were waiting to lift him out. Horses were standing ready at the door. "Blaine! Britric! Take Owain to Tavistock," ordered Tessa. "The mage there will take care of him, no questions asked. The rest of you know your instructions. Duncan and I will meet you at the rendezvous point tomorrow morning . . ."

The party broke up speedily and went their separate ways. As the hoofbeats thundered away into the night, Duncan turned to Tessa. "So what's it to be for us, Captain?" he asked.

"We ride to Rhylnie," said Tessa thinly. "I have a feeling Vult Hemmling and his men will have something to say about hostages being marched east through their territory."

THE PLAGUE-BEARER

THE PERNATHAN SEAPORT OF GHAZARAH was a city of terraces. Looped in a close crescent about the zircon-blue basin of the harbor, the shops and taverns, hostels, houses and gardens rose steeply tier above tier from the water's edge to the top of the cliff that sheltered the bay from the east. Seen from the waterfront, all white walls and red roofs, Ghazarah by day looked like an elaborate sculpture in sugar and cinnamon. After sunset, lit by strings of lamps, it looked like a haven for fireflies dancing in the dark.

Even though it was late in October, the night was mild. Down by the quayside, taverna owners threw open their doors and shutters to catch the light breezes that drifted in off the sea. Rough laughter and the harsh twang of chitarras spilled out into the darkness where the usual nighttime assortment of sailors and stevedores, hawkers, idlers, and prostitutes roved from street to street in pursuit of business or pleasure. When two men in dark clothing emerged from a shadowy side alley to join the general throng, they attracted no more than a few disinterested glances from the other passersby.

The big man in Garillan clothing and his small wiry associate followed the uneven line of the mole until they came to a salt-eroded flight of stairs leading down to the water. Two oarsmen in a ship's cockboat were waiting for them at the bottom of the steps. As soon as the big man and his companion had taken their seats, the rowers pushed off from the landing. Oar-strokes muted, they struck out through the floating press of Garillan merchantmen and native dromonds toward a sleek black caravel anchored just inside the breakwaters that marked the boundary of the bay.

They arrived in a pale ripple of foam. At a whistled signal from one of the oarsmen, anonymous hands lowered a stout rope ladder over the *Night-Raven*'s portside railing. The big man riding in the stern of the cockboat was the first to make the ascent, his massive weight dragging the ropes perilously taut. As he heaved his muscular bulk heavily on board, the *Raven*'s captain came forward to greet him. "Here's a piece of news for you, Muirtagh: the *Yusufa*'s crew took on their last load of provisions just before sunset. It looks as if they're expecting to set sail soon—maybe even tonight. Do you want me to have the hands standing by in case we have to raise anchor in a hurry?"

"We'll see." Muirtagh's broad, flat-featured face was impassive as ever. "I'm going to my cabin. Keep an eye on our visitor till I send for him."

The *Night-Raven*'s captain stole a glance over the rail. "Who is he?"

Muirtagh shrugged a massive shoulder. "A thief. Somebody Kislar dug up. If you want his name, you can get it from him."

"What do we want with a thief?"

Muirtagh's pebble-colored eyes were opaque as two chips of slate. "When that becomes any concern of yours, you'll be told about it," he growled. "Give him food if he wants it, but no drink, understand? And make sure I'm not disturbed for the next half hour . . ."

The open windows of the *Night-Raven*'s great stern cabin afforded a panoramic view of the lights along the shore, seen through the black latticework of neighboring spars and rigging. Muirtagh paused to lock the cabin door behind him. After pocketing the key, he made his stooped way across the room to close first the casements and then the shutters, plunging the room into sudden stagnant warmth.

The ensuing silence was broken only by the dull creaking of the ship's timbers and the hiss of hot oil burning away in the lamp suspended from the ceiling. Muirtagh withdrew from the windows and went to seat himself at the table under the lantern. Flanked by his own mammoth shadow, he reached into the breast of his jerkin and drew out a small packet wrapped in soft chamois. His coarse fingers unusually delicate, he gingerly peeled the wrappings away to expose an orb made of something that looked like pale green crystal.

Slightly larger than a hen's egg, the orb glimmered unctuously in the lamplight, as though it had been dipped in oil before being exposed to the air. Initially it was icy cold to the touch. Cradling the stone between his broad callused palms, Muirtagh bent his head to gaze fixedly into its pale murky depths. For several minutes nothing happened. Then, as the orb warmed to the heat of the big man's flesh, the clouds inside of it began to dissipate.

For the space of a few heartbeats, it seemed to Muirtagh as if he were peering down into a bottomless void. The accompanying sense of vertigo was something he had experienced before; even so, beads of cold sweat broke out along his hairline. He drew breath to steady his hands. As he did so, a dense black mote appeared in the midst of the nothingness at the center of the crystal.

Initially remote, like some black bird of prey suspended in flight against the sun, the distant fleck of darkness began to converge, growing larger as it advanced until the interior of the orb seemed full of shadow. As Muirtagh continued to stare into the stone, the shadow began to resolve itself into a coherent image. Details sharpened until he found himself confronting a human face.

A dark, saturnine face, the patrician structure of its bones offset by an arrogant full-lipped mouth and dusky, heavy-lidded eyes. "Ah, Muirtagh—punctual as ever," said Borthen Berigeld. "Have you been in contact with Kislar Al Khaffir?"

"Aye. He was able to buy us a sorry enough bit of gaol bait for what you've got in mind." Muirtagh curled a sneering lip. "The winkle-picker was all set to be executed in the morning, so you can bet *he* wasn't going to ask any questions. I brought him on board a few minutes ago."

"Good." Borthen's tone was unusually clipped. "Has he received the mark yet?"

"Aye. I took care of that." Muirtagh was watching his employer's inflexible face. "He's all ready. We can plant him aboard the *Yusufa* whenever you like."

"Excellent," said Borthen. "Send him across tonight."

"Tonight?" Muirtagh was startled out of his habitual phlegm.

"That's what I said." Borthen's black gaze showed glints of cold viciousness. He was looking unwontedly haggard.

"So you still haven't figured out what went wrong," said Muirtagh.

This bald statement of fact earned him a glance like a dagger thrust. "Not yet," said Borthen with chill emphasis. "And until I do, I want to make sure that *nobody* leaves Ghazarah after tonight—beginning with the crew of the *Yusufa* . . ."

The tide was due to turn an hour past midnight. Even as the current reached the high-water marks all along the bay-front, the *Night-Raven*'s cockboat returned to the water for another journey.

The sky was cloudless but hazy. Less than a week past the full, the rising moon cast light enough to open up deep wells of shadow between one ship's hull and the next. Squatting on skinny haunches in the bow of the cockboat, the convicted thief Durbak peered nervously ahead of him as the men at the oars eased their light craft stealthily from darkness to darkness.

The noisome stink of the oubliette still clung to his clothing, reminding him that only hours ago he had lain groveling in the rank straw of his cell, paralyzed with horror at the knowledge that he was soon to face execution by dismemberment. No prisoner, he realized, snatched from the very jaws of death as he had been, had any right to quarrel with the conditions attending his reprieve. Nevertheless, thinking back over all that had happened in the short time since he had been released,

Durbak could not repress a small shiver of uneasiness.

His uneasiness had little to do in principle with the fact that he now found himself expected to carry out a theft on behalf of the man who had secured his release. The instructions Durbak had been given on that account were clear enough: he was to sneak aboard the galleass *Yusufa*, rifle the captain's strongbox, and abstract from it a sheaf of documents which he was subsequently to deliver to his employer. What Durbak found difficult to understand was why he had been chosen for the mission in the first place. A skeptic could argue that anyone previously convicted of thievery might well be somewhat lacking in competence.

Then there was the curious business of the tattoo. Squinting down at his bony chest, Durbak could just make out the strange red glyph that had been etched on his skin earlier that evening. The big Garillan merchant named Muirtagh had let it be known in no uncertain terms that Durbak's release from the oubliette depended upon his consenting to receive the mark. At the time it had seemed a small price to pay for life and ultimately freedom. But Durbak couldn't help wishing he had dared to question the significance of the design.

A hand jogged his elbow from behind, disturbing his reverie. As he started round, one of the rowers thrust a small flask at him. "We're almost there," whispered the oarsman. "Orders are you're to drink that before you make your move."

Durbak eyed the bottle with misgivings. "What is it, effendi?"

His informant shrugged. "Something to steady the nerves, most likely. Muirtagh doesn't want any slipups."

"Please, effendi—"

"Drink it down," hissed the oarsman, "or we put you overboard."

"B-but effendi, I cannot swim!"

"Aye. Well. The choice is yours, ain't it?" said his informant with brutal simplicity.

Durbak swallowed hard. Then he took the flask and removed the cork.

The liquor in the flask was acrid enough to snatch the thief's breath away. The oarsman who had given him the flask sniggered unkindly. "Some potion, eh? Heads up—that's the *Yusufa* dead in front of us."

Oars neatly feathered to cut no ripples, the cockboat's crew of two sent their small craft coasting noiselessly into the inky blackness beneath the galleass's overhanging stern. When all remained quiet topside, the taller of the two men from the *Night-Raven* passed a mooring line around the *Yusufa*'s sternpost, drawing it taut so that the cockboat was braced firmly against the larger vessel's rudder. His companion stood up, weighing a steel grappling hook in his right hand. A quick accurate toss sent the implement sailing over the galleass's after-rail, trailing a stout length of rope behind it. The oarsman gave the rope an expert tug to make sure the hook was firmly grounded, then turned to Durbak. "All right, barnacle, here's where you prove your worth," he growled. "Up you go and make it quiet!"

Durbak considered the last injunction unnecessary. His heart thudding dully against his sternum beneath the arcane tracery of his fresh tattoo, he took a firm hold on the rope, bounced once to give himself momentum, and began shinning his way up toward the nearest of four square dark cabin-ports.

The shutter protecting the port was unlatched, and the window itself was ajar. Teetering perilously ten feet above the water, Durbak loosened his grip on the cable long enough to nudge the casement wide open, then swung himself feetfirst through the narrow gap.

The unlighted cabin beyond was redolent of assorted cargo smells, from peppercorns and dye-alum to turpentine and rotten oranges. Durbak crouched on the floor below the windowsill and paused a moment to listen. When his straining ears picked up no sound of anyone approaching, he fumbled in the pouch at his belt for matches and warily struck a light.

The captain's cabin was half as long as it was wide. The furnishings were sparse, limited to a box-bunk, a stout wooden table with three chairs, and a large iron-bound sea chest standing against the far wall next to a built-in cabinet. There was a branched candlestick nailed to the tabletop. Durbak appropriated one of the candlestubs, then ducked under the table to examine the drawer beneath its fly-leaf.

The drawer slid open easily, but proved to contain nothing more interesting than a bundle of sea charts and a disappointing collection of worthless oddments. The cabinet, similarly, held nothing of importance. By the time he finished rifling its contents his head was aching and he had developed a curious buzzing in his ears. Feeling feverish and unwell, he turned his attention to the sea chest.

The chest was locked. Hunkering down in front of the receptacle, he braced himself to pick the lock. The air in the cabin felt thick and close, increasing his discomfort. He gave his head a shake to clear the fog away from his eyes, then leaned forward to insert a metal pick into the lock's casing.

In the same instant, someone kicked open the cabin door.

The crash as it struck the inside wall sent Durbak diving for cover. Three burly figures shot forward to intercept him as he rolled under the table. A sinewy hand laid hold of one of his ankles. He kicked his foot loose and lunged for the open window.

He was head and shoulders over the windowsill before he realized that the cockboat from the *Night-Raven* was not waiting where it should have been. A second glance told him that in fact it was nowhere in sight. He knew a brief moment of mingled panic and indignation before strong fingers latched onto his belt and hauled him back inside.

Escorted by his captors, he was marched rudely forward, out onto the maindeck. By then, the noise of a disturbance had brought the rest of the hands topside to see what was afoot. His escort deposited him in front of the *Yusufa's* first mate. Conscious of a cold knot of nausea in the pit of his stomach, Durbak steeled himself for questioning.

They wanted to know, of course, who he was and what he had been doing in their captain's quarters. Shaky on his feet, Durbak did not need any threat of physical violence to persuade him to tell his captors whatever they might ask of him. His tongue was hot and swollen as though he had accidentally bitten down on a wasp, but he managed to pronounce his own name, along with a halting explanation for his presence. Then he tried to give them the name of the man who had sent him.

He had to draw breath twice before he succeeded in gasping out the first syllable, "Muir—" As the second syllable escaped his lips, he was transfixed by a twisting stab of excruciating pain centered in the middle of his chest.

It was almost as though his speaking Muirtagh's name had touched off the attack. Writhing in helpless anguish, Durbak bowed his head over his breastbone. There was a venomous crimson glare pulsating from the mark that had been tattooed over his heart.

The two men holding his arms leaped away from him, jabbering to each other in sudden alarm. Without the aid of their support, Durbak folded to his knees, clawing at the incandescent rune on his chest. Scarlet smoke shot hissing through his clamped fingers, lashing out like whips at the nearest bystanders.

Men howled and convulsed as the red thongs of smoke flogged the air around them. Thrashing about on the deck in the midst of a sudden wave of panic, Durbak mouthed a noiseless ongoing scream as the blood in his veins began to boil. The blood-steam erupted through his skin to feed the nightmare cloud that was expanding to engulf the ship. When at last he stopped moving, his corpse was blackened with lesions like buboes.

Within seconds the waves on either side of the galleass were chopped white with swimmers trying frantically to escape. Those left behind on the ship expired in agony, their bodies murderously drained of vitality. Swollen with death, the plague-cloud hovered for a moment like a carrion bird over a clean-picked carcass. Then slowly it began to lift.

Its vaporous mass was shot through with capillaries of dark red shadow that pulsed like blood vessels. Abandoning the lifeless hulk that had been the *Yusufa*, the cloud swept over the ship's forecastle and rolled turgidly after the men in the water as they threshed their way toward the shoreline.

Its advancing presence cast an eerie glimmer over the foam kicked up by the swimmers. Men dived for the sanctuary of deeper water, only to be forced up again when the oxygen in their lungs gave out. They surfaced, inescapably, into the blood-red glare of the death-cloud, and perished with their first intake of breath. The cloud sucked their bodies dry and left the corpses floating in its wake as it surged on, seeking new prey among the other vessels that lay anchored between the *Yusufa* and the shore.

Then, bloated as a vampire, it carried on toward the sleeping precincts of the Ghazaran waterfront.

By then, the black caravel *Night-Raven* was well out to sea. Not even Muirtagh guessed the extent of the carnage his ship had left behind it. Running fast before the wind, the caravel turned her prow westward on the first leg of the voyage that would take her to the East Garillan city of Tyrantir.

DANGEROUS SUMMONS

Dusk fell early on All Hallows Eve, throwing the cold purple shadow of Mount Cormallon over all the upland vale of Dyrnhallow. As the wan autumn light faded and died, grey mists began to gather on the heights, rising like spirits of the drowned out of the many hidden pools and water-courses. The mist-patches drifted noiselessly down the mountainside, meeting and merging in the hollows. Within the space of an hour, the whole mountaintop was blanketed behind a silent, impenetrable wall of cloud.

Thick and dank as the exhalations of a peat bog, the fog continued to build as it moved farther down into the valley. In the town of Dyrnhallow itself, people hastened inside to close shutters and bolt doors. A mile above the town, perched on the outflung knee of the mountain, the Hospitallers' abbey of Llewyscairn was visible for a time as an isolated island of lights in an ocean of fog. Then the rising mist overwhelmed it, and it sank from view like a ship foundering at sea.

If any of the members of the Llewyscairn community considered the fog unusual or uncanny, they did not allow their apprehensions to interfere with their duties. Punctually at seven o'clock the resident mages and novices gathered in the abbey's chapel to celebrate All Hallows mass. Normally the sacrament would have been administered by Llewyscairn's Magister General. On this occasion, however, the mage-superior had willingly yielded precedence to his honored guest, Earlis Ap Eadric, Prior of Kirkwell and Inquisitor of Farrowaithe.

His Eminence the Inquisitor was a frequent visitor to Llewyscairn, drawn there by the special nature of the abbey's library, which boasted the most comprehensive collection of arcane books to be found in all East Garillon. Most of these were locked away in the undercroft of the library, safely out of reach of curious neophytes, but those whose interest in such ordinarily forbidden matters was sanctioned by episcopal authority could browse freely among the holdings there. Earlis had found the Llewyscairn library a treasure trove of information.

It also held other secrets, as disturbing as the contents of the restricted books. Following the completion of mass, Earlis returned to the apartment that had been assigned to him, there to await an expected visitation.

The fruits of two days' worth of intensive research lay scattered across the wooden worktable facing the window. In the midst of the litter of books and loose manuscripts squatted a small iron-bound chest. Earlis locked the door behind him and went to seat himself at the table. He stared at the chest for a moment, then raised the lid.

The assortment of items inside had been acquired from many sources over many years: a bone-handled dagger whose serpent blade had been forged from the iron heart of a meteor; a bowl fashioned from the inverted skull of a murdered child; a stole and chasuble sewn from human skin; a medallion cast in lead and brass in obscene phallic parody of the Hospitallers' star. All were perverted counterparts to sacred vessels and sacramental vestures. And all were intended to be used that very night in the performance of a blasphemous Rite of Summoning.

No one knew better than Earlis how dangerous such a ceremony might prove. In attempting to call a spirit into the material world, the summoner pitted his own strength against that of the entity he was seeking to dominate. If he hesitated—even briefly—in the midst of his conjuring, he could be seized in his turn and sucked down into the pathless realms of shadow. And if that happened, nothing on earth or in heaven could save him.

It was risky enough to seek commerce with lost souls that had once been men. Only a madman would attempt to invoke one of the true powers of darkness. A madman —or a master necromancer, confident enough of his own power to venture all in such a deadly contest of wills. But who could tell the one from the other, until the struggle was over? Gripped by rising fear and uncertainty, Earlis abruptly abandoned his inventory and reached for one of the books at his elbow.

It was an ancient thing, its leather binding crusty with age. The letters on its cover were only just readable: *On Negromancie ond ye Divers Ordres of Daemonkynde.* Earlis nudged the chest aside and set the book squarely in front of him. His refined fingers cold and trembling, he began turning pages, skimming past woodcuts and chapter headings until he arrived at the entry "Erinys."

The text seemed to leap out at him from the vellum upon which it was written:

ERINYS ys ye name bye whiche we signify ony unclaene spirite whiche doth inhabit as bye possessione a livynge personne—inne bodie, minde, ond soule—ond dwelleth thereinne to ye grete harme of yts hoste whome yt doth tormente withe foulest fantasies ond imaginings.

For yt ys saide of these unclaene spirites that they do derive theyre sustenance from alle mannere of peine ond drede visited uponne the onne possessed. Ond so yt ys that ye ERINYS doth delite to trouble yts hoste allwise, nevere suffering hym to forget the smerte of passt afflictions, alle the while prickinge hym to freshe hertesache. Fore bye these means ys ERINYS evere the mare enlarged ond made proofe against the rite of exorcisme . . .

The Prior of Kirkwell stared at the page in front of him. "It *should* have worked," he muttered distractedly. "The boy was already in a state of subjection when that thing was given charge over him. How could the brat possibly have broken free?"

"That is precisely what we are going to try and find out," said a sardonic voice from the direction of the window.

The Inquisitor of Farrowaithe looked up with a start, then dropped the book. There was a face not his own gazing back at him from the windowpane.

Earlis instinctively recoiled, then relaxed his guard as he realized that the other man was present in image only. The voice that accompanied the face spoke from the projection on the glass with characteristic acrid mockery. "You seem surprised to see me, Narcissus. Were you thinking I might change my mind about tonight?"

"I know you better than that." Earlis moistened his

lips, then smoothed back his fine silvery hair. "The time is running short. Where do you want me to meet you?"

"On the lower level, in the cavern of the cromlechs," said his contact. "You were able to procure all the necessary properties?"

"There." Earlis indicated the chest on the table.

"Excellent." The other man nodded cool approval. "I shall await your coming, eager as a bridegroom for his bride."

The image in the glass winked out like a snuffed flame. "I wish I could believe that," murmured the Prior of Kirkwell aloud. Then abruptly he turned away.

A few moments later, carrying a shuttered lantern, he slipped from his room with the chest concealed beneath the folds of a heavy cloak. He paused briefly at the head of the night stairs. When his sharp ears detected no activity below, he continued on across the corridor that led into the upper floor of the library.

The library was dark and deserted. Earlis made his way swiftly and silently to the stairway in the south wall and descended two flights of steps to the door of the basement vault. The door to the undercroft was locked, but Earlis had been issued a key by the Master of the Archives. He used that key now to let himself into a low cryptlike chamber centuries older than the stonework above ground.

When the archdiocese of Farrowaithe had commissioned the building of Llewyscairn three hundred years before, the masons in charge of laying the foundations had discovered on the site the sunken remains of an ancient vault. Since the old stonework was still sound, and since there was no evidence to suggest that the vault had ever been used as either an idol-fane or a tomb, the workmen were allowed to take advantage of it in constructing the undercroft of the library. What they never suspected, and consequently never found out, was that the vault was merely the antechamber to a vast underground labyrinth of artificial catacombs reaching into the mountain's bowels.

There were two ways to reach the catacombs. The first involved a grueling climb down a vertical chimney shaft from a concealed opening on the mountaintop. The other way was Earlis's own discovery. Stepping up now to the second of three pilasters on the west side of the room, he ran sensitive fingers over the friezework that encircled the column. Hidden gears responded with a muted growl, and a narrow rectangular panel shifted inward to reveal a cramped stone-walled tunnel.

Bringing the lantern with him, Earlis entered the tunnel and closed the panel behind him. Ahead of him, the passageway branched out to become a bewildering network of twists, turns, and junctions. Guided by marks he himself had left behind on previous excursions to this level of the maze, Earlis threaded an unerring course through the tangle of converging corridors. Circumventing several cunningly placed traps along the way, he arrived at the top of a steep stairway that plunged downward into a stagnant well of shadows. He paused to take a firmer grip on the lantern, then started to descend.

The steps were treacherous, no two of them the same height. At the bottom the floor broadened out before a tall archway leading into a second labyrinth, the walls of which were painted over with strange polymorphic designs. It cost Earlis a sustained effort of concentration to follow the clues embedded among the interlacing forms that seemed now and then to shift queasily in ways that defied analysis. Despite the dank chill of the underground chambers, he was perspiring freely by the time he finally reached the archway at the farther end of the maze.

He passed under the arch onto a stone ledge suspended midway between the roof and the floor of a vast echoing cavern. Forty feet below him, a succession of massive stone dolmens formed a circular ring fifty paces across. In the middle of the circle, dwarfed to insignificance by the brooding weight of the surrounding darkness, stood a single flickering lantern.

Earlis made his way down to floor level by means of

a sloping ramp that had been gouged out of the rock of the east wall. At the foot of the ramp he halted and cast a searching glance around him in a vain effort to penetrate the shadows on the dark side of the standing stones. "Borthen," he said. "Borthen, where are you?"

"Here," said an inimitable voice that resonated among the looming monoliths. A tall cloaked figure detached itself with feral grace from the murk at the base of one of the great dolmens and sauntered forward into the compass of the light. "Welcome, Grimalkin," said Borthen Berigeld with biting cordiality, and gestured toward the center of the stone circle. "Won't you step into my parlor?"

"Have I a choice?" Earlis gathered his cloak more tightly about his slim shoulders, his ascetic face showing its bones in the shifting glow of the lamp. He added aggrievedly, "I've put myself through a lot of trouble on your account, you know. You might at least pretend to be glad to see me."

His companion paused in the act of turning away. "Forgive me," said Borthen crisply, "but this is hardly the time or the place to indulge in effusive professions of regard. We have far too much work to do."

"*Do* we?" Earlis hung back, a sudden desperation breaking through the veneer of self-control. "Are you *sure* there's no other possible way to get at the information you want?"

"Quite sure," said his companion with chill finality. "Are you coming? Then be quick about it. We've no more time to lose . . ."

In the middle of the circle of dolmens, a great slab of basalt had been raised up on two lesser boulders to form a rude altar. Using chalk dyed red with goat's blood, the two men marked out a pentacle on the floor surrounding the stone table, and set a lighted taper at each of the symbol's five boundary points. Acrid black smoke coiled sluggishly toward the roof. Smiling down at his white-faced accomplice, Borthen ran a stroking finger lightly along the other man's strained jawline. "I am trusting you, Earlis, as I would trust no one else, to uphold me in this venture," he said softly. "You aren't going to fail me. Are you?"

The Grand Prior's eyes were bright and unblinking as those of a shrew mesmerized by a snake. "No," he said huskily. "Never, while we both live."

Borthen withdrew his hand. "Good," he said. "Then let us begin . . ."

Robed in the vestments his chosen acolyte had provided, he set a brazier of black incense to burn before him on the altar. When the air was thick with the cloying reek of decaying flowers, he threw back his head and opened wide his arms like a victim being offered up for slaughter. Drawing breath harshly, he began to chant. The opening cantrips of power rolled sonorously off his tongue in phrases that rang hard as a brazen bell.

The echoes generated by his voice seemed to take on an eerie life of their own. Standing at Borthen's right hand behind the altar, Earlis listened in frozen fascination as the guttural syllables washed over one another without seeming to dissipate. The dissonances multiplied and grew in warring intensity. Earlis was at the point of crying out in protest when Borthen abruptly let fall his arms and all the echoes died.

The stillness that followed was even more uncanny than the cacophony that had preceded it. His own mage-trained senses straining outward, Earlis became aware of a dark presence gathering beyond the confines of the vault in which he stood. The presence savored of unearthly cold and ravenous, imperishable hunger. The blood running chill in his veins, Earlis glanced nervously over at Borthen.

Borthen's eyes were fixed with blind concentration upon a point of darkness above and in front of him. As his acolyte watched, he bared his left arm from elbow to wrist and seized the sacrificial dagger in his right. Earlis snatched up the skull-bowl and stood ready. Borthen raised the dagger before him at eye level.

Poised at his full height, he entered into a second invocation. He spoke softly at first, but as the cadence of the incantation changed, his voice gained volume and power until every syllable was a dagger stroke aimed at the enveloping blackness. As his canticle shrilled to a crescendo, the hand that held the knife made a swooping pass through the air to slash open the vein at the base of his opposite wrist.

Earlis leaped to catch the blood that jetted from the gash. When the bowl was full, he placed it on the altar, then returned to whip a twist of black cloth tightly about Borthen's extended forearm. Even as the bleeding subsided, there was a sharp crackle of rending stone, and a jagged seam appeared in the face of the opposite wall.

The floor underfoot was simultaneously shivered by a series of earth-tremors. Borthen spared Earlis a brief piercing glance, then stretched forth his arms again and cried out in a voice that rolled like thunder, "Come to me, Herech Thanatos! Come, Prince of Necrophages— Dark Devourer! By Bethe and by Baphethe, and by the seven one-eyed skulls of Araphire I lay this summons upon you—and by the black flame of Guryak Zigguroth I bid you to appear!"

TEST OF STRENGTH

THE LAST WORD CRASHED LIKE a great wave against the cavern's vaulted roof. As the shivering echoes subsided, there was a raw, rending sound, like the ripping of a bone from its flesh. The rock along the seam in the wall began to crumble as the two sides of the crevice strained apart. Borthen took the sacrificial cup and stepped from behind the altar. Brandishing the vessel before him, he strode to the edge of the pentacle and set the cup down on the floor outside the boundary marked in chalk. "Here is wine, Herech Thanatos!" he called. "Come, and drink!"

There was an eldritch ululating howl, and the jagged

line in the wall was wrenched wide. Borthen leaped back within the protection of the pentacle as a darkness that was all eyes and teeth boiled out of the gap and lunged for him.

It fetched up against the rim of the pentacle with another ear-piercing howl, then wheeled and regathered over the vessel of blood. There was a slavering sound in the dim fire-shot air, before the thing swooped up again, circling the pentacle like a predatory beast. Voices thin and rough hissed in unison out of the many revolving mouths. "Who daress to call upon the ancient name of Herech Thanatoss?"

"I do!" Buffeted by foul carrion exhalations, Borthen matched challenge with challenge.

"And who art thou, rassh mortal?" sneered the chorus.

"One who seeks knowledge!" Borthen's tone conceded nothing. "I have questions that only the powers of darkness can answer."

The myriad eyes danced and flickered like mirror shards fallen among live coals. "What price art thou willing to pay for thiss knowledge?"

"The price—as you well know—is paid already!" said Borthen. "At Ghazarah, by the Rune of Samael, I gave you the lifeblood of a hundred men to drink, and you have tasted my own besides, on the threshold of the land of the living. For that blood-feast you owe me recompense. That is the law, as it is graven in the Cthonologica."

"Law?" The bloated darkness reared up until it overarched the pentacle. "There iss no law," hissed the manifold voices in sibilant contempt. "There iss only hunger . . ."

Like an insurgent tidal wave, the shadow massed, then toppled, surrounding the pentacle on all sides. Even as Borthen fought to keep his feet, the engulfing blackness erupted into a hoard of gaping mouths, sucking up to the invisible barrier like vampire bats in a feeding frenzy.

The atmospheric pressure inside the pentacle collapsed. Pinned against the altar, Earlis choked and clawed at his chest as the breath was whipped from his lungs. The sudden suffocating drain on the air brought Borthen to his knees. Breathing hard in a space that was threatening to become a vacuum, he twisted the ring on his right hand and closed his fingers tightly over the large green gemstone within the bezel.

Verdant light flared up within his grasp, strong enough to silhouette the web of his knucklebones. Hackling like a dire-wolf, Borthen braced himself and made a sharp casting motion with his ring hand. As his fingers unclenched, a bolt of green flame flew from his grasp like an assassin's dagger.

Mindlessly voracious, a dozen slavering maws converged to engorge it. As the fireball vanished into the starved belly of the void, the darkness shuddered in sudden dread premonition. The howling of the vortex subsided, to be overtaken by a deep subterranean rumble that shook the floor.

The jostling mouths of the Devourer convulsed in sudden torment, then began spewing out gouts of viridian light. Air, tainted but breathable, flooded the cavern again. Gasping, Borthen hauled himself upright.

Behind him Earlis lay slumped across the altar, blood oozing sluggishly from his nose and mouth. Standing unbowed, Borthen waited until the fiery paroxysms ceased, then smiled thinly up at his adversary. "Be warned, Herech Thanatos!" he called. "I am master of the Magia, the same celestial fire that hurled you from the Empyrean. So do not think to prevail against me. Unlike other mages, I know how to fight—and how to kill."

He raised his arm again. The demonic presence hissed at him and retreated, writhing in rage and capitulation. "Forbear, Masster of the power. What iss it that thou dosst wish uss to tell thee?"

"First this." Borthen did not lower his hand. "I committed Evelake Whitfauconer into the guardianship of an erinys. How has it come about that the boy is not only alive, but free of spiritual possession?"

The darkness surged uneasily. "The erinyss wass driven forth by one like unto thysself—a wielder of the ssacred flame."

Borthen's eyes were diamond-hard. "Who is this wielder-of-power? What name does he go by in the land of the living?"

"Caradoc . . ." The three syllables reverberated hollowly throughout the shadowy vault. "Caradoc Penlluathe . . ."

There was a steely pause. "That is a lie," said Borthen in a voice of icy calm. "Caradoc Penlluathe is only mortal. And like any other mortal, he must have a magestone if he is to enter into effective communion with the High Power. I myself took away the stone that once was his."

"That ssignifiess nothing," breathed the shadowy voices in sullen chorus. "Caradoc Penlluathe hass no need of ssuch a sstone ass thou dosst sspeak of."

Borthen's coal-black gaze held the hot, hard glow of burning anthracite. "Have a care, Herech Thanatos," he said. "No man can unlock a gate without a key—or carry water without a vessel."

The demon's corporate substance writhed uneasily. "Caradoc iss himsself the key . . . he iss the chossen vessel . . ."

"Chosen?" Borthen's tone was edged with razors. "Chosen by *whom*?"

"By the Victor . . ." rasped the legion mouths. "The One we are forbidden to name . . ."

The presence outside the pentacle retreated, shuddering and gibbering darkly to itself. As Borthen silently pondered the answers he had been given, his features paled and hardened, as though the bones beneath the fire-burnished skin had turned to iron. "Nothing comes without a price," he said with soft malice. "I have traded away mastery over my own immortal soul in exchange for knowledge, and the power to command men and spirits. Tell me, Herech Thanatos: what price did Caradoc Penlluathe have to pay to gain his power?"

"We cannot ssay. . . ."

"Why not?"

"Becausse we do not know," whispered the Devourer. "The wayss of the Immortal Wissdom are ever hidden from uss—"

"But not, I think, the ways of the underworld. The Book of the Damned lies open to you," said Borthen. "Is Caradoc's name enrolled there?"

"We have not sseen it. . . ."

Borthen's mouth tightened in a grimace of cold displeasure. "Think again, Herech Thanatos. I will not be mocked."

The demon-spirit shuddered. "We can tell thee only sso much ass iss given uss to know. Thiss mortal'ss desstiny hass not yet been decided."

"This mortal's destiny," said Borthen, "is bound up with that of the Most Holy Order of Mage Hospitallers. And I intend to be the bane of all of them."

The chilly gleam of calculation lingered on in his gaze as he surveyed the shadowy presence hovering in the gateway between two worlds. "The time to move against the Order is now, while Caradoc Penlluathe is still in exile. Herech Thanatos, I can offer you payment richer than a feast of blood, if you will consent to an alliance with me."

The darkness swelled and rippled. "Thou art flessh, Masster of Ssorcery, and we are sspirit. What have we to do with thee and thine enemies?"

"My enemies serve your Enemy," said Borthen. "Is that not reason enough for us to join forces?"

He paused a moment, then continued. "Tell me this, Prince of Necrophages: what do mortal men possess that the fallen angels do not have?"

The shadow writhed in hatred and envy. "Two things, Masster of Ssorcery: the ssanction of grace to contemplate their Creator, and the ssensibility to experience the world He made for them. . . ."

Raw with resentment, more voices rose out of the bowels of the darkness. "That world sshould have been ourss to enjoy, jusst ass men sshould have been ordained to be our sservantss. Insstead the Creator demanded that we humble oursselvess to minisster to them—ass though *we* were the inferior creaturess. Dosst thou wonder that ssome of uss chosse to rule in hell, rather than sserve in heaven?"

"No. I would have chosen to do likewise," said Borthen, "knowing that sooner or later I would find occasion to revenge myself upon my Judge, destroying what He held dear and taking by force what ought to have been mine by right."

The gleam in his half-veiled eyes matched the deep glow of his magestone as he surveyed the entity he had summoned. "The payment I am offering you, Herech Thanatos, is your chance to seek the vengeance you have long been denied. Strike a bargain with me, and I will furnish you with the means to manifest yourself physically in the world of men."

The darkness mantled like some monstrous bird of prey. "That iss not possible, mortal. It hass been decreed that our ssubsstance sshall become inchoate the moment we trespass beyond the boundariess that sset our world apart from all otherss. . . ."

"I tell you, there is a way," said Borthen. "Will you hear me out?"

There was a susurrant pause. "Yess!" breathed the Devourer. "Yess, we will hear thee. . . ."

Helplessly sprawled across the altar, Earlis was at first aware of nothing beyond a blinding pain in his head. Only as he groped his way closer to consciousness did he realise that the tooth-jarring burr in his ears was actually a colloquy divided between one voice and a chorus of many. Even as he strove to identify the single speaker, the discussion came abruptly to an end.

The ensuing moment of silence was broken by a low rumble from deep within the earth. Even as the floor underfoot began to tremble, Earlis was caught from behind by a rising gust of sulphurous air. The wind tore at his robes as it rushed past him. Then all at once all was still again.

Lying prone in the wake of the receding whirlwind, Earlis remained motionless, listening to the dry panting of his own breath. A lesser sound penetrated his breathless daze: the sound of approaching footsteps. The steps came to a halt beside him. "You can wake up now, Cock-Valiant," said Borthen Berigeld acidly. "The excitement's all over for the time being."

A sinewy hand took Earlis firmly under the chin and gave his face a light admonitory shake. The Grand Prior groaned and forced open his burning eyes. "What happened?" he stammered weakly. "Where did the demon go?"

"I sent it back to the Pit," said Borthen crisply. "Once we'd concluded our business."

Earlis gathered his aching limbs and raised himself painfully off the basalt table. "You took an awful risk," he said, and shuddered. "We might both have been killed."

Borthen shrugged. "Nothing ventured, nothing gained. In the end I got what I wanted."

"Yes. You generally do." Earlis drew a shaking hand reflexively across his mouth, then stopped short as his fingers encountered a sticky smear. He whipped his hand away and stared transfixed at the blood on his fingertips. His chest heaved. "God damn you, Borthen!" he exclaimed in a choked voice. "There isn't anything you wouldn't sacrifice to serve your purposes—including me."

Borthen lifted a winged eyebrow. "If that were true, my sweet virago, you would not now be standing here before me, free and self-possessed."

Earlis's silver-grey eyes flew wide. "You don't mean to tell me that that *thing* would have . . . ?" He swallowed hard and bit his lip.

"You see, I *do* appreciate you and your talents," said Borthen silkily.

There was a moment of silence. "Did you get the information you wanted?" asked Earlis.

"That," said Borthen, "and more."

He flung back his head so that the flickering glow of the altar lights irradiated the hard sardonic cast of his features. "It seems that we have in Caradoc Penlluathe an awkward prodigy: a hierophant who possesses free and possibly limitless access to the power of the Magia."

Earlis stared at him. "Can that really be true?"

"Our supernatural informant says so. There is no accounting," said Borthen viciously, "for divine caprice."

His expression turned speculative. "I must confess I'm surprised: Caradoc's slate is not exactly unblemished. Still, ours is not to reason why. Ours is to seek out—and if possible, to destroy."

A mirthless smile thinned his full lips. "Our precious little miracle worker won't be able to hide from me indefinitely. As long as I retain possession of his magestone, he will never be able to cut himself off from me completely. As for destroying him . . ."

The smile became wolfishly indulgent. "Elect or not, Caradoc Penlluathe can accomplish only so much on his own. Whatever other goals he may have set for himself, he is sure to need the help of his former colleagues the Hospitallers if he hopes to see Evelake Whitfauconer restored to eminence as Lord Warden of East Garillon. I have no doubt that the present Arch Mage would receive the boy and his protectors with sympathy. But that situation can readily be altered."

A taper guttered and went out. "All right," said Earlis. "What's our next move?"

"Our next move," said Borthen, "is to approach Lady Gwynmira Du Bors."

"The Regent of East Garillon?" Earlis was taken aback.

"Certainly. Why waste resources?" said Borthen. "I have good reason to believe that Gwynmira and her son would give their very souls for the power to destroy their political enemies, among whom should be included the Mage Hospitallers. . . ."

CASTLE PERILOUS

STANDING EXPOSED ON ITS GAUNT island rock, Gand Castle had weathered its share of storms. The same thick walls and strong towers that kept out the incursions of wind and water were equally well designed to keep out human enemies. The site had been chosen nearly three hundred years before by Adrien Du Penfallon, the fourth Seneschal of Gand. Subsequent generations of Du Penfallons had expanded the fortifications in their efforts to render the Keep secure and defensible. Whether or not they had succeeded in making it impregnable was an issue soon to be tested by an expeditionary army of three thousand men in the service of Gwynmira Du Bors, the Dowager-Regent of East Garillon.

The troops were commanded by Lord Khevyn Ap Khorrasel, Baron of Kirkwell. Under his generalship, they had successfully captured the city of Gand itself and were in the process of establishing control over the outlying townships. That they had not succeeded in seizing the castle as well was due to a miscalculation on the part of their commander, Lord Khevyn. Having failed initially to anticipate the tenacity of the Keep's resident defenders, the baron was anxious for a variety of reasons to have the situation resolved as quickly as possible. And so on the first day of November, in the year of the Red Boar 1347, he called together an assemblage of his officers and advisors in order to plan a full-scale assault.

The session began with a general briefing. "Gentlemen, I can hardly overemphasize how important it is that the castle should be taken as quickly as possible," said Lord Khevyn, surveying the attentive faces of his subordinates. "Our control over this region will never be complete so long as the garrison remains entrenched inside the Keep walls. The longer their defiance is allowed to go unpunished, the greater the danger that the general populace will be inclined to emulate it."

His face darkened. "This is not mere speculation on my part. You all know how we have become increasingly plagued by acts of civil disobedience. What you may *not* be aware of is the rather more serious fact that yesterday we lost twenty of our most valuable hostages to the forces of these so-called loyalists."

A murmur of indignation and dismay went round the room, instantly suppressed when Lord Khevyn gestured for silence. He continued bitterly. "The hostages in question—all members of the leading families here in Gand—were being taken west under guard to Farrowaithe when their escort was attacked by a sizable band of masked woodsmen. The ambush was well planned and efficiently carried out—to our discomfiture. I leave it to you to imagine what the consequences are likely to be once the city's aldermen learn that their relatives are no longer under threat."

"No longer under threat?" inquired one of the adjutants. "Surely there has been enough provocation to justify our taking stiff reprisals against these aldermen themselves."

Lord Khevyn lifted an eyebrow. "What measures would you propose?"

"A lottery," said his subordinate promptly. "Out of all those burghers whose families were involved, select four or five at random and have them publicly executed as an example to the rest—and to those who conducted the raid. Once we demonstrate that we intend to counter violence with violence, these townsfolk will think twice before they provoke us further."

"The idea has some merit, and I will consider it," acknowledged the baron. "But the fact remains unaltered that the castle and its defenders represent a major source of trouble. As long as Devon Du Penfallon is free, he remains a rallying point for his former subjects."

"But the brat's a cripple!" exclaimed another adjutant incredulously. "He's worth nothing!"

"He is certainly of no personal account," agreed Lord Khevyn. "But he comes from an important family. If the people of this province are prepared to accept his birthright, we can't afford to ignore it."

"According to all of our reports, the Keep is undermanned and ill-provisioned," said one of the other members of staff. "All we have to do is wait, and let hunger work for us in the course of time."

"Time," said his superior cuttingly, "is no friend to us, either. Haven't you been listening? We need to bring this affair to a speedy conclusion—before the citizens of this province forget completely that Devon Du Penfallon is only a cripple with an illustrious name and start thinking of him as a hero."

He paused to get a grip on his temper before going on. "Admiral Lord Gervaise Du Lacque should be arriving any day now with a shipload of heavy ordnance. I had word by special courier that the *White Mermaid* left Ambrothen twelve days ago. By the time she gets here, I want everything in readiness. This is what I propose we do . . ."

The first sign of trouble visible to the watchmen posted along the guard towers of the besieged castle was the sudden reawakening of activity out in the bay. For days—ever since Lord Khevyn Ap Khorrasel had imposed a blockade on the harbor—the waters east of the castle rock had been quiet as a millpond. It had been a fortnight since Gand's fleet of fishermen had been allowed to do anything more than sit on the quayside mending their nets while their empty boats lolled at their anchors offshore. Even the oystermen had been forced to beach their coracles, leaving them to dry on the sand. Outside the harbor mouth, two tall-masted carracks of war prowled up and down the coast like cats keeping watch at a mousehole.

But now some of the small craft were moving again,

swarming out like fish-fry past the loaf-shaped mass of Dinty Rock in mid-channel toward the deeper waters off Godelyn Point to the north. The sentries on the castle walls were quick to spot the preponderance of crimson uniforms among the boat crews. While his subordinates remained on lookout, the sergeant went off in search of the lord of the castle to warn him that something was afoot.

Lord Devon Du Penfallon was not in his rooms on the uppermost level of the donjon. Nor was he outside in the forecourt, where at least a full quarter of the castle's civilian residents were gathered together for archery practice. Several of the sergeant's colleagues were supervising the shooting from a safe distance behind the firing line. From them, he learned that the young seneschal had been last seen heading toward the south rampart to inspect a weakness that had been detected in the structure of the curtain-wall.

A ditch ten feet deep separated the wide expanse of the forecourt from the grassy compound on the southern side of the Keep itself. Crossing over the movable bridge that spanned the fosse, the sergeant bypassed a terraced exercise area where some of the more professional members of the garrison were refining their skills at hand-to-hand combat. Beyond the drillground, at the southernmost point of the triangular green, a small flock of sheep was grazing in the shadow of the great circular bastion of the Peacock Tower. His eye traveling east from the tower along the baseline of the rampart, the sergeant spotted the slender, slightly unbalanced figure of Devon Du Penfallon. He was examining a section of the wall in the company of the castle's resident stonemason and another man: Jorvald Ekhanghar, the marshall of the Keep.

Jorvald was the first to notice the sergeant approaching. After thirty years spent in military service, the marshall was quick to read trouble in the expression on his subordinate's lantern-jawed face. Stiffening inwardly, he laid a cautionary hand on Devon's shoulder. "Don't

look now, my lord," he muttered, "but I think we're
about to hear news not very much to our liking."

The sergeant's report was darkly colored with suspicion. "Mark my words, sir, those lobsterbacks are up to
something," he concluded. "I don't know what that may
be, but I don't like the smell of the wind from that
quarter."

Devon traded glances with his master-at-arms.
"Neither do I," said the young seneschal. "Jorvald, I
think you and I had better fetch a watchglass and go up
to the Eagle's Rood to get a bird's-eye view of the
situation."

The Eagle's Rood crowned the roof of the donjon
like a finial surmounting a coronet. It could only be
reached by means of a narrow, winding stair-passage
built into the north wall of the seneschal's bedchamber.
The way up was steep, the steps little more than toe-hold
ledges. Jorvald waited until he and Devon were alone at
the entrance to the tower, then said abruptly, "You don't
have to make this climb, if you don't want to. You can
trust me to give you a thorough account of all that's
visible from here."

Devon turned to him, level-eyed. "I know that,"
agreed the young seneschal simply. "But all the same, I'd
feel better if I could look for myself." Seeing Jorvald's
dubious expression, he added with a wry smile, "Don't
worry: actually I find a steep, narrow stairway like this
one much easier to deal with than one that's broad and
shallow."

Once they began their ascent, Jorvald saw what the
boy meant. Inside the stairwell Devon used his arms
with practiced efficiency to take the strain off his weak
leg. Jorvald was surprised to see him move so swiftly and
surely. The Marshall of Gand realized that his young
overlord had unexpected reserves of hidden strength.

The tight curl of the stairway ended beneath a
trapdoor. The door panel yielded without resistance in
well-oiled response to Devon's one-handed push. They
emerged through the accessway onto a square platform a

mere six feet across. Encircling parapets three feet thick
protected the platform from the winds off the sea. Even
so, Jorvald could feel a slight tremor in the wood beneath
his feet.

Supported by thirty feet of human construction
work on top of sixty feet of bedrock, the Eagle's Rood
commanded a dizzying panorama of the surrounding
land and sea. To the south, the cliffs bordering the
Amberhyl Estuary were as high and as rugged as the
castle-isle itself, but on the opposite side of the bay, the
ground leveled out, sloping seaward at a gentle incline as
far as the beach at Godelyn Point. Standing out beyond
the harbor, midway between the headland and the
horizon line, the two blockading warships rode the ocean
swells like a pair of floating gulls. But close inshore, on
the far side of the point, a third tall ship rolled at her
anchor in the midst of a school of little boats.

The newcomer was a sleek, triple-masted caravel.
Redonda-rigged, she had been built for speed, her hull
lines clean and sharp. Even at a distance, there was
something about her that Devon found oddly familiar.
"Jorvald," he said with a slight frown, "I'd like a closer
look at her. May I have the glass for a moment?"

The marshall nodded and handed the instrument
over. Devon trained the lens on the newly arrived caravel
and scanned her from stem to stern. After a moment, he
uttered an exclamation of grim satisfaction. "I *thought*
I'd seen that caravel before! She's the *White Mermaid*.
When she last put into port here, she belonged to a man
named Gudmar Ap Gorvald."

Jorvald knew something of Gudmar's reputation.
"The *White Mermaid*?" he exclaimed in surprise. "Here,
let me take a look."

Devon returned the watchman's glass. "You're right,
at that!" conceded Jorvald, after peering down the
eyepiece at the stately vessel in the water. He added, "By
my daughter Tessa's account, Gwynmira Du Bors had
Gudmar declared a traitor before the Great Council at
Kirkwell. In which case—"

"In which case, that's not Gudmar in command of her now," finished Devon. "I wonder what she's doing here."

"Landing a consignment of heavy ordnance—judging by the look of things," said Jorvald darkly. "See for yourself."

It was true. Taking a second look through the glass, Devon watched as a squat tubular bundle wrapped in strong netting was lowered from davits overhanging the caravel's port railing. Pale November sunlight glinted coldly off the bronze casting of breech and casing as the field piece settled ponderously onto the deck of the waiting transport barge. Weighed down almost to the gunwales, the small craft edged out from under the *Mermaid*'s lea, to make room for another to come alongside.

Short in the barrel and wide in the bore, the piece being rowed ashore was conspicuously a siege-mortar, capable of hoisting hundredweight projectiles at the acute angle necessary to assault an enemy bastion from below. Several other similar siege guns had already been landed on the beach where parties of civilian conscripts were laboring to load them onto oxcarts. "That's six ashore, one in transit, and five still to come off the ship," said Devon.

"And all for our benefit. Well, it was only a matter of time," said Jorvald with sour resignation.

"I don't see them unloading any powder or shot," said Devon.

"They wouldn't need to ship those in. All the necessary materials are easy enough to come by locally," said Jorvald. "Not to mention skilled craftsmen whose labors can be engaged without charge under the articles of martial law."

The oxcarts were getting on the move, trundling with painful slowness up through the dunes toward the outlying houses on the point. "Where do you think Khevyn Ap Khorrasel will be placing those guns?" asked Devon.

Jorvald pursed his lips. "Where he stands the best chance of hitting something worthwhile. If it were up to me, I'd deploy them all along the bluff directly opposite the castle barbican. It's a mere forty yards across the gap from the shoreline to the foot of the castle rock, and the shelf on which the barbican is built is only ten or twelve feet higher than the housetops on the city side."

"The barbican *is* the most obvious target," acknowledged Devon soberly. "What can we do to defend it, if Khevyn fulfills your expectations?"

"Given our present resources, not very much," said Jorvald candidly. "Not against heavy artillery. We have enough of our own ordnance in place on this side of the Keep to trade shots with the enemy, but our firing will have to be selective. We can't afford simply to blanket the gap with shot, hoping for a lucky strike here and there to put the enemy guns out of action. We haven't the supplies to waste."

"If we don't put up enough of a gun battle, the baron is likely to send men across the beach to storm the rock," said Devon. "We'd better be prepared to change to hand-to-hand combat at a moment's notice, if it comes to that."

"There again, we'll have to allow for the fact that our resources are limited," said Jorvald. "The numbers are far better than we expected when we started—thanks to some scare-mongering during the days leading up to the invasion. But we're short on seasoned soldiers: besides your own retainers, there are the Keep's auxiliaries, but the rest of the people inside these walls are just civilians who came to us two steps ahead of Baron Khevyn's army, in the hope of finding protection."

He shook his head. "Granted, most of them have since been making an effort to learn how to defend themselves, but they're hardly crack troops. We're going to have to start taxing our imaginations to come up with ways to compensate for the fact that the barbican is likely to prove vulnerable."

Devon appreciated the necessity. The barbican,

with its heavy portcullis and four box towers, was a relatively late addition to the fortress. The original entrance to the castle lay behind it, carved out of solid rock—a subterranean complex consisting of two adjoining guardrooms and a tunnel shaft leading upward at an oblique angle into the undercroft of the gatehouse a level above. The early residents of the Keep had stabled their animals in the undercroft; a later generation of builders had replaced the narrow stair-exit with a horseramp that opened into the yard behind the gatehouse. The defenders of the Keep had already taken the precaution of dismantling the ramp, but Devon shared his companion's fears about the general layout.

"Any enemy party strong enough to penetrate the barbican," continued Jorvald, "would stand a good chance of forcing their way up through the tunnel into the gatehouse. We'll have to do something about that. Here's what I have in mind . . ."

THUNDER AND SMOKE

JORVALD EKHANGHAR'S PREDICTIONS CONCERNING THE placement of the siege-mortars proved well founded. On the enemy-occupied side of the gap, a small army of conscript workmen spent the rest of that afternoon razing the buildings in the immediate neighborhood to obtain enough stone and timber for constructing breastworks along the cliff facing the castle's barbican. By sunset, all the houses along the street nearest the fortress had been reduced to their skeletal foundations. All along the cliffside, the corresponding mounds of rubble began to assume the shape of revetments.

The effort of field construction carried on into the night. On the opposite side of the gap, the castle's defenders were also making preparations against the coming assault. Torches flared red and yellow within the enclosure of the barbican where men and women worked side by side in teams. Some had been assigned to build up a buffer of sandbags behind the portcullis; others labored to erect a redoubt in front of the entrance to the underground tunnel.

Higher up on the ramparts of the gatehouse, the gun crews in charge of the castle's first level of ordnance checked over the condition of their weaponry. That task completed, they broke up into work parties to transfer a carefully rationed complement of powder and shot from the underground magazine in the main Keep, down to the level where most of the firing action was expected to take place. Down in the tunnel between the barbican and the gatehouse, Jorvald Ekhanghar and a small group of handpicked followers likewise had some special work to do. But their actions went concealed even from the eyes of their own people.

Devon kept constantly on the move throughout the evening. With his elderly manservant Brachen dogging his heels like an anxious spaniel, he carried out an exhaustive tour of the fortifications on the west side of the Keep, inspecting the work being done, conferring, advising, encouraging. His self-imposed duties cost him all the energy he had to give. By midnight, he was shaking with fatigue, his lame leg throbbing on the edge of agony.

Experience had taught him that once his body reached that stage, there was nothing to be gained from trying to force the issue any further. Yielding to necessity, he abandoned his pilgrimage and retired to the Keep to seek the sanctuary of his own apartments.

It was a profound relief to shed the weight of the chain-mail shirt he now felt obliged to wear outside the privacy of his own quarters. Once free of it, he sank down in the nearest chair and allowed Brachen to draw off his shoes. A month ago, he would never have stood up to the physical demands of his inherited responsibility. Thanks to four rigorous weeks of preparation, he had

gained strength and stamina, but the price he paid for it
was pain.

Everything hurt—his neck and shoulders, back and
legs. Brachen's face was furrowed with concern as he
assisted Devon out of his clothes. Once the boy was in
his bed, the old man arranged the blankets and pillows
with the gentle efficiency of long practice to ease his
young master's aching limbs. Devon submitted quietly
to his valet's ministrations, grateful for such knowledgeable service.

As a matter of habit, Brachen left a candle burning
on the sideboard next to the door that divided his room
from his master's. Once his manservant had withdrawn,
Devon lay motionless for some time, waiting with self-
willed patience for the moment when his need for sleep
would overcome his awareness of pain. Tired out as he
was, he expected that moment to come soon. But in spite
of his weariness of body, his mind remained alert,
plagued with fears and doubts.

Doubts as to the wisdom of his decision to defy the
armed might of the Du Bors family, whose lust for
dominion had scarcely been whetted when young Gythe
Du Bors had been elevated to the highest office in all East
Garillon. Hungry for revenge over the death of his uncle
Fyanor, hungrier still to consolidate his power as a ruler,
Gythe had been persuaded by his Regent mother to send
an army to invade the territories presided over by the
city of Gand. Faced with the prospect of war, Gand's
council of burgesses had argued in favor of appeasement
in the hope of avoiding havoc and bloodshed. Reviewing
the situation in the dark night of his own conscience,
Devon wondered wearily if perhaps they had been right
to reject the course of action he himself had chosen.

He had committed himself and his castle to uncon-
ditional resistance at the urgent behest of his sister,
Kherryn. She had sent him a message from the Great
Council at Kirkwell, warning him of the coming attack
and urging him to fight, regardless of the cost. The
reasons that she had given were not those of a counselor,
but those of a prophetess: solemn attestations that the

new rulers of East Garillon had gone beyond mere political aggrandizement to enter into an unholy alliance with men who dealt with forces of darkness.

By her own admission, her knowledge was the fruit not of empirical study, but of revelation. Devon still trusted the clarity of his sister's vision, which the turn of events had validated. But his own abilities had yet to be tested. Whether he could live up to the demands of faith remained to be seen. He hoped his loyal followers would not have cause to regret putting their trust in him, once battle was joined in bitter earnest.

What he feared most—more than any weapon or device of his enemies—was his own rank inexperience. His father, Arvech, morbidly conscious of his son's physical disability, had actively discouraged him from taking any interest in matters of warfare. What Devon knew of strategy and tactics he had learned from books secretly pirated from his father's library. What he knew of the arts of personal combat, he had garnered through observing other boys as they performed their exercises on the drill field.

His book-learning would supply him with the basis for ideas. But if he stood any chance at all now of defending himself in a hand-to-hand engagement, it was because of his vanished friend Evelake Whitfauconer, who had made him the coveted present of a sword. The sword in question was lying with Devon's other discarded equipment on top of the chest at the foot of his bed. It was an elegant weapon, its hilt decorated with intricate giltwork. Evelake had worn it only as a dress sword on high occasions, but in spite of its ornamental appearance, it was still a serviceable blade.

For months after Evelake's disappearance, Devon had labored to teach himself how to handle his treasured weapon, practicing in solitary secrecy in front of a mirror. It had been heartbreaking work at first, but he had persevered, learning by difficult degrees to compensate for his poor balance and lack of agility. In time he had come to feel at ease with the sword in his hand.

Once he had assumed his right to carry a blade openly, Devon might have relinquished his damascened weapon at any time, in preference for one less ornate. But he had elected to keep it. The sword was his legacy from Evelake Whitfauconer. And as long as Devon wore it, it was almost as if his friend were still at his side.

He wondered—not for the first time—what had become of Evelake since the other boy had been captured by brigands seven months before. By now most people—even Jorvald—were prepared to believe that Evelake was dead. But Devon was not entirely convinced. His sister, Kherryn, certainly, had never given up hope that one day Gythe Du Bors's lost half brother would return, giving the lie to every rumor concerning his death. Devon was sure that Kherryn, of all people, could not be easily deceived where Evelake was concerned.

For there had been a special bond between Kherryn and Evelake. They were by nature two very different people: Evelake lighthearted and quick-witted; Kherryn serious and reflective. But their differences had been complementary. Evelake had used his own aptitude for laughter and invention to brighten Kherryn's more sober spirits. And she, for her part, had awakened his deeper qualities of heart and mind.

They had been happy in one another's company. But their contentment had been cut short when Evelake had been recalled to Farrowaithe. From the very moment of his departure, Kherryn had seemed unable to find any lasting peace of mind. Certainly, it was during the weeks and months following his disappearance that her gifts of prescience had begun to manifest themselves with strange, often frightening clarity.

Loving his sister as he did, Devon wanted to see her hopes concerning Evelake rewarded. Her prophetic insight had shown her so much darkness; she deserved that her one bright vision should be fulfilled. It was this thought that he carried with him as he slipped at last into worn-out sleep.

Brachen roused him five hours later. Struggling back to consciousness, Devon opened beclouded eyes to find that Jorvald was also present in the room. "I'm sorry to wake you so early, my lord," said the marshall, "but the watchmen on the west ramparts report that the civilian labor crews have finished work on the shoreline barricades. That means we can expect the enemy to start bringing his guns forward within the hour. I thought you would want to view the situation for yourself before the firing starts. . . ."

Hostilities broke out shortly after daybreak. The first clash occurred between rival ranks of archers. For the better part of two hours, the castle militia traded arrows with enemy marksmen posted along the newly constructed earthworks. In trenches behind the enemy line of fire, the siege-mortars crawled like slow reptiles toward their emplacements.

The castle batteries held their fire, reduced to inaction by the realization that there were still groups of civilians toiling under duress within close target range. Having the advantage of elevation, the defending bowmen did all they could to hinder the guns' progress. But without the support of their own artillery, they could do little more than postpone the inevitable.

By mid-morning the mortars were all in position. The first shots sent up by the shoreline batteries went wide and wild. Working under a thickening pall of acrid smoke, the enemy gunners spent another hour experimenting to correct the range. As Jorvald had anticipated, they were concentrating their fire on the castle barbican. By noon they had their chosen target well in their sights and embarked on their attempt to pound the barbican's portcullis and foretowers into rubble.

Something had to be done, even though there was no guarantee that all the townsfolk had been withdrawn from the area. Watchglass in hand, Devon braced himself against the tremors of bombardment and scanned the smoke-wreathed installations inshore from the height of the gatehouse rampart. His survey, however, told him very little, thanks to the overhanging cloud of powder fumes blanketing the shore. After a brief consultation with Jorvald Ekhanghar, the young seneschal at last gave his own men the order to open fire.

The first response came from the two drakonets mounted on the roof of the gatehouse. Under the careful direction of one of the castle's four experienced gunners, the shots skipped over the crest of the landside fortifications to sow red confusion among the baron's reserve troops, holding back from the firing line. While the smoke was still clearing, the Keep's three tower batteries followed up on the initial salvo, raking the enemy's earthworks with flying stone. There was a momentary cesura in mortar fire as Lord Khevyn's men paused to reload; then the thunder of guns resumed.

The booming of ordnance carried on throughout the rest of the afternoon. Having no need to conserve resources, Lord Khevyn's gun crews fired off round after round, battering ceaselessly at the barbican and its supporting cliff-rock. Unable to afford a similar expenditure of materials, the defenders were forced to hold back, taking elaborate pains to ensure that every shot would tell. By dusk they had succeeded in putting four of the enemy guns out of action. But the bombardment still continued on into the night.

No one on either side of the gap managed more than a few intermittent winks of sleep during the rare lulls between salvos. Huddled in the relative safety of the underground vaults beneath the castle donjon, women and children whimpered and cringed as each fresh assault shook the rock walls of their refuge. Above ground on the battlements, men struggled to carry out their assigned duties, half deafened by the noise, half choked by the roiling smoke, the darkness below them bloodshot with fire.

For Devon the black night seemed interminable. After enduring long hours on his feet, his body at last grew numb to its own protests, as if all capacity to feel had been drubbed out of his nerves by the rumble and roll of the detonating guns. But that was no consolation as, all around him, he saw the casualties beginning to mount up. By midnight there had been only two deaths. But he needed none of Kherryn's powers of foresight to know that there would be more before dawn.

Although he could not sleep, Devon forced himself to take what rest he could, stretched out on a pallet in one of the guardrooms at the base of the south tower. All around him, the bellow of conflicting ordnance continued to shake the foundations of the Keep. After several more hours of continual crossfire, Devon was beginning to wonder how much more any of them would be able to stand, when all at once the deafening cannonade ceased.

The sudden silence was unnerving. Devon struggled up off his comfortless bed and limped outside. To the east, a sullen dawn was breaking through leaden clouds above the cold grey sea. The air stank of niter and violence.

He looked west, toward the city. Jorvald Ekhanghar was striding toward him up the steep path from the level of the gatehouse. Devon gathered his heavy cloak more tightly around his stiff, aching shoulders and hobbled forward to meet him.

The marshall was looking grim. His heart sinking, Devon asked, "Why have the guns stopped firing?"

"Because the mortars have done enough damage for one night," said Jorvald. "You'd better come have a look."

Seen from the gatehouse, the barbican was in shambles, its corbeled foretowers reduced to toothless stumps of broken stone. The portcullis had been hammered into scrap iron. Thanks to the fortification work carried out the day before, the entry-way was still partially blocked, but the walls had been breached and the secondary towers were leaning. "Let's just be thankful the tide is in at the moment," said Jorvald. "When it goes out again, we'd better all be ready and waiting to repel a sortie. . . ."

FIRE BY DAY

"We have broken the castle barbican, my lord," reported the young aide-de-camp, standing stiffly at attention beside the breakfast table of his commanding officer. "The portcullis is down and the flanking towers all but dismantled. Captains Darnely and Saddlyr are ready to proceed on your orders."

Lord Khevyn Ap Khorrasel, who had slept no better than anyone else the night before, received the information without any trace of commendation. "I expected this report hours ago," he said acidly. "Given our resources, our gunnery crew should have been able to level those outworks to the ground by midnight."

The baron's tone demanded an explanation. The messenger tightened his shoulders an uneasy fraction further. "I'm sorry, my lord. The resistance from the Keep was sharper than we had anticipated—"

"Indeed? To what effect?" inquired Lord Khevyn.

The aide was looking increasingly uncomfortable. "Nineteen men dead, my lord, including three gunnery engineers. Another twenty-seven injured. Seven of the mortars out of action—"

Lord Khevyn's jaw hardened with an audible grinding of teeth. "*How many?*"

"S-seven, my lord," muttered his subordinate in subdued tones. He added defensively, "Those bloody bastards on the ramparts were having the devil's own luck! You'd have thought—"

"I don't believe in luck!" snapped his commanding officer. "And I have no patience with sniveling excuses. Tell my orderly to saddle my horse. I'm going down to the harbor to review the situation in person."

Arriving at the waterfront half an hour later, the baron found his men working to clear the space behind the revetments. The sheer quantity of debris testified to the accuracy of the enemy's range fire. The ruined mortars were having to be dug out of mounds of rubble, along with the corpses of those who had been manning them. The loss of ordnance was strategically more damaging than the incidental loss of lives. Khevyn transferred his embittered gaze to the enemy Keep, perched on its steep island offshore.

The barbican had been badly damaged, but it had been a costly piece of demolition, and not as thorough as Lord Khevyn might have wished. There were signs of activity going on behind the walls to suggest that the castle garrison was busily making repairs. That and the sight of the Du Penfallon standard flying defiantly above the donjon seemed to mock the baron for his previous failure to occupy the castle. Stony-faced with fury at the thought that the Keep's defenders might again succeed in resisting him with impunity, Lord Khevyn turned on his heel and stalked back to the pavilion where his aides and officers were waiting to receive their instructions.

The baron got to the point with brutal candor. "Thanks to what I can only describe as incompetence aggravated by misadventure, we find ourselves in no position to continue an effective campaign of bombardment against the castle," he said in icy tones of disparagement. "Since I do not propose to oblige our enemies by giving them time to rebuild their low-line defenses, I suggest that we consider seriously the possibility of launching a manned assault on the barbican as soon as the tide goes out."

This proposal was greeted with consternation. "But my lord!" protested one of his senior adjutants. "That's little more than five hours from now. It will still be broad daylight!"

"Thank you, I am aware of that," agreed Lord Khevyn tartly.

"But—" The adjutant hesitated, then struggled on.

"Forgive me, my lord, but the castle bowmen aren't blind. If we send troops across the gap before sunset, most of them will be cut down before they get anywhere near the base of the castle rock."

"I think not," said the Baron of Kirkwell with acid indulgence. "If fighting is our profession, it's time we demonstrated that we are capable of professional ingenuity. . . ."

As the tide receded, the castle's defenders redoubled their efforts to shore up the ruined fortifications below the gatehouse. Under the direction of the castle mason, men plied picks and spades in hurried relays, using rubble from the foretowers to fill in the cavity left by the destruction of the portcullis. Another group of volunteers under Jorvald's supervision deployed themselves in two parallel lines stretching the length of the tunnel between the exit from the barbican to the undercroft of the gatehouse. These constituted a carrying-brigade, transferring buckets of soda-ash and flasks of oil hand to hand from the storage vaults in the main Keep to the endangered precinct of the foregate.

Set back behind the towers flanking the gateway, with thirty feet of rampart between them, the barbican's two auxiliary box-turrets were still partly intact. Screened from the wind by the parapet of the right-hand turret, Devon Du Penfallon kept an eye on the situation ashore with the aid of his watchglass. The amount of industrious activity going on behind the earthworks left him in no doubt that the enemy commander was planning to take some form of offensive action. But it wasn't until he paused momentarily to rest his aching neck and shoulders that a flicker of crimson-clad movement farther up the beach alerted him to a new development.

Several dozen of Khevyn Ap Khorrasel's men-at-arms were trudging along the water's edge toward the shingle where the oystermen's unused coracles were lying bottom-up, like so many sea turtles on the sand. As Devon bemusedly looked on, the group broke up into parties of four. Each party seized upon a coracle and hoisted it to shoulder level. Carrying the coracles like coffins, they began making their way back toward their main entrenchment.

Devon was at a loss to account for the purpose behind this exercise. Lowering his glass, he waved a hand to attract Jorvald's attention. The marshall looked up, nodded, and came bounding up the outside stairway to join the young seneschal at his vantage point. "There's something odd going on down there," said Devon, pointing toward the straggling procession of boat-bearers. "Take a look and see if you know what to make of it all."

Jorvald took the watchglass and did as Devon had directed. After a moment he gave a grunt of mirthless laughter. "There's only one reason that I can think of why the Black Baron would be interested in those coracles," he said tightly. "I imagine they'll make very good substitutes for arrow screens."

"Tough, easy to carry, reasonably fireproof—I see what you mean," said Devon with a grimace. "Well, it's not as if we weren't expecting something like this. How are your preparations coming along?"

"My men and I will be ready when the time comes," said Jorvald.

"If Khevyn's waiting on the tide, that'll be about an hour from now," said Devon. He added abruptly, "I wish I could stand beside you."

His voice held mixed intensities. "That is not your office," said Jorvald calmly, "any more than it was your father's before you. As Seneschal of Gand, you are supposed to keep back and give the orders."

His tone was devoid of either indulgence or conde-scension. Devon gave him a crooked grin. "In that case, here are my orders for you: remember that I need you as a counselor as much as I need you as a champion, and don't take any unnecessary chances once the fighting starts!"

* * *

By mid-afternoon, the tide had receded until the waters separating the castle rock from the mainland were only a few feet deep. Standing at the head of what had once been the castle causeway, Lord Khevyn Ap Khorrasel cast a critical eye over the company of men-at-arms assembled behind the earthen barricades at the cliff's edge. Satisfied at their state of readiness, he summoned the company captain to his side and pointed out across the water toward the base of the island, to a spot where the rock had been gnawed by erosion.

"Start your ascent from there," he told his subordinate. "Our crossbowmen will cover your advance across the gap, but once you and your men are on your way up, they will have to desist. You've seen the diagrams of the castle's interior, so you know what to go for once you're inside the barbican enclosure. Have you any questions?"

"Only one, my lord," said the captain. "Do you want Devon Du Penfallon alive?"

"Yes, if that can be arranged," said the Baron of Kirkwell coldly. "Anything else? Very well, you may give the trumpeter the order to sound the charge."

Brazen as pot metal, the horn call rebounded off the rocks. There was a concerted clatter of chain mail and weaponry as the first rank of the attack force poured through the gap between the breastworks and bounded down the embankment. Carrying their coracle-shields with them, they ploughed into the shallows and surged forward, thrusting their improvised arrow screens aloft to form a broken roof above their heads.

Whooping like game-beaters, kicking up fountains of seaspray, Lord Khevyn's soldiers thrashed and floundered toward the cliff base. Some lost their footing and fell, to be picked off by archers shooting from behind the covering palisade at the barbican's gateway. The response from the shore was a whizzing battery of crossbow bolts. Within seconds, the air between the island and the shore was thick with missiles. "Watch yourselves! They're firing in ranks!" Jorvald called to his bowmen. "Keep back until you're sure of a clear shot!"

The first wave of attackers abandoned their shields at the base of the castle rock. Armed with ropes and grappling hooks, they swarmed up the cliff face as far as a crooked ledge twenty feet below the foot of the barbican walls, where the leaders paused to take aim for the broken parapets above them. Within seconds a whole stringcourse of cables took root. Short swords swinging free from leather wrist loops, men flocked to the ropes and began to climb.

On Jorvald's signal, the Keep's defenders began emptying bucketfuls of caustic soda over the barricades. Before the attackers could react, a swirling downdraft of sea air swept a white cloud of chemical ash into their startled faces. Those at the top of the ropes cursed and choked and clawed at their streaming eyes. As the lines of climbers faltered to a standstill, a second wave of defenders rushed forward with hand axes.

Men screamed and plummeted, still clutching severed bights of rope. More crowded in to take their places. Within minutes, the cliff below the barricades was black with jostling figures. A single glance told Jorvald they were losing ground to sheer numbers.

A reaching arm clutched at the top of the parapet a few feet to his left. He knocked it loose with a sweep of his sword, then shouted to his civilian auxiliaries, "Fall back! We'll cover your retreat!"

Watching from one of the gatehouse oillets, Devon saw his people break for the entrance to the tunnel. Jorvald and his men-at-arms were the last to leave the ramparts. Devon could hear the heavy clash of weaponry as they fought their way back to the redoubt. He turned to Brachen, his face pale but decisive. "Jorvald and his men have done all they could," he said grimly. "If our enemies insist on forcing the issue, we'll have to carry out the plan as arranged . . ."

The redoubt was a makeshift affair, and Khevyn's men had it down in minutes. The defenders' grey-haired commander, flanked by two sergeants-at-arms, confronted them with cold steel at the mouth of the tunnel.

"I'd advise you to back off, if you value your lives," said the Marshall of Gand in a voice that carried to the back of the ranks. "This tunnel has been mined with explosives. If you try to force your way in, we will bury you alive."

He spoke with chill deliberation, but the mercenary captain uttered a derisive crack of laughter. "The dog with the loudest bark is the one with no teeth! Don't listen to him, lads. That's a loser's bluff if ever I heard one."

The marshall's eyes were glinting. "I'm not bluffing. Order your men to proceed, and you take their deaths upon yourself."

A desultory murmur ran through the mercenary assembly, but the captain quelled it with a glare. Turning back to his opponent, he said sneeringly, "Out of my way, old man, before I decide to trim off your beard at your throat."

Someone up on the battlements overhead blew three high, trilling notes on a silver pipe. It was the signal Jorvald had been waiting for, telling him that everyone had left the gatehouse. His two sergeants stiffened, poised to move on his signal. "You've all been warned," he told the enemy company. "Follow us now at your peril!"

His broadsword flashed out in a sudden lightning arc. The captain started back with a curse as the point of the marshall's weapon nicked the front of his surcoat. In that instant, the three men defending the tunnel wheeled and bolted up the shadowy passageway.

There was a moment's indecision among the invaders. Seeing his men hanging back, the captain snarled, "After them, you fools!" And led the way into the tunnel behind the fleeing men from the Keep.

Fired by their officer's example, the rest of Khevyn's attack force packed in behind their leader. Thundering up to the top of the passageway, they spilled out into the gatehouse undercroft in time to see the trapdoor in the ceiling slam shut.

It was not the only way out of the undercroft. There was a door big enough to accommodate a wagon set into the far wall. Recalling that this ought to lead to an outside courtyard, the captain gave his men the order to break the door down.

More men came up through the tunnel, jostling for position among their companions. The air was thick with the reek of sweat and fuming torches. The stench masked the acid hiss of burning slowmatch, creeping by accelerating inches across the floor of the gatehouse overhead, where the castle's defenders had left a sizable cache of gunpowder.

The explosion blew out the lower walls of the gatehouse, bringing the upper level, with all its tons of masonry, crashing down into the yawning pit of the undercroft. The thunder of falling rock drowned the shrieks of those trapped under the killing weight of it. The rending shock was enough to collapse the supporting roof of the adjoining tunnel. First with a rumble, then with a roar, the passageway shuddered and began to cave in.

The paroxysm reached as far as the barbican. Already weakened by bombardment, the ledge on which the walls rested heaved and groaned. Before the disbelieving eyes of the watchers on the shore, a crack appeared at the base of the supporting bastion. Throwing off rocks and boulders, the ledge parted company with the parent cliff, sweeping everything below it toward the water below.

Brown foam sheeted skyward, gnashing at the base of the island. When it settled, there remained a raw scarp of sheer cliff where the barbican had been, and above that, a heap of ruined stone that was now a tomb.

Shaken to the marrow, Khevyn Ap Khorrasel lifted incredulous eyes higher still, toward the crown of the castle rock. To his fury and amazement, the donjon and its outbuildings stood intact, more unattainable than ever. For a long moment he was incapable of speech. When he at last found his voice again, it was to summon the captain of the *Mermaid*.

THE FEAST OF ST. ALANIN

EVERY YEAR ON THE FIFTH of November, the citizens of Farrowaithe turned out into the streets and waterways of the city to celebrate the Feast of St. Alanin, their spiritual protector.

Preparations for the day traditionally began weeks ahead of time as the city's guilds and merchant companies vied with one another to produce the finest pageants in honor of their patron saint. As the day itself drew nearer, vendors and performers of every description began flocking into the city from the surrounding townships, clamoring at the great guild hall for permits to erect stalls and stages in every market square. The city burghers turned out in force to set festive torches ready for burning at every bridgehead and street corner, and the shore patrols towed floating platforms laden with fireworks out into the lake.

Normally, the Feast of St. Alanin was an occasion set aside for feasting and dancing, mirth and merriment. In the year of the Red Boar 1347, however, the prospect of the day's revels was overshadowed by confusion and uncertainty. Confusion over the radical political changes that had taken place in the past few weeks. Uncertainty as to how those changes would shape the future.

For according to a decretal handed down by the parliament of lords at Kirkwell, there were to be no more seneschals in Ambrothen, Gand, or Farrowaithe, and no more Lord Wardens of East Garillon as a whole. Instead, the Five Cities would be united under the rule of a king: His Majesty Gythe the First.

The one openly critical voice had been that of Dorian Du Ghelleryn, the old Seneschal of Glyn Regis. Crooked as a winter ash, his joints stiff with arthritis and

ocean damp, he had nevertheless been a formidable
warrior in his youth, taller and broader even than
Delsidor Whitfauconer, who had taken Dorian's only
child, Marissa, to be his first wife. Lissome as a hawthorn
blossom, Marissa had been her father's greatest pride—
some said his only joy—and she had died giving
Delsidor his firstborn son. Dorian had neither forgotten
nor forgiven her loss.

His grief and resentment had given rise to a complicated tangle of grudges against his son-in-law, Delsidor,
who had wooed Marissa and won her, and against his
grandson, Evelake, whose birth had cost his mother her
life. Delsidor's subsequent remarriage to Gwynmira Du
Bors had widened the breach between the two men
seemingly beyond all hope of reconciliation. None of the
events of the past eight months—neither Evelake's disappearance, nor Delsidor's murder—had quenched the
smoldering embers of Dorian Du Ghelleryn's abiding
bitterness.

Since he had never made any secret of his feelings, it
was common knowledge that the old Seneschal of Glyn
Regis disliked Gwynmira for reasons that had nothing to
do with politics. When the new Dowager-Regent had
summoned him, along with the other twenty-three standing representatives of East Garillon's higher nobility, to
a formal meeting of the parliment of lords, no one had
expected Dorian to behave in a particularly conciliatory
manner.

Deep-set eyes narrowly agleam beneath lowering
brows, the old man had contributed nothing but silence
to his colleagues' guarded endorsement of the policies
Gwynmira had outlined for them—until she had moved
on from matters of state to raise the issue of kingship on
behalf of her son. Then, without warning, he had flung
back his head with a single harsh crack of derisive
laughter.

It had taken everyone present by surprise, so that
they turned to stare at the gnarled and hulking figure in
their midst. Weathered skin stretched taut over the
prominent bones of his face, Dorian had favored

Gwynmira with a coldly admiring stare. "Ever since the days of Evelain Whitfauconer, we've had seneschals to rule the cities, and a Lord Warden to mediate among them," he growled. "Now *you* say it's time we chose ourselves a king—and no one here in this room seems prepared to argue the point!"

Half turning, he had raked the hushed ranks of his peers with a withering glare, before returning his attention to Gwynmira. "You know, madam, I begin to think you may be right: if we haven't the sense to look after ourselves, we deserve no better than we get. I hope you relish your success."

"May I take it," Gwynmira had said silkily, "that you accede to my proposition?"

The old man's response had been a thin smile. "You may take it, madam, that I don't consider it worth my while to fight other men's battles for them."

He had risen then from his seat, a tall, gaunt figure in ceremonial velvet, out of place as a death's head at a wedding. "There is a certain justice in the ways of the world—for people as well as nations. Delsidor Whitfauconer, for instance, got his just deserts when he married you, milady. And as for you and that whelp of yours—well, we shall see."

Having delivered this parting shot, he had stalked out of the council chamber, leaving a stunned silence behind him. Since there was nothing to be gained by attempting to forestall him, Gwynmira had let him go. Three hours later, Gythe Du Bors Whitfauconer had been proclaimed King of East Garillon before a hastily convened assemblage of burghers on the steps of Farrowaithe's great guild hall. But by that time, Dorian and his entourage had already set sail upriver for the Firth of Verendvoe on the first stage of their voyage home to Glyn Regis.

Thus he had not been on hand to emulate the rest of the parliament in swearing fealty to the newly created boy-monarch. Since then, war had broken out in Gand, following young Devon Du Penfallon's refusal to surrender Gand Castle into the hands of the military commander Gwynmira had sent to take possession of it. As of the fifth of November, the situation in Gand remained unresolved, and Dorian Du Ghelleryn's neutrality remained a matter for uneasy conjecture. But as the chilly autumn dusk settled in over the city of Farrowaithe, Gwynmira Du Bors and her son had more immediate obligations to fulfill.

It had long been customary for the Seneschal of Farrowaithe to celebrate the feast of St. Alanin by hosting a banquet at the castle for the city's aldermen, their wives, and selected members of their families. Gwynmira had no particular respect for tradition, but she was quick to perceive how such occasions could be exploited to personal advantage. Endowed with the striking good looks of the Du Bors family, Gythe could be winningly engaging when it suited him. The Festival of St. Alanin offered an appropriate opportunity for him to display his gifts and talents.

Following the completion of her own fashionable toilette, Gwynmira paid a visit to her son's dressing room and found him in buoyant high spirits. Dark eyes sparkling like the gems that patterned his collar and sleeves, he smiled at her reflection as she came through the door, then turned and stood up, pivoting to show off the immaculate cut of his brocaded doublet.

Tall for the thirteen years of his age, he wore his clothes with a muscular grace that would have done credit to a professional courtier. As his mother advanced farther into the room, he made her a flourishing obeisance, then struck an august pose, chin regally uplifted, sword hand resting lightly on his hip. "Well, what do you think?" he inquired brightly. "Shall I have my portrait painted like this?"

Gwynmira did not answer. Her brow darkening ominously, she summoned her son's attendant valet with a curt flick of an imperious forefinger. As the little man leaped to obey, she pointed to the narrow fillet of gold that crowned Gythe's luxuriant dark hair.

"What," she demanded icily, "is this?"

"A—a coronal, milady."

"Remove it."

"M-milady?"

"I said remove it!" repeated Gwynmira sharply. "What the devil possessed you to put it there in the first place?"

The valet cast a mute beseeching glance over at his master. "Oh, don't be angry with poor old Draycott, Mother," said Gythe. "It wasn't his idea, it was mine."

He eyed Gwynmira in some surprise. "What's the matter? Doesn't it suit me?"

"It suits you admirably," said Gwynmira tartly. "But you are not yet supposed to wear a crown—or anything resembling one—in public."

It was Gythe's turn to be displeased. "Why not? I'm king now, aren't I?"

"Yes," said Gwynmira. "But you have yet to go through the ceremony of coronation. Until then, it will be in your best interests to observe a few painless restrictions."

Gythe snorted. "How can a few muttered words of mumbo jumbo and a penny's worth of rose oil make that much difference?"

"Common people," said his mother, "are notoriously superstitious. They set great store by ritual—especially when it purports to carry supernatural significance."

She raised a slim jeweled hand to caress her son's flushed cheek. "Come—don't quarrel with me. I know what I'm talking about. Do as I ask, and I promise you I shall see to it that you are crowned as soon as possible."

Gythe made a petulant move as if to jerk his head away. "And how soon will that be?"

"As soon as affairs in Gand are brought to a satisfactory conclusion."

Gythe went rigid with dismay. "But that could take months!"

"I don't think so." Gwynmira's voice was firm. "Devon Du Penfallon is sickly, and his followers are ill-prepared to withstand a long siege. With winter coming on, all the advantages are on our side. We need only be patient."

"Patient!" Gythe shot an exasperated glance toward the ceiling. "If that's all you can suggest, I've got a better idea."

He lowered his voice. "Kherryn Du Penfallon is in sanctuary up at Kirkwell—practically under our very noses. It shouldn't be too hard to hire a few ruffians to go in and drag her out. Once we had her in our hands as a hostage, her brother would come to heel in no time at all."

"Except that then we would have the whole of the Hospitallers' Order up in arms against us," said his mother dryly.

"What of that?" Gythe tossed his head. "The mages haven't been exactly helpful to us so far. Certainly, if old Baldwyn Vladhallyn has his way, I'll never be crowned."

His lip curled as he considered the Arch Mage of East Garillon. "Preachy old meddler! I wish he'd drop dead in the middle of one of his own long-winded lectures! How he ever came to be elected head of the whole Order, I'll never know."

Gwynmira's expression was veiled. "He is said to possess considerable affinity for the power of the Magia."

"You'd never know it, to look at him," declared Gythe. "Mage power!" he went on in disgust. "If the Magia is all the mages claim it is, why don't they do something worthwhile with it, instead of wasting all that energy curing warts and carbuncles?"

His dark eyes turned speculative. "I wish *I* knew how to call up the Magia," he said. "I'd soon put it to some better use than coddling sick old women and scrofulous beggar's brats!"

A deferential knock at the outer door forestalled him from elaborating further. The valet Draycott withdrew in silence to answer the summons. After a brief whispered dialogue with someone on the other side of the threshold, he rejoined his employers, his expression one of studied neutrality. "My lord, Lady Gwynmira—the Master of Revels informs me that your guests are beginning to arrive. He reminds me that the presentations are to begin in another quarter of an hour."

"Fifteen minutes? All right." With a petulant twitch of his shoulders, Gythe turned back to the mirror, tilting his head this way and that so that the golden circlet caught the light in mercurial flashes. His mother watched him for a moment, then slipped a slender forearm delicately around his neck, so that his face in turning came to rest against her open palm.

"For thirteen years," said Gwynmira softly, "I have pursued my one desire, which was to see you raised to eminence as ruler of all East Garillon. Believe me when I tell you that a few weeks—or even a few months—is not a long time to wait for what you want."

Seeing that Gythe was still looking stormy, she continued. "The formal privilege of wearing a king's crown is of trivial importance compared with the right to wield a king's authority. You have the authority now. The trifling matter of regalia can wait."

The angry color subsided from Gythe's cheeks as he considered what she had said. Then all at once he shrugged and plucked the fillet from his hair. "Oh, very well. Have it your way," he said grudgingly. And added, "This circlet isn't nearly grand enough for a crown anyway."

He was rewarded with a smile from his mother. "When the time comes, you shall choose the jewels yourself from your father's treasury," said Gwynmira. "As for tonight: let Draycott choose a cap for you and I shall give you a ruby brooch to gladden it. . . ."

The banquet, along with the entertainments that had been arranged to go with it, was scheduled to begin at eight o'clock. While the kitchen staff were still rushing about, garnishing plates and putting the finishing touches on the table decorations, the invited guests assembled in the arras-hung anteroom before being ushered into the great dining hall, where the young king-elect and his mother were waiting to greet them.

The high table stood on an elevated dais at the western end of the hall, commanding an unobstructed view of the open performance area that had been left in the center of the floor. The rest of the tables had been arranged to form two parallel galleries, one on either side of the improvised stage. The guests took their seats in a rich rustle of expensive cloth. Once they were all in their places, the heralds withdrew, leaving the leading burghers of Farrowaithe alone with their new overlord.

Gythe himself read out the traditional invocation for St. Alanin's Day. As the company voiced the traditional response, Gwynmira signaled the servants to bring in the first course of the meal. Music filtered discreetly down from the minstrels' balcony, softening the clatter of cutlery long enough to allow conversation to get started. The mood among those present, noticeably wary at first, became gradually more relaxed under the influence of food and wine. By the time the first group of performers took to the center of the floor, the initial chill in the atmosphere had thawed to a more congenial air of conviviality.

The dancers and acrobats, jugglers and animal trainers all received a good-humored share of approbation. But, as everyone expected, the crowning event of the evening was the presentation of a miracle play portraying the life of St. Alanin himself.

The original story, preserved in the Book of Caer Ellyn, was a popular one, and had been the subject of many ballads and plays. The version which the Du Bors guests were to see was a new one, commissioned by the Dowager-Regent in honor of the occasion. Gwynmira had given the script her perfunctory approval, leaving the Master of Revels to hire the actors and supervise the production of set pieces, costumes, and properties. Only mildly curious to see the play itself, she was roused to sudden interest when a tall male figure, robed head to foot in black, emerged from the wings and advanced to the center of the stage.

His face was hidden by the cowl of his hood, but he commanded attention with his mere presence. As an expectant hush settled over the company, he faced the high table and bowed low in a susurrant flurry of black robes and shadows. When he spoke, his voice carried musically over all the room, hovering rhythmically between song and recitation.

"Health to you all, masters and mistresses—you who are gathered to keep the high feast of Alanin Penrithyn, saint and sage, magister of mages, preceptor of princes, he by whose rede was established the Order, the Brotherhood of Healers, the Mage Hospitallers.

"Exemplary were his deeds, admirable his merits, and we who stand ready to enact his story ask only this: that you, our worthy patrons, should take instruction from this play of ours. Seek to know your enemies for what they are. Search for a power to shape your own destiny."

A sudden chill laid hold of Gwynmira, as she realized that the man in black was speaking directly to her.

AIRS OF MYSTERY

THE IMPRESSION WAS SO KEEN that she started forward in her seat. The sharpness of her involuntary movement caused Gythe to look around in surprise. "What's the matter, Mother?" he asked in an undertone. "Is anything wrong?"

Despite the heat within the hall, Gwynmira's upper body was tingling with gooseflesh, as though she had been stripped to the waist. Only the realization that her son was staring at her prevented her from making a reflexive movement to cover her breasts. "Nothing. Merely a slight draft," she murmured, annoyed to discover that her cheeks were burning. "Perhaps you would be good enough to assist me with my mantle?"

The garment in question was draped across the back of her chair. "Are you sure you really feel the need of it? The air seems more than warm enough in here to me," said Gythe.

His mother did not respond. Her attention had been drawn back to the tall man in black who still held the center of the stage. As Gythe, scowling slightly, followed the direction of Gwynmira's eyes, the hooded play-actor executed another graceful obeisance and pivoted to face the opposite end of the long dining room, arms uplifted in a theatrical gesture of summoning.

The twilight areas in the far corners of the hall came to life in a sudden burst of activity. Dim figures, bristling with anonymous pieces of hardware, made a concerted rush for the middle of the floor. The hooded man stepped into the midst of them and disappeared from view behind a swiftly assembled screen of canvas panels. None of the members of his audience had been permitted to catch so much as a glimpse of what he looked like.

Which left Gythe at a loss to account for his mother's interest in the tall actor. Though the man was no longer among the figures on stage, Gwynmira continued to gaze abstractedly ahead of her, a small crease pleating the skin between her winged eyebrows. Mildly vexed to see her for once completely unmindful of himself, Gythe turned and beckoned to the Master of Revels, who was standing at the back of the dais. "Who is the actor who delivered the prologue?" he demanded in a whisper. "What's his name and where does he come from?"

The Master of Revels looked slightly askance. "He calls himself Rothben Pendarion, my liege. I believe he comes from Baileywell."

"What do you know about him?"

"N-not a great deal, my lord—except that he has considerable talent, as you will soon see. He has been cast," explained the master, "in the role of St. Alanin himself."

The set crew were returning to the wings, leaving behind a simulated outdoor scene: the forecourt of a stone fortress set against a painted backdrop of snow-capped mountains. "Everything stands ready now, my lord," continued the Master of Revels. "May I give the actors their signal?"

Gythe had already arrived at a private resolution to keep an eye on his mother during the course of the performance. "Yes," he said to the waiting master. "Let the play begin."

The first act of the miracle play was set in the mountain retreat of the Corrianon chieftain Widsith Whitfauconer. Ringed round by the members of his comitatus, the legendary warlord bewailed the woes of his people: how they had been overwhelmed by their Ap Lliar neighbors and forced into serfdom, forbidden on pain of death to practice the miraculous rites of their ancient religion. "Alas that the arts of the Magi are lost," lamented the chieftain in the words of the playwright. "Else might we have seen the deliverance of my daughter, Aelwyn of the White Brow, she who this morning's dawn was struck down by the blood-feathered arrows of our enemies. . . ."

There was a flicker of movement between two sections of painted canvas on the left side of the stage. A heartbeat later, a tall cloaked figure stepped forward through the gap into the light. "My lord, the gifts of the Magi are *not* lost," said the golden inimitable voice of Rothben Pendarion. "All the skills and powers of the elder days have I gathered into my hands so that a new princedom may arise from the ashes of the old."

Infused with all the rich vocal melody at the speaker's command, the words resonated with intimations of promised glory. Her pulse quickening, Gwynmira tensed, waiting with keen anticipation for her first glimpse of the face that went with the voice. On the stage below, the player-Widsith girded himself up and advanced upon the newcomer. "Who are you, wanderer?" he demanded. "And what manner of man are you that you come upon us like a thief in the night, silent and alone?"

The cloaked figure lifted back his hood. "I am called

Alanin Penrithyn," said the speaker. "I am the sword hand of high destiny. I am the harbinger of a new order."

The speech was melodramatic. The effect was anything but that. Gazing down at the actor Rothben Pendarion, Gwynmira felt her bone marrow turn to water.

Standing bareheaded in the full glow of the stagelamps, he was all lights and shadows, from the pale sheen of candlelight that lay like a halo on his night-black hair, to the iconlike folds of his dark robe. The cultivated austerity of his features was offset by an incontestable air of virility. Gwynmira was left feeling sensually vulnerable, as though her nerves were made of glass.

She was not allowed license to analyze the ambivalence of her own reactions. Even as she became aware that her son, Gythe, was staring at her, the player-Widsith struck a pose and demanded of his counterpart, "By whose authority are you here?"

Rothben Pendarion lifted up his right hand. Light flickered green off the jewel set in the ring he wore on his middle finger. "The authority is my own—by virtue of the power vested in me," he said, his voice floating like a clarion call toward the oak-timbered rafters. "If you believe in me and follow my counsel, you shall have victory over your enemies, and your descendants shall rule this land. If not, your people will be scattered like chaff before the wind, and not even the wind shall remember your name."

In one breath a promise. In the next a warning. It seemed to Gwynmira that she was being offered a choice between two genuine alternatives. Even as she groped for the logic to explain such a fanciful notion, Rothben Pendarion's brilliant glance leaped upward like an arc of lightning to engage with hers. Staring back at him over the heads of his fellow players, she felt herself begin to dissolve in the onyx-glitter of that compelling gaze.

A hand touched her arm. "That's not right," protested Gythe's voice in her ear. "That wasn't in the script."

Gwynmira's senses were swimming. "What does it matter?" she murmured absently, and felt a slight pull at her sleeve as Gythe whipped his hand away.

Such adolescent petulance at that particular moment came as an unwelcome distraction. Gwynmira said with brittle temperance, "I daresay the playwright made some last-minute changes. You may take him to task, if you choose, once the performance is over."

Stung into silence, Gythe glowered down at the tall man in black who seemed to have taken command of Gwynmira's regard. The young king-elect was annoyed that his mother should display such interest in a common play-actor. At the same time, he caught himself admiring Rothben Pendarion's enviable grace of movement and force of character.

Fascinated in spite of his resentment, Gythe began paying closer attention to the play. The script had been conceived to present episodes from the saint's life with the conventional stylism of stained-glass windows, like pictures within a frame: St. Alanin using Orison to heal Widsith's injured daughter; St. Alanin guiding the Whitfauconer chieftain down out of the mountains through a black winter fog to meet Evelain Du Morrigan, sea-lord of Vesteroe; St. Alanin mystically purging a traitor's poison from the cup that Widsith and Evelain were to share in celebration of their alliance. Well-known to every person present, the incidents might have come across as so many formulaic tableaux. Instead, Rothben Pendarion infused every scene with a passion and mystery that seemed to bring the old legend glowingly to life.

So persuasive was his performance that Gythe found himself spontaneously caught up in the events unfolding before his eyes. Both his imagination and his pride were kindled by the later scenes of the play which dealt with the founding of his own family line.

Acting upon St. Alanin's advice, Evelain Du Morrigan had married Aelwyn Whitfauconer, taking her name in token of the unity they hoped to forge between their peoples. With St. Alanin to guide them, Evelain

and Aelwyn had gone on to reconcile the warring popu-
lations of old Dunsinar under one rule. After founding
the city of Farrowaithe, Evelain had assumed the title
Lord Warden, establishing at the same time his family's
preeminence among the nobility of the realm.

Once political stability had been achieved, St.
Alanin had sought the new ruler's support in carrying
out his own religious mission. Evelain had gladly consented, and out of this union of spiritual and temporal
powers was born the kingdom of East Garillon and the
Order of Mage Hospitallers.

A new kingdom. A new order. Contemplating the
sweeping achievements of his own forebear, the young
king-elect of latter-day East Garillon was powerfully
moved to think of himself in a whole new light. Words
that Rothben Pendarion spoke to the player-Evelain rang
out with emphasis that seemed to Gythe to be personally
significant:

"You stand, my lord, upon a threshold in time.
Behind you lie the old days. Turn your back on them, for
they are dead. Before you stretches a new age. Step
forward with stern resolution, for there all your aspirations will be fulfilled, and all your dreams will come to
ripeness. . . ."

Aspirations. Dreams of power and glory. The power
to command individuals and armies. The glory of
personal conquest. Sailing dreamily from vision to shimmering golden vision, Gythe lost the thread of the play.
He was not aware that the performance had ended until a
burst of applause jolted him to earth. He was himself still
clapping enthusiastically when a deferential voice spoke
in his ear. "I beg your pardon, my lord, but one of the
players has requested a few words with you in private.
Will it please you to grant him a brief audience?"

Recalled from the dizzy spiraling heights of his own
imagination, Gythe looked up to find the Master of
Revels standing over him. From his opposite side,
Gwynmira spoke up with suave curiosity. "Which player, Master Raedmon?"

"Rothben Pendarion, milady," said the master, with

an apologetic glance at Gythe. "He played the role of St. Alanin."

"Indeed? I wonder what he has to say for himself." Gwynmira's long-lashed eyes were veiled. She ran a teasing forefinger along the line of her son's jaw. "Well, my lord? Shall we allow this fellow a moment or two of your precious time?"

Gythe would have preferred to speak with Rothben Pendarion alone, but one glance at his mother's face assured him that she had every intention of being present. Less than pleased, but unable to think of a sufficiently plausible excuse for excluding her, he surveyed the Master of Revels with an air of hauteur and said grandly, "We can see no one, Master Raedmon, until we have first done our guests the courtesy of bidding them farewell. After that, we will receive this play-actor in the Pelican Chamber."

The room in question was situated at the western end of the dining hall, separated from the main room by a short, discreet length of passageway. It had been constructed as a useful retreat for anyone wishing to pursue business too sensitive to be discussed in more public surroundings. In keeping with standing custom, the servants had left a fire burning on the hearth. Gythe led the way into the warm glow of lamplight and woolen tapestries, and took a seat on the brocaded divan to the right of the fireplace. Catching sight of her own reflection in the gilt-edged mirror just inside the door, Gwynmira paused to make sure that she was looking her best. No sooner had she reassured herself concerning the state of her makeup and the placement of her jewels than a soft knock at the door announced the arrival of the Master of Revels with Rothben Pendarion.

At a spoken word from his mistress, the master ushered the tall play-actor across the threshold and then withdrew with well-trained alacrity. As the door closed behind him, Rothben Pendarion advanced three graceful steps toward the Dowager-Regent and bowed deeply, affording her a fleeting view of wide shoulders and a supple well-muscled back. Veiling her appreciation be-

hind lowered eyelashes, Gwynmira offered him a slender
perfumed hand to kiss. "I am most pleased to make your
acquaintance, sir," she said dulcetly. "Allow me to
congratulate you upon your consummate performance.
A man of your talents must surely go far."

The light, experienced touch of his lips against her
fingers seemed to leave a glowing, invisible imprint on
her skin. "Thank you, milady, for the compliment," said
Rothben Pendarion. "The same might be said about
you—if there is any truth in rumor."

The audacity of his remark earned him a sparkling
rebuke from the Dowager-Regent's dark amber eyes.
"You are forward, Master Pendarion. What has rumor
led you to expect of me?"

The player's full sensual mouth lifted at the corners.
"That you are as ambitious as you are beautiful, milady.
And as resolute as you are ambitious."

Tall and clean-favored, his black hair glossy as a
raven's wing, he radiated a potent male vitality. Again
Gwynmira experienced a misting of her senses. She said,
"Are you presuming to criticize me, sir?"

He laughed, shaking his head in urbane disclaimer.
"Never, milady. On the contrary, your qualities are
those I most admire. I hope your son shares them."

Left fuming on the outside edge of the conversation,
Gythe decided he had gone unnoticed long enough. He
said with waspish emphasis, "I understand, Master
Pendarion, that you want to speak with me about
something."

The tall black-haired man did not appear to notice
the shrill pitch of immaturity in his questioner's voice.
Turning, he surveyed the boy with a cool assumption of
gravity. "Forgive me, my prince. You are correct. I am
here because I happen to have come across information
of a highly confidential nature which you and your lady
mother need to know about."

Gythe rose to his feet, glaring at his visitor through
narrowed eyes. "What kind of information?"

Rothben adjusted his position so that his gaze

included Gwynmira. His pupils held a queer inner luminance. "This won't be pleasant for you to hear," he said warningly. "But it is in your own best interests that you should find out now, while there is still time for you to make preparations. Your brother, Evelake, is not so dead as you have been led to suppose. He is alive and well, and even as we speak, he is making plans to return to East Garillon, intending most certainly to launch a campaign to reclaim his inheritance."

A thunderstricken silence greeted this astonishing announcement. The silence grew, until Gythe suddenly drew a sharp breath. "I don't believe you!" he spat. "How do you know this? What kind of proof do you have?"

Rothben's gaze flickered aside toward Gwynmira. She was standing pale and still as a sculpture in snow. "Proof of a kind accessible to the mages and their disciples," he said to Gythe. "My affinity with Alanin Penrithyn is more than coincidental."

He lifted a shapely hand, turning it from the wrist so that the stone in his ring drew the firelight and converted it into a flickering corona of emerald glints. Gythe's jaw dropped slightly as he stared at it. Then he recovered himself with a shake. "That jewel," he breathed. "It's not a smaragdus. Is it?"

Rothben nodded. "You are astute, my prince."

"But—" Gythe paused and began again. "I thought only mages were allowed to wear magestones."

"That is a matter of legal convention," said Rothben gently. "It is not a matter of fact. I do not, I admit, have the sanction of the Order. But my gifts—for the Magia and other powers—are genuine. If you will allow me, my prince, I will be happy to furnish you with a demonstration."

Gythe's expression was black, but Rothben's suggestion aroused a keen glimmer of interest. "Yes!" said the young king-elect, his voice quivering with eagerness. "Show me what you are capable of doing with these powers of yours."

"I shall need a focus of some kind," said Rothben. "Is there any place in the castle that was particularly associated with your brother—for example, the rooms he occupied while he was still in residence here."

"There is the southeast tower," said Gwynmira. Her voice rang hollow. "We can take you there now."

"As it pleases you, milady." Rothben was all deference.

"Good!" said Gythe grimly. "I'll fetch a guardsman or two to light the way."

He made a bound for the door and stepped outside. Left briefly alone with the man who called himself Rothben Pendarion, Gwynmira subjected him to a searching look. Meeting her gaze, he lifted a quizzical eyebrow. "Are you having doubts, milady? You may be sure I am telling you the truth."

"I don't doubt your word," said the Dowager-Regent. "But I can't help wondering why you should feel impelled to warn me—warn us that my son's position is not secure."

Her companion's smile was caressing. "Did I not say that your qualities are those I most admired? There, and nowhere else, lies your answer. Shall we go . . . ?"

WINDOW OF VISION

THE TOWER GWYNMIRA HAD DESIGNATED lay at the farther end of the south wing which for several generations had housed the Lord Wardens, their families, and their intimate attendants. Getting there from the Pelican Chamber on the ground floor involved traversing three levels of stairs and as many separate lengths of passageway. Two Farrowaithe Guards with lanterns accompanied the party as far as the last flight of steps. When they arrived, Gwynmira took one of the lamps to light the rest of the way.

"Wait for us here," she said to their escort. "Either I or my son will call you if you are needed. Otherwise, we are not to be disturbed."

The door leading into Evelake's long-disused apartment was accessible from below by means of an open stairway which ascended along the cylindrical curve of the outer wall. The circular chamber beyond had been divided into sitting room and sleeping loft. A small lozenge-shaped oriel opened off the opposite side of the circle to form an eyrielike reading nook. Six long window panels yielded a segmented view of the black midnight sky.

The apartment had been stripped bare of all its hangings and most of its furniture. Gwynmira set the lamp down on the one remaining lampstand and drew her cloak more closely about her with a small shiver of disdain. "Some of the servants still come up here regularly to dust and sweep the floor. I'm sure I don't know why," she said. Then turned to Rothben. "Will this take long?"

The man known to his enemies as Borthen Berigeld shook his sleek black head. "There are one or two preparations I must make first, before we may begin," he said with a thin smile. "If you will permit me . . . ?"

There was a small wooden table by the door. Borthen moved it to the center of the room. From the pouch at his belt he produced a shallow black bowl and a vial of pale oily liquid, which he emptied into the bowl with a muttered phrase too low for his companions to catch. Leaving the vial on the table, he reached into an inner pocket of his doublet and drew out a jeweled pendant. The stone flashed emerald-green as it caught the light, and Gythe repressed a slight gasp. The gem was the twin of the one the dark mage was wearing.

Holding the bowl in one hand and the pendant in the other, Borthen stood motionless for a long moment, wrapped in deep concentration. Then he beckoned

Gythe and Gwynmira to join him. "We three must be in physical contact if you are to participate in my vision," he said. "My lord, place your hand on my right shoulder, and you, milady, place yours on my left. Do not speak or call out. If you do, you will shatter the image."

Gythe did as Borthen had instructed. "What are we going to see?"

"Your brother and his confederates," answered Borthen, "as they are at this very moment in time."

He closed his eyes, lips moving in silent invocation. After a short time, Gythe became aware of a tingling in the fingers that rested on the dark mage's arm. Small noises, hitherto unheard, became distinctly audible— the sound of his mother's shallow breathing, the skitter of a mouse in the wainscot, the scrape of boots on stone as the soldiers downstairs shuffled their feet to alleviate the tedium of waiting. Even as the boy marveled at his new enhanced perception, Borthen lowered the pendant into the black bowl.

The dark mage uttered a single guttural syllable of command, and a plume of murky green smoke boiled up hissing from the bottom of the bowl. At once the walls of the surrounding room began to fade from view. For a moment, all was cloudy. Then a new scene began to take shape.

Breathless with amazement, Gythe looked around him. He seemed to be standing in the middle of a sandy clearing. Embers glowed red and gold in a firepit a few yards away, throwing a dim yellow light over an area bordered by outcroppings of stone. Beyond the enclosure, barren miles of starlit desert stretched away into the night.

There were people sleeping around the campfire, discernible as dim blanket-wrapped bundles on the ground. Other human forms prowled wakefully along the camp's perimeter. Two robed figures were sitting side by side on a large flat boulder several feet to the right of the firepit. Even as Gythe stared at them, the smaller and slighter of the pair straightened up and stretched, turning his head so that his face was visible in profile. Gythe bit his tongue hard to keep from crying out in shocked disbelief. For the face belonged to his brother, Evelake.

Not, however, as he remembered seeing it last. This Evelake was plainly older, his features sharpened as though by a grave illness from which he had only recently recovered. His fair hair, uncharacteristically unclipped, fell in tumbled locks across the shoulders of the white cotton garments he was wearing. Recognizing the Pernathan design of the clothing, Gythe felt his mouth go dry.

Something intrinsically uncontrived about the scene left Gythe convinced that what he was seeing had the substance of truth. Scarcely able to contain his feelings of having somehow been cheated by fate, he wrenched his angry gaze away from Evelake's thoughtful mien to take stock of the tall man who sat next to him.

Evelake's companion had a striking face, constructed along uncompromising lines of severity and strength. The man himself was young, but his aggressive aquiline features bore the stamp of hard-won experience. His hair, a rich shade of auburn, showed streaks of white at the temples.

Power seemed to emanate from him in invisible waves. The tangible force of his personality reminded Gythe eerily of Rothben Pendarion.

Evelake and his companion seemed to be in the midst of a serious conversation, but nothing of what passed between them was audible to their secret audience. Even as Gythe squinted in an attempt to read their lips, the auburn-haired man abruptly stiffened up, pulling back his broad shoulders as though he felt the prickle of a knifepoint against his spine.

Evelake leaned in toward his companion, brown eyes startled and inquiring. The auburn-haired man forestalled him with a gesture and sprang to his feet.

His handsome face had taken on an intense abstracted look, as though he were striving to identify the source of some elusive sound or smell. Gythe felt a sudden irrational desire to turn and run before he could be spotted.

Brows drawn tightly together in a frown of concentration, Evelake's companion circled around the rock on which he had been sitting until he was facing the direction of the unseen onlookers. Here he came to a bristling halt, eyes narrowed to emerald slits.

His glance wavered for a moment, like a compass needle seeking its point of orientation. Then his gaze steadied and gravitated toward the very spot on which Borthen was standing.

The black mage uttered a hissing imprecation and overturned the bowl in his hand. Even as the magestone pendant spilled toward the tabletop in a splatter of oil, Gythe experienced a sudden wrenching sensation in his gut. The nausea blinded him momentarily to all else around him. When the paroxysm subsided, he found himself back again in the impoverished confines of his brother's abandoned rooms.

Gwynmira was leaning over the table, her eyes closed, her face as white as chalk. The mage Rothben was glaring down at the fallen magestone as though it were a scorpion. "What happened? Why did you break off your trance?" panted Gythe. Then voiced a more fearful question. "Who was that tall man with the red hair?"

Borthen raised his head, his hooded eyes malevolent as a cobra's. "That, my prince, was the rogue-mage who has attached himself to your brother's cause. His name is Caradoc Penlluathe."

He bent to retrieve the pendant. Holding the jewel up to the light, he said, "Caradoc is highly gifted—more gifted, it appears, than I previously suspected. If I hadn't severed contact when I did, he almost certainly would have penetrated our field of perception. We had better not risk spying on him again for a while. He mustn't guess that I am helping you until we are better prepared."

"I remember Caradoc Penlluathe. He was to have been executed in Ambrothen for necromancy," said

Gwynmira. Her hollow eyes searched Borthen's face. "You sound as though you know this man well."

"He and I have been adversaries for quite some time now," said Borthen. "Which is one more reason why I hope you will accept the aid I can give you."

"Caradoc Penlluathe, as I recall, was in league with the men who abducted my stepson in the first place," said Gwynmira. "Why has he changed his coat?"

"He hopes to win his way back into favor with the Hospitallers' Order," said Borthen. "Evelake Whitfauconer has everything to gain from soliciting the aid and influence of the mages. Baldwyn Vladhallyn, certainly, would support him, and would use his authority as Arch Mage to rally the rest of the Order against you. If that happens, you are going to need more than military forces to retain your throne."

He turned to Gythe. "Have you ever been tested for affinity for the Magia?"

Gythe bit his lip in vexation. "Yes—three years ago, by Arch Mage Baldwyn himself. But it didn't work. I mean, I didn't show any latent sensitivity."

"Still, I gather the idea of wielding that kind of power is not unattractive to you?" Borthen was watching the boy closely.

"I would have given almost anything—" Gythe cut himself short with a scowl. "It hardly matters now, does it?"

"It might. The Magia is not the only supernatural force at work in the cosmos," said Borthen.

His gaze became more intent as he continued speaking. "There are other powers, equally potent, equally accessible—given the right conditions. If you were to ally yourself with one of these other principles, you would be in a position to defend yourself against any outside threat."

Gythe's dark eyes flew wide at the prospect. "What would I have to do? To gain control of a power like the Magia?"

"You must learn the techniques by which an individual can summon a principle of power and bind it to do his bidding," said Borthen. "I can teach you if you are truly willing to learn."

Gythe's handsome face was flushed with eager enthusiasm. "Please!" he declared fervently, then checked himself as a belated thought occurred to him. "Will it be very difficult?"

"It is not easy." Borthen's expression was inscrutable. "It will require a certain amount of . . . self-sacrifice."

"If it means I'll be able to show the Hospitallers a thing or two, I don't mind!" declared Gythe with ringing conviction. "How soon could we start?"

"We could begin tomorrow," said Borthen. "If your lady mother gives her consent?"

He turned to Gwynmira and arched an inquiring eyebrow. The Dowager-Regent's chiseled face had taken on the sunken malevolence of a skull. "I would consent to anything, Master Pendarion, that would enhance my son's chances for achieving victory over his enemies," she said coldly. "If you return to the castle tomorrow afternoon, you shall find him—and me—waiting to receive you."

The following day the weather turned to heavy rain. As the autumn daylight began to fade away into a showery evening, Gythe retired with his favorite deerhound to the somber ancestral opulence of the family's trophy room. Curled up on the hearth rug, the deerhound Chluan watched with liquid brown eyes as his young master paced restlessly up and down beneath the many rows of deer antlers displayed on the walls. It was approaching five o'clock when a soft-footed manservant brought word that Gythe's new tutor had arrived and was waiting in the anteroom.

When Borthen was ushered into his presence a moment later, Gythe waited with ill-concealed excitement until the servant had withdrawn. As the door swung shut, leaving them alone, he turned to look up at the tall man standing at his side. "I was beginning to think you'd never get here!" he exclaimed. Then his eager gaze lighted upon the small silk-wrapped bundle that the dark mage was holding in one gloved hand. "What have you got there?" he asked.

Borthen's smile left his eyes unreadable as ever. "A gift for you, my prince," he said doucely, and placed the packet in the boy's cupped hands.

The hard object within the wrappings weighed strangely heavy for its size. Gythe peeled away the layers of silk with gingerly care, then caught his breath as he glimpsed what lay beneath.

It was a smoothly polished gemstone the same size and shape as a pigeon's egg. Its heart glowed with a baleful crimson light that seemed to churn like a pool of molten magma. The animated radiance of it reflected luridly up into his face as he gazed at it in rapt fascination. "It's a pretty thing," murmured Borthen. "Isn't it?"

His voice was low, almost caressing. Gythe nodded, hardly able to tear his mesmerized attention away from the shimmering activity at the heart of the jewel he held between his palms. "What is this?" he breathed, almost reverently.

"It is a pyrope," said Borthen. "Like the gems wielded by the Hospitallers, it is a talisman—a conductor of spiritual energy."

It seemed to Gythe as he stared at the stone that he could hear many voices calling out to him in an inviting chorus from the depths of the jewel's interior flame. Charged with seductive melody, the voices throbbed with dulcet promises that set his blood racing even though he only half understood them. He said huskily, "Is it the Magia that makes the stone glow?"

"No," said Borthen. "It is Aeshma—the power of the denizens of Topheth."

The names meant nothing to Gythe. His cheeks hectically flushed, he said, "Will this stone allow me to draw on the Aeshma the way the mages draw on the Magia?"

"Yes—provided that you succeed in arranging an alliance with the spiritual entity who has brought the pyrope to life," said Borthen. "It will entail an exchange of favors. If you want this spirit to loan you a measure of its power, you must give it something in return— something that it wants as much as you want the ability to perform marvels."

Gythe's smooth brow developed a crease of uncertainty. "What have I got to offer?"

"At the very least, all the gifts and virtues that come from having a physical body," said Borthen softly. "Taste and touch, sight, smell, and hearing—all the manifold pleasures of sensory experience. The opportunity for power and intellect to become for a while incarnate."

Gythe's pupils were dilated. He said falteringly, "Are you suggesting that this creature wants to take possession of my body?"

"You misunderstand, my prince. What your ally desires," said Borthen gently, "is the chance to *share* your sensory experiences at the same time that it shares with you its power."

As Gythe considered this, the voices from the heart of the stone renewed their suppliant murmuring in tones tender as a lullaby. They seemed to plead beseechingly for his trust and indulgence, offering in exchange all manner of hitherto unimagined delights. "Caution is not always a virtue," continued Borthen, giving the boy a glinting look from under his heavy lids. "Have you forgotten that your brother has already found *his* ally?"

The reminder stung. Recalling the aura of power that had surrounded the mage Caradoc Penlluathe, Gythe drew himself up, his face hardening. He said thinly, "What have I got to do?"

"You must seek to enter into direct communion with your ally," said Borthen. "Look deep into the very center of the stone. See if you can find a center point to the light."

"All right," said Gythe. "I'll try."

He bent his gaze upon the glowing jewel in his hands. After an interval of several heartbeats, his dark eyes focused and sharpened. "I—I've found it!" he stammered excitedly. "It's like a star . . . at the bottom of a volcano!"

Red as blood, the star sang out to him with the voices of a thousand sirens. The song inflamed him with a host of half-realized yearnings and desires. "Now that you have found the origin of the light," said Borthen, "you must call it to you."

"By what name shall I call it?" whispered Gythe.

A growing sense of voluptuous warmth was embracing him. Half-intoxicated, the boy did not see his dark companion's glittering smile. "Call it Herech," said Borthen softly. "Herech Thanatos."

"Herech . . . Thanatos. . . ." The name seemed to resonate with dark music on Gythe's tongue. He pronounced it again, giving the individual syllables weight and stress. The rocking three-beat rhythm gave him pleasure, and he began to chant the name as though it were a litany: 'Her—ech . . . Than—atos . . . Her —ech . . . Than—atos. . . ."

And from the heart of the pyrope, the legion voices called sibilantly in answer, "Here . . . we are . . . here. . . ."

Enthralled, Gythe felt as though his blood had caught fire. He burned suddenly with longing. "Come . . ." he breathed devoutly. "Come to me. . . ."

"We come!" sang the voices. And in that instant, the red star at the center of the stone flowered into a thousand fiery eyes.

Like myriad sparks fleeing a smelter's forge, the eye-motes shot upward, bursting out of the gemstone to sweep Gythe into a scintillating storm of crimson lights. Blinded and bedazzled, he was caught up in the whirlwind of their wanton dance. His lingering shreds of doubt flew from him like so many scattered garments. In a delectable twinkling of surrender, he yielded himself up to his many-eyed ravisher, and moaned in painful ecstacy to feel the molten blaze of eldritch power surge throughout all his members.

Through scarlet veils of incarnality, remote as from a great distance, he heard the voice of his black-browed mentor. "The Aeshma has been kindled within you. Now open the eyes of your mind!"

Gythe, however, had no need of any outside prompting. Like an embryo quickening in the womb, a strange newly-conceived part of himself was rousing to awareness, clamoring hungrily for license to explore its virgin environment. Seized by a sudden lust for sensual impressions, he directed his attention outside of his augmented self and discovered that all his sensory perceptions had been heightened to an exquisite pitch of sensibility.

Ordinary noises—the crackle of the fire on the hearth, the spatter of rain against the windowpanes— had taken on symphonic intensity. Glancing around him, he noted with magnified exactitude the cellular grain of the wood paneling, the moth flecks scattered among the stitches of the tapestries. He felt the individual fibers of the carpet give way underfoot as he turned on his heel, scanning the room at large. Avid for details, his roving gaze lighted upon the deerhound Chluan among the shadows by the far wall.

Transfixed in the act of lifting a paw to scratch, the rough-coated animal started up under the piercing impact of his master's lambent eyes. His hackles rose. All four legs braced as though to spring, he drew back his lips and uttered a low rasping growl.

Abrasive as the grating of chalk on slate, the noise set Gythe's teeth on edge. Nostrils twitching at the ripe effluence of brute fear, he took a step forward. The dog shrank back, its snarling muzzle flecked with froth. Gythe noted its reactions with interest. He wondered how the animal would respond to a psychic form of attack.

Concentrating all his enhanced powers of perception, he studied the dog carefully. It was possible, he discovered, to see through fur and hide as through a pane of glass. He noted the quivering knots of pink muscle overlaying white bone, the autonomic activity of the viscera. Then he focused his surgical gaze upon the animal's beating heart.

Amplified a hundredfold, the sound of the heart's beating crashed against Gythe's eardrums like waves against a seawall: The noise sent sympathetic vibrations racing in ripples up from the base of his own throat. He watched for a time, studying the regulated flow of blood through the heart's chambers until he could anticipate the lag between systole and diastole. Then, prompted by curiosity, he seized the instant of caesura and held on to it.

Like a shaft shot through the spokes of a rolling wheel, the brief delay was enough to bring the natural rhythm of the organ to a shattering standstill. The dog shuddered convulsively as its heart faltered. For a moment it trembled on the brink of collapse. Then out of the chaotic flash-fire of nerve impulses, the heart-pattern reemerged.

Gythe observed the animal's innate reflex for survival. Intrigued by the prospect of a challenge, he waited long enough to allow the dog's heart to settle back into its regular beat, then moved to arrest it a second time.

This time he entered actively into the struggle, opposing the resistance of living flesh with his own overriding will. His own control, he discovered, drew force from his victim's ebbing strength. His own veins throbbing with the thrill of anticipated conquest, he brought more power to bear.

The sense of his own virility was euphoric. Greedy for victory, he pressed his advantage to its extremity. The dog's life-energy flickered before him like a wayward candle flame. Even as he reached out to crush it, something that was neither light nor heat flared up into his face.

The rich hot savor of triumph suffused all his senses. For a moment he languished half swooning in the embrace of an exquisite pleasure. Then he felt something stir deep in his bowels.

Rousing, he attempted to repress it. Instead of subsiding, pain struck him like a dagger in the gut. The dagger of pain twisted, then withdrew, tearing at his entrails. His recent conquest forgotten, he screamed like a woman in childbirth as his body expelled a burden of power it could no longer contain. In the instant of separation he lost consciousness.

When he regained his senses, he was lying prone on a low divan. Gone was the luxurious acuity of perception, and with it the exhilarating power to command. His body ached in every limb as though he had been engaged in hard labor. His groin felt hot and sore.

He groaned and tried to sit up. An impersonal hand seconded his efforts. Feeling weak and shaken, he opened his throbbing eyes to find the man he knew as Rothben Pendarion sitting beside him. "W-what happened?" he stammered.

"Nothing untoward." The dark mage was matter-of-fact. "Your body is simply not yet conditioned to the demands you impose upon it under the influence of Aeshma. The duration of your periods of rapport with your ally will increase as your corporal frame grows more accustomed to such usage. Your abilities, likewise, will be subject to further enhancement in due course."

Gythe had stopped listening. His gaze had been drawn to an inert heap of grey fur on the floor by the north wall. A cold knot of dread tightened in the pit of his stomach. Shaking off Borthen's hand, he swung his legs over the side of the couch and called his deerhound by name. "Chluan!"

The shape on the floor did not move. "The beast is dead," said Borthen.

Gythe rounded on him, his dark eyes smoldering with anger and distress. "What have you done to him?" he demanded.

"I? Nothing," said Borthen with a faint twist to his long mouth. "If your pet is no longer alive, it is because you willed it to be so."

Gythe struggled for a moment with the memory of his first exercise in the use of power. He felt as if he might be sick. "That's not true," he protested. "I never meant to kill him!"

"No. Probably not," agreed Borthen calmly. "Experience will teach you how to regulate the effects of your power."

Gythe's face was ashen. "I don't think I want that kind of power," he said mutinously.

"Then what kind *do* you want?" inquired a brittle female voice from behind him.

Gythe had not realized that his mother was present. He whipped around to find her gazing at him in cool displeasure. "Nothing comes without a price, my dear," said Gwynmira. "Stop mewling like a greensick girl."

She came forward to stand over him. "If you reject the gift that has been offered you on account of some flea-ridden cur," she said with measured coldness, "may God curse me for having bred you a feeble-witted coward."

Her words stung like a birch-rod. Gythe started up, his white lips trembling. "I'm *not* a coward!" he objected.

"Then stop sniveling like one," said Gwynmira. She pointed to the glowing red jewel resting in its wrapping on the table beside the divan. "*That* represents power that will make you invincible. If you decline to take advantage of it, I shall begin to wonder if you are any true son of mine!"

"Patience, milady!" Borthen's musical voice was coolly forbearing. "Your son has done very well. He deserves an explanation rather than a scolding."

He turned to Gythe. "You are upset because you are wondering what could have prompted you to kill something you cared for. I can tell you why you did it: because it gave you greater pleasure than any other experience you have ever known before."

He smiled aridly. "That is why you will not renounce the Aeshma, even though it has cost you some minor distress. Now that you have tasted its solaces, you will never be content with lesser satisfactions. For you will always know that there will never be any pleasure in life greater than the thrill of absolute mastery."

There was a long silence. "Now then," said Borthen softly. "Will it please you, my prince, to keep the stone?"

Gythe's cheeks were pale, but his eyes burned with the remembrance of searing delight. "Yes," he whispered. "Yes, I will keep it. . . ."

SHERAT JESHUEL

THOUGH MOST OF THE TRAFFIC that passed through the Pernathan port of Ghazarah came and went by sea, the city was also accessible by three separate routes overland. One road followed the seacoast west and then south, passing through the lesser haven of Khadesh on its way to the greater city of Pirzen It'za. A second highway ran a level, well-tended course due east toward the wealthy enclave of Telphar, city of pomegranates, where five generations of sultans had wintered in their marble palaces among gardens fragrant with cinnamon and sandalwood. The third road had originally been little more than a crude track of hard-trodden earth used by the shepherds that pastured their herds on the desiccated grasses of the Ghaza foothills. Later it had been extended to accommodate traffic to and from the quarries of Sul Khabir, a penal settlement hacked out of the bare desert rock of the parched inland plateau of Khazar Mu'Jakr—the "Anvil of the Sun."

The mule drivers, carters, and soldiers who made regular forays back and forth from the quarries knew they were within a day's ride of the coast when they began to catch distant glimpses of dusty greenery on the

high ground to the northwest. Within the space of a mere
few miles, bare rock and sandy scree gave way to short
sun-browned turf dotted here and there with clumps of
hard-bitten brushwood. From that point on, goat paths
could be seen branching off into the hills on either side of
the road.

The herdsmen who roamed the foothills in all
seasons knew when and where to find hidden wells
among the arid slopes and deep ravines. Travelers less
familiar with the terrain could count on finding sweet
water all year round at Sherat Jeshuel, a natural spring
that flowed out of a cleft in the rocks at the foot of
Mohrab Gilead, the Mound of Cedars. It was at Sherat
Jeshuel that a mounted party of sixteen, en route northwest from Sul Khabir, decided to break their journey for
one night before pressing on to Ghazarah in the morning.

The waters that spilled out of the grotto of Sherat
Jeshuel were gathered first into a clear rock-bound pool.
The overflow from the pool created a clean shallow
rivulet that flowed south for half a mile along a pebbly
watercourse flanked by cedar trees and camphire before
fading away again into the porous ground. The riders
from Sul Khabir unsaddled the horses and led them
downstream to drink. Then, leaving their tethered
mounts to graze on the grass that grew among the cedars,
they returned to the water to bathe and refresh themselves before setting up camp.

The sun by that time was westering, but there was
still plenty of light in the sky. His brown hair still wet
from his ablutions, Serdor Sulamith—musician by
trade, adventurer by chance—had just finished shaking
the travel dust from his bedroll when he felt a hand on
his shoulder.

Blunt-fingered and powerfully capable, the hand
belonged to Gudmar Ap Gorvald, organizer of the
expedition that had set out from Ghazarah nearly a
fortnight ago. Under Gudmar's direction, the party had
carried out a successful raid on the slave pits of Sul

Khabir to rescue a fifteen-year-old boy named Evelake
Whitfauconer. Back in East Garillon, Evelake's political
enemies had murdered his father and laid claim to his
birthright as hereditary Lord Warden of East Garillon.
His friends were grimly determined not to let the conspiracy go unchallenged.

Gudmar had two swords slung over one broad
shoulder, their blades bound up in strips of cotton
quilting so that neither edge nor point could cut.
"Margoth informs me that we can expect nothing in the
way of supper for a while yet," he announced in response
to an owlish look from the minstrel. "I thought you
might be game for some drill work in the meantime."

"'The practyss of swerdsplaye,'" quoted Serdor
with dignity, "'ys a moste praiseworthie occupatione,
forbye yt doth enhance the quicknesse of the eye ond
begetteth in the bodie a pleasinge supplenesse of
grace—'"

"Besides possibly saving your life one of these
days," said Gudmar practically. "Are you coming?"

His pupil pulled a wry face. "It rather looks that
way, doesn't it?"

"Just what I like to see—a spirited show of enthusiasm," said Gudmar, clapping the younger man affably
on the back. "Come along—there's a very good spot not
far from where we left the horses."

Gudmar's choice of a fencing ground was a level
stretch of firm white sand down by the water. There,
screened from view of the camp by a feathery stand of
young evergreens, the two men stripped to the waist.
Chest and arms muscled like the forequarters of a
he-lion, his tawny hair and beard showing glints of gold
in the sunlight, Gudmar sketched out a few boundary
lines in the sand with the toe of his boot. Taking up his
drill sword by the hilt, Serdor made a few experimental
passes through the air to limber up his wrist.

The minstrel had had his right arm badly broken
several weeks before in a shipwreck off the coast of
Khadesh. The break had been set and sealed through the

magecraft of his friend Caradoc Penlluathe, but there remained some temporary stiffness in the ligaments. Serdor had begun his training in the use of the sword on the way to Sul Khabir. Since then, his movements had grown progressively more fluid. "Your arm looks good as new to me," remarked Gudmar as he watched his pupil's preliminary exercises. "How does it feel?"

"Better than my backside, after riding up and down hill over rocks for most of the day," said Serdor with rueful candor. "I'm ready any time you are."

"All right," said Gudmar, coming forward to take up his fencer's stance opposite the minstrel. "We'll take it slowly to begin with. En garde!"

Teacher and pupil saluted one another and crossed blades. "From the starting position, on my instructions," said Gudmar. "Now . . . disengage—straight thrust— recover! Thrust in prime—beat—thrust in tierce! Cut over—parry—riposte! . . ."

Body poised and quivering, grey eyes intent, Serdor devoted his full attention to following each clipped command as it was given. Quilted blades thudded more vigorously off one another as the pace of the drill accelerated, punctuated by barked words of praise or admonishment from Gudmar. Before long the two men were perspiring. "Hard to believe it's November back in Garillon!" panted Serdor as they both paused for breath.

"You'll believe it once the sun goes down," said Gudmar. He surveyed his pupil appraisingly. "I've done enough shouting for one day. Now it's time for you to let your own instincts give the orders."

Serdor grimaced. "I wouldn't mind so much if it weren't for the bruising jabs I take every time you break through my guard."

"Then you'll just have to perfect your guard so that it can't be broken," said a voice matter-of-factly from the sidelines.

Serdor and Gudmar looked around to discover a slim fair-haired boy sitting cross-legged in the soft sand higher up the bank. Serdor lifted an eyebrow in pained disapprobation. "That, my lord, is all very easy for *you* to say."

Evelake Whitfauconer was far too well acquainted with the minstrel's ironic manner of address to take umbrage at either the look or the tone. He grinned back at his friend and said reprovingly, "Don't be stuffy, Serdor. That recommendation is every fencing master's stock-in-trade."

"And not without good reason," agreed Gudmar. His hazel-gold eyes warming, he gave the boy a quizzical smile. "How long have you been watching? We never noticed you come up."

"That doesn't surprise me. From what I could see from here, neither of you had any attention to spare," said Evelake. He got to his feet and brushed the sand from his clothing, before adding casually, "I've been thinking it's time I started getting into a bit of training. Do you mind if I take a turn?"

Once he was standing, the loose flow of his Pernathan garments was no longer any disguise for the thinness of his frame; his face showed its bones too sharply for health. Gazing up at the son of his murdered friend, Gudmar found it all too easy to recall how ill the boy had been when his companions had finally found him.

The mage Caradoc had saved Evelake's life, but he had been unable to restore more than a vital measure of strength to the youth's dangerously depleted body. Only time could repair the long-term effects of prolonged hunger and exhaustion combined with soul-rape. And there had not yet been enough time. He cast an oblique glance at Serdor before speaking to Evelake. "Are you sure you're feeling fit enough?"

Evelake shrugged angular shoulders. "I've got to start somewhere."

Gudmar could not dispute this, much as he would have liked to. "Very well," he said. "Which one of us do you want for a fencing partner?"

Before Evelake could respond, Serdor interposed.

"Unless you have any violent objections," he said, "I imagine it probably ought to be me. I wouldn't be much use as a spectator, whereas Gudmar knows enough to school us both."

"That sounds fine to me," said Evelake. "Give me half a minute—"

He shrugged himself out of burnoose and shirt, and left them lying folded on the sand before coming to join his companions. Grasping his weapon by the foible, Gudmar presented Evelake with the hilt. "Take a moment or two to get your bearings," he advised. "I'll go find myself a suitable vantage point."

The thonging that bound the hilt was worn with sweat and use. Evelake felt for a comfortable grip, conscious of a tingling in his palm. He flicked the blade up and down, testing its weight and balance. As reflexes long-disused began sluggishly to awaken, he tried to recall the last time he had found an occasion to put a sword to use. And was chilled into sudden immobility when he remembered.

It had been the day of his capture by Borthen Berigeld.

His blade point faltered to the ground. Blind to his present surroundings, he seemed to be standing once more amid the hot clouds of swirling dust in a narrow pass between two flanking hills. He heard again in his own mind the clash of weaponry and the screams of wounded men as the members of his escort were cut down without mercy by their ambushers. He had himself crossed blades with one sallow-faced brigand who had died, accidentally self-impaled, on the shard of the boy's broken rapier. But then Borthen Berigeld had arrived to take up the challenge.

Evelake recalled the mortifying ease with which the necromancer had been able to subdue him. And that had been only the beginning. Even as he shied away from reliving the even blacker experiences of the hours following his capture, a light hand touched his bare shoulder in sympathy. "Evelake? Are you all right?" asked Serdor.

The sane reassuring sound of the minstrel's voice dispersed the evil shadows of eight months before. Evelake drew breath and gave himself a shake: whatever had happened in the past, he was now among friends. And for the moment, that knowledge was sufficient to allay his fears for the future. He lifted his eyes to meet concern in Serdor's grey gaze. "Don't mind me," he said firmly. "Let's get down to some serious fencing practice. . . ."

Back at the main campsite by the pool of Jeshuel, well away from the padded thump-thunk of mock swordplay, Margoth Penlluathe was devoting her energies to the task of organizing what everyone expected to be their last evening meal on the road to Ghazarah. Earlier in the day, Houssein Al Nas'ra, the pilot from the *Yusufa*, had brought down a wild sheep with a well-placed arrow. After ten uninspiring days of ship's stores—salt fish, dried fruit, and unleavened biscuit made from coarsely ground flour—the addition of fresh meat to the party's bill of fare offered Margoth a chance to display something of her flair for cookery.

Harlech Hardrada, owner and captain of the *Yusufa*, had placed two of his men at her disposal to help out with the heavier duties. Leaving Houssein to dress out the mutton he had provided, Margoth dispatched his assistants to fetch firewood and draw water. While they were gone, she delved deep into her own pack and dragged out a small pouch containing the slender store of herbs and spices she had brought with her on the outward journey.

There wasn't much left—some pepper, a little thyme, and a clove of garlic—but it was enough to help her make the most of what they had. When Houssein brought her the meat he had prepared, Margoth received it with a sunny smile of thanks. She said, in cautious Pernathe, "Tonight, I think, we should celebrate a little."

Stocky as a bullock, the big pilot grinned back at her. "If thou sayst it, it shall be so. Perhaps thy friend with the silver tongue will tell us more tales of Simbaya the Mariner. And perhaps, little marmoset, thou wilt show us again the art of juggling with knives?"

Harlech had assured Margoth that the nickname was intended to be taken as a compliment, reflecting his men's admiration for her exceptional dexterity. "I will show thee how it is done to juggle with knives," said Margoth, "if thou wilt teach me the use of the bow."

She realized that her grasp of Pernathe must be improving, for the pilot chuckled good-humoredly. "A small price to pay, little marmoset. In Ghazarah we shall seek out a bow suited to thy strength. And then let the birds in the air, the goats on the mountain, and all thy lord's enemies be wary for their very lives."

"All thy lord's enemies . . ." The words echoed on in Margoth's head after Houssein himself had departed. Despite the lingering heat of late afternoon, she experienced a small thrill of cold, as if a cloud had passed over the sun. The enemy they all had most to fear was the necromancer Borthen Berigeld. Although she had never set eyes on Borthen, Margoth knew how implacably ruthless he could be, corrupting those he sought to use, killing those he could not corrupt.

His victims included all the people Margoth Penlluathe held most dear. He had seduced her brother Caradoc into forswearing his vows as a Mage Hospitaller. He had slain Caradoc's teacher, Forgoyle Finlevyn, and had murdered their good friend Arn Aldarshot. Serdor Sulamith had suffered brutal physical violence at the hands of Borthen's henchmen. Evelake Whitfauconer had been so poisoned in spirit that it had taken all the strength that Caradoc had to give in order to save him.

Reviewing all of Borthen Berigeld's cold unbridled cruelties, Margoth tasted an anger that burned hot and bitter as gall. "Warlock or not, you bloodsucking bastard," she muttered grimly, "if I ever *should* get the chance to put an arrow through your black heart, may God have mercy on my soul, for I won't miss!"

CLOUDS OVER GHAZARAH

THE LIGHT BREEZES OF EARLY evening carried the savory scent of roasting meat as far as the makeshift training ground downstream. Narrowly escaping untouched from a feverish tac-au-tac exchange with his opponent, Serdor beat a hasty retreat to his own end of the fencing strip and flung up a hand in a gesture of capitulation. "Stop—hold off a moment!" he panted.

His own chest heaving with exertion, Evelake relaxed and lowered his guard. He said haltingly between breaths, "What's . . . the matter?"

Serdor dropped his blade point to the sand. Massaging his sword arm with his free hand, he announced with a grimace, "I think I just twisted something too far the wrong way."

Evelake promptly abandoned his aggressive position and went to join his friend. He plucked the rapier out of Serdor's slackened grip and said contritely, "I'm sorry—that might have been my fault. I wasn't entirely in control of my blade on that last engagement."

"Neither of you were," said Gudmar tartly, coming forward out of the lengthening shadows. He surveyed his pupils with a critical eye. "You're both getting tired. That's why your form is deteriorating. You'd better stop for tonight."

"If you say so." His breathing still somewhat disordered, Evelake handed over the drill weapons to Gudmar, then wiped his perspiring forehead with the back of his hand. "Whew! That was too much like hard work," he said. "I could use another dip in the water."

"Me, too," agreed Serdor.

"There's no reason why you shouldn't have one,"

said Gudmar. "If you want to stay here and freshen up, I'll go back to camp and see how supper's coming along. If there's any need to rush, I'll come back to let you know."

The stream was refreshingly cold after the warmth of the sun and the heat of physical exercise. Lying back on his elbows, Evelake shivered pleasurably as the clear water coursed smoothly over his prone body. "It feels good to be clean," he said, sighing.

Serdor was lying on his belly a few yards away, supporting his chin in his hands. He paused to dunk his head before nodding. "Even when I was very young— before I went to work for Holbein the Lutemaker—I never understood how some of my mates could go about for weeks without washing."

Evelake paddled lazily with his feet in the shallows. "Margoth told me you used to run with a gang of street thieves. She said they were the ones who taught you everything you know about juggling and sleight of hand."

"It was all part of the game," said Serdor. "A small group of us would stage a show on a public street corner. Once we'd attracted an audience, the others would make their way through the crowd picking pockets and cutting purses."

He paused to splash water over his back. "Not a very admirable way to make a living, I'm afraid, but it kept us fed and clothed."

"What happened to make you change your . . . profession?" asked Evelake, intrigued.

Serdor pulled a wry face. "I tried to pick Forgoyle's pocket. Naturally, I got caught."

Caradoc's teacher, Forgoyle Finlevyn, had been a mage of considerable talent. Evelake's brown eyes went owlish. "Didn't you realize he was a Hospitaller?"

"He wasn't wearing his magister's robes at the time," said Serdor ruefully. "The revelation came as quite a shock."

His expression turned reminiscent. "Two officers of

the Watch marched me off to gaol at Ambrothen Castle. I spent the next three days in custody, scrubbing floors, blacking boots, and doing all manner of other odd jobs about the place. And at the end of those three days, Forgoyle came and fetched me away."

He smiled crookedly. "Needless to say, we came to a gentlemen's agreement. Forgoyle's friend Holbein took me on as an apprentice, and Forgoyle himself enrolled me in the choristers' school at the cathedral. No more picking pockets or breaking locks for me."

"Until you and I came back to Ambrothen and discovered Caradoc had been incarcerated in the castle oubliette. I seem to recall," said Evelake dryly, "that you were all set to crack every lock in the place, if necessary, in order to get him out."

"I was all set to *try*," amended Serdor. He peered down at his wet hands. "If Margoth hadn't volunteered to come along, that whole affair might have ended very differently. Ten years is a long time to be out of practice."

"I can well believe that. Even eight months is a long time," said Evelake feelingly. He clucked his tongue in self-reproach. "You wouldn't know it from this afternoon's performance, but I used to be reasonably proficient at fencing. I don't even want to imagine what Jorvald Ekhanghar would have had to say if he'd seen me today."

"Who's Jorvald Ekhanghar?" asked Serdor.

"The Marshall of Gand. He was my arms instructor while I was serving as esquire under Arvech Du Penfallon," said Evelake. He added reflectively, "He was a formidable hand at most forms of combat. Apart from the seneschal himself, the only person I ever knew who could stand up to Jorvald was his own daughter, Tessa."

He smiled to see Serdor's nonplussed expression. "Jorvald must have taught her everything he knew—not that either of them ever advertised the fact. But Tessa and I used to fence together in private. Sometimes Arvech's son Devon came along to watch and cheer us on, but he was only one of a very favored few."

"Didn't Devon ever take part himself?" Serdor was mildly surprised.

"No." Evelake shook his head. "Devon's incurably crippled in his right leg. Jorvald, I think, would have encouraged him in spite of his handicap, but Lord Arvech wouldn't hear of his son's engaging in any kind of weapons training. I never could understand why."

"Maybe Lord Arvech thought he was doing the right thing by protecting his son against any chance of further injury," suggested the minstrel.

"Maybe. But he ought to have known better than that," said Evelake. He paused a moment, then continued. "Arvech Du Penfallon is a man of highest integrity. No one could have been more honorable than he was in all his dealings with me. All the same, he was less than just in his assessment of his own children."

Serdor was reminded of the fact that the Seneschal of Gand also had a daughter. "The girl's name is Kherryn, isn't it?" he said.

Evelake confirmed it with a nod. "She's a year younger than I am. And *very* serious."

The dawning lightness of his tone told Serdor that the boy was only half serious himself. "Like her brother, she spends too much time alone with her books," continued Evelake. "But I could almost always make her laugh."

The boy's simple pride in that one particular accomplishment brought an involuntary smile to the minstrel's expressive mouth. But Evelake sobered almost at once. "I hope we have a fair wind at our backs all the way to Gand," he said quietly. "I can't seem to shake off the fear that all may not be as well there now, as it was when I left eight months ago."

Gand—home of Delsidor Whitfauconer's old friend and ally—was where Delsidor's son and his friends were hoping to find support against their enemies. A fitful gust of wind rippled the face of the water, cool with the approach of dusk. Seeing the boy shudder slightly, Serdor cast a quick glance around them and realized that they had been overtaken by shadows. He gathered himself to his feet and extended a hand to Evelake. "It's going to be dark in another quarter of an hour," he said. "Time we started thinking about heading back to camp. . . ."

They arrived just as the other members of the party were gathering around the cookfire where Margoth and her two assistants were preparing to serve the company's evening meal. Catching sight of Serdor and Evelake as they emerged into the camp clearing, Margoth greeted them with a wave of her hand and beckoned them to join her. "I was all set to send someone down to the water to see if the pair of you had drowned," she said, handing Evelake a laden trencher. "Where's Caradoc? I thought he was with you."

Serdor's expression, as he accepted the plate she held out to him, was one of mild surprise. "No—the last I saw of him, he was pitching a tent on the north side of camp."

A tousled black head appeared at Margoth's shoulder. "Is it Caradoc you're missin', lassie?" inquired Harlech Hardrada, captain of the *Yusufa*. "If he's left ye guessin', I can tell ye where he's got to."

Reaching a knotty arm around her, he pointed across her nose in the direction of the spring. "See yon clump of brush just there, where the rock meets the sand? If ye look, ye'll see the beginnings of a trail—aye, that's it. I saw your brother head out that way about twenty minutes ago."

"Where does the trail lead to?" asked Serdor.

"Nowhere in particular," said Harlech. "From what I could see of it, it's just another goat track."

Margoth knit a puzzled brow. "Why would he wander off in that direction?"

Her male companions exchanged modest glances. Margoth clucked her tongue in asperity. "Don't be coy," she snapped. "If he was just off to relieve himself, he should have been back by now."

"If you want my opinion," said Serdor, "I think he

simply wanted to be alone for a little while, and has since lost track of the time. In which case, he won't have strayed very far. I'll go fetch him."

He handed his untouched plate to Harlech. "Would you like me to come with you?" asked Evelake.

"It's not really worth the bother," said Serdor frankly. "I won't be gone long. Just make sure there's some food left for me when I get back."

He plucked a resinous brand from the firepit to serve as a torch and made off in the direction that Harlech had indicated. A lingering ribbon of crimson sky was still visible above the low hills that shaped the western horizon, but overhead the darkness was pricked with stars. The minstrel located the head of the path by the yellow flare of his makeshift taper. Pocked with goat tracks, the trail skirted the rockbound bank of the pool, then zigzagged off among the odorous evergreens toward the back side of the hill.

Superimposed over the wedge-shaped hoofmarks of numerous wild goats were the prints left by the boots of a tall man with a long stride. The trail of footprints led down into and back out of the shallow tree-lined ravine that separated the squat mound of Sherat Jeshuel from the low hog-backed ridge of neighboring Sherat Ephatha.

All the signs indicated that Caradoc had made the hundred-and-fifty-yard climb to the top of the ridge. As he picked his own way along the narrow switch-backed path, Serdor began to have second thoughts about his own light words to Margoth. It was beginning to look as if something more serious than a mere desire for solitude had driven his friend out of earshot of the main camp.

The crown of Sherat Ephatha was bare of trees, an irregular concave depression ringed round about with boulders. As the minstrel reached the southern edge of the hollow, a familiar baritone voice spoke curtly from the shadows on the opposite side of the bowl. "I'm over here, Serdor."

The minstrel followed the rim of the bowl around to his right. He found Caradoc sitting cross-legged on the ground with his back propped against a large rock. Though the arid air of the foothills had not yet lost its warmth, the mage had drawn his cloak tightly around him, as though he felt cold. "What on earth are you doing all the way out here?" asked Serdor.

"Trying to get a little peace and quiet," said Caradoc. "I couldn't think straight with all that camp commotion going on around me."

He sounded testy and ill at ease. In the torchlight his handsome, strongly molded features showed traces of strain. "You look more than a little worried," said Serdor. "What's wrong?"

"Plenty—if my instincts are at all to be trusted." Caradoc stirred restlessly, his green eyes drawn almost against his will toward the dark line of hills to the north. "Tell me—does the air feel strange to you?"

"In what way?"

"Does it seem to be—I don't know—*shrill* . . . as if there were people wailing just out of hearing range?"

Serdor concentrated for a moment, then shook his head. "I don't feel anything."

"Well, I do," said Caradoc grimly. "I woke up to it this morning, and it's been nagging at me ever since. The closer we come to Ghazarah, the worse it gets."

Serdor stared at the mage, his grey eyes solemnly attentive. "Do you know what it is—or what's causing it?"

"Not yet," said Caradoc. "I can't make anything of it by myself. I need the aid of the Magia."

He flexed stiff back muscles and sighed. "So far, my attempts to enter into Orison have failed. All I can do is keep trying."

His voice betrayed impatience with himself. "My presence here will only complicate matters," said Serdor. "I'll leave you alone—"

"No, wait!" Caradoc sounded definite. "It would be better, I think, if you stay. Just put out the torch. We can always rekindle it if we need to."

Serdor snuffed the flame in the sand, then sat down

nearby to keep watch beside his friend. As darkness enveloped them, Caradoc composed himself in an attitude of contemplation, head erect, hands resting palm upward on his bent knees. Closing his eyes, he drew upon ten years' training as a Hospitaller for the discipline to regulate his breathing in defiance of fear and uncertainty.

The familiar exercise in self-control steadied his nerves. By degrees his rate of respiration decreased; his heartbeat slowed in sympathy. Once the agitations of his body had subsided, he turned inward in spirit, seeking the sublime elusive detachment of interior silence.

Sight . . . sound . . . taste . . . smell . . . He divested himself of each of them in turn, knowing that all his powers of perception would be enhanced by the Magia when they returned to him in the midst of Orison. At last only the capability of touch remained to anchor him to the physical world. But even as he steeled himself to sever that final sensory link with his surroundings, he was assailed by sudden doubts that made him hesitate.

Eight months had passed since he had lost his magestone to Borthen Berigeld. Since then, in spite of his loss, he had several times been granted the grace to use the virtue of the Magia on behalf of himself and his friends. But always the experience had been a gift: the Magia had visited him not at his command, as a servant summoned, but at his urgent request, as a master might answer a servant's earnest plea. Like wildfire on the mountains—like thunder on the hills—the visitations of mage power were not subject to his human authority. The thought that the Magia might deny him now, despite the keenness of his desire, made him suddenly fearful of sundering all his ties with the realm of sensible experience.

His imagination conjured up daunting visions of nothingness, and he wavered for a moment, torn between the impulse to retreat and the need to go on. Then in a resolute impulse of self-abandonment, he made the necessary blind leap of faith.

And found the keeper of the Magia waiting to receive him.

In the instant of contact, all his chilling fears of nullity evaporated in a warm glow of affirmation. Drawing strength and solace from this, the source of his comfort, he framed without words his appeal for the gift of discernment. The response was swifter than a stroke of summer lightning, generous as a summer shower. Like a tree parched by drought, he felt his deadened nerves spring back to life, vibrant with regenerated power.

His whole body tingled with heightened awareness. He could sense the presence of tree roots in the earth around him; the scent of aromatic herbs was like a cloud of altar smoke. He could hear voices from the camp on the far side of Sherat Jeshuel, and near at hand Serdor's light, even breathing.

He opened his eyes. The rocks and trees bordering the hollow stood out in luminous relief against the darkness, their outlines finely drawn as etchings in silver. The minstrel's slender, loosely gathered figure was surrounded by an ethereal pearllike glow—a pale light that enveloped him like a pair of folded wings.

Caradoc's moment of spiritual awakening invested everything near him with supernal beauty. But as he turned his attention outward, north toward Ghazarah, the disturbing subliminal whining that had plagued him all day became at once audible as the harsh funereal wailing of many voices—male and female, young and old—rising and falling in a choral extremity of bereavement.

Caradoc listened aghast as the voices keened and sobbed, their grief darkly infused with penitential bitterness, as if the mourners could find no explanation for their loss other than divine retribution. The despairing force of so much collective sorrow was unbearable. Feeling like a clumsy intruder, Caradoc was forced to turn helplessly away.

His withdrawal was attended by a dark rush of images. Skimming overland in his mind's eye, he saw miles of intervening hills as a succession of treeless hummocks shimmering with starlight. The ground north of Sherat Ephatha was seamed and broken. As he rode the wings of his vision back across a series of shallow ravines, he was transfixed in flight by a piercing stab of unmistakably physical pain.

Pain—and thirst. Excruciating thirst. Caradoc leaped to his feet in a scatter of small stones. His sudden movement startled Serdor out of his studied immobility. "What is it?" asked the minstrel, scrambling upright.

"There's a man lying injured at the foot of this hill," said Caradoc tersely. "Quick—light your torch and follow me!"

NEW DIRECTIONS

THE TALL MAGE LED THE way down the slope, his heightened powers of perception allowing him to spot every obstacle and pitfall even in the dark. Dependent on the light thrown off by the taper in his hand, Serdor came after as swiftly as he dared. He knew they had found what they were looking for when Caradoc fetched up short at the top of a shallow gully and turned back to beckon his friend forward. "He's down there," reported the mage. "Find a place to leave the light and give me a hand."

The walls of the gully were steep. There was a dusty figure sprawled facedown in the loose stones that filled the bottom of the fold. Kneeling beside the fallen man, Caradoc laid swift, knowledgeable hands on him. "He's got a sprained ankle and lots of bruises, but no bones actually broken," he said over his shoulder to Serdor. "It's safe for us to move him."

The man was completely unconscious. It required

the combined efforts of his two rescuers to shift his limp weight to the top of the bank. The torchlight picked out the man's slack features as he lay flaccid upon his back. Gazing down at him, Serdor gave a sharp exclamation of surprise and dismay. "Good God, Caradoc—do you know who this is?"

The mage nodded. "Aengus Cullen. From the *Yusufa*."

"But—what's he doing *here*?"

"We'll know soon enough," said Caradoc grimly.

He detached his water bottle from the clip on his belt. Taking the stopper from the neck, he tipped a small measure of water into his patient's parched mouth. For a heartbeat or two there was no response. Then abruptly the man Aengus shuddered and gulped convulsively.

Satisfied that his charge was capable of swallowing, Caradoc gave him more water, a sip at a time, until the flask was half-empty. As he knelt beside Aengus in the dark, his senses lost by degrees their enhanced acuity until all seemed dim around him. Serdor stood by, his thin face shadowy and anxious.

They were both so intent on attempting to revive the man they had found that neither of them noticed lights bobbing toward them until two newcomers were almost upon them. Warned by the sound of crackling brush, Serdor and Caradoc turned around as Gudmar, with Evelake at his heels, pushed through the last of the scrub growth to join them.

"There you are at last!" exclaimed Evelake in tones of mingled relief and reproach. "What happened? Did you get lost?"

"I wish that were our excuse," said Caradoc grimly, and beckoned the big merchant-adventurer to come closer. "Look here, Gudmar. It's Aengus Cullen from the *Yusufa*."

Gudmar's golden eyes narrowed sharply. "Aengus? What the devil is he doing *here*?"

"We haven't been able to get any information out of him yet—he's in a pretty bad way between exhaustion

and exposure," said Caradoc. "But he must have fled
Ghazarah in desperate haste. He didn't even have a
water bottle on him when we found him."

He gnawed his lip. "This confirms what my instincts
have been telling me all day: that some kind of disaster
has overtaken the city since we left it. I tried investigat-
ing by means of Orison, but all I got were jumbled
impressions of mass mourning—as if a lot of people had
died suddenly and unexpectedly. Aengus, no doubt, will
tell us more."

"Quite," agreed Gudmar succinctly. "I'd better see
if I can attract Harlech's attention." He put two fingers
between his lips and blew a piercing whistle.

Stumping stolidly through the bracken that covered
the western spur of Sherat Ephatha, Harlech Hardrada
stopped dead in his tracks at the sound of a sustained,
high-pitched trill coming from somewhere ahead and to
his right. Following close behind him, Margoth narrowly
missed treading on her companion's heels. She clutched
at his sleeve and peered over his shoulder into the
darkness beyond the cone of light thrown out by their
lantern. "That's Gudmar's signal," she said. "I hope that
means he and Evelake have managed to locate our
truants."

"Whatever else it may mean, they've made it round
tae the far side of this hummock ahead of us," said
Harlech. "We'd better mend our pace a bit if we dinnae
want them goin' daft for wonderin' if we've gone missin'
as well."

The ground on the north side of Sherat Ephatha was
slashed with small ravines. Margoth and Harlech found
the other members of their party waiting for them out in
the open beyond a giant's playground of tumbled boulders. Gudmar was the first to spot them as they approached, and came forward to meet them. Poised to
deliver an astringent observation at her brother's ex-
pense, Margoth took one look at the blond man's stern
face and swallowed her flippancy with a shiver of premonition.

The big merchant-adventurer wasted few words in getting to the point. "Before you go any farther, I'd better warn you that you may be in for some bad news," he said to Harlech, and proceeded to explain what had happened.

Harlech's swarthy face lost no apparent color during Gudmar's brief recital, but his cheek and jaw muscles hardened until they were set like wrought iron. "I dinnae doubt but there's some deviltry let loose in Ghazarah," he growled when Gudmar had finished. "Let me see Aengus. If we can rouse him, maybe I can get him tae tell me what's become of his shipmates."

Caradoc was bathing his patient's sun-blistered face with a cloth moistened from Serdor's canteen. Serdor and Evelake wordlessly drew aside as Harlech knelt down beside the red-haired mage. "He's starting to come around," said Caradoc. "Your voice is one he's bound to recognize. Call him by name—it'll give him something to focus on."

Harlech nodded. Black eyebrows bristling fiercely, he leaned over the injured man. "Aengus!" he urged. "Aengus, can ye hear me?"

The man stretched out on the ground stirred feebly and uttered a low groan. Harlech cast a sideways look at Caradoc, then repeated himself. "Aengus! Open your eyes, laddie."

Sunburned eyelids quivered, then retracted a painful chink. The seaman inhaled stertorously, then ran a swollen tongue over cracked lips. "C-Cap'n Harlech?" he whispered.

Harlech clapped him reassuringly on the shoulder. "Aye, Aengus, it's me."

Instead of relaxing, the crewman from the *Yusufa* lurched forward in an attempt to sit up. Failing, he clawed at Harlech's arm. "They're dead, Cap'n!" he choked. "They're all of 'em dead!"

Harlech's black eyes were sharp as gimlets. "Who's dead, Aengus?"

The sailor's bloodshot gaze was haunted. "Everyone you left aboard the *Yusufa*, sir—Haroun . . . Tregar . . .

Fergie—all of 'em but me. It was the cloud that killed 'em. The red cloud—"

He broke off short, his mouth working. "What red cloud?" demanded Harlech. "Where did it come from?"

A shudder racked the injured man from head to foot, but he pulled himself together to answer, "Some of the lads caught a wee fellow snooping about your cabin, sir. Duote had him hauled up on deck for questioning. The next thing we knew, he . . . it . . . it was like a demon burst out of this little sneak-thief—all red and crackling like it was full of lightning. It took Fergie and Timms . . . sucked the life right out of 'em. Then it spread. . . ."

He gulped for air and got his breathing back under control. "We abandoned ship, but this cloud-thing came after us . . . overtook us as we swam for the shore. We all dived deep, trying to get away from it. . . ."

He shook his head bemusedly. "I was toward the rear. I guess I was so blind with fear I lost my bearings. Anyway, when I came up I found myself back almost under the lea of the *Yusufa*. The cloud had moved on—toward the Ghazaran waterfront."

He shivered at the memory. "It was red havoc there, Cap'n, like some kind of plague. The sultan's men have since sealed off the port from all sides. No one can get in or out, either by land or by sea."

His hollow eyes searched Harlech's grim face. "I came ashore on the other side of Ghazra Point. I was pretty sure you'd have to stop for water at Sherat Jeshuel, so I set out overland, hoping I could warn you off."

His voice was beginning to crack, but he kept on, though tears of weakness were brimming in his eyes. "You can't get back to the *Yusufa*—she's nothing but driftwood and cinders now," he moaned. "They set her on fire and left her to burn . . ."

His speech trailed off into incoherent whimpering. Caradoc laid a quieting hand on his patient's furrowed brow. "That's enough—don't try to talk any more," he said softly. "You've done your duty. Now rest."

The mage's lowered voice exerted a calming effect

on the injured sailor. As his harsh breathing eased, he lapsed into exhausted sleep. "Let's get him back to camp," said Gudmar.

Harlech's expression was black. For all his small stature, he looked in that moment fully capable of committing murder. "Aye," he muttered darkly. "It'll take me just about that long tae figure out how I'm tae break this news tae the rest of my men."

The ten remaining crewmen from the *Yusufa* responded first with shock and then with anger. Later that evening, once the storm of grief and outrage had subsided into vengeful muttering, the leaders of the party withdrew to take counsel among themselves around one of the outlying campfires on the east side of the bivouac. "You're the only one among us who's ever had direct dealings with supernatural powers," said Gudmar to Caradoc. "This 'cloud' Aengus spoke of—have you any notion what it might have been?"

Caradoc shook his head. "I've never encountered anything like what he described, either by experience or by report."

He scanned the faces of his companions. "No mage below the rank of magister is encouraged to seek knowledge of any spiritual power other than the Magia. Such knowledge is judged dangerous, for reasons I'm sure you can appreciate. But consider what we all know. This *thing* was powerfully evil; it pursued its victims with malice and intention. And it was unleashed on the *Yusufa* under circumstances which plainly indicate a premeditated attack."

He shivered slightly, his green eyes troubled. "I don't know about the rest of you," he concluded, "but when I think about who might be capable of contriving anything as fiendish as this, only one name comes to mind."

"Aye." Harlech Hardrada's voice grated like filed iron. "Borthen Berigeld."

"But Borthen wasn't in Ghazarah," protested Margoth.

"He wouldn't have to be," said her brother thinly. "His henchman was there to do his dirty work for him."

"Muirtagh!" exclaimed Harlech in bitter disgust. "I knew we should ha' scuttled that stinking bastard while we had the chance!"

He dug the point of his hand-hook savagely into the sand in front of him. Gudmar reached out wordlessly and clasped the smaller man's wiry shoulder. A sympathetic silence prevailed for a long moment before Serdor ventured to speak. "This may be little more than cold consolation," he said diffidently, "but I think we may guardedly assume that Borthen—at least for the time being—must not be capable of launching a direct attack on us. Otherwise, he most assuredly would have done so before now."

He hugged his knees more tightly. "As it is, the best—or worst—he could do is take steps to delay us from returning to East Garillon. Which is reason enough for us to try to get home as soon as possible."

"I couldn't agree with you more," said Margoth. "The only question is *how*."

"That's going to be a tricky one to answer, given the fact that our financial assets are pretty well exhausted," said Gudmar. "At the very least, we require as fast a ship as we can find, and the money to equip ourselves decently. Even assuming we are rigorously frugal, that's going to cost more than we have at the moment—"

"Which means we're going to need outside help," concluded Caradoc. "You must have made plenty of professional contacts here in the past, during your missions as merchant-diplomat. Would any of these people be willing to assist us?"

"Maybe," said Gudmar. "But it's bound to be a bit chancy approaching anyone with financial or political obligations to consider. By now my membership in the Merchant-Adventurers has probably been revoked, which means I cannot rely on either the support or the discretion of my fellow guildsmen. And the first loyalty of the Pernathan alcaids must be to their ruler the sultan,

whose interests are unlikely to embrace ours. No, I have
a better idea."

This statement penetrated Harlech's heavy mood of
smoldering ire. He jerked a tousled head upright to gaze
at Gudmar unwinkingly. "Ye're thinkin' of Fayah," he
said. "Aren't ye?"

Gudmar nodded. His eyes were for a moment
unreadable. "Whatever reservations you and I may
share, she's her own mistress—at least for the moment.
And she knows how to keep a secret."

He glanced around at his companions. "The lady we
are speaking of—Fayah Rashotep Assad, to give you her
full name—has a winter villa in Telphar, about four
days' journey from here. We're admittedly low on food
supplies, but if we tighten our belts and are careful with
our water, we should weather the trip without too much
discomfort. Harlech, do you think any of your men will
want to accompany us?"

The little sea captain scrubbed his bearded chin
with a gnarled hand. "They're a loyal bunch, this lot. No
doubt they'd honor their oaths of service if I was tae ask
it of 'em. But after what's happened tae the *Yusufa* . . ."

The lines in his weather-beaten face deepened. "I'm
thinkin' I ought tae send 'em on their way. I dinnae want
any more of my lads gettin' themselves killed on account
o' Borthen's grudges."

"I understand." Gudmar's tone conveyed his respect for his friend's grievous loss. He turned his attention to Evelake, sitting thoughtfully silent next to Serdor.
"You've heard us out, my lord," said the former
merchant-adventurer. "Does the plan meet with your
approval?"

Evelake nodded, knowing that Gudmar's judgment
could be relied upon. His own mind was overclouded
with dark speculations. He realized that for the past few
days he had been permitting himself the luxury of not
dwelling too long upon the dangers that might await him
and his friends back in East Garillon. But that time was
past; the disaster that Borthen's agent had unleashed in

Ghazarah had demonstrated, brutally, the magnitude of the necromancer's malice and power.

He shuddered to think what might have been happening at home during the past two and a half months since his father, Delsidor, had been murdered before the altar in Ambrothen's cathedral. The events of that night had revealed chillingly how deeply his own half brother's family had become enmeshed in Borthen Berigeld's affairs. "He must have offered the Du Bors something they wanted very badly," Evelake observed grimly to himself. "Like the chance to set Gythe in my place."

Certainly, his younger brother by this time would have been invested as Lord Warden. "I wonder if he knows his uncle Fyanor murdered our father—that his mother tried to murder me," he thought. "Has he any idea the kind of monster they've been trafficking with?" And was driven to ask himself, "Would it make any difference if he knew?"

Not for the first time he found himself regretting that he and Gythe had never gotten to know one another very well. Had never, in fact, been *allowed* to do so; Gwynmira had somehow always managed to keep them separated. Gazing into the red heart of the campfire, he felt oddly compelled to call his brother's face to mind.

The general shape of the face was reminiscent of Delsidor's—the cheekbones higher, the jaw more square than Evelake's own. And the coloring was richer by far: Gythe had inherited his mother's raven hair and warmly tinted skin along with her imperious mouth and brilliant eyes. Evelake discovered he could picture his brother's image clearly among the dancing tongues of the firelight.

So clearly, the image seemed almost alive. As Evelake stared at the simulacrum in shrinking fascination, the full lips parted in a smile . . . the dark eyes focused. . . .

The expression in them was so inhumanly malevolent that Evelake uttered a choked exclamation of revulsion. In the same heartbeat, the slow-burning watchfire exploded with a bang into sudden full-bodied flame.

THE FIRE-CHILD

SPARKS FLEW IN ALL DIRECTIONS. "What the devil—" exclaimed Gudmar, then swore in earnest as a shooting mote of hot ash stung his right cheek. The fire whirled and spat like a fizgig. Margoth cried out and reeled back, both hands outflung before her face to ward off a blistering wave of intense heat.

There was another earsplitting bang, and the flames jetted higher. "Get back!" shouted Caradoc.

Gudmar and Harlech dive-rolled in opposite directions. Serdor caught Margoth by the arm and dragged her with him out of the thickening rain of burning cinders. Only Evelake remained motionless, gazing as if mesmerized into the heart of the blaze. "Get away from here!" urged Caradoc.

The air stank of brimstone. The rising bonfire shot skyward like a rocket, then fell back, coalescing into a writhing pillar of bloodred heat. The wildfire shimmered like blown silk. In the midst of it appeared the standing figure of a boy, his naked body sheathed in flames.

The fire-child threw back his head and laughed, his voice echoing eerily above the hungry crackle of the blaze. Huddled at the feet of the glowing apparition, Evelake seemed incapable of moving. Still laughing, refulgent as an angel of death, the other boy flung back his hand, its taloned fingers tipped with crimson lightnings. "Evelake!" shouted Caradoc. *"Look out!"*

His voice broke through the heat-haze that held the young Warden paralyzed. Rousing with a start, Evelake saw his danger and made a scrambling attempt to get out of the way.

He was a split second too late. Bubbling with malignant mirth, the fire-child let fly at him with its lash

of flame. The limber thong of balefire snapped at
Evelake's averted back, setting his outer robe alight. He
pitched to his knees and hurled himself to the ground.

Floundering in the sand, he struggled to throw off
his burnoose. Two pairs of hands came to his assistance,
ripping him free of his charred clothing. He raised
himself on his elbows to find Serdor and Margoth
kneeling over him. "Quick! Fall back!" cried the minstrel.

Evelake managed a breathless nod. His two companions snatched him to his feet. Gouts of fire like
burning hailstones pelted the earth around them as they
raced toward the water. Behind them the fire-child
shrieked with unholy delight and let fly again with its
flaming scourge.

Webbed like a gladiator's net, the serpent-tongues of
fire caught Evelake's legs in a searing tangle. The leather
of his boots smoked and shriveled as he fought to keep
his balance. "Caradoc, help!" shrilled Margoth.

The conflagration was spreading out along the
ground. Oblivious to the cries and confusion from other
parts of the camp, Caradoc flinched aside as a blast of
energy singed the left side of his face. "Bury the firepit!"
he shouted across to Gudmar and Harlech. "Start throwing earth over it!"

Dragging up his hood to shield his hair, he himself
darted forward and kicked a heavy spray of dirt over the
glowing embers between the feet of Evelake's attacker.
Leaping like corybants, Gudmar and Harlech followed
his example. The fire-child turned on them with a roar
and spat flames like a salamander.

Caradoc's cloak went up like dry tinder. He hurled it
from him in a blaze of scarlet sparks. Gudmar and
Harlech cursed and slapped at the burning holes in their
clothes. Rocking with demonic merriment, the fire-child
drove them back with a second burst of flame, then
jerked back on the fiery net that held Evelake captive.

The young Warden tumbled to the ground. Chor-
tling to itself, the fire-child began to gather in the net.
Evelake struggled to kick himself free, but in spite of his

efforts, he was drawn inexorably backward toward the firepit. Serdor and Margoth seized his wrists, adding their resistance to his.

It wasn't enough. Serdor could feel his heels ploughing furrows in the sand. "We're still slipping!" he yelled over to Caradoc.

Evelake's boots were disintegrating into smoldering scrap leather. He bit back an involuntary gasp of pain as the fire seared flesh. "Please, Caradoc," begged Margoth, *"do something!"*

Desperate, buffeted by searing gusts of hot air, Caradoc could think of only one thing to do. Refusing even to consider the possible consequences, he took three running steps and hurled himself recklessly into the web of flame projected by Evelake's attacker.

Fire scorched through his jerkin as he became enmeshed among the beams of power. Evelake tumbled free, slamming into Serdor as the minstrel fell back on his haunches. Balked of its intended prey, the fire-child hissed at Caradoc in black malevolence, then lashed out at him with all its force.

Crimson tentacles of raw energy whipped him in a crackling embrace, fastening themselves like fiery shackles about his wrists and neck. Fighting blind in a red haze of agony, Caradoc struggled in vain to pull free. The web of power yielded, but did not break. Trapped, he moaned in anguish.

Fire lashed his flesh in wanton touches, vicious enough to punish, not heavy enough to kill. Caradoc sensed that his enemy was prolonging his torment in order to revel in his pain. The Magia might save him from immolation if he could only keep from fainting. But even as he fought to stay conscious enough to call for help, the night air was riven suddenly by a shrill, unearthly howl.

Heart-stopping as the wail of a lost soul, the cry echoed and reechoed as it soared to a piercing note that knifed the eardrums. The cords of flame disintegrated, leaving Caradoc lying breathless on the charred earth.

The fire-child went rigid, limbs stiffly splayed like those of a man struck by lightning.

Its legs trembled. There was a tearing sound, and fire erupted like lava from the child's straining loins. Screaming like a banshee, it flickered before Caradoc's aching eyes like a soul in purgatory. Then all at once it winked out.

Darkness flooded the camp. Only dimly aware of the continuing thud of footbeats and buzz of voices, Caradoc attempted to draw air into his lungs, then choked as multiple bands of lingering fire squeezed his ribs. From the paralyzing intensity of his pain, he knew the burns he had taken were deep. Half swooning, he could make nothing but incoherent fragments of thought. But his anguish spoke for itself.

The Magia came upon him tenderly, soothing his fever with ineffable gentleness. Its presence drew the cankerous heat from his wounds. He yielded himself gratefully, without reservation, into its solacing power and rested while the Magia itself brought his sorely injured flesh under its healing governance.

Hands tugged at his arm—anxiously, insistently. Margoth's voice broke half-sobbing through the peace and quiet of spontaneous Orison. "Caradoc! Oh, Caradoc, are you all right?"

Surfacing through drowsy veils of interior silence, he heard the panic in her tone and made an effort to reassure her. "Don't worry," he murmured. "I haven't taken any lasting harm."

He opened his eyes. Margoth was kneeling over him, her face white and drawn. There was an ugly burn on her left forearm. Frowning slightly, he reached out to touch the mark with gentle fingers.

She started to flinch, then uttered a small gasp of astonishment. Her expression one of wonder, she stared down at her arm as the raw weal left by the fire began to seal itself before her very eyes. She said rather breathlessly, "Of course—the Magia! I should have thought—"

Then abruptly she snatched her arm away and stood

up. "No, Caradoc, leave it. If you're *really* all right, don't waste time on me. Evelake's the one who needs you."

Her words acted as a spur to Caradoc's still-groggy wits. He sat up, marveling to discover that his own injuries were all but healed. A warm tingling in his nerve ends told him that the Magia's influence was with him still. He leaped to his feet.

Her brother's movements were fluid enough to show Margoth that he was miraculously recovered. "Evelake's down there," she said, pointing toward the pool. "Gudmar carried him down to the spring."

Together they ran to the water's edge. They arrived to find Evelake half sitting, half lying on the bank, his head cradled against Serdor's supporting shoulder. The boy's legs from the knee down were swathed in wet cloths. Gudmar was keeping the wrappings saturated with cupfuls of cold water dipped from the spring, but as soon as he saw Caradoc, he drew back to make room for the mage.

Evelake was clinging fast to Serdor's sleeve with hands that were white at the knuckles. The look he gave Caradoc was one of speechless appeal. Kneeling down next to the boy, Caradoc said reassuringly, "Courage! It won't hurt like this for much longer." Then he bent to unwind the soaking rags.

The young Warden's feet and legs were deeply scored with angry burns. The brandings had a venomous look to them, as if they had been infused with some unnatural elemental poison. Grave-faced, Caradoc laid hands on the boy and immediately felt the dark stirrings of some baleful influence.

Skin and muscle touched by the bane resisted healing. It taxed Caradoc's powers heavily to overcome the poison so that the regenerative capabilities of his patient's own body could be brought to work through the gift of the Magia. Success came in the end, but it was costly and hard-won. When Caradoc roused himself at last from Orison, he was shaking with fatigue.

His vision was blurred and his ears were ringing. A

voice called sharply, "Watch out! I think he's going to faint!"

Strong hands gripped Caradoc by the shoulders. He opened his eyes to find Gudmar supporting him. Someone else thrust a cup into his lax hands. "Here, Caradoc—drink this!" ordered Margoth.

The smell told him it was aqua vitae. With Margoth helping, he took a gingerly sip and said thickly, "I'm fine now. How's Evelake?"

He got an answer from the young Warden himself. "Better than I would have thought possible," said Evelake. "But you shouldn't have driven yourself so hard."

Though the boy was still pale, the pain had gone out of his brown eyes. Caradoc discovered that his own vitality was slowly beginning to come back to him. He summoned a fragmentary smile. "It was a case of all or nothing, I'm afraid," he said. "Just don't ask me to run any races for the next hour or two."

Footsteps were approaching from off to his right. "Could ha' been worse. None o' my lads have taken more than a spattering of blisters," said Harlech, stumping to a halt with arms akimbo. "Still, we're no' likely tae forget tonight in a hurry."

The little sea captain was sporting a singed beard and a raw red streak across the bridge of his nose. His black eyes held a militant sparkle as he peered down at Caradoc. "That was as glaikit a thing as ever I saw anyone do—throwin' yourself at that fire-bogey like ye did. Ye could ha' got yourself killed!"

"Probably," agreed Caradoc dryly. "But fortunately, I got lucky instead."

Harlech grunted. "Any notion which quarter o' hell the thing came from?"

"None, I'm afraid." Caradoc shook his head.

"Well, just let me get my hands on the de'il that turned it loose on us," growled Harlech, "and I'll show him the real meaning of *hot*!"

"I think we've all got a pretty good idea who the

devil is," said Gudmar grimly. "Let's just hope it's not a foretaste of what he's prepared to serve up to us once we reach East Garillon."

A grave silence fell. "Gudmar," said Evelake diffidently. "The figure in the fire—did you happen to get a glimpse of its face?"

The big merchant-adventurer frowned. "Not a clear view, no. Why?"

"It didn't look like Borthen," said Evelake. "It looked . . . it looked like my brother, Gythe—no!" he amended with sudden certitude. "It *was* Gythe. Whatever else it may have been besides, its *presence* was my brother's. I could feel it somehow in my own blood."

"Surely that's not possible!" exclaimed Gudmar. His tone was one of protest rather than doubt.

"I dinnae ken why not," said Harlech with a black scowl. "It's no secret here that the Du Bors have been hand in glove wi' Borthen for months—"

"That's not my point," said Gudmar. "Gythe was tested a few years ago to see if he had any aptitude for magecraft. He showed none whatsoever."

"All that means," said Caradoc, "is that he may have shown no affinity for the *Magia*. But there are other, darker powers in the world. And Borthen, of all people, knows how to gain access to them."

He reflected a moment in grim silence before going on. "There may very well be a connection between the force this demon-child let loose on us tonight and the crimson cloud that killed the crew aboard the *Yusufa*. If that's so, we got off lightly. The consequences might have been far worse."

"Only they weren't, thanks to you!" said Margoth, pressing her cheek impulsively against her brother's shoulder.

"No," said Caradoc. "No thanks to me."

Margoth blinked at him. "What do you mean? You're the one who dispelled that creature."

"I didn't dispel it," said her brother. "The attack

caught me off guard as much as the rest of you. By the time I got a chance to call upon the Magia, the demon was already gone."

There was an uncomfortable pause. "If you *didn't* dispel that thing," mused Serdor, "why did it break off the attack? Why didn't Gythe—or whatever is using his aspect—do his worst when he had the chance?"

"Good question," said Caradoc. "My guess, judging from what I saw, is that the entity must have only a limited amount of power at its disposal—or else is capable of wielding its power for only a limited period of time."

He bit his lip. "What appeared before us was a psychic manifestation, projected—presumably—over some considerable distance. I imagine it involved a vast expenditure of energy to sustain the manifestation with all its destructive capabilities. We were just fortunate that there were enough of us on hand to keep the creature busy, so that its power ran out before it managed to do any lethal damage."

Serdor was eyeing the array of superficial burns on his arms and legs. "If this is a sample of what our fire-imp can do at a distance," he said with a grimace, "I don't think I relish the idea of meeting up with him at close range."

"Me neither," said Margoth with a shudder, and cast an uneasy glance around her. "What's to prevent him from attacking us again whenever he pleases?"

Her brother thought a moment. "It takes great strength to wield and control great power. Gythe exhausted himself tonight. He'll have to rest—rebuild his strength—before he can try again."

"How much grace does that buy us?" asked Gudmar.

"I wish I knew," said Caradoc frankly. "Probably at least a day or two. With luck, a week or more. But there are no guarantees. We'll have to be on our guard at all times."

THE CITY OF POMEGRANATES

THE PARTY THAT SET OUT the following morning in
the direction of Telphar numbered only six. Apart from
Gudmar, Evelake Whitfauconer's companions included
only Harlech Hardrada and Evelake's three friends from
Ambrothen: Caradoc, Margoth, and Serdor Sulamith.

Shortly after dawn, the little sea captain had called
together the eleven surviving members of his crew in
order to inform them that he was releasing them from all
further obligation. His announcement had occasioned
some argument from the men who had been with the
Yusufa the longest, among them the navigator Houssein.
In the end, however, Harlech had prevailed upon them
to accept the wisdom in choosing a path separate from
his own. Farewells, when it came to the point, were brief:
those who were being left behind knew full well that the
six who were leaving had every need to make haste.

Half a day's ride north of Sherat Jeshuel, the party
reached the road that ran east-west between Ghazarah
and Telphar. The rest of the journey passed without
incident. Toward mid-afternoon of their fourth day of
traveling, they reached the summit of a tall conical hill.
From there they caught their first distant glimpse of the
white stone watchtowers and delicate needle-tipped min-
arets of their destination.

Another hour's riding brought them down off the
high ground into the fertile crescent of orchards and
olive groves that surrounded the City of Pomegranates.
As they approached the gates, they sighted on either side
of the road the rooftops of outlying villas glowing
warmly in the late sunshine. One of the porters on duty
at the town gates supplied Gudmar with the name of a

respectable hospice, along with directions on how to reach it. Gudmar returned the favor in coin, and the party was allowed to proceed into the city.

The hospice was located on a small side street in one of the more modest quarters of the town. Inside, it proved reasonably clean and quiet, with a shed large enough to accommodate their horses. The proprietor made three rooms available to them, and having been paid, showed them the way to a small court behind the kitchen, equipped with a well and a hand pump.

The whole party took their evening meal together in a small common room downstairs from the sleeping quarters. As they worked their way through trenchers of couscous and spiced mutton, Margoth's mind was occupied less with food than with matters of finance. "We can't possibly have more than a few beggarly denarii left in the communal purse," she observed to Gudmar. "How soon are you planning to visit our prospective benefactress?"

The former merchant-adventurer smiled. "Very soon," he assured her.

There was an odd glint lurking deep down in his golden eyes. Margoth wondered if she had perhaps missed something. Curiosity prompted her to remark, "So far you haven't told us very much about this Lady Fayah. Who is she? Or are we not supposed to ask?"

The second question drew a chuckle from her companion, but the mysterious glint, she noticed, still remained. "It's hardly a great secret," said Gudmar. "She is—or rather, was—the wife of Sulimar Al Khumram, Agha of Sultan Saladir's imperial dromonds."

"Was?"

"The agha died a year ago last spring. Since then, she's been officially in mourning," said Gudmar. He added, "She might have gone back to Nhubor, but she has two children, both sons. For their sake, she has remained here in Pernatha, living in seclusion until the accepted time of purification is over."

"So she isn't Pernathan at all?" Margoth was intrigued.

"No," said Gudmar. "Her father, N'gobi Kaunda, is prince of the province of Ghat, on Pernatha's south border. Her marriage to Sulimar was intended to keep peace on both sides of the boundary."

Margoth was about to inquire how he had become acquainted with someone as exotic as a Nhuboran princess, but at that moment the big merchant's attention strayed across the table to where Evelake was poking abstractedly at the food on his plate. "You're looking more than a little tired, my lord," said Gudmar kindly. "Since there's no more to be accomplished before tomorrow morning, maybe it wouldn't be a bad idea for us all to adjourn early for the night, and try to get some rest."

Evelake had no objections to offer. His back and legs were aching from the long ride, and his spirits were heavy. His companions, he knew, had been glad, for all normal and practical reasons, to reach Telphar. His own feelings were less clearly defined. He was grateful for the three unbroken nights they had enjoyed upon the road, but he was painfully aware that the mere fact that they were sleeping under a roof tonight in the middle of a populous city did not make them any safer against arcane attacks than they had been sleeping rough in the wild.

He and Serdor had elected to share a room, leaving Margoth to lodge with her brother. As they passed through the doorway, the minstrel noticed the boy's air of uneasiness. "What's the matter?" he asked, as Evelake sank down on one of the two pallets in their small chamber. "Are you worrying about your brother?"

"Other things too, but that mostly," admitted Evelake. "It's not just being afraid," he continued, struggling to put his disquiet into words. "It's just that I didn't think . . . I never before suspected how deeply Gythe might be capable of hating me."

Serdor sat down on the opposite bunk, his grey eyes

very steady as he studied the boy's distressed face. "I don't *think* I ever did anything to him to make him resent me so bitterly," murmured Evelake. "How could I? We hardly ever spent any time together."

"Maybe that's part of the problem," said Serdor quietly. "If you don't really know someone very well, there's not much to stop you from believing the worst of him. Especially if the person in question has something you think you're entitled to—in this case, the right to rule." He paused, then added, "If Gythe has chosen to follow Borthen, it certainly isn't your fault."

"No. Probably not," said Evelake wearily. "But that won't make much difference when it comes to my friends. If Gythe and Gwynmira don't succeed in destroying me, the next best thing for them to do is to try and destroy all the people in East Garillon who would support me if I were to challenge the Du Bors claims."

"Beginning, I suppose," said Serdor, "with the Du Penfallons of Gand."

"That's what I'm afraid of," said Evelake. "What makes it even worse is that Gythe knows I'm alive, but they don't. They may not even see a blow coming until it strikes them down."

"Or they may be vigilant enough in their own right to keep their guard up," said Serdor. "We'll nose around for news first thing tomorrow. But in the meantime, have a little trust in your friends. There's still plenty of room in this situation for something better than complete pessimism."

Evelake's face lightened. "You're right, of course. I've no more reason to fear the worst than to hope for the best."

"That's a good thought to sleep on," said Serdor with one of his wry smiles.

Nodding, Evelake lay back and drew his blankets over him. After a moment he said dreamily, "Would you tell me a story? Perhaps that bit from the chronicles of Simbaya the Mariner where he visits the Temple of Silence?"

"Anything to oblige," said Serdor. And drawing up his knees, tailor-fashion, he began to recite the tale. . . .

Some time after the minstrel's voice had fallen silent, a dark figure tiptoed past the threshold outside. Light as a shadow, for all its size, the figure padded noiselessly on down the passageway and descended the stairs to the ground floor. It let itself out into the courtyard through a side door and melted into the general darkness next to the outside wall. There was a soft click as the dark figure shifted the bolt that closed the inn-yard gate from the inside. The gate creaked twice—once opening, once closing. Then all was still again.

The big man slipped through the Telpharan streets like a wraith, keeping away from lighted doorways and late passersby. Eventually a narrow lane took him down to the waterfront. There was no moon, but out in the bay, lights burned yellow along the walls of the island fortress of Al'Cantra. Skirting the taverns and the red lanterns of the brothel district, the man continued on up the wharf until he reached a point where the buildings came to an abrupt end.

Beyond, an elevated strip of land thrust itself out into the waters of the bay. The breeze floating down off the headland was redolent of cinnamon and sweet-gum, for it was here that many of the sultan's officers and favorites kept their winter estates. A narrow strip of pebbly beach lay exposed by the tide at the base of the shallow bluff. The big man took a quick look behind him, then scrambled down the sea-sculpted embankment to the damp sand below. Once there, he began working his way around to the opposite side of the tonguelike peninsula where the bay cut inland into a deep and narrow estuary—the entrance to the sheltered basin where no fewer than twenty great war dromonds at any given time rested at their anchors.

Across the estuary, colored lights flickered and flashed like countless flitting tropical fish among the shrubs and fountains and ornamental outbuildings of the sultan's sprawling and opulent palace. The man followed the beach for as long as it lasted. When the sand came to an end, he waded out into the black tide-freshened waters of the channel and began to swim.

Sleek as a seal, his strokes measured and effortless, he propelled himself two hundred yards up the estuary and grounded himself in a small backwater concealed in the shadow of an overhanging guard wall. There was a guard pacing the top of the wall. The swimmer waited until the turbaned figure had moved on before clambering nimbly up the bank to the foot of the wall.

There in the cover of impenetrable darkness, he paused to unwind a length of rope from about his waist. One end of the rope he attached with deft fingers to the stout steel hook he had carried strapped to his belt. Once he had made his grappling line secure, he stood back and gave the spike shank a practiced twirl before launching it at the top of the wall.

The hook fell back on the first cast with a scrape and a thud. On the second cast, the claw found purchase and lodged fast. The man in the shadows gave the rope an experimental tug, then swarmed up the cable like a monkey.

Astride the copestones, he stopped long enough to dislodge the grappling hook before dropping lightly to the ground inside the wall. A slithering crawl through a stand of shrubbery brought him to the edge of a clipped lawn. Here his pricked ears picked up sounds—the stealthy pad of paws, the hot suspicious panting of animal breath. He paused where he lay as the two mastiffs edged closer.

Schooled to attack in silence, they moved in without baying. Then they caught his scent and realized who he was. Wet noses poked questioningly at his ears and open hands. He pushed them off with rough caresses and a whispered word of dismissal. Satisfied, the pair faded back again into the night.

The house itself had been built on the highest of

three terraces. Flitting in and out among trees and statuary, the intruder twice went to earth to allow other household guards to pass him by. He reached the house undiscovered and again unlimbered his grappling hook. Again luck and skill were with him, and within minutes he had gained the roof.

The villa had been built in a square around an inner courtyard. The apartment he was looking for was located in the northeast corner of the building. He let himself down into a wrought-iron balcony in the middle of the same wing. The casement, being on the upper floor, was not locked. He opened it and slipped inside.

The room by which he had entered opened into a lighted corridor. The left-hand branch of the passage ended in a door. In front of the door stood the hulking figure of a bare-chested man, his black skin gleaming dully in the lamplight, his broad face impassive as a sphinx's.

Leaving the door to his hiding place ajar, the intruder knelt on the floor by the threshold and took off the ring he wore on the third finger of his right hand. With a quick flick of the wrist, he sent the ring rolling along the hallway to the feet of the huge black guard.

The big Nhuboran started at the sight of something small and bright winking toward him on the floor. The ring came to rest between his feet. Frowning deeply, he stooped to pick it up, then paused to examine the device inscribed within the bezel.

The symbol was that of a rigged ship within the compass of a star. As the lines came to light, the black man stiffened and blinked. A slow knowing smile crept over his lips. Clutching the ring in his hand, he turned toward the doorway where the door stood cracked and beckoned. . . .

Lady Fayah Rashotep Assad heard the outer door of her bedchamber swing open. Her silk gown trailing unheeded off her shoulders, she sat up in bed as the massive figure of Mackai, her bodyguard since child-hood, stepped into the archway leading into her inner-

most sanctum. Light from a lamp glowed golden behind
him so that he was all silhouette.

"Mistress of Lions, here is someone to see you,"
said Mackai in the native tongue of their people. "Someone," he added, "whom you have long missed." He
stepped forward to press something small and hard—a
ring—into her hand, and immediately slipped back
through the archway to allow another man to enter. The
outer door closed.

The newcomer was broad-shouldered and compact-
ly powerful, and his damp hair glimmered golden above
the light he carried between his hands. Fayah's fingers
tightened on the ring, but she did not need to look at it.
Her visitor placed the lamp on the lampstand just inside
the arch, then spoke from the shimmering interplay of
fire and shadows.

"Dusky art thou, huntress of leopards,
  Yet fairer than the morning, daughter of princes.
  As a pillar of ebony is thy gem-encircled throat,
  And thy mouth a sweet nectary of honey. . . ."

The words belonged to the poet Khalibram, but the
voice was inimitably that of one she loved above all
others. Supple as a lioness, she slipped from the bed.
From the impassioned pen of the same poet came her
own words of greeting as she gave him back his ring:

"Like the hart on the mountaintop,
  Even as the young roe on the high mountain,
  Is to me my Beloved.
  Let him kiss me with the kisses of his mouth.
  Let him wound me with his love among the
  roses—"

Then all at once she was in his arms, and all poetry
between them ceased, subsumed in a moment of ravish-
ing silence.

THE WIDOW OF TELPHAR

ANY PROTESTS FAYAH MIGHT HAVE uttered melted away into sun-colored insignificance before the glowing warmth of Gudmar's presence. Only after their lips had parted did the world begin to right itself. Still entwined in his arms, she whispered in a mixture of her language and his, "Gudmar! *Daia'tama*, what are you doing here?"

His clothes were soaked through with seawater, and his skin smelled of brine. He said with a deep chuckle, "Kissing you—and getting your nightgown wet, I'm afraid. Shall we move off the rug before I ruin it as well?"

"The rug," said Fayah, "is of no consequence. You, however, are another matter. First Mackai shall bring you a dry robe and some *kjaffe*. Then you shall tell me what you're really doing here."

Gudmar's golden eyes were lazily amused, like those of a lion at rest. "You seem very sure, *Uvanyah*, that it was not solely for the delight of seeing you again."

The endearment, lifted from her own language, stirred many memories. Fayah's dusky full-blown mouth framed a smile. "I know you better than that, *Daia'tama*. Were that your only reason, you would have waited three months longer—until I was no longer in mourning—so that you might come to me openly as a suitor, not clandestinely as now, like a thief in the night."

There was an odd note of seriousness underlying her teasing tone. Before Gudmar could remark upon it, she disengaged herself with a small twist of her hips and stepped away from him to give a single tug at the silken bell-cord that hung beside her curtained bed. Gazing after her, Gudmar forgot his momentary pang of disquiet in the pleasure of watching her move.

Fayah had already been twelve months a wife when she and Gudmar had first been introduced to one another ten years before at the court of her grandfather, Prince N'jembi Kaunda. But neither the constraints of a political marriage nor the passage of time had dimmed the beauty that he remembered from that day: her short tightly-wound hair was still soft and fine as the wool of a coal-black virgin ewe, and her eyes still as limpid as those of a young gazelle. Gudmar's heart stirred within him in mingled admiration and yearning. The years he had spent in waiting seemed all at once no more than a watch in the night, with dawn not far away.

And for her, the time had not been wholly without its compensations. Catching her glance in the nearest mirror, he said, "Your children—how are they?"

She turned her head to look at him, wide-eyed, over one smooth shoulder. "They do very well, *Daia'tama*. Sharif is showing an interest in falconry, and Shahiar is almost big enough to be taught how to ride a horse. But they are not here just now," she continued. "Their uncle has taken them off to stay with him and his family at their villa in Khoorish."

Again, there was the odd note of restraint that conflicted strangely with her evident gladness that he was there. Gudmar sensed that there was something she wasn't telling him. The softness left his eyes as an unpleasant suspicion took shape in his mind. "Their uncle *took* them?" he said. "Are they perhaps being held as hostages to ensure your good conduct?"

Fayah turned to face him, and he saw from her eyes that he had guessed rightly. "The decision," said Fayah quietly, "was made not by my brother-in-law Hassim, but by the sultan himself."

"On account of me." Gudmar made it a statement, not a question.

"A new ambassador arrived from East Garillon four days ago," said Fayah. "Among the documents he presented to Saladir was a writ declaring you an outlaw. In the event that you approach any of your former associates at the Pernathan Court, they are to detain you, if possible, so that you may be sent back to East Garillon under guard to be tried as a traitor."

Gudmar muttered an expletive under his breath. "Fool that I am, I should have expected something like this!" he growled. "Fayah, forgive me! It seems I've put both you and your children at risk by coming here. I'll go at once. Just give me ten minutes' head start before you alert your husband's guards—"

"No," said Fayah flatly. She interposed herself between him and the door, and faced him squarely, chin held high. "When the Inyumi hemmed us in among the ruins of Kumbikuru, did I not stand firm at your side?" she challenged softly. "Then do not ask me to behave as though I had never shown courage."

Her words brought Gudmar to a standstill. "No one knows the extent of your courage better than I, *Uvanyah*," he said. "But it isn't courage at stake here, it's the welfare of your children—"

"Did anyone see you enter here?"

"I took every precaution, of course," said Gudmar.

"Then I am satisfied that no harm will come of your remaining here for a while," said Fayah. "And even if I am wrong," she continued, "will you not trust me to make good a tale of the robber who was too cunning even for Mackai?"

She knew she had won when he smiled in spite of the trouble in his eyes. "That is better, *Daia'tama*," she said approvingly. "I promise you I will be none the worse for the time we shall spend together. And the Dowager-Regent in Farrowaithe will be none the wiser."

"The *Dowager*-Regent?" Gudmar's smile vanished abruptly.

Fayah nodded. "Gwynmira Du Bors. She was appointed by the Great Council at Kirkwell a few weeks ago. Had you not heard?"

"No," said Gudmar bluntly. His golden eyes were stormy. "The members of the council must have taken leave of their senses!" he muttered, then shook his head. "Wait—I can't believe this sorry situation could have

come about without some strong opposition from somewhere. At the very least Arvech Du Penfallon of Gand
would have had a few words to say against the Du
Bors—"

"He said them." Fayah's normally velvety contralto
had taken on an edge. "Those words cost him his life."

"What?" Gudmar went rigid. "Lord Arvech is
dead?" When Fayah inclined her head in sober confirmation, he drew a deep breath as if to restrain himself.
When he spoke, it was in a voice of deadly quiet. "How
did it happen?"

"I only know what Hassim was able to tell me," said
Fayah. "Apparently the Seneschal of Gand went up
before the council and accused the Du Bors of conspiracy and murder. He claimed to have a witness, but the
man could not be found for testimony. Rather than
retract his charges, Lord Arvech elected to settle the
issue by assay of arms."

"A trial by combat . . ." Gudmar's face was hard as
stone. "Who took up the gauntlet?"

"Lady Gwynmira's brother," said Fayah. "The Seneschal of Ambrothen."

"A man more canny with words than with weapons.
If Fyanor Du Bors agreed to fight," said Gudmar grimly,
"it was only because he had good reason to be sure he
would win." He gave a short, bitter laugh. "The devil
takes good care of his own."

"Not good enough in this instance," said Fayah.
"Lord Arvech took his adversary with him over N'gai
Farangi."

N'gai Farangi . . . the Bridge of Shadows. "So
Fyanor's dead, too? The devil, it seems, knows how to
drive a cheater's bargain," said Gudmar.

He scowled deeply. "Lord Arvech left two
children—a boy and a girl. Have you heard any word
concerning what's become of them?"

"About the girl I have heard nothing," said Fayah.
"The boy, however . . ." She paused, then went on.
"This news will not be welcome either: the Du Bors sent
an army into Gandia to seize the city, as a gesture of

retribution. The castle itself, however—at last report, anyway—was still free. The boy is said to be numbered among the Keep's defenders—"

She broke off as a soft stir from the doorway heralded the return of the servant Mackai, carrying a laden tray in his hands and a robe of tawny-colored damask draped over one powerful arm. Fayah wordlessly took the robe and held it in readiness while her retainer helped Gudmar divest himself of his wet garments.

Strong-boned and hard-muscled, his body showed fighting scars, and other marks more recent: an array of half-healed burns scattered over his torso and arms. Fayah said nothing until they were alone again. Then, after drawing him down beside her on a low divan, she broke her silence. "Trouble, it seems, has overtaken you more than once on this visit to Pernatha. Tell me, *Daia'tama*, why does Gwynmira Du Bors want you dead?"

Despite the wealth of soft cushions, Gudmar had not relaxed. He said bluntly, "It's because I support her son's rival for the rulership of East Garillon."

"Her son's *rival?*" Fayah frowned. "But surely there aren't any other legitimate claimants for the office of Lord Warden?"

"There is one," said Gudmar, with a smile thin and white as the flash of a drawn blade. "There is his elder half brother, Evelake."

For a moment Fayah merely stared at him, full lips parted in astonishment. Then she gave herself a shake. "I don't understand, *Daia'tama*. We were given to believe that the older boy was dead, killed by brigands."

"That's the way the Du Bors originally planned it," said Gudmar. "And that's the story they've been telling ever since, hoping to make everyone accept it. But Evelake Whitfauconer is very much alive. And I intend —God willing—to see that he gets the chance to regain his birthright."

He gave her then a concise account of his long search that had begun months earlier in Farrowaithe, and had ended only a fortnight before amid the heat and squalor of the quarries at Sul Khabir. When he described the attack on the camp at Sherat Jeshuel, Fayah's face reflected a growing concern. "You begin to frighten me, *Daia'tama*," she said gravely. "Are you sure you are doing the right thing in seeking to return with the boy to East Garillon? How can you hope to prevail against enemies with power such as this?"

"I don't know," said Gudmar honestly. "But we've got to *try*."

There was a long moment of silence. "Very well," said Fayah. "I will do all I can to help you. What is it that you need most?"

"Just now we need money," said Gudmar. "Enough to get us back to East Garillon. Once there, we will be able to contact the Mage Hospitallers. With their help, we will be in a position to rally more support elsewhere."

"Will the mages believe you?"

"I hope so," said Gudmar. "But even if they doubt my word, they'll have to believe Evelake." He added heavily, "God knows, the boy carries scars enough—in mind as well as body—to uphold the truth of his story."

He raised a hand to caress her brow with almost reverent gentleness. "I have no illusions, *Uvanyah*, about this venture we are about to undertake. It may well cost all of us our lives. If that should prove to be the case, I ask your forgiveness, now and for all time."

Fayah's dark eyes were suspiciously bright. "If I am to be denied the fulfillment of my hopes, I would rather share your death than grant you pardon."

"And what then would become of your sons?" asked Gudmar quietly. "No, it is better this way. I shall be all the more resolute, knowing you are safe."

"We both know where our duty lies," said Fayah. "It has kept us apart all too long. But since you must go, grant me one favor in exchange for what you have asked of me tonight."

"If it is within my power, *Uvanyah*."

"Stay with me for but an hour longer, *Daia'tama*," said Fayah softly, "and for that little while, let us pretend there is no duty and no danger—only such love as men and women share tirelessly and stainlessly in the gardens of paradise. . . ."

Dawn was still two hours away when Gudmar left Sulimar Al Khumram's winter villa the same way he had entered it, in darkness and stealthy silence. Reclad in his old garments, he carried with him, strapped securely beneath his shirt, a leather wallet containing a small fortune in Nhuboran gemstones. Unhampered by this slight encumbrance, he slipped unchallenged across the gardens and scaled the restraining seawall with only a minor scuffle. Once safely outside the grounds, he returned to the water and struck out, strong-swimming as a selkie, for the sparse scattering of winking lights that marked the waterfront purlieus of Telphar.

He spent more time in the water on his return trip than he had going out. During the hours he had spent in Fayah's company, the tide had come in, covering over the beach that earlier had girdled the base of the headland. Stroking his way smoothly inshore amid only traces of ripples, he found his feet within thirty yards of the stone-built quay that ran the length of the harborfront. He waded into the shallows and followed the line of the wall until he came to a flight of barnacle-covered steps leading up to the street level above.

The buildings that fronted this section of the quay were unlighted, but Gudmar's eyes by this time were accustomed enough to the darkness for him to tell that most of the structures were warehouses. Slab-sided and windowless, they clustered together in untidy irregular clumps, like children's building blocks, with dark alleys forcing spaces between them. Disinclined to risk getting entangled among the disorderly sprawl of narrow byways, Gudmar kept to the open wharf for a hundred yards until the expanse of cobblestones broadened out into a rubbish-strewn receiving yard. Here he paused to reconnoiter.

One corner of the yard was contained by the flanking walls of two adjoining warehouses. The open space was blocked off on its opposite side by a straight row of storage sheds. The mole continued on around the southern end of the shed row before hooking back on itself behind the buildings to follow the natural line of the shore. A ten-foot gap between the sheds and the warehouses formed an alleyway dark as the inside of a coal scuttle. Satisfied that the area was deserted, Gudmar moved on again.

He was almost even with the mouth of the alley when his quick ears picked up the sound of footsteps pattering nervously along the back sides of the sheds. Even as he took an instinctive stride toward the nearest dark doorway, there was a sudden triumphant outcry from the same direction. "Look, there he is! After him!"

The shouts were in Garillan. The pattering feet sprang instantly into a pelting run, with other footsteps hammering after. Gudmar withdrew noiselessly into the concealing shadow of the door. A dark figure shot around the corner into the receiving yard and made a frantic dash for the alley.

He swept past Gudmar's hiding place in a hard-driven burst of speed. Behind him, light flared wildly in splashes across the cobbles as three men with a lantern pounded after the fugitive. As the pursuers flashed by him, Gudmar caught a passing glimpse of their livery: crimson and black, with three golden chevrons emblazoned on their billowing cloaks.

The livery of the Du Bors family!

The sight of men-at-arms wearing enemy colors was all Gudmar needed. Eyes narrowed to hard chinks of topaz, he stepped out into the lane. The ground at his feet was littered with broken boards and brickbats. He snatched up a conveniently short length of wood and started forward.

Fifty feet farther up the alley, the muddy paving doglegged abruptly to the left. The fleeing man skidded around the bend only a few strides ahead of his pursuers. Armed and purposeful, Gudmar shot after them soft-footed as a lynx.

Ten yards beyond the first junction, the cobbles

made another sharp turn to the right. As Gudmar
slipped swiftly up on the second corner, the sound of
running feet ahead of him came to a shattering standstill.
Tall black shadows danced across the walls of the adjacent buildings to the accompaniment of grunts and
stamping feet. There was a crash as the lantern hit the
ground.

"Hold still, you miserable weasel, before you force
me to cut your throat!" wheezed a harsh voice angrily,
then choked out a curse in response to the thud of a
shrewd blow.

The struggling redoubled in a brief burst of fierce
intensity. "No, you fool!" snarled a second voice. "We
need this one alive, at least until we get back to East
Garillon."

"You may as well do your worst!" panted a third
voice in reckless defiance. "For I swear I'll put the
Mermaid on a rock before I let you bloody buggers sail
her into Gand Harbor with a hold full of Pernathan
devil-fire on board!"

Whether or not the prisoner's captors would have
taken him at his word was a question never resolved, for
at that moment, Gudmar launched himself with a flying
leap for the ringleader's unguarded back.

A warning shout from the leader's two companions
came a split instant too late. The equerry spun about in
time to take a cracking blow across the face that broke
his nose and laid open his left cheek. The force of the
impact sent him reeling to the pavement. He groped for
his sword hilt, only to have the weapon snatched from
his hand an instant before someone put a dent in his
helmet that sent him abruptly to sleep.

The prisoner, who was shorter than the two remaining livery men, gave a raucous whoop and butted one of
his captors in the mouth with the point of his head. The
victim grunted and let go, his front teeth palpably
loosened. The other guardsman cursed and whipped out
his dagger, but before he could use it, a blade point
insinuated itself coldly under his left ear to rest, razor-
sharp, against a vulnerable pulse point. "Drop your

weapon," growled the deep voice of his attacker, "before it costs you your life."

Gripping the poniard haft uncertainly, the guardsman cast a furtive glance around him and discovered that both of his colleagues were now lying unconscious on the ground. Gritting his teeth in impotent fury, he loosened his grip on his blade and heard the dull clatter as it struck the cobbles. It was the last sound to meet his ears before his erstwhile prisoner clocked him vigorously from behind with a loose chunk of paving stone. He folded to the street and lay still.

Gudmar and the fugitive stared at each other through a smoky haze of burning lamp oil. "Jamie Greenham!" exclaimed Gudmar in a measured tone between vindication and bewonderment. "I thought that voice sounded somehow familiar!"

The smaller man grinned broadly, despite a split lip. "Lord have mercy, if it isn't Master Gudmar! So those Du Bors maw-worms haven't got you after all. . . ."

THE WHITE MERMAID

IT WAS STILL DARK WHEN Margoth awoke to the sound of muffled voices. Groggily, without opening her eyes, she rolled over and reached out a hand to shake her brother by the shoulder. Her groping fingers encountered only blankets. Caradoc was not there.

The discovery roused Margoth to full awareness. Throwing off her own bed coverings, she sat up and swung her legs over the edge of the narrow bed. Light showed dimly around the cracks in the door. She stood up and reached for her outer robe where it lay across the foot of her pallet.

As she thrust her arms into the sleeves, there was a soft knock from outside. "Half a moment," called

Margoth huskily. She dragged the garment over her head, pausing only to shake down its voluminous folds before padding over to answer the summons.

The rangy figure on the threshold was Caradoc's. He gave her a cursory look and said, "Good: you're dressed. Come next door. It's important."

He gestured toward Gudmar's room. The light in the corridor was coming from the open doorway. "What's going on?" demanded Margoth, running a hand through her tangled coppery hair.

"Gudmar will explain everything once we're all gathered together," said her brother. "Go on in. I'll rouse Serdor and Evelake."

The third door in the passage swung open. "We're already roused, thank you," said Serdor, leaning around the doorframe. "We'll be with you in a trice."

Margoth expected to find only Gudmar and Harlech in the room. To her surprise, there was a third man present whom she had never seen before. The newcomer was short, round, and burly, with a rubicund snub-nosed face and a deep tan. "Come in, all of you," said Gudmar, beckoning. "Allow me to present Jamison Greenham, for five years now pilot aboard my ship the *White Mermaid*, and the best of his trade ever to serve in my employ."

The *White Mermaid*, as the whole party was subsequently informed, was anchored just offshore in the Bay of Telphar. Gudmar left it to Jamie Greenham to explain how she came to be there.

"When we were in Ambrothen back in the spring, Master Gudmar left us with orders to take the *Mermaid* south to Zhengipal in Lower Nhubor," began the pilot. "We were to pick up a cargo of teakwood and carry it back to Ambrothen, where there were cabinetmakers waiting to receive it. The voyage itself came off without a hitch," finished Jamie sourly. "The trouble started after we made landfall."

He paused to rub his chin reminiscently before going on. "We hadn't been in port half an hour before we were all at once surrounded by customs boats all loaded to the guntels with Fyanor Du Bors's lobsterbacks. They swarmed all over us like cockroaches in a corncrib. Before we knew it, they were marching us off to gaol at Ambrothen Castle."

He glowered at the memory. "I never managed to make much sense of the charges—it was all some trumped-up gibberish about conspiracy. And anyway, it was Master Gudmar they really wanted to get their hands on. Seneschal Fyanor and that hellcat sister of his actually called in a mage-inquisitor to put me and our sailing master Giles Penrith to the question, to see if we knew where our employer was likely to be found. I'm pleased to say they got precious little for their trouble. All the Du Bors could do to salve their itchy pride was impound the *Mermaid* and press us into service to sail her."

He grinned with crooked pride. "She's a fast ship, with a sweet turn of speed to her when she's properly handled. I guess that's why we got sent out on this particular mission. The Black Baron of Kirkwell wanted his *bashanti* as soon as possible."

"Bashanti?" said Caradoc. "What's that?"

"Translated, it means 'dung of the fire-djinn,'" said Gudmar. "I had a small quantity of the stuff with me at Thyle Tarn, if you recall. It has the nasty property of burning in the presence of water."

"What does the baron want *bashanti* for?" asked Evelake.

Gudmar grimaced. "That's where I think I'd better take up the tale."

He gave them then the gist of all Fayah had told him concerning recent affairs in East Garillon. Evelake listened in tight-lipped silence. All his waking nightmares about what might be happening to his friends in Gand seemed to have come to bleak fulfillment: Arvech Du Penfallon dead, Devon left to defend Gand Castle against overwhelming odds, Kherryn unaccounted for. The implications made him feel sick.

Standing beside the boy, Margoth watched the color drain from his face, leaving it all but bloodless. He looked so vulnerable in that moment that she felt an almost overpowering impulse to throw her arms about him and shield him with her comfort. But brutal necessity dictated that he must find his own strength unaided. She held herself in check until Gudmar had finished speaking.

At first Evelake said nothing, and she began to fear that after all he had endured, he might now falter. Then all at once he drew a breath, and she saw that there was fire in his eyes. He spoke with quiet intensity. "If I've learned nothing else in these past eight months, I've at least come to know something of what it's like to live in fear. What Borthen Berigeld did to me is what Gwynmira and my brother are now seeking, with the aid of his counsel, to do to the people of East Garillon. They see inflicting misery on others as a means of demonstrating how powerful they are. And it's not because they need to, it's because they enjoy using force."

He shivered slightly, but his voice continued firm and true. "Even if Gand Castle fell tomorrow, and I were to give up all claim to my birthright, the violence and bloodshed would still continue, because the power that now rules in Farrowaithe is the kind that demands sacrifices. For that reason, I don't care if our enemies seem to have all the might on their side. We've still got to try and stop them—somehow!"

Never before had Margoth heard Evelake speak with such grim authority of purpose. "You speak for all of us, my lord!" declared Gudmar in tones of quiet affirmation. But Margoth noticed that he gave full weight to the title of respect.

"Thanks to the generosity of the Lady Fayah, we now have the funds to equip ourselves, and thanks to a fair wind of Providence, we have a ship to carry us home," continued the big merchant-adventurer with a hard grin. "All we have to do is take her—and for that, Jamie and I have come up with a plan. . . ."

Apart from the stark walls of the fortress that guarded the bay, one of the most distinctive landmarks to be seen along the waterfront in Telphar by the light of day was a long wooden pier jutting three hundred feet out into the waters of the bay. Supported from beneath by massive pilings of seasoned oak, the pier in turn provided the base for a lofty two-story edifice almost as long as the pier itself. The building had been erected three decades before to serve as the principal clearing-house for grain imported by sea into the city. From its rooftop, it was possible to survey the whole of the harbor as from a watchtower.

Shortly after eight o'clock in the morning, three people—apparently two men and a boy—walked west along the quayside in search of a rowboat for hire. They found one to their satisfaction tied up at a landing not far from the grain-market pier, and paid the owner enough to forestall any misgivings he might otherwise have had about letting them take the boat out unattended. Once the transaction had been completed, the trio stepped into the boat and put out from the shore. Within a matter of minutes, they were lost from view among the many other small craft moored in the shallows.

Farther out in the harbor, the deeper water was dotted with large vessels—carracks, caravels, and sea-going galleys: merchantmen from a score of different home ports. Stationed forward of the rowing bench in the front end of the cockleboat, Margoth shook back the disguising folds of her headgear and kept watch ahead of the bow. Serdor and Evelake sat with their backs to her and plied the oars in tandem. Under her guidance they steered a meandering course out past the shorebreak toward the end of the long pier.

Their arrival disturbed half a dozen herring gulls perched among the heavy truss beams that shored up the pierhead. Ignoring the chorus of protesting squawks as the birds took flight, Margoth whipped a mooring line around the nearest piling and secured it with two half hitches. "That should keep our cockleshell from going anywhere for a little while," she said. "From here it's up to you two."

Serdor peered up through the intersecting network

of crossplanks. "It looks like a relatively easy climb," he said. "All the same, I'd better go first."

"All right," said Evelake. "Do you want the sack?"

"Not yet," said Serdor. "We'll send the rope down for it once we're safely up ourselves."

Using Evelake's shoulder as a prop, he eased himself upright. While Margoth held the little boat steady against the piling he set first one foot and then the other on the rowing bench and extended an arm over his head. The lower of two thick horizontal beams loomed within ten inches of his outstretched fingers. "On the count of three I'm going to jump, so brace yourselves," he told his two companions. "One . . . two . . . *three!*"

The cockleboat gave a violent lurch as he launched himself for the beam. His strong musician's hands gripped wood and hung on. For a moment he dangled by his arms over the water, then jackknifed and got one leg over the bar. An instant later, he was astride it.

Evelake was already on his feet, balancing precariously on the rowing bench in preparation to follow. Wrapping one arm around the piling, Serdor leaned down and offered the boy his free hand. "Whenever you're ready," he called down.

Evelake nodded and tensed his leg muscles. "Here I come!" he announced, and leaped.

Serdor's fingers meshed firmly with his. The minstrel gave an arm-wrenching tug, lifting the boy within reach of the beam. Evelake scrabbled for purchase and found it with more effectiveness than grace. Lying bellydown across the bar, he panted, "Thanks! I've got it now."

Serdor promptly let go of him and left him to right himself. Above them, a series of crossties provided a ready-made set of hand- and footholds. With Serdor leading, they gained the foundation of the platform without difficulty. Here they paused to catch their breath while they waited for Margoth to send up the bundle they had left behind.

There was a yard of clearance between the edge of the pier and the base of the building. A rusty metal ladder, clamped to the outside wall, gave access to the roof. Letting the minstrel go first, Evelake paused on the topmost rung and cast a shaded glance over the array of merchant ships anchored on the west side of the pier. "There she is! That's the *Mermaid!*" he exclaimed, and pointed out a sleek lateen-rigged caravel riding the swells of the incoming tide. "She looks just as I remember her."

Serdor looked. The figurehead—a coquettish golden-haired mermaid with a white tail—was proof enough of the ship's identity. He counted the figures on deck and grinned. "It looks as if we're in good time. They don't appear to have sent anyone ashore."

"Jamie did say the landing parties probably wouldn't leave the ship much before nine o'clock," said Evelake, climbing off the ladder to join Serdor. Turning, he scanned the waters east of the pier. "I don't see any sign of Gudmar and the others yet. I hope they managed to find the rowing-gig those mercenaries came ashore in."

"If they didn't, there's always a harbor dory," said Serdor, kneeling down to undo the bag. He took out two coarse brushes and a canister which looked as if it might contain tar. He handed one of the brushes to Evelake. As he took it, the boy remarked, "You don't suppose anyone might have found those three soldiers?"

"I doubt it. Not where Gudmar left them," said Serdor. "Besides, without their uniforms, they have nothing to back up any story they might have to tell. You watch the *Mermaid* and I'll look out for Gudmar's party. Don't forget to look busy. If anybody happens to notice us up here, we want him to think we're just workmen tarring the roof. . . ."

Gudmar's party found the *Mermaid's* cockleboat floating at the end of her mooring line not far from the place where Jamie Greenham had been cornered by the three men sent to apprehend him. "No sooner had I taken to the water than somebody spotted me and sang out," said Jamie with a deprecating shake of his head. "When I couldn't swim fast enough to outpace them, I decided to come ashore. I couldn't have picked a better place, either—luckily for me."

Caradoc flexed his shoulders uncomfortably within the confines of his borrowed tunic, cut to fit a man five inches shorter. "I don't know about this, Gudmar," he said dubiously. "You and I look about as convincing as two scarecrows in these uniforms."

"Don't worry. Just keep your helmet on and your cloak drawn," said the big merchant-adventurer with a wolfish grin. "When we're in close enough for these hired brigands to take our tailor's measurements, it'll be too late for them."

Once they had retrieved the boat, Jamie volunteered to do the rowing singlehanded. "It's what the lobsterbacks will be expecting to see," he explained. "They never do anything for themselves if they can order someone else to do it for 'em."

Jamie, in any case, handled the oars with easy competence. Sitting in the stern next to Harlech, Caradoc kept watch as they approached the grain-market pier from the east with the sun at their backs. There were two small dark figures on top of the building at the far end of the pier. They seemed to be doing some work on the roof.

"I've just spotted Serdor and Evelake—they're in position," he reported to Gudmar.

"Excellent," said Gudmar. "Jamie, take us in closer. It shouldn't be long now."

Lord Gervaise Du Lacque, the Du Bors emissary to Pernatha, had come on board the *White Mermaid* at Ambrothen, bringing with him one manservant to look after his personal comfort and fifteen men-at-arms to keep the *Mermaid*'s resident crew of thirty-seven under tight control for the duration of the voyage. On the morning of the *Mermaid*'s last day in Telphar, the lieutenant in charge of the military detachment came on deck after breakfast to be greeted with the news that the pilot who had jumped ship during the night was still unaccounted for. Already displeased, he was even more annoyed to be further informed that the three men who had been sent to track down the runaway had not yet returned.

There were three possible explanations. Either they were still hunting the fugitive. Or, having failed to find him, they had turned aside from their duty to sample the enticements offered by the Telpharan dens of pleasure. Or they had somehow gotten themselves into trouble. In any case, their absence had left the lieutenant short-handed, which was a major inconvenience. Not only were there ship's stores to be fetched from a storage depot inland, but there was also the Baron Du Lacque's personal baggage to be transferred aboard the *Mermaid* from his residence ashore.

As the provisions were indispensable for the voyage home, and since the king's emissary intended to leave Telphar on the noonday tide, there could be no delays in sending landing parties ashore to undertake the necessary donkeywork involved. Swearing awful retribution on his three missing subordinates, should they fail to produce a satisfactory explanation for their failure to return to the ship on time, the lieutenant summoned his two sergeants-at-arms and instructed them to get their shore parties in order.

Twenty minutes later, two large rowing gigs put out from the *Mermaid*. The lieutenant watched the longboats' departure from the upper deck. Below on the maindeck, the four members of the crew who had not been confined to quarters prepared to go about their assigned duties under the supervision of two of the three remaining soldiers. Neither they, nor the lieutenant, noticed the workmen on the roof of the grain-market pier.

Shading his eyes with the blade of his hand, Evelake counted heads as the two ship's gigs sculled past his vantage point on their way inshore. "One officer, three regulars, and thirteen sailors in each boat," he reported.

"If Jamie has his figures right, there will be ten crewmen left on board," said Serdor. "And only four Du Bors mercenaries."

He tossed aside his brush and stood up. Fifty feet to the opposite side of the pier, the four men in a cockboat stiffened expectantly. After reading the minstrel's sharply delineated hand signals, Gudmar uttered a short exclamation of satisfaction. "Let's be off, gentlemen," he said in a voice edged with steely laughter. "The ship's virtually ours for the taking. . . ."

Once the gigs had been launched, the lieutenant aboard the *Mermaid* retired to his cabin. His two subordinates remained on deck, while the third stayed below to make sure that the rest of the crew caused no trouble during their confinement. Outside in the open air, the ship's carpenter and three assistants were grudgingly constructing something that resembled a gun carriage. The staccato thud of their hammers had scarcely begun, however, before a loud hail in Garillan from off the port bow drew the two men-at-arms to the portside railing.

Peering down, they saw directly below them four men in a small rowboat drawn up at the ship's side. Three of the men were anonymously familiar in their crimson uniforms, with the Du Bors chevrons worked in gold down the backs of their cloaks. The glare of the morning sun off the water rendered their faces indistinct beneath their helmets, but the fourth man was recognizable by his clothes as the pilot who had jumped overboard six hours earlier. "Oi, Dougal!" called a voice from below. "Break out the grog! We're back with the bacon!"

The speaker's voice was half-drowned in the clatter of carpentry tools, but the sense was clear enough. "Here, you barnacles, give it a rest!" called Dougal peremptorily to the four workmen clustered around their unfinished construction. "Rhodri! Stoat! Dovy! You three go fetch a rope ladder and bring our friends on board. Malco, you go inform the lieutenant that the chickens have come home to roost."

Down below, the four men in the rowboat were surreptitiously checking their weaponry. "Do you think they bought it?" muttered Caradoc, squinting up from under the brow-piece of his helmet.

A bundle of hemp cascaded down the ship's side. "There's your answer, I think," said Gudmar. "Everybody get ready. . . ."

Rhodri Blantyn, the ship's carpenter, was standing by when his friend Jamie swung himself over the railing looking somewhat the worse for wear. "Tough luck, Jamie boy," he murmured as the pilot edged past him. Then choked back a gasp of surprise as he caught sight of the long dagger strapped behind the other man's back.

Nonplussed, Rhodri cast a lightning glance over the side and found himself gazing point-blank into a pair of bright golden eyes. For an instant he merely goggled. Then he grinned from ear to ear.

The mercenary who stepped forward to take charge of Jamie Greenham was dumbfounded when his intended prisoner flicked a poniard from behind his back and jabbed the point of it against the underside of his chin. Snarling, he struck the pilot's hand away and leaped back. "Look out, this bugger's armed!" he shouted to the man who had just stepped over the railing. "I know," agreed the red-haired newcomer, and leaped for his throat.

Grappling, they both went down. Whooping enthusiastically, Jamie and Rhodri joined in. The other guardsman howled and made a dash for the hatchway astern. Gudmar vaulted over the rail at a bound and charged after him.

He overtook the fleeing regular in four strides and shouldered the other man violently into the wall beside the hatchway door. The liveryman grunted and clattered to the deck. Before he could draw a weapon, a second figure in crimson landed heavily astride his chest and snared his right nostril with the talon-sharp point of a steel hook. "Make one false move, laddie, and I'll carve your face like a capon," said his assailant. "You lot, come get his weapons—"

Leaving Harlech to deal with the man he had

downed, Gudmar whipped out his sword and threw wide the door into the stern-castle just as two armed figures stumbled out into the companionway. The man in the lead fetched up short mere inches from impaling himself on the point of Gudmar's weapon. He recoiled with a curse, his eyes wildly staring. The man behind him barred his retreat with a stiff arm and demanded sharply of Gudmar, "Who the devil are you?"

"I'm the rightful owner of this ship," said his adversary with chilly civility. "I hope you have the good sense to surrender her without a fight."

Instead of answering, the lieutenant caught his subordinate by the shoulders and hurled him forward. Gudmar sprang back, but the guardsman's falling body fouled his blade. The lieutenant wrenched his own weapon from its sheath and lashed out at his adversary's extended sword arm. To his astonishment, the blade clashed off steel instead of flesh.

His wrist jarred, the lieutenant realized belatedly that his opponent was also wielding a poniard. Showing teeth in a tigerish smile, Gudmar flexed his dagger hand, using the full strength of his forearm to force the lieutenant's point toward the floor. Unable to break free of the bind, the officer aimed a kick at the man on the floor. "Get him, you fool!" he snarled.

His subordinate made a floundering attempt to reach his weapon. His movement freed Gudmar's sword. "That's your second mistake," said Gudmar succinctly, and executed a swift angled thrust to ram his point home beneath the lieutenant's exposed ribs.

The officer dropped his blade and clutched at the wound in his side. Blood welled between his fingers as he folded to the deck. Gudmar nudged the fallen sword out of reach with the toe of his boot and gazed down dispassionately at the other mercenary still sprawled at his feet. "Well?" said the big merchant-adventurer. "Have *you* any further quarrel with me?"

The man's attention strayed aside to where his superior was lying in a widening spill of crimson. Raising his eyes to meet Gudmar's, he wordlessly shook his head.

"Very wise," said Gudmar with an approving nod. "Once you've disarmed yourself, we'll take this rather feckless gentleman out on deck and see what can be done to keep him from bleeding to death. . . ."

Come fresh from the siege of Gand to the court of His Magnificence Sulimar the Deep-Minded of Pernatha, Admiral Lord Gervaise Du Lacque was accorded a diplomatic welcome upon his arrival in Telphar, and was housed with all due consideration in one of the opulent guest-villas that adjoined the imperial palace itself.

Rising in pale marble eminence above the cultivated lushness of the sultan's pleasure gardens, the villa overlooked the harbor from the west. It had been built by Sulimar's great-uncle, the corsair-prince Feyseid Al Sir'dhar, and still, as in the days of Prince Feyseid, the sultan's great war dromonds sailed past its windows on the way in and out of their sheltered anchorage inland. From the state apartments on the upper floor, the villa's present occupant could survey the whole harbor from the teeming quay to the rocky fortified island of Al'Cantra at the entrance to the bay. For the moment, however, Lord Gervaise's main object of interest was an elegant carvel-built caravel anchored just beyond the end of the grain-market pier.

Even at a distance, she was distinguishable by the lateen rake of her mizzenmast and the general sleekness of her design. Standing at the window, splendidly attired in silk brocade, the baron sipped his *kjaffe* and congratulated himself on his choice of vessels. Fast and seaworthy, despite the surliness of her crew, the *White Mermaid* had shown an admirable turn of speed on her outbound voyage to Pernatha. The success of the first part of Lord Gervaise's mission had depended upon his own gifts for diplomatic negotiation, but the success of the next part of his mission was likely to depend on the *Mermaid*'s swiftness and maneuverability. From Telphar, Lord Gervaise intended to return with all possible dispatch to Gand, where he was to assist his army counterpart Lord

Khevyn Ap Khorrasel in forcing the defenders of the castle to surrender.

In preparation for carrying out the second part of Lord Gervaise's orders, the *Mermaid* had taken on board in the last two days a total of thirty-five lead-lined kegs of *bashanti*, a substance whose strange incendiary properties rendered it one of the most fearsome weapons in the sultan's military arsenal. The process involved in its manufacture was a secret so closely guarded that the full details were known only by the sultan himself and his minister of war. But Saladir was not entirely averse to selling a quantity of the material itself when the buying price amounted to something approaching a king's ransom.

Besides the *bashanti* itself, Lord Gervaise had also succeeded in purchasing the services of two Pernathan engineers who possessed the knowledge to construct and operate a flame-throwing device known in Pernathan terms as a "salamander." Properly handled, the salamander was capable of projecting burning jets of *bashanti* for distances in excess of fifty feet. The Dowager-Regent had reason to hope that such a weapon might succeed against Gand Castle and its stubborn garrison where ordinary ordnance had so far failed.

The component parts to the *Mermaid*'s salamander, like the *bashanti*, had been taken on board after the diplomatic compact had been signed and sealed. The parts would be fully assembled once the ship's carpenter and his mates finished constructing the carriage to house the mechanism. His own voluminous baggage having been dispatched within the past hour, Lord Gervaise was waiting only to be joined by the two engineers before setting out under royal escort for the ship. He looked forward to the moment when he and the *Mermaid* would be off.

A light breeze stirred the tops of the pomegranate trees below his windows, reflecting a change in the wind. It was a sign that the tide would soon be turning. Lord Gervaise scowled, impatient for the Pernathans' arrival. One or two of the smaller vessels near at hand had raised anchor and were already starting to edge their way toward the harbor-bar. Watching their drift from his vantage point, the baron suddenly became aware of another source of movement farther out beyond the grain-market pier.

The *White Mermaid* appeared to be shifting her position.

Starting forward, Lord Gervaise took a second dumbfounded look, then groped for the small ship's glass that swung from a chain from his belt. Snapping the lens to his right eye, he trained the glass on the *Mermaid*. Men were racing to and fro in a flurry of disciplined activity, with a conspicuous absence of red uniforms. The big blond man at the wheel was someone the baron had never seen before.

Lord Gervaise dropped the glass with a curse and bellowed for his valet.

The tone and volume of his roar brought the servant on the run. "Call Alhef Al Bek'r immediately and have him signal the fort," snarled Lord Gervaise. "Someone's in the process of trying to steal my ship!"

The land breeze was rising. Breaking out of the tangle of stationary vessels, the *White Mermaid* forged forward under the outbound pull of the changing tide. Her lateen sail aft caught the wind with a crack as the canvas sprang taut. Foam curled away from her keel in a widening vee as she gathered speed, making for the open sea beyond the confines of the harbor.

To reach it, she had to run the quarter-mile gap between two arms of land that pinched the neck of the bay like the claws of a crab. Up on the forecastle, Margoth clung to the railing with both hands and braced herself against the canting motion of the deck. Off to her right, the white marble walls of the sultan's palace glistened like loaf-sugar above the green lawns that crowned the headland. Even as she studied the confectioner's fantasy of domes and arches, from the tallest of five faerielike towers came an agitated flicker of lights, like sunlight dancing off a large moving mirror.

A shout went up from the masthead lookout. "Captain, they're signaling the fort!"

Standing next to Gudmar at the wheel, Harlech marked a responding flash of lights from the crenellated walls of the Al'Cantra. "I had a notion we wouldnae slip away unnoticed," rumbled the little seafarer. "They've been ordered tae run out their guns."

"Our best defense at this point lies in speed," said Gudmar. Inflating his lungs, he called out to the *Mermaid*'s sailing master, "Master Penrith, let go the main sail!"

In response to a shouted relay of commands, topmen leaped for the ratlines and swarmed aloft. Loosed from the main yard, the great square of canvas unfurled like an arras. As it swelled to take the wind, Gudmar brought the ship around a few points to port. Close-hauled, she surged ahead in a creamy flume of foam.

The Al'Cantra's high walls loomed tall off the port bow, rising off a barren foundation of sea rock. Harlech counted gun muzzles as they appeared along the fort's east rampart and pulled a beetling scowl. "Eight culverins and six basilisks, by my count," he muttered. "I wonder what kind of range they've got—"

He was interrupted by a belching roar from above. A fifty-pound ball of stoneshot dashed up a fountain of sea spray a chain's length off to starboard. "Long enough, I'd say, to hit us anywhere between here and Sulimar's dining room," said Gudmar. "Well, if we can't get on the outside of their arc of fire, maybe we can get on the *inside* of it. Master Penrith!"

"Aye, sir?"

"How much water are we drawing?"

"About ten feet, sir."

"I want two men on the port bow with a leadline," said Gudmar. "We're going in close, so tell 'em to keep their eyes on the bottom and nowhere else!"

All along the east wall of the fort, the basilisks bellowed in enfilade. One ball clipped the top off the

Mermaid's foremast. Another punched a hole through the mainsail. The caravel faltered, lost a brief moment's headway, then recovered. Held hard before the wind, she cut bravely into the shallows under the lea of the fortress.

The rampart boiled with activity as the fort's gun crews labored frantically to reduce the range. The stink of brimstone settled like volcanic ash. One by one, the culverins roared flame as their crews brought them to bear on the passing ship. Several balls went wide. One smashed away six feet of starboard railing and covered the deck with flying splinters.

Two men went down wounded. Ahead of the bowsprit, the water paled from sapphire to aquamarine. "Captain!" yelped one of the leadsmen. "Two fathoms!"

Harlech swore, then abruptly shut his mouth. Strong hands locked firmly to the wheel, Gudmar set his teeth. "Come on, princess," he urged his ship silently. "Don't leave us stranded now. . . ."

There was a crunch as the rudder scraped bottom. The *Mermaid* lurched, then broke free with a shudder. Churning up sand in watery clouds behind her, she slithered past the last of the outlying reef rocks with mere yards to spare. "Two fathoms, mark three!" called the leadsman. "Three fathoms—she's coming clear, sir!"

There were some jeering catcalls from the men amidships. "Don't get cocky, you lot!" snapped the sailing master. "We might still get our tails peppered from the fort's seaward batteries."

"Or maybe we could give 'em a taste of their own medicine," skirled an anonymous voice from somewhere forward. "How about it, Master Gudmar? Shall we run out the stern-chasers and give those misbegotten moldywarps a few pops to teach 'em respect for a lady?"

"Just keep your heads down," Gudmar called back, "and prepare to go about."

He put the helm hard over. The water boiled around the *Mermaid's* rudder as she heeled sharply to the windward and began to turn. Her sails slackened briefly as she changed tacks, then swelled again as she recaptured the wind from a new quarter. Reaching another twenty degrees to starboard, she sped for the sanctuary of the open sea.

The Al'Cantra's guns laid down a volley of shots in her wake. An oblique hit astern smashed through a bulkhead, leaving a gaping hole in the upper level of the sterncastle. More shots whizzed through the rigging, tearing shrouds and rending canvas. Despite the punishment she was taking, the *Mermaid* steadily gained headway. Before the fort batteries could organize a last salvo, she pulled out of range.

The achievement drew cheers from all sides. Margoth ducked out of the sheltering overhang of the forecastle and planted a resounding kiss on Serdor's cheek. Then she turned to her brother and threw both arms around him. "We did it!" she cried jubilantly. "We're on our way!"

All over the ship, men were either clapping each other on the shoulder, or else waving derisive fists at the walls of the Al'Cantra, dropping farther and farther astern. Harlech and Jamie Greenham were dancing an impromptu hornpipe in the middle of the deck. Evelake was with them, flushed and triumphant. Leaving the helm to Giles Penrith, Gudmar joined them, throwing a strong arm around the boy's slight shoulders. Raising her eyes to meet Caradoc's, Margoth discovered that he alone of all the ship's company was showing no sign of elation.

"What's the matter with you?" she asked, giving his arm a tug. "In case you hadn't noticed, today has just become an occasion for celebrating."

"Has it?" Caradoc's green eyes were troubled. "Margoth, what's to cheer about when we're going straight back to a country at war with itself—quite possibly to get ourselves killed? Has everyone forgotten that but me?"

"No one's forgotten," said Margoth quietly. "That's why we're all the readier to give today's success its full share of appreciation."

Her cornflower eyes challenged him to argue the

issue. Instead, his anxious look softened into a reluctant smile. "I never seem to win a point over you, do I?" he said with a rueful shake of his head. "Never mind—I'm just as happy for you to be in the right this time."

Hugging her to him, he waved a hand in Gudmar's direction. "Oi, Captain!" he called. "If you've any decent wine aboard this scow, let's break it out and drink a toast. . . ."

A GARDEN FULL OF ROSES

IT TOOK GUDMAR AND HIS crew the rest of the afternoon to work the *Mermaid* north as far as Qu'rash Point, a rugged peninsula jutting seaward like an outthrust tongue between Telphar and Ghurbek, a day's journey up the coast. The *Mermaid* anchored off Qu'rash long enough for her captain to put ashore the Du Bors mercenaries who had been captured along with the ship. Then the caravel pressed on again, striking out for the open waters of the Straits of Belvidar.

During the night, the wind shifted round to the east. The following morning, the sun rose bloodred through an ominous haze of impending storm. Keeping a wary eye on the sea and sky, the *Mermaid*'s carpenter and his mates worked feverishly to finish repairing the damage inflicted by the guns of the Al'Cantra. They had scarcely completed the task of resetting the broken section of the ship's foremast when it became clear to everyone on board that they were heading into a squall.

The dirty weather held unbroken for the next two days. Buffeted by wind and rain, the *Mermaid* ploughed her course laboriously through white-capped waters, her momentum reduced to a snail's pace. Her crew spent half their time aloft, trimming her sails to make the best of contrary gales. Below, in the state cabin astern,

Gudmar and Harlech pored over sea charts and argued over points of navigation, while Evelake and Serdor played war games with an assortment of makeshift counters. Caradoc joined them whenever he found time to spare from looking after the men who had been injured in their flight from Telphar.

Margoth firmly excused herself from taking part, having some very specific plans of her own to pursue. She and her companions had come aboard the *Mermaid* wearing either borrowed Du Bors uniforms or else their own tattered, travel-stained garments. Unable to envision anything less in keeping with the party's intentions than their clothes, she made up her mind to do something to rectify the situation.

Among the goods brought on board the *Mermaid* at the last minute had been several large iron-bound sea chests, all of them belonging to her late captain, Baron Gervaise Du Lacque. As far as Margoth was concerned, the fact that there were no keys to the locks was an irrelevance. Once she had them open, the first few chests yielded up not only several complete changes of clothing, but also a quantity of shirts, linen, footwear, and other accessories. One of the other boxes contained bales of fine uncut cloth. Satisfied that she had plenty to work with, Margoth took what she wanted to start with, and left the rest for later depredations.

Having a berth to herself, she proceeded to convert it into a seamstress's workshop. First on her list was Evelake. His Pernathan garments—haphazardly borrowed in the first place from the command post at Sul Khabir—had been reduced to little better than beggar's rags in his encounter with his brother's fiery alter-ego. He had since traded these in for some spare seaman's clothing, but he still looked like nothing so much as an adolescent scarecrow. Having at long last a pair of sharp scissors and sufficient opportunity, Margoth captured him long enough to trim back his shaggy blond hair to a neat silken cap. Then she set out to refurbish the rest of his appearance.

He submitted somewhat self-consciously to being

measured and fitted, but Margoth ruthlessly disregarded his shyness. A needlewoman second to none, she pursued her task with as much determination as skill. By noon the next day, she had ready for him a doublet of dark blue velvet, quilted for warmth against the coming winter, and woolen breech hose in a shade to match.

He went away to try them on, and returned several minutes later so that she could inspect her handiwork. After walking all the way around him so that she could survey him from all angles, Margoth was able to congratulate herself on her tailoring. The fit was close, but comfortable, and the somber richness of the cloth not only set off the sun-brightened fairness of his hair, but lent depth to the amber-brown of his eyes. He seemed all at once a very different creature from the scrawny waif Serdor had brought home with him from his travels at the end of the summer.

The owlish expression on his face, however, belonged as much to Rhan Hallender as to Evelake Whitfauconer, reminding her that the one was never truly to be separated from the other. He said with wry diffidence, "Well? Do I pass muster?"

"You do indeed!" said Margoth, dusting off her hands with an air of satisfaction. Seeing that he was looking slightly abashed, she gave him a grin. "It's a pity we haven't got a full-length mirror. You'll just have to take my word for it that you look every inch a nobleman!"

This assurance made him chuckle. With great deliberation, he walked over and kissed her warmly on the cheek. "No one could ask for better friends than I have," he said. "Thanks, Margoth—you're a marvel!"

"I have my moments," agreed Margoth cheerfully. "And this was one of my best. Even if I do say so myself. . . ."

She received further commendations from the other members of the party when the group gathered in the state cabin for their evening meal. Even Harlech was moved to voice his approval. "People are gey queer in the matter of looks," he observed sapiently. "Now *we* ken brawlie that the laddie's Lord Delsidor's son—but if ye want the rest of the world tae believe it, ye've got tae show 'em what they'd expect tae see: a bird with fine plumage."

"In other words," said Serdor, " 'If thou wouldst be captain to men's souls, thee needs must first command their admiration.' Merit, unfortunately, isn't everything. You've got to have appearances on your side."

Margoth had good reason to know that the minstrel was speaking from experience. Though he was superbly gifted as a musician, his talents had never brought him prosperity—largely because his threadbare clothes and general air of poverty had always excluded him from circles where he might otherwise have sought to win a patron. As the meal progressed, Margoth found herself recalling a conversation she had once had with Arn Aldarshot, the owner of the Beldame Inn back in Ambrothen.

That had been many months ago. Serdor had been performing at the Beldame that night, to the thorough appreciation of Arn's customers. "What fairly puzzles me," the little innkeeper had said, "is why some lord high-muckety-muck hasn't swept him off the street corner and into the manor house to lead a fat, pampered life as the family songbird." To which Margoth had replied, not without a certain bitterness, "For one thing, he has no influential connections. For another, he's not nearly decorative enough."

The second point, however, was open to argument. Certainly Serdor lacked the striking degree of good looks that had always caused Caradoc to turn female heads in the street. But he had his own assets, well worth considering: a strong, lightweight body, graceful in all its movements, and a matchless pair of wide grey eyes. Even if she hadn't known him for his quick wits and warm heart, Margoth would have taken pleasure in watching him.

And she had found herself watching him more and more closely during the past few weeks.

When he wasn't troubling to hide his feelings, his spirit expressed itself freely in his eyes and his unstudied gestures. But lately he had seemed less open, as if he were holding himself under a tight rein. Margoth was puzzled by his behavior, especially this diffidence where she was concerned.

She knew that passion ran strong in him: like Caradoc, he had had his share of amorous adventures in the past. And she knew that he cared for her in a way he had never cared for anyone else—with deep conviction and abiding loyalty. But for all that, he had never in her company allowed himself to trespass beyond the bounds of courtesy. Why he should have imposed such restraint upon himself, when everything in his nature opposed it, was something Margoth had yet to account for.

Whatever his reasons might be, she was firmly convinced that his scruples were doing him no good. Ever since the party had left Sul Khabir three weeks ago, he had been growing increasingly restless, as if even the rigors of hard traveling could not ease the tensions under which he was laboring—tensions that she knew full well had nothing to do with the whole party's fears for the future, but were rather signs of his personal need.

Sitting by him at the table now, she could see he was merely toying with his food. There were traces of strain in the unconscious set of his mouth, and his grey eyes were heavy, as though he might not have slept well the night before. Taking stock of his demeanor, Margoth decided that it was high time the two of them had a talk.

She had scarcely arrived at this resolution when Gudmar, who was sitting at the head of the table, pushed back his chair and stood up. "The wind's changing again—I can feel it in our timbers," he said. "If you all will excuse me, I'd better go topside and see how the weather's shaping up for the night."

"If ye've no objection, I'll bear ye company," said Harlech. "I fancy a breath of air that doesna stink of wet woolens. How about you, milord?"

"No, thanks," said Evelake with a laugh. "Serdor

and I are locked in mortal combat on the Hills of Ardmuir. If he doesn't watch himself, I'm going to overrun his left flank on my next move."

Serdor roused himself to glare at his opponent. "You sound awfully sure of yourself."

"Nothing but a really bad roll of the ship can save you now," declared Evelake with unblushing conviction.

"Those sound like fighting words to me," said the minstrel. "Come on, then."

He and the boy made for the chartroom. Seeing her hopes for a private conversation disintegrating before her eyes, Margoth turned to Caradoc and said pessimistically, "I don't suppose I could persuade you to come back to my berth so that I can take your measurements for some new clothes?"

Her brother was already on his feet. Keeping a wary eye on the cabin's low ceiling, he said apologetically, "Could it wait till tomorrow? One of my patients in the forecastle has fallen into a fever, and I'm thinking I'd better not leave him unattended tonight."

"No. Tomorrow will do just as well," said Margoth with sour resignation. Glowering after him as he made for the door, she muttered, "Don't worry about me—I'll just amuse myself darning my stockings."

Upon reflection, she decided to have a bath instead. With this object in mind, she arrested the cook's mate when he came to collect the dirty dishes and besought him to bring her a basin, along with a canister of warm water from the galley. He did as she asked, and stayed long enough to light her lamp for her before taking himself off to his more regular duties. Left alone, Margoth caught herself drifting off into wistful reflection. She drew herself up with a cluck of her tongue, and got down to the practical business of personal cleanliness.

It was chilly in the berth, despite the heat from a charcoal brazier bolted to the floor in one corner. After sponging herself down from head to foot, Margoth dried hastily and struggled back into her petticoat and skirt.

She was just putting out a hand for her camisole when there was a knock at the door. A voice said hesitantly, "Margoth? Have you got a few minutes to spare?"

It was Serdor. Margoth's pulse gave an odd leap. She said, "Of course. Just give me half a moment here—"

She reached for her bodice again, then paused as a sudden thought occurred to her. Without bothering to reconsider, she whisked the garment away out of sight under a heap of sewing materials and caught up her shawl instead.

It settled warmly round her shoulders. She drew it close so that no betraying flicker of skin would show, then moved to open the door.

Serdor was looking slightly distrait. As he edged past her into the tiny room, Margoth sensed his unrest. Not wanting to let her own nervousness show, she said prosaically, "It certainly didn't take you long to finish off your game. Evelake must have made good his boast."

Serdor grimaced. "With a vengeance." After a pause, he added, "Evelake's got a good head for strategy. Which is probably just as well, considering what we're likely to find waiting for us once we reach East Garillon."

Margoth closed the door, then unostentatiously latched it. She asked, "Has Gudmar decided yet where's the best place for us to make landfall?"

"He seems to think," said Serdor, "that Falmyth offers certain material advantages."

"To begin with, the fact that it's not too close to Ambrothen, and not too far from Gand," said Margoth thoughtfully. She sat down on the bunk and tilted her gaze upward to meet Serdor's. "I imagine there are other reasons."

The minstrel braced his back against the bulkhead opposite, scarcely more than an arm's length away. "For one thing, the Hospitallers maintain a sizable community there—the largest one this side of Gand, with five ranking magisters in residence. That's important, since the first thing we have to do is prove that Evelake is who he says he is. Once the magisters at Falmyth have verified his story, they will be able to communicate their findings to other hospices in the area."

He rubbed the bridge of his nose with a contemplative forefinger. "The other advantage to landing at Falmyth lies in the fact that the place is virtually ruled by the Merchant-Adventurers. Gudmar is firmly convinced that once his colleagues are presented with a true and proven account of what the Du Bors have been up to, they'll be prepared to give Evelake their staunch support."

Margoth was silent for a moment. Then she said wistfully, "Serdor, do you remember that night back in the spring, when we had the dance at the Beldame Inn?"

The minstrel nodded. "Yes, I do. It was great fun—till Caradoc got into a fight."

"And a lot of hopes went down in ruins for no good reason," said Margoth with a sigh. She added, "Haven't you ever wondered what our lives might have been like now, if Caradoc hadn't lost his temper that night?"

"Of course I have," said Serdor. "But every time I do, I end up deciding that it's best the way it is. If Caradoc hadn't fallen out with the Order, Evelake would probably be dead now. And I wouldn't be here, about to make the most important speech of my life."

His tone was wry, but Margoth's pulse quickened. "What I have to say would be much better said elsewhere —in a garden full of roses, maybe—or by the side of a brook in high summer," he announced ruefully. "But we haven't come across any rose gardens since we left Ambrothen, and summer's too far away. The way things are going, this may be my one and only chance to tell you—formally in words—what you've probably already guessed: I'm in love with you—so much in love that nothing else in the world seems to matter, except the hope that you'll marry me."

He was watching her closely. Her heart all at once full to overflowing, Margoth gave him a misty smile. "Serdor, you dear, silly fool, my heart has been yours for the asking ever since I was old enough to know what I really wanted—and that's been for quite some time now! What made you wait so long?"

He lowered his gaze to his hands. "Several reasons, I suppose. Back in Ambrothen, I didn't want to make things any more complicated than they were already. Above all, I didn't want to risk spoiling things for you—"

"*Spoiling* things?" Margoth was genuinely puzzled. "Whatever are you talking about?"

"Well," said Serdor with a lopsided grin, "it isn't as if you've ever suffered any lack of suitors. Any one of them would have been able to give you a far more comfortable life than I could ever hope to provide. It would have been unjust of me to have taken advantage of our childhood friendship, just as it would have been unfair of me to have pressed my suit while Caradoc needed my help. And since then," he ended, "we've been too bloody busy running away from trouble for me to find time to pursue anything like a courtship.

"I have so little to offer, when you deserve so much!" he added recklessly. "But all I am, and all I ever hope to have or be, is yours if you'll accept it."

"I'm going to hold you to that vow!" said Margoth. "Starting this very night."

He was too quick not to catch the subtle change of inflection in her voice. Eyeing her quizzically, he said, "Why do I suddenly have the feeling that I'm about to be outmaneuvered for the second time tonight?"

"I don't know," said Margoth. "Don't you think it's high time you kissed me?"

She gave her head a small backward toss, roguishly inviting him to take her at her word. Provoked into laughter himself, Serdor said, "*More* than high time, if you're going to put it like that!" Catching hold of her hands, he pulled her toward him. Before he could realize what was happening, Margoth shook the shawl from her shoulders and stepped half-naked into his embrace.

His initial response was an audible gasp. Without giving him any chance to school his more instinctive reactions, Margoth twined both bare arms around his neck and pressed her lips firmly to his. For a heartbeat or two, he struggled to resist his own impulses. Then his hands moved, one sliding caressingly down her back to press her closer to him, the other drifting upward to cup her left breast with possessive delicacy. His mouth still close to hers, he murmured, "Margoth, you *minx*! You planned this!"

His pulse was racing with excited abandon. Her own reflexes pleasurably disordered, Margoth gave an unsteady chuckle. "I did indeed. There are times when you're too much of a gentleman for your own good."

She traced the sharp-cut line of his lips with light fingers, stroking downward toward the base of his throat where she began loosening the lacing of his collar. Without letting go of her, Serdor said huskily, "If you're going to keep that up, I won't be responsible for the consequences."

Margoth paused, her blue eyes brimming with dizzy exhilaration. "Nothing could please me more than to hear you say so!" she assured him. "Now, why don't you let me help you off with that shirt . . . ?"

THE PENITENT OF KIRKWELL

FAR FROM THE WINDSWEPT COAST of Gand, where her older brother, Devon, was desperately defending Gand Castle against an implacable host of enemy attackers, Kherryn Du Penfallon lay in a troubled sleep, her dreams haunted with visions of danger and death.

Within the frame of her nightmare it seemed that she was locked up in a dungeon cell—dark, apart from a subdued glimmer of pale light filtering through a square grating in the heavy cell door. She could hear, but not see, the water that trickled ceaselessly down the muck-encrusted walls. Underfoot, the floor was dank and slick with unspeakable ordure. There were bones scattered throughout the lice-ridden straw. Some of the bones were human.

Kherryn knew that she was dreaming. That knowledge prevented her from surrendering to the slimy horror of her surroundings. Even during her waking hours, she was capable of shutting out the world around her, retreating into her own mind whenever the stress of the moment became more than she could bear. Experience had taught her that this same instinct for self-defense would cause her to waken if the horrors of her dream should threaten to overwhelm her.

Even so, in her present dream, she was reluctant to venture away from the light that shone from the doorway. Eyes wide, face pressed hard against the grimy bars of the grate, she watched the light, burning steadily with a soft silver-green glow. All her spirit, all her concentration was centered on the starlike point of radiance. Her heart pierced with a sudden yearning, she thrust thin fingers through the mesh of wrought iron, straining as if to touch the light. "I cannot reach you," she told the star-glow in a whisper. "Please, will you come to me?"

As if in response to her pleading request, the light quickened to fresh and vibrant intensity. Like a jewel flowering, it burst into life, putting out shoots and blossoms of sparkling radiance. Entranced, Kherryn held her breath and watched it grow until it filled her vision with scintillating beauty.

The grid to her cell door melted away under the touch of the light, dissolving like dirty snow. The heavy lock fell away, transformed into a shower of mud. The door swung open on hinges brittle as glass. Her heart leaping, Kherryn drifted across the threshold and found herself at the foot of an ascending flight of stairs.

She could not see the top of the stairs for the brightness of the intervening light. Blinking, she raised a hand to shield her eyes from it. At once, the light diminished, contracting until it resumed its former soft, lamplike shimmer. It hovered a moment above her head, then, like a guiding star, began to rise.

Kherryn followed it up the stairs, stumbling a little because her eyes were watching the light rather than the steps. The climb seemed endless, the steps without number, but she persevered, drawn on by the light that moved before her. Then, just as she was beginning to fear that she might never reach the top, she caught sight at last of her goal.

There was a tall door at the head of the stairs. It was intricately carven in designs disturbing to the eyes. Feeling all at once dizzy and unbalanced, Kherryn looked sharply away. As she did so, her guiding star blazed out with sudden angry ardor.

Spinning like a top, throwing off light in searing green-white flares, the ball of flame leaped forward like a missile shot from an arbalest. It struck the door in a shower of sparks. The carvings fell away in ashes as the star passed through the center of the portal, leaving a gap wide enough to admit Kherryn to the room beyond. Holding her skirts carefully, she stepped between two still-smoldering panels, then froze in her tracks.

The chamber she had entered was circular, its walls smothered in black draperies. A round table had been set in the center of the floor beneath a hanging lamp fashioned from the horned skulls of four he-goats. Four people—a woman, two men, and a boy—were seated at the table, all gazing inward, their faces rapt in concentration. Kherryn's heart leaped into her mouth as she stared at them aghast. At least three of those present at the table were known to her.

The first was Lady Gwynmira Du Bors, her lovely face hard as a sculpture in ivory. To her right sat Earlis Ap Eadric, the Grand Prior of Kirkwell Abbey. The third, sitting opposite his mother, was Gythe Du Bors, half brother to the missing Evelake. The fourth member of the group had his back to Kherryn. His face wasn't visible, but his presence filled Kherryn with cold dread.

The four seemed oblivious to the fact that she was there. All their attention was centered inward on a small object lying in the middle of the table.

Kherryn remained where she was for a long moment, uncertain what to do. But as the people at the table continued to ignore her, she plucked up the courage to move closer, curious to see what was holding their interest.

The object in the middle of the table was a small box, wrought of clear quartz crystal. On its lid, its maker had carved the image of a hawk in flight. Staring at it, Kherryn bit back a gasp of astonishment. The box was something she knew had once belonged to Evelake Whitfauconer.

The man whose face she could not see stretched out his hands over the box and muttered a phrase in a language that made her flinch even though she could make no sense of the words. Gythe leaned forward, the corners of his mouth upturned in a smile of vindictive anticipation. His eyes burned in their sockets, crimson as living coals.

Transfixed with horror and revulsion, Kherryn could only watch in paralyzed dread as the boy with the eyes of a demon gathered into his hands the pendant that hung from an iron chain about his neck. The crimson stone set within the pendant glittered malevolently with the same baleful fire that blazed within the containment of Gythe's flesh and bone. With a shudder of unholy ecstasy, the boy clasped the jewel between his palms and bent his fiery gaze upon the crystal box with his family's crest inscribed upon its lid.

For a moment nothing appeared to happen, but Kherryn could feel the invisible crackle of power charging the atmosphere within the room. The air began to throb with a pulse inaudible but punishingly palpable. Thin tendrils of smoke began to rise from the crystal box. Out of the smoke above the tabletop an image began to form.

The image of Evelake Whitfauconer!

But not quite the same Evelake who used to surprise her with gifts and invent preposterous lighthearted games for her and her brother, Devon, to play. This Evelake was taller, thinner, his face and manner showing the restraint of a grave sense of purpose. The truth struck home to Kherryn like a physical blow. "He's *alive!*" she thought dazedly. "He's alive—*and he's in danger!*"

Intent upon his victim, Gythe raised a hand taloned like the foot of a bird of prey. Chuckling softly, he paused a moment, flexing his elongated fingers as if to test their predatory strength. Then, moving with savage swiftness, he reached out to seize his half brother by the throat.

Evelake's head snapped back. Rigid with shocked incomprehension, he choked and clawed at his windpipe. His brown eyes clouded. Quivering with almost sexual delight, Gythe began inexorably to tighten his murderous grip—

"No!" screamed Kherryn in desperate denial, and threw herself across the table.

Her fingers closed around the crystal box. Fire shot up her arm, scorching every nerve, but she held on to the box for dear life. Evelake's image dissolved in an explosive crackle of broken energies. There was an unearthly shriek of hatred and frustration before the room was thrown into total darkness.

Then the darkness itself dissolved.

She was no longer pressed against a tabletop in a necromancer's chamber. Instead, she was lying in a narrow bed. Bare stone walls encompassed her, somber and cheerless. The cold light of morning glanced in through two lancet windows on the opposite side of the room, sparsely furnished as the cell of an anchorite.

She was not in a conjurer's tower. She was not in a dungeon. She was in her room at Kirkwell Abbey.

The dream was over, for the moment. Gasping for breath, she told herself, "It's all right. Calm down. And for God's sake, don't let Brother Tyrvald find you like this, or they'll start questioning you all over again."

She was shaking from head to foot. Ever since her coming to Kirkwell, she had been visited by nightmares like the one from which she had just wakened. In each one, she either sought someone she could not find, or else fled from some ghastly danger she could not name. The mages at Kirkwell—especially Rouault Du Bracy, the subprior—had been eager to pry into her visions of the night, but she had been steadfast in her refusal to allow any of them to engage her in Orison. "I don't want them to know anything more about me than what they see with their eyes," she whispered fiercely. "They have no right to know more!"

Whatever horrors might haunt her in the realms of shadow, these were less deadly to the spirit than the grey suffocating atmosphere that prevailed at Kirkwell. After her father, Arvech, had met his death in mortal combat against Fyanor Du Bors of Ambrothen, Kherryn had sought sanctuary at Kirkwell, only a short distance from the place where he had died. But she knew it now for what it was—not a refuge, but a prison.

The mages here, she had discovered, were not healers, but gaolers. And soon—too soon—one of them would be coming to bring her food and check up on her. Fighting to recover a convincing measure of equanimity, Kherryn struggled up into a sitting position, and realized with a stab of chill astonishment that she was clutching something small and hard in her right hand.

Her heart gave a queer, incredulous lurch. Quaking again, she slowly pulled her hand out from under her blankets. Her fingers were clenched tight as a fist around an object that seemed to fit familiarly into her palm. Casting a nervous glance in the direction of the door, she gathered herself into a small huddle of limbs and willed herself to relax her grip.

The object that met her eyes was a small box carven out of clear rock crystal, its four sides decorated in patterns of lines as delicate as frost. The lid of the box was surmounted by the image of a striking hawk, executed with exquisite skill. Kherryn uttered a repressed cry as she stared at the little box in near disbelief. "In my dream I picked up a box—this box!" she murmured breathlessly. "And now I've got it! I've actually got it back!"

Her voice broke in a sob, half delighted, half hysterical. For this crystal box that she now held in her hands was one of the things she had been forced to hand over to the sacristan of Kirkwell on the day she was admitted to the abbey. Since then she had more than once wept over its loss. For the box had been Evelake Whitfauconer's parting gift to her, bestowed on the morning in spring when he had left Gand to return to Farrowaithe—the last time she had seen him in the flesh.

When she had first applied for sanctuary, Magister Roualt, acting proxy for his superior, Earlis Ap Eadric, had agreed to accept her only under the most rigorous constraints. He had insisted that she observe all conditions imposed by canon law upon criminals applying for the protection of the Order. In compliance with his sternly worded edict, Kherryn had been obliged to relinquish what little personal property she had brought with her—even the clothes she had been wearing. Nerveless with shock over her father's violent death, she had submitted to every demand without protest until the time had come for her to surrender Evelake's pledge.

She had pleaded in vain for the favor of retaining this one small token. The subprior, however, had been adamant in his insistence, and in the end, had wrested the box from her. Too numb after that even to weep, she had donned the black robes of a penitent, and had allowed them to lead her—with bare feet and the Hospitallers' symbol traced in ashes on her forehead— to this stark and isolated chamber, with no comforts and only the most meager of necessities. The whole ritual had been an obscenity.

Only now this box—Evelake's box—was back in her possession by some mysterious means that defied explanation. Kherryn fingered the hawk image with fearful tenderness, hardly able to believe her eyes, still less account for what had happened. The more she thought about it, the more convinced she became that the other images she had encountered in her dream must have been expressing desperate incontrovertible truths. On the one hand, the certainty that Evelake was still alive, and might yet be restored to her. On the other, the realization that something dark and deadly was about to be unleashed on East Garillon at the hands of Evelake's half brother.

"I wish Ulbrecht were here!" she muttered distractedly to herself. "He would be able to explain this—or at least tell me what to do next."

But that kind of wishing was as foolish as it was futile. Her friend and mentor, Ulbrecht Rathmuir, the one mage in whom she had confidently placed her trust and affection, had been detained in Farrowaithe following a stormy confrontation with his superiors who made up the College of Magisters. Possessing information damaging to Gwynmira Du Bors, Ulbrecht had strongly urged that he be allowed to publish it, but his petition had been denied on the grounds that he was not an inquisitor. His response to the ruling of the college had been more honest than prudent—a circumstance which had prompted the college to take disciplinary action against him. Having been severely reprimanded, Ulbrecht had been required to undertake a rigorous series of penitential exercises and activities under the supervision of the head of the college: Earlis Ap Eadric.

It was all beginning to make hideous sense in the light of her vision of the night before. As High Inquisitor of Farrowaithe, Earlis had used his authority to keep her from warning her father of his danger until it was too late. And it was he who had cut short all subsequent investigations into the charges her father had made against Gwynmira Du Bors. Clearly, the High Inquisitor was involved in some deadly game of power. He had effectively silenced Ulbrecht, and would silence anyone else who interfered with the plans he shared with the Du Bors and their unknown confederate.

Kherryn's blood ran cold as she continued to stare at the little crystal casket. Prisoner as she was—here, in Earlis Ap Eadric's own ecclesiastical retreat—she would be completely at his mercy if he were to discover that she was the one responsible for the box's disappearance. "I've got to hide it!" she thought. "And for Evelake's sake, it's got to be someplace where no one else will find it."

But where? Certainly not in her room. Kherryn had every reason to believe that the premises were searched on a regular basis during periods when she herself was absent. Nor would it be safe to carry the box around with her on her person for any longer than was absolutely necessary. She did not trust herself to deceive her gaolers, whose trained intuitions would alert them all too readily to the fact that she had something she wanted to hide.

Time was running short. Brother Tyrvald would soon be arriving with her breakfast. She scrambled out of bed and hastily exchanged her nightgown for her day clothes. As a temporary measure, she secreted the box away among the coarse and clumsy folds of her overrobe, above the cincture of hemp that gathered the garment in at the waist. She had scarcely finished dragging a comb through her long fine hair when the sound of ponderous footsteps approaching the threshold to her room warned her that her dreary day's routine was about to begin.

DREAD ENQUIRY

BREAKFAST WAS PORRIDGE—COLD, LEATHERY, and wholly unappetizing. Brother Tyrvald stood over her as she sat with her spoon in her hand and stared down helplessly into the bowl, unable to force herself to do more than taste what was in it. The ordinaire's brown robe was redolent of sweat and stale bacon fat. The smell, combined with the looming closeness of his presence, all but turned her stomach. She bore it as long as she could, then abruptly pushed the tray away and stood up.

With breakfast over and done with, she faced a burdensome round of activities prescribed for her as a matter of routine by Magister Roualt. Tyrvald as usual remained to see that she carried them out. He watched her put on her cloak, then accompanied her out of her room and down the back stairway of the abbey's guesthouse to the small private chapel on the ground floor.

Tyrvald followed her inside and took up his station at the threshold as she walked away from him up the short central aisle and went down on her knees at the chancel rail. It was cold in the chapel, but as long as she kept her back to her unwanted attendant, she was guaranteed some small measure of privacy in which to think. Bracing herself against the penetrating chill of wandering floor drafts, she adopted an attitude of contemplation, acutely conscious of the little casket resting next to her skin. Without moving her head, she covertly scanned her immediate surroundings.

They offered little by way of inspiration. The chapel's interior was plain, the austerity of its wood and stonework unalleviated by any softening touches of ornamentation. The furnishings of the small altar were confined to a linen cloth and a brace of brass candlesticks. The window bays were shallow, their frames finished with functional simplicity. No generosity of depth or contour anywhere. No place to hide even so small a thing as the casket.

By Roualt's inflexible decree, Kherryn was obliged to remain in chapel until after the office of terce. By the time the bell in the tower of the main church tolled out the hour of nine, she was shivering with cold, her knees throbbing from long contact with the floor. Tyrvald made no move to help her as she struggled to her feet against the numbed stiffness in her joints. Remembering Ulbrecht Rathmuir's irrepressible compassion, Kherryn shuddered at the contrast. "I don't know what you are," she told Tyrvald silently, "but you are no mage! Whatever powers you profess, you and your superior may as well be dead men!"

Dead men. Bodies without souls. Tyrvald's eyes had a cold reptilian glitter to them as he stared back at her. Kherryn looked away, her skin crawling. She had to make an effort of will to step past him into the hall beyond.

Leaving the guesthouse by the front door, she made her cheerless customary pilgrimage across the abbey's forecourt, past the west porch of the church to the west entrance of Kirkwell's extensive library. Once inside, she was presented to the chief curator, who led her away to a small windowless cubicle in the northeast corner of the building. There was a book waiting for her on the desk. "Magister Roualt has left instructions that you are to read the first three entries," said the curator in a flat voice that rustled like vellum. "Should you complete the assignment before noon, you may take some exercise in the garden under Brother Tyrvald's supervision. But bear in mind that you will be examined on your readings in the usual manner."

Which was just another way of reminding her that the subprior would be questioning her to see how well she had complied with his orders. If she failed to perform satisfactorily, she could expect to spend extra time on her knees in the chapel, or have her evening meal restricted to bread and water. But at the moment Kherryn was less concerned about avoiding penalties than she was about avoiding discovery. "I've got to get rid of Evelake's box," she thought. "And I've got to do it before Roualt sends for me."

The reading cubicle, however, was too sparsely furnished to afford her any safe hiding place for her dangerous treasure. Which left only the garden—a square quarter acre of cultivated ground between the library and the hospital. It was an area amply large enough to lose a trinket in. The trick would be finding a place where she could be reasonably sure this particular trinket would remain lost.

She had perhaps two hours' grace before her interview with Magister Roualt. A large part of that time would have to be spent in the library: if she left too soon, someone would be bound to get suspicious. And for the same reason, she would have to make at least a token effort to acquaint herself with the contents of the chapters Roualt had left for her to read, little as she might relish the task.

The thought of the subprior's scowling heavy-jowled face and his censorious manner made her grit her teeth in resentment, but she dragged the dusty book toward her across the desktop. It proved to be a collection of polemical treatises, deliberately chosen, she had no doubt, for the weight of vinegary erudition that had gone into their writing. The first entry was a discourse sourly entitled "Concerninge ye Wantonne Natur of Womankynde," and turned out to be a catalogue of female vices, complete with exempla. Kherryn fixed her eyes to the first page with mingled antipathy and resolve. "You've got to try and remember all you can," she told herself. "Don't afford them the satisfaction of finding reasons to punish you."

Even so, in spite of her resolution, her mind kept harking back to her vision of the night before, wholly mystifying in its material consequences. "The ability to 'see afar' is one of the special gifts of the Magia," Ulbrecht Rathmuir had told her. "We don't know—yet —the magnitude of your ability, but I suspect it must be very great, to manifest itself spontaneously in the manner that it has. For that very reason, it's important that you learn how to control and direct this talent of yours. The sooner I start teaching you some magecraft, the better!"

He had intended to remain with her as her instructor, but the subsequent turn of events had prevented it.

Now, more than ever, Kherryn felt the burden of her own ignorance and inexperience. "Why do they call this ability a gift?" she wondered distractedly. "It's more like a curse!"

But she corrected herself almost immediately. Frightening and bewildering as her unexplored and ungovernable talent might be, it had nevertheless given her the priceless assurance that Evelake Whitfauconer still lived. And it had lent her the means to interfere with the designs of those who meant to harm him. "There's got to be some purpose in all this," she whispered. "I just wish I knew what it was."

Time crawled by at a snail's pace. Too unsettled to read, Kherryn finally abandoned her efforts when the church bell struck eleven. The idea of spending any more time in the library was intolerable. Rising from her chair, she picked up Magister Roualt's book and stepped out of her cubicle.

The curator started up from his desk and came across the room to meet her. He regarded her with some suspicion as she returned the volume into his keeping, but she met his curious gaze with wooden determination. After a moment, he turned away and set the book aside on a shelf. Then he sent a servitor to fetch Brother Tyrvald.

With the ordinaire back in attendance, she left the library by the north door, which opened onto the abbey cloister. Beyond lay the cloister garden. The outside air was dank and grey, with a wintery nip to it. A light wind was blowing off the river. She could hear the surge and splash of the current rolling past the bank outside the abbey walls. Gathering the folds of her cloak tightly around her, she stepped out of the shelter of the portico onto a stretch of withered grass.

Everything in the garden looked moribund, as if it had been stricken by a blight and left to die. Leaves three weeks dead lay everywhere in brown drifts. The flowerbeds had been reduced to pallid graveyards of dry stalks. The stone fountain in the center of the garden was clogged with cankerous-looking lichens. As Kherryn looked around her in growing dismay, a sharp breeze sent the moldy leaves whirling across the ground. Its bite made her shiver. Even Tyrvald paused to shrug his cloak closer.

Hope stirred in her heart that the inclement weather would prompt him to hang back and watch her from the shelter of the cloister walk, rather than dogging her steps everywhere she went. But that hope proved dismally short-lived. After a moment's hesitation, he drew up his hood and laced it tight at his throat. Then he left the cloister to join her.

The realization that she was going to continue to be plagued with his company brought Kherryn almost to the brink of angry tears. Digging her fingernails hard into the palms of her hands to steady her nerves, she set out on a wandering course among the skeletal remains of quince and plum trees.

The unsightly carpeting of fallen leaves and twigs was deep, but Kherryn dared not simply let the tiny casket fall amid the forming mulch, trusting to luck to keep it from coming to light again. For Evelake's sake, she had to do better than that. Had she not been so closely supervised, she would have hollowed out a hiding place for the box at the base of one of the trees where no novice, assigned to a day's gardening, would be likely to rake it up. As it was, with Tyrvald following only a few paces behind her, she was forced to seek a better place of concealment.

On the north side of the garden, the cloister walkway was succeeded by a solid section of stone wall. Three espaliered apple trees had been planted in a row along the base of the building, their bare branches forcibly outspread like crucified limbs. Feeling obscurely akin to them, Kherryn slowed to a halt, her pitying glance ranging over their splayed forms.

Only the central tree showed any sign of life. Its younger boughs had put out a scattering of winter buds. The main trunk was pockmarked with blemishes.

Kherryn took a closer look, then stopped short, her pulse quickening. There was a knothole a few inches below the crux of the tree's two main branches.

Her hand crept involuntarily toward the small bulge that rested above the knotted cord at her waist, then stopped as she felt the weight of Tyrvald's gaze upon her. Before she could make any decisive move to divert his interest away from the tree, the sound of a door opening off to her right made them both look around. A bulky figure in grey appeared at one of the archways on the hospital side of the cloister. "Brother Tyrvald!" called the newcomer. "Will you be so good as to join me for a moment? Lady Kherryn may remain where she is. I want a brief word in private with you."

Kherryn recognized the voice. It belonged to Magister Roualt. His tone, however, betrayed an unwonted degree of agitation. The realization made her heart beat faster. If the subprior was disturbed about something, there was a chance that he and his subordinate might take their eyes off her for a few seconds.

As Tyrvald turned his back on her, she pressed a hand to her midriff beneath the cover of her cloak and began surreptitiously to work the box upward toward the loose neck of her gown. Her fingers were trembling as she plucked it free. She cast a furtive glance at Earlis Ap Eadric's two henchmen. They had their heads together, absorbed in their muttered colloquy. Catching her breath, Kherryn took two quick steps sideways and slipped the crystal box into the hollow of the apple tree. It dropped noiselessly out of sight.

When her two gaolers looked up a moment later, she was back in her original position, quaking with apprehension. Far from feeling relieved over her successful piece of legerdemain, she had a sick premonition that she was already in trouble. Her fears were confirmed when Magister Roualt beckoned her to approach him.

She obeyed with reluctance, hardly knowing what to expect. "Lady Kherryn, your recent behavior has given us some cause for concern," announced the subprior, in a voice heavy with sententious foreboding. "His Eminence the Grand Prior himself has ridden up from Farrowaithe this morning in order to speak with you. He is waiting for you now in his study."

He was moving purposefully closer as he spoke. Had there been any place to run to, Kherryn would have turned and fled. As it was, she stood wide-eyed and helpless as a leveret in the presence of a snake as the two men closed in on her from either side and caught her by the arms. "Now, my lady," said Roualt with chilly unction, "shall we go?"

Kherryn placed little faith in her own fortitude. As she trod her way along the corridors of the mages' hall of residence, she could foresee no way of keeping her secret if her present guardians resorted to the use of force. Her brother, Devon, whose disability had made his whole life an apprenticeship to pain, would have been far less vulnerable. Lacking his experience, she knew she had no such will to endure.

Earlis Ap Eadric's private suite of rooms occupied the southeast corner of the upper floor. A paragon of elegance from the shining crown of his silver-fair head to his slender high-arched feet, the Grand Prior of Kirkwell rose fluidly out of the depths of a brocaded wing chair as Kherryn's escort hustled her through the door to his study. Coming forward, pale and graceful as a narcissus in flower, Earlis halted an arm's length away from her and bent his luminous grey gaze upon her ashen face.

"Good afternoon, Lady Kherryn," he said. "I see I have not come any too soon. It has come to my attention that you have been troubled by some rather extraordinary dreams of late. I hope you will see fit to confide in me, as in a confessor."

His tone was gentle, but there was a sharp gleam in his eyes that made a mockery of his apparent solicitude. Kherryn made a futile attempt to moisten her dry lips. "I have nothing to confess," she said huskily.

"Your manner and appearance, I'm afraid, tell another story," said Earlis with a fleet half-smile. "As an inquisitor it is my business to sift the minds and hearts of other men and women—sometimes against their wills, if the situation warrants it. However, it is infinitely less painful—believe me—if the individual can bring himself voluntarily to unburden his conscience."

The warning was obvious. Tongue-tied with apprehension, Kherryn merely stared at him. "Come now," said the grand prior reasonably. "There is really no need to dissemble. A small crystal box—you remember the one—vanished out of the possession of its keepers last night. We have good reason to think you know what became of it. And we'd like you to tell us about it."

Which was just another way of letting her know she had betrayed herself the instant she had invaded the necromancers' circle to save Evelake from injury. She bowed her head to avoid meeting his piercing gaze and murmured numbly, "It was an accident. I can't tell you any more than that."

"Oh, yes you can," said Earlis, with sudden hard-mouthed impatience. "And I'm here to see that you do it."

He gestured curtly to her two attendants. They dragged her over to the chair Earlis had vacated and forced her down into it in spite of her struggles. The grand prior waited until his henchmen had her firmly pinned, then came to join them, his ascetic mouth twisted with malice. "This is your last chance, girl," he said. "If you force me to use my powers against you, I will make sure you regret the experience."

Her small face blanched white, Kherryn mutely shook her head. Earlis shrugged and reached for his magestone. Watching as he prepared himself for his self-appointed task, Kherryn swallowed hard, her stomach knotting itself into a cold ball of terror. "I did my best," she thought wretchedly, "but it wasn't good enough. . . ."

A shadow loomed over her. She glanced up and encountered Earlis's ruthless gaze. Her gaolers tightened their hold on her wrists as the grand prior released his magestone and reached out with both slender hands to cup her face between his palms. She closed her eyes and braced herself to endure his touch as best she could, hoping she wouldn't scream. "Oh, Evelake," she thought disjointedly, "I'm so sorry. . . ."

Then all at once, her skull seemed to break wide open.

Exposed, her conscious thoughts went up in flames. Like a rag of silk, her subliminal self was sucked into the firestorm of the inquisitor's kindled power. The barriers between her mind and his began to burn away in the blistering heat of a forced psychic encounter. As the last membrane of resistance disintegrated, he plunged thirstily into the secret well of her soul.

And was caught, out of all depth with his intention, as the fire with which he had so confidently invested himself flickered out without warning, leaving him submerged in a sea of formless darkness.

For Kherryn, the agony of spiritual dismemberment ended in sudden resolution. Trapped below the surface of his victim's liberated consciousness, Earlis struggled frantically to recover his own integrity. Like shock waves coursing through water, the resonances of his battle for identity penetrated Kherryn's field of awareness in fragments of thought and feeling. Before she could dissociate herself, it was given her to share in the counsels of his mind.

Like the sea casting up flotsam after a storm, his being yielded up fragments of its troubled existence. She saw him briefly in his nakedness of spirit, stung by a swarm of jealousies and scarred by the feverish corrosion of passions he could neither exorcise nor fulfill. Above him loomed the shadow of one he hated and adored, for whose sake, like a slave, he had bent time and again to kiss the fiery rod of servile obedience.

A man tall and dark, with some hint about him of the soul-destroying beauty of a fallen angel. Kherryn had seen him before, in Farrowaithe—had glimpsed his face for one brief unforgettable instant among the many faces

clustered around the bier of Delsidor Whitfauconer in
St. Alanin's cathedral. His name was Borthen, and he
had been posing as Earlis's acolyte. . . .

Through Earlis's eyes she saw again the great sweep
of the nave, the ribbed marble columns blossoming
overhead into starbursts of tierceron vaulting. Only now
the nave was empty. A group of grey-robed magisters was
clustered together at the far end of the great aisle beyond
the chancel arch. In the midst of them stood a slight
stooping figure in white—Baldwyn Vladhallyn, Arch
Mage of East Garillon.

Her vision precipitated her dizzyingly into the
midst of them. His aged face worn and troubled, the
Arch Mage seemed at the point of addressing the gathering. But even as he opened his mouth to speak, the
surrounding air seemed all at once to tremble. In her
inner ear Kherryn heard a sudden low-pitched subterranean rumble.

The walls started to shake. Small outcrops of sculpture began crumbling away from capitals and friezes.
Within seconds the chancel was full of dust. Startled out
of a brief moment's paralysis, the men present broke
formation and scattered in a rush for the exits.

The rumbling grew louder, rocking the stone floor so
that many were hurled off their feet. As those still
standing struggled to help the fallen, there was an
ear-splitting roar, and a jagged rift burst open at the base
of the pulpit, swallowing up everything and everyone in
its path. The rumble of rock merged with the thunder of
toppling masonry. Men screamed and died under the
crushing weight of falling stones.

Two younger mages shouldered Baldwyn Vladhallyn away from the pulpit. As they fled, one of
them was struck down by a collapsing beam. The old
man reeled to his knees beside his dead companion,
arms helplessly upflung above his head as a huge granite
gargoyle came hurtling down on him from above—

Kherryn's own scream of horror shattered her rapport with Earlis Ap Eadric. She groped blindly toward
independent awareness, knowing that what she had just

witnessed was nothing less than the shape of her enemies' intentions: Unless circumstances could be diverted
to prevent it, the disaster would be realized in time and
space. "Who—or what—wields that kind of power?"
she wondered.

Somewhere close by her, someone was being violently sick. She forced open her aching eyes and was
shocked to see the Grand Prior of Kirkwell stagger up off
his knees. He was clutching a napkin to his mouth, his
face pale as cerecloth. When he saw she was conscious,
he went rigid, his visage contorted with rage. "You little
squeaking *bitch*!" he hissed at her. "You are going to pay
for this!"

He was trembling with almost ungovernable fury.
Cornered in her chair, Kherryn shrank back as he
advanced on her with twitching fingers. As soon as she
was within easy reach, he fetched up short, breathing
hard. Then in a sudden explosion of anger, he dashed the
back of his hand across her face.

His knuckles broke open her lower lip. Half-blind
with tears of pain and shock, she gave a small protesting
whimper as he raised his hand to her again. The second
blow hurled her against the arm of the chair. The
crushing throb of her bruised cheek and jaw was her last
waking impression before she collapsed in a dead faint.

FLIGHT IN THE FOG

WHEN THE GIRL KHERRYN FAILED to revive of her own
accord, she was removed from the grand prior's study to
a windowless cell on the upper floor of the infirmary.
Having watched the door to the room being locked,
Earlis Ap Eadric called Magister Rouault aside. "I want
Lady Kherryn kept under constant surveillance," said
the grand prior, his voice under grinding restraint. "But

make sure these fools on duty here understand that they are to have as little direct contact with her as possible. As soon as she shows signs of waking up, I am to be notified immediately."

Roualt's pendulous face was bluish with shock. "I shall see to it, Your Eminence," he promised. And added, "Don't worry, my lord. Whatever her powers may be, she won't get another chance to use them."

"I trust not," said Earlis viciously. "Nothing—do you hear me?—*nothing* must be allowed to interfere with the preparations for tomorrow noon. . . ."

For the next few hours, stretched out on a narrow hospital pallet under the eyes of an attendant, Kherryn Du Penfallon lay pale and still as a corpse, the contusions on her face showing dark as smudges of soot in the dim light of a guttering bedside lantern. Outside, cold rain battered intermittently at the roof with a tattoo hollow as the drum of dead men's fingers. When the passing hours of the afternoon brought no observable change in the girl's condition, the senior ordinaire approached subprior Roualt with the practical suggestion that some measure of treatment might be called for. He was dismissed with a curt denial and a sharp injunction not to meddle with affairs that were not his concern.

Twilight came early, the fitful falling rain giving way to rising fog. It rolled in off the river in ever-thickening waves, blanketing the abbey and its environs under a moist pall of obscurity. By the time the ordinary brethren of Kirkwell assembled in the refectory for their evening meal, the grounds enclosed within the walls had become a well of cloud.

Left behind in the infirmary while his colleagues went off to their suppers, young Brother Nichol was not especially cheered by the prospect of spending the better part of an hour alone in the presence of the girl who had reportedly given the Grand Prior of Kirkwell a very unpleasant turn. There had been rumors of witchcraft circulating among the abbey's lower orders—the speculation that Lady Kherryn Du Penfallon might possess some uncanny and dangerous powers. Shivering at the notion of necromancy, Nichol thought he could understand why his superiors had kept such close watch on her since the day of her arrival.

Lying before him, white and still, she certainly didn't *look* dangerous. Disturbed by her extreme pallor and the continued shallowness of her breathing, Nichol reached out a tentative hand and felt her pulse. Her skin was icy-cold beneath his fingers, her heartbeat sluggish. Professional judgment told him that she needed, at the very least, more than a single coverlet. He had, however, been strictly enjoined on the pain of severest displeasure, not to let her out of his sight even for a moment.

It posed something of a dilemma. Nichol's own feet were growing numb with cold after nearly two hours of sitting idle. He stood up and paced the length of the little room. Outside, the bell in the church tower tolled six times. That meant it would be at least half an hour longer before any of his colleagues would be returning.

He glanced over at the girl on the bed. She had stirred not so much as an eyelash since he had first entered the room. In view of her state and appearance, the strictness of the grand prior's orders seemed uncalled for. "It wouldn't take me more than half a minute to fetch a few more blankets," he muttered to himself. "Even if she were to rouse, where could she go in that short a time?"

Satisfied with his own logic, he marched over to the threshold and turned the key in the lock. The door swung open with a creak. Stepping out into the hall, he started to secure the room behind him, then thought better of it. "If she moves, I'll be more likely to hear her if I leave the way open," he thought. After a last half-guilty glance over his shoulder, he left the door standing ajar and set out up the corridor toward the upstairs storage closet.

Located midway between the ward rooms and the stairs, the storeroom held a variety of supplies. Nichol made his way to a cabinet against the back wall where the spare bed linens were kept. Keeping his ears dutifully pricked for any slight rustle of movement from back down the hall, he dragged two blankets down out of the topmost compartment. As he paused to tuck them under his arm, he caught a sudden flicker of motion out of the very corner of his eye.

Startled, he whipped around in time to catch a fleeting glimpse of someone small and dark flitting noiselessly past the closet doorway. Astonishment rooted him to the spot for half a second. Then with a strangled cry, he hurled the blankets from him and made a bound for the threshold.

He gained the passageway just as the slight skirted figure reached the head of the stairs. "Stop!" shouted Nichol. "Hold it right there!"

The girl merely kept moving. Aghast, Nichol leaped forward, hoping to seize her. To his horror, she seemed to float down the steps like a ghost. Thrusting aside all sick notions about what Earlis Ap Eadric was probably going to do to him, Nichol uttered another futile shout and started down after her in thundering pursuit.

He lost sight of her briefly at the corner where the stairwell turned and doubled back on itself. His own footbeats rattling like a drumroll, he gained the landing with a flying bound, crashed off the wall, and cast a searching look down the next staircourse. There was no one on the steps, and the vestibule at the bottom was empty. "My God!" he wondered disjointedly as he pounded on down the remaining steps. "How could she possibly be moving that fast?"

The stairwell opened into the southern end of the main corridor downstairs. Breathing hard, Nichol burst through the doorway and caught sight of his shadowy quarry again. She was making for the far end of the passageway in a shimmer of speed and darkness. Opening his stride to the fullest, he shot after her.

The corridor ended in a right-angle turn. By the time he reached the corner, she was again out of sight. The door at the end of the adjoining hall led to the kitchen and was standing ajar. Nichol bolted for the gap and collided full-tilt with one of the kitchen servitors coming from the opposite direction.

They both hit the floor in a disorderly jumble of arms, legs, and curses. "The girl!" Nichol managed to blurt out. "Which way did she go?"

"Who? What girl?" wheezed his colleague.

"The Du Penfallon girl!" snapped Nichol. "Didn't you see her?"

"I didn't see anyone—"

"But you must have! She was heading this way, toward the kitchen!" exclaimed Nichol.

"I tell you, I didn't see anybody," protested his companion. "Not even you. What's this all about?"

Nichol groaned. "She got away from me. I took my eyes off her for a few seconds, and suddenly she was gone!"

He began scrambling to his feet, his expression distracted. "It was uncanny, I tell you. I'm beginning to think all those rumors about her might be true—"

"You mean that she really is some kind of witch?"

"All I know is that she seemed to be gliding faster than I could run," said Nichol grimly. "And now she's disappeared."

He cast a worried eye over the kitchen. "There are still people eating in the dining room. She couldn't have gone in there," said his colleague with a glance aside toward the large door on the right-hand side of the room. "That leaves only the cellar."

They both turned to stare at the smaller door in the far left-hand corner of the kitchen. "Maybe I'd better go call His Eminence," suggested the kitchen servitor, sidling toward the dining-room exit.

"No, wait! Before you do that," said Nichol, "I'd better take a look."

While his companion hung back, he gingerly approached the cellar door. After pausing to dry his perspiring palms on the front of his robe, he resolutely took hold of the knob. When nothing alarming happened, he gave the knob a turn and pulled the door open.

A course of wooden steps descended into inky blackness below. "See anything?" called the servitor.

"No. Bring me a lantern or something," said Nichol. Scowling, his companion lifted the nearest cruse lamp from its wall bracket and delivered it at arm's length before beating a hasty retreat. Nichol drew breath at a gulp, then thrust the lamp through the opening.

Light splashed pallidly over ale kegs, wine casks, and bins of root vegetables. A corresponding tide of flickering shadows threw their shapes against the walls. Nichol anxiously scanned the floor through a gridwork of posts and rafters. Then he sighted an elfin silhouette lurking in the darkest of the room's four corners.

He jerked back the lamp and slammed the door shut. "She's down there!" he announced. "*Now* we'll call Lord Earlis. . . ."

Kherryn Du Penfallon surfaced with a start out of a sea of chaotic dreams that were filled with impressions of desperation and breathless flight. Her first conscious realization was that her face hurt. Her second was that she was not in a dark root cellar, where she had somehow expected to find herself, but in an unfamiliar dimly lit room.

"Either I must have been dreaming about the cellar," she thought dizzily, "or else I'm dreaming now." However, the cot on which she was lying felt too hard and solid to be part of her nightmares, and the pain in her head was sharp enough to convince her that she was after all wide awake.

She remembered with frightful clarity Earlis Ap Eadric's vicious assault. She opened her eyes wider, half expecting to find him bending over her, preparing to strike her again. To her relief and surprise, the chair next to the bed was vacant. She was all alone in the small chilly room.

More surprising still, the door was standing open.

She struggled up on one elbow. The cot creaked when she shifted her position, but the sound drew no immediate response from the corridor. Moving with care, she slowly sat up and swung her legs over the edge of the narrow bed. When her feet found the floor, she braced herself and tried to stand.

Her first attempt was a failure, but on the second try she managed to keep her knees from buckling. Keenly aware of the cold, she paused shakily to tug the blanket off the bed. Hitching it clumsily around her shoulders, she shuffled unsteadily to the door and peered out.

The passage outside her room was empty. A series of hanging oil lamps lighted the way down the hall to the head of a staircase leading down. Spurred by an awakening sense of urgency, she abandoned the support of the doorframe and made for the head of the steps.

The all-pervasive smell of medicinal herbs told her that she was probably in the infirmary. As she started down the stairs, she began to be aware of feverish activity going on somewhere else in the building. Her sense of impending danger growing more insistent, she stumbled as quickly as she could from step to step, pausing only when the pain in her head threatened to overset her balance. It was a relief to reach the bottom.

She emerged from the stairwell at the end of a long corridor. Borne up by her compulsion to get out of the building, she approached the first door on the left side of the passage. When she tried the latch, it swung open.

Beyond lay an unoccupied examination room. She closed the door and hurried along to the next. This door opened into the infirmary's entrance hall. She stumbled across to the outer port and tugged the bolt aside to let herself out.

It was like stepping out of a mountain cave into a low-hanging cloud. She was astonished to discover that day had turned into a night thick with fog. The dank air made her shiver, but its sharp bite helped to clear her head a little. In that instant, she recalled Evelake's crystal box. "I can't go anywhere else until I've retrieved it!" she thought.

The mist was so dense she could scarcely see, despite

the lantern suspended above the hospital porch. Laying her left hand against the wall, she groped her way like a blind woman toward the southern corner of the building until a variation in the texture of the stonework told her she had reached the west wall of the cloister garden. She found the gateway by touch and followed the inside of the wall back in the direction of the apple trees.

After twenty steps, her outstretched fingers encountered the gnarled skeleton of a lifeless apple bough. She bypassed the first tree and went on to the second. Feeling her way down the trunk, she located the knothole she had found that morning. Furling her fingers tight, she slipped them into the small cavity that lay on the other side of the opening.

The box came readily enough to hand, though it cost her some skin off her knuckles to get it out. Even as she tucked the little casket away in the safety of the front of her dress, she heard the sound of a door being thrown open on the east side of the cloister. As she shrank back into the shelter of the trees, the fog blossomed into clusters of pale lights to the suddenly audible rumble of excited voices. "All right, this way!" called one authoritative voice. "The witch can't have gone far!"

The asters of torchlight bobbed swiftly from archway to archway. The procession was heading her way. Hugging the wall, Kherryn retreated toward the gateway, praying that the thickness of the fog would help conceal her. Heart pounding, she gained the opening without drawing notice. In the darkness of the forecourt she paused briefly to reconnoiter.

Her head by this time was pounding. Not even her desperate desire to escape could compensate for a growing sense of debility. But lights were multiplying along the upper windows of the mages' hall of residence, and she could hear the rising tumult from within. She had perhaps minutes before the hue and cry spilled out into the courtyard.

If she surrendered now to her body's weakness, it would probably cost her her life—and Evelake's. Pulling herself sternly together, she got her bearings and made the short diagonal run from the cloister wall to the abbey stable.

She knew there was a small postern gate set into the wall between the stable and the granary. Even as she reached it, the mists behind her lit up in a smoky blaze of torchlight. Setting her teeth, she tripped the gate latch. The gate itself opened almost without a sound.

But her pursuers were bound, at any moment, to call upon gifts of heightened perception. Once outside the abbey wall, Kherryn wheeled and set out along the ruts of a sunken path at the best pace she could manage.

Her shoes were thin-soled enough to allow her to feel her way through the murk along the trail. Knowing that it would take her down to the river's edge, she accepted it as her surest guide to whatever hope she had for escape.

The ground fell away in a steep slope toward the water. Shouts broke out behind her as her pursuers picked up her trail. Half reeling now with exhaustion, Kherryn struggled to quicken her stride. Her dragging feet entangled themselves among the coarse riverside grasses and pitched her forward into a tumbling slide that ended at the bottom of the bank.

She fetched up short against a wooden bollard. Wet, scratched, and winded, she dragged herself to her knees and felt the ground ahead of her. Her fingers met wood instead of earth. She had come to the land's end of a small boat dock.

The air throbbed with the drum of approaching feet. She cast a fearful glance over her shoulder as the vanguard of her pursuers appeared in torchlit silhouette at the top of the embankment. Too spent to stand, she half crawled, half scrambled out along the dock as Earlis Ap Eadric's hunting party surged down the path toward the water's edge.

There was a small rowing boat moored up to a post at the dock's end. Her hands trembling with haste, Kherryn tugged at the knot that held the rope in place.

Its end came free in her hand as the first of her pursuers reached the other end of the dock. Clutching the line to her chest, Kherryn summoned her last ounce of strength and made a blind leap for the center of the rowboat.

The shock of her landing sent the small craft lurching violently away from the pilings. The swollen river current caught the boat broadside and spun it around in a hungry gurgle of foam. Lying in a shivering heap in the stern, Kherryn lacked the ability to pull herself up. She could only stare helplessly up into the swirling mists while the boat took to the mainstream under its own guidance.

Behind her the air was loud with splashing and shouting, as men cast about in the shallows for some trace of her. Drifting ever deeper into the chill embrace of the fog, the boat submitted silently to the flow of the current. The noise from the shore receded into the distance and at last was no longer audible. But by then, Kherryn was past all caring.

THE ORDINAIRE'S AWAKENING

IN FARROWAITHE, THE HEAVY VAPORS of the night dissipated like a host of unquiet spirits before cockcrow. The early rays of the pale November sun glanced first off the donjon towers of Farrowaithe Castle, then off the stepped spires of St. Alanin's Cathedral, separated from the island Keep by the peat-stained waters of the Castle Tarn.

Within the hemispherical bay of the cathedral's rose chapel, at the easternmost end of the chancel, a man wearing the hooded grey robe of a magister felt the light against his closed eyelids as he knelt in an attitude of meditation at one of the chapel's praying desks. He opened bleary eyes to find himself surrounded by a mosaic of colored lights thrown down from all sides by the chapel's five stained-glass windows. As he attempted to blink away a beclouding film of weariness, the door to the sacristy opened and closed. Soft, slightly hesitant footsteps made their way through the sanctuary toward the rose chapel, and came at last to a halt a few paces behind him. A voice pitched to the level of gentle admonition called softly, "Ulbrecht? My son, are you awake?"

Ulbrecht Rathmuir, formerly a resident of Ambrothen, unbowed the aching curve in his spine and turned his head. "Yes, Your Holiness," he said. "I have been quite faithful in my prescribed observances."

Baldwyn Vladhallyn, Arch Mage of East Garillon, sighed inwardly to hear the slight edge of bitterness in the younger man's tone. Studying Ulbrecht's worn face with mild blue eyes, he said quietly, "I have never had any reason to complain of you for lack of diligence, my son. We both know that your faults are of another order. Has this morning brought you any fresh counsel?"

"Have I found any reason to change my beliefs concerning Earlis Ap Eadric? No, Your Holiness," said Ulbrecht, with a troubled shake of his head. "I'm sorry if it grieves you to hear it, but I remain convinced that His Eminence has allowed himself to fall under the influence of powers inimical to the Order and all the Order stands for. There is a darkness—a perversity—that surrounds him like a cloud. You endanger yourself by taking him into your confidence."

"I will be the judge of that, my son," said Baldwyn gravely. "Lord Earlis has given me no just cause to question his integrity."

"But Your Holiness," protested Ulbrecht, "surely it has not escaped your attention that he has been showing a keen interest in matters related to necromancy."

"I am aware of his interest," said Baldwyn, "and I consider it fully justified. We need to know the nature of the dangers facing us. Even as we speak, Lord Earlis is preparing a report which he is to deliver today before the members of the general synod."

The purpose for which the synod was being convened was a grimly open secret. Nine days earlier, the mage-hospice of St. Dysmas's in Tyrantir had been assaulted by a demonic manifestation in the form of a crimson cloud that had seemed to materialize out of nowhere. Those engulfed by the cloud had died hideously, their blood evaporating from their veins in a matter of seconds. The Hospitallers in residence had suffered heavy casualties before the survivors managed to summon the Magia to their defense. After a severe struggle, they had successfully exorcized the entity, driving it back across the threshold of the material world into unknown darkness. The attack had left them without any clue as to who might have conjured the cloud in the first place.

Those mages who had escaped with their lives were not sure whether to speak of the cloud as a force or a presence. But they were quite sure that it had been unleashed on them through an act of necromancy. Their fears had spread like wildfire throughout the rest of the Order. Baldwyn had summoned his fellow prelates to consider their own defense, but Ulbrecht was afraid they might have left it too late.

It wasn't as though the attack on St. Dysmas's had been the first sign of serious trouble in East Garillon. Two months before, Ulbrecht's good friend and colleague Forgoyle Finlevyn had been killed in arcane combat against a renegade mage by the name of Borthen Berigeld. Borthen had escaped, leaving Ambrothen's great cathedral in ruins. The Arch Mage might have called a general synod then and there; instead, he had entrusted the matter to Earlis Ap Eadric.

Earlis's investigations into the events at Ambrothen had come to nothing. Similarly, all the questions surrounding the death of Arvech Du Penfallon, Seneschal of Gand, had been allowed to die unanswered. Looking back over the events of the past two months, Ulbrecht was certain that the High Inquisitor had been deliberately discouraging his colleagues from taking any form of decisive action. He said diffidently, "Your Holiness, isn't it just barely possible that Lord Earlis might be tempted to put his knowledge to use to serve his own ends?"

"In theory, it's possible," agreed Baldwyn. "But in practice—no, I cannot see it. Earlis is one of the most talented and reverent members of our community. I have every confidence in his virtue."

He eyed Ulbrecht more closely. "You claim to perceive a shadow hanging over Earlis. Might this darkness not be simply a reflection of your own ill will or jealousy?"

"I assure you, Your Holiness, that I do not covet anything that appertains to the Grand Prior of Kirkwell," said Ulbrecht. "Neither his eminence, his offices, nor his talents. The perversity I spoke of stems from Earlis's own heart. I can *feel* it.

"I'm not talking about gut emotions, either," he continued. "What I'm talking about is a host of psychic impressions. I can't help what my spirit-sense is telling me. If I'm to believe in anything spiritual, I've got to believe in the validity of this kind of revelation."

"The choice is hardly as absolute as that," said Baldwyn reprovingly. "I suspect you would realize as much if you would only examine your own conscience impartially." He sighed deeply, his faded eyes distressed. "I had hoped to be able to release you from all further exercises in penitence, but you have made such remission impossible. I'm afraid I must ask that you continue to mortify your flesh in the days to come, to the ultimate benefit of your soul."

Ulbrecht veiled his smoldering eyes and inclined his head in grim submission. "If you so order it, Your Holiness," he said. "Do I take it that you wish me to extend my vigil here and now?"

"No," said the Arch Mage. "You have already watched the night through. To ask any more of you at the present moment would be to exceed what is fair and reasonable. After you have broken your fast, you may retire to your cell for a period of rest and reflection. We will talk again this evening."

Ulbrecht left the basilica by the north door, conscious of a grinding sense of frustration. He realized that he had been hoping for the chance to speak his mind without reservation. Instead, he had been dismissed before he could question his superior concerning the welfare and safety of his former pupil, Kherryn Du Penfallon, daughter of the late Seneschal of Gand.

Following the death of her father, she had been sent into supposed sanctuary at Kirkwell Abbey. Since that day, Ulbrecht had heard no news of her, and his fears on her behalf were growing daily, fueled by his distrust of Kirkwell's grand prior. He had asked several times for permission to visit her, but each time his request had been denied. It made him afraid that she might have come to harm.

He trudged across the frosty expanse of grass and trees that separated the cathedral from the resident-quarters of the mages of St. Alanin's. As he walked he found himself seriously thinking about defying the orders of his superiors, who had decreed that he should not set foot outside the abbey's high walls. At his ordination he had sworn a holy oath of obedience, to honor the authority vested in the hierarchy of the Order. So far he had been faithful to that oath, but his patience was wearing thin as his anxiety mounted. "Oath of obedience be damned!" he told himself with sudden anger. "I've got to do something!"

Even as the idea crossed his mind, he caught sight of three figures emerging into the yard from the refectory. Two of them wore grey robes; the third wore white. But even without the distinctive livery of his office, Ulbrecht would have recognized An'char Maeldrake, Grand Master of Ambrothen.

They were in Farrowaithe, of course, to attend the synod. But having served the Order for eight years under An'char's direction, Ulbrecht was sure he could prevail upon the older man to listen to him where others had not. At least An'char would be able to learn whether or not Kherryn was all right. Quickly he stepped down into the leaf-strewn path behind the receding forms of his three former colleagues. But before he could carry out his intention to hurry after them, a melodious voice called out to him from the adjoining herb garden, "Brother Ulbrecht! Where are you going?"

The voice belonged to Earlis Ap Eadric. The grand prior's tone was superficially affable, but Ulbrecht felt the short hairs at the back of his neck begin to prickle. He paused a brief moment to assume an expression of bland inscrutability before turning around to face his questioner.

The Grand Prior of Kirkwell was standing at the low garden gate. He had his hood thrown back, and his fair hair glistened like spun glass in the wintery sunshine. "Good morning, Your Eminence," said Ulbrecht with wooden civility. "As you can see, I am just on my way to my quarters."

"Without first paying a visit to the dining hall? You astonish me, Brother Magister," said Earlis with a vixenish smile. "One would have thought that after a day of fasting you would have been glad of some sustaining refreshment to restore your spirits."

Aware that the grand prior was deliberately baiting him, Ulbrecht cocked an eyebrow and said shortly, "And so I should be, Your Eminence—only I had thought the hour for breakfast was past."

"Not at all," said Earlis with sugared cordiality. "If you go now, you will be certain to find food still on the table, even if you prove to be somewhat at a loss for company. I suggest you repair to the refectory without further delay."

The three mages from Ambrothen had passed beyond the garden gate. In another moment it would be too late for Ulbrecht to catch them. But Earlis's suggestion carried the weight of a direct order. Anything less than immediate compliance would be reported as insubordination. Effectively outmaneuvered, Ulbrecht summoned a frosty smile and said, "Your concern for my material welfare is very gracious, Your Eminence. I will, of course, avail myself of your advice."

"Of course," said Earlis smoothly. And waited to see that his instructions were carried out.

Grinding his teeth in silent frustration, Ulbrecht stalked into the dining room a few minutes later to find the long trestle tables only thinly populated. There was no one present above the rank of ordinaire. Ulbrecht's entrance drew one or two furtive sidelong glances, but most of the other diners kept their eyes nervously to themselves. The air seemed oddly heavy, full of unvoiced uncertainties. "There's a threat of some kind hanging over this whole place," thought Ulbrecht. "And I'm not the only one who's feeling it."

Which made it all the more important that he should find some way to speak with An'char. Caught up in his troubled meditations, he ate what the kitchen servitor put before him, hardly noticing what was on his plate. It wasn't until a shadow fell across his shoulder that he roused himself from his reverie and discovered that two burly figures were standing over him.

One of them was wearing ordinaire's brown, the other servitor's blue. Both were men Ulbrecht had seen before as frequent attendants of Earlis Ap Eadric. Their presence spelled fresh trouble. Ulbrecht said testily, "Yes? What is it?"

The ordinaire squared bulky shoulders. "I'm Brother Tyrvald, and this is Brother Gille. We've been instructed by His Eminence Lord Earlis to escort you to your room."

"That's very thoughtful of Lord Earlis," said Ulbrecht, "but I don't need an escort. I know my own way perfectly well, thank you."

He made a move to stand up, and promptly felt the warning pressure of two heavy hands on his shoulders. "All the same, Brother Ulbrecht, we'd better go with you," said the one who had given his name as Tyrvald. "Orders are orders, don't you see?"

The dual grip on Ulbrecht's collarbone was just

short of being painful. "I think I'm beginning to," said Ulbrecht with a grimace. "I take it I'm supposed to go now?"

"That's right," said the servitor in blue. "After being up all night, you must be needing your rest. . . ."

Ulbrecht's assigned cubicle was located in the northwest corner of the north wing. He arrived there somewhat bruised, in a state of cold fury. As his escort chivied him toward the threshold, he inquired tartly, "Just how long does His Eminence expect me to remain here?"

"Till he calls for you," said Tyrvald. The servitor sniggered. Both men seemed queerly excited, as though they were expecting soon to be able to gratify some unwholesome appetite. Catching the odd, almost feverish gleam in Tyrvald's bloodshot eyes, Ulbrecht all at once began to wonder if the actions he had so far interpreted as petty harassment might actually be foreshadowing something far more sinister.

The servitor relaxed his grip and stepped forward to open the door. "Upon reflection," said Ulbrecht, "I'd rather set my own schedule." And jabbed the point of his elbow into Tyrvald's unguarded midriff.

The ordinaire doubled over with a grunt. Jerking himself free of the other man's slackened grip, Ulbrecht spun on his heel. He bolted for the stairs at the opposite end of the corridor. "Gille! Stop him!" wheezed Tyrvald.

The servitor bulled his way past his puffing superior and dashed after their fleeing quarry. Hearing the heavy thud of overtaking footsteps at his back, Ulbrecht attempted to put on an extra burst of speed and discovered to his dismay that he had failed to reckon with the debilitating effects of fasting and sleeplessness. His head swimming, he forced his faltering legs to stagger on for another half-dozen paces before his pursuer caught up with him and slammed him to the floor with a flying tackle.

Struggling under the weight of the other man's body, Ulbrecht struck out with one purposeful fist and managed to bloody his assailant's nose. The servitor cursed and tumbled aside. Ulbrecht scrambled to his knees. Before he could regain his feet, his other opponent lumbered up and dealt him a lashing blow across the back of the head with a wooden candlestick. The crack of something breaking was the last thing Ulbrecht remembered before his mind abruptly went black.

When he saw light again, it came to him first as a pale blur. As his vision sharpened by aching degrees, the blur resolved itself into differentiated shapes and forms —the bright oblong shape of a casement window, the outline of a human form silhouetted against the light. The figure was too small and slight to be either of Earlis Ap Eadric's two minions. Curious, despite a crashing pain at the base of his skull, Ulbrecht made a concentrated effort to focus on details.

His companion was female. Frowning, he tried to piece together the individual features of her appearance. Frail shoulders, weighed down by a heavy soot-colored gown . . . long black hair, trailing loose like seaweed . . . great dark eyes in a small bruised face. . . .

Recognition hit him like a lightning stroke. "Kherryn!" he gasped, and struggled upright to stare at her in blank amazement.

Standing before him, mute and motionless, she looked almost like the ghost of one drowned. The sight of her in such a pitiable state made Ulbrecht forget everything else. "Kherryn, dear heart, you're soaked to the skin!" he said in stricken remonstrance. "Come, let me put some warmth back into your bones before you perish with cold!"

He held out his arms. Without a sound, without a word, she ran to him. He reached out to gather her into a comforting embrace. It wasn't until the instant of contact that he realized that she was form without substance.

The shock of this discovery took Ulbrecht's breath away, but in the same twinkling of an eye, he experienced an ineffable sense of Kherryn's own very real presence—

as though the insubstantial shade that had passed through his arms were as much a part of Kherryn as her physical body. Without stopping to wonder how or why, he threw wide the doors of his spirit to welcome her in. Like a nestling seeking the shelter of its parent's wings, she entered into his heart of hearts.

She brought with her both the verity of her affection for him and a sense that she desperately needed his help. Ulbrecht's mere desire to know more brought him a flood of sharp impressions—being harried like a hunted rabbit through a dense black fog . . . embarking on a dark journey over water . . . being lifted out of the boat and carried somewhere. Through her eyes he caught a glimpse of a squat stone tower perched at the end of a low headland. The pennon flying above the rooftop bore the device of a wheel cloven by lightning: the sign of St. Burneas.

But Kherryn's strength was waning. Like a candle guttering in a strong wind, he felt the life force within her falter, and knew that her physical body must be dangerously near to collapse. He sensed the struggle as she fought to keep in contact with him, and realized that it was this effort that was draining her of vital energy. "Kherryn, let go!" he urged her. "You'll kill yourself if you don't! From what you've shown me, I know now how to find you. Let go, and I'll come to you as quickly as I can."

His assurance won her consent. To his relief, she stopped fighting. He felt the instant of separation like a daughter's kiss of parting. Then she was gone.

Her leave-taking left him clearheaded, as if she had taken some of the pain of his injuries upon herself in order to render him free to act. It was up to him to match the depth of her self-sacrifice. But first he had to escape the confines of St. Alanin's.

RACE AGAINST TIME

THE CUBICLE THAT HAD BEEN assigned to Ulbrecht overlooked a narrow ledge of brown grass running along the bank of one of Farrowaithe's main canals. Levering himself to his feet, he went to the window and threw it open. A twelve-foot drop separated him from the ground. Too far to hazard a leap, but still safer than trying to sneak out through the building—if he could find a way to make less of the distance.

The bed on which he had been lying was sturdily constructed of oak, with slats instead of strapping to support the mattress from beneath. He hauled it over to the window and stripped off the blanket with the sheet. He knotted the two together and looped one end around the bed's footboard, securing it in place with another knot.

Profoundly hoping it would hold, he gripped the other end of his improvised rope in one hand and backed out onto the windowsill. Clinging to the right-hand mullion with his free hand, he dropped first one leg and then the other. As soon as he managed to get a toehold, he shifted his full weight onto the knotted lifeline.

The bedframe struck the inside wall with a bang, but the knots held. Ulbrecht lowered himself hand over hand until the length of blanket played out, then dropped the remaining four feet to the ground. As soon as his feet struck turf, he sprang for the bank and clambered down the slope to the water's edge.

The canal was near to flood level after the heavy rains of the day before. Listening anxiously for any sound of pursuit, Ulbrecht heard instead the measured splash of oars coming toward him up the channel. He floundered crabwise along the bank for another twenty yards until he reached a small crescent of higher ground. Here he halted and waited for the boat to heave into view.

The craft proved to be one of the many flat-bottomed rowing barges that daily plied their way up and down the canals of Farrowaithe, transporting goods and passengers. This one was carrying only the boatman himself, a brawny individual with a bushy head of ginger hair. After casting a swift glance over his shoulder in the direction of the dormitory, Ulbrecht called out to him and beckoned him in toward the shore.

The barge grounded with a bump. "This is an emergency," said Ulbrecht. "I'm afraid I must invoke Hospitallers' Privilege and divert you from whatever other business you may be engaged in. On behalf of the Order, I guarantee your fee."

"That's no hardship to me, sir—I was just doing my usual rounds," said the boatman with a genial shrug. He watched as Ulbrecht stepped hastily down into the bow seat, then inquired, "So what is it, twins?"

"I only wish it were!" said Ulbrecht. "Which of the city guardposts mounts the sign of St. Burneas?"

"St. Burneas?" The boatman pushed off from the bank. "That's up at the northernmost tip of the city."

"Can you get me there?"

"Aye, sir. Nothing simpler," said the boatman.

"Good!" said Ulbrecht. "Get me there quickly, and I'll pledge you double your usual rate."

"You certainly *are* in a hurry!" exclaimed the boatman. "Well, if speed's what you want, sir, Colby Sims'll be more than willing to put his back into it. . . ."

The boatman Colby turned out to be as good as his word. Forging along more quickly than Ulbrecht had dared to hope, they overtook several other barges on their way to Marischal's Bridge, a quarter of a mile north of St. Alanin's.

Beyond the bridge the canal carried on for another two furlongs, before dividing into two branches, east and west. With hardly a hitch in his stroke, Colby brought his craft smoothly around the bend to the east. Anxiously craning his neck, Ulbrecht saw the arch of another stone bridge looming up ahead of them. "That's St. Burneas's Bridge," said the boatman between breaths. "The guardtower's not far beyond it."

They passed under the bridge, leaving a wake of ripples. Gazing ahead, Ulbrecht marked the crenellated rooftop of a boxlike tower on the north side of the canal, standing higher than the thin scattering of other buildings. The tower matched up with the one Kherryn had shown him in their shared vision. He drummed nervous fingers on the gunwale, silently willing the boatman to make even greater haste.

The tower occupied the boot end of a miniature peninsula, flanked on one side by the river Mistrhyl and on the other by the mouth of the canal. As Colby brought his barge in close at the base of the embankment, Ulbrecht caught sight of a small rowboat drawn up on the shingle above the waterline. "Let me out here," he told the boatman.

Sand grated under the prow as Colby wordlessly sent the barge ploughing into the bank. "Thank you!" called Ulbrecht over his shoulder as he scrambled out of the boat. "I would be obliged if you could wait here for me."

Red-faced with exertion, the boatman nodded his acknowledgment. Leaving him to regain his breath, Ulbrecht scuffed his way through soft wet sand to the base of a shallow slope and began clambering up an eroded path to the top of the low bluff. A short sprint brought him around to the entrance to the guardtower. The oaken door was standing ajar.

He could hear voices coming from the interior of the ground floor: "Who d'you suppose she is?" "More to the point, what are we to do with her?" "Better wrap her up and take her to St. Alanin's. This looks like Hospitallers' business . . . ."

The ongoing murmur of concerned debate told Ulbrecht that his vision had led him unerringly aright.

He struck the door a perfunctory rap with his knuckles, then pushed it open.

The chamber beyond was empty, but as Ulbrecht entered from outside, a fair-haired man in the blue and white livery of the Farrowaithe Guard appeared at the threshold of a side room. Blue eyes widened in astonishment. "Good God!" exclaimed the guardsman, surveying Ulbrecht from head to foot. "What brings you here? No, forget I asked. Miracle or mystery, we've got a patient for you. She's in there."

He pointed back toward the room from which he had just come. With a nod of thanks, Ulbrecht brushed past the younger man and stepped through the doorway. Two other guardsmen started up at his entry, then moved aside at a sign from their fair-haired superior. "I'm Lieutenant Geston Du Maris, by the way," said the officer, following Ulbrecht into the room. "My sergeant and I were out making our regular rounds when we spotted what looked like an empty boat tangled up in the reeds close to shore. When we went down to check it out, we found this little lady lying unconscious in the stern."

Kherryn was lying on a wooden bench by the far wall, wrapped in her rescuers' two cloaks. Only half listening to the lieutenant, Ulbrecht knelt down beside her and gently smoothed her damp hair back from her bruised face. She was scarcely breathing, her skin icy-cold to his touch.

"There was nothing said in this morning's dispatches from the Commandery about a young girl's having gone missing," continued Lieutenant Geston, looking soberly over Ulbrecht's shoulder, "but seeing how she's been mistreated, it's just possible somebody was hoping she wouldn't be found." He added, "You obviously knew enough to come looking for her here, so perhaps you could give us some information about her—for example, who might have marked up her face. It would give me personal satisfaction to see to his arrest."

"I'll be glad to tell you what I can," said Ulbrecht,

"but not now. For the moment I must ask you and your men to leave the room."

"I understand," said the lieutenant, and turned to his two subordinates. "All right, you heard the reverend brother. Let's take ourselves off."

The three withdrew speedily, closing the door behind them. Left alone in the room with Kherryn, Ulbrecht pressed his magestone between his palms and breathed a brief prayer of supplication. Fervidly responsive, the power of the Magia welled up within him. Like swelling chords of music, it swept him out of his own interior silence toward rarified heights of sensibility. From the hallowed eminence of Orison, he reached out to take Kherryn in his arms.

His first impressions upon touching her were of extreme cold, extreme exhaustion. Holding her close, he poured the living heat of the Magia into her chilled flesh and bones to ease away the icy rigor of exposure. By degrees her light frame relaxed under the influence of the Magia's comfortable warmth. When she was at last resting naturally, Ulbrecht moved on to the task of restoring some measure of her strength.

As a man might use a pitcher to dip water from a stream, so he used his own body as a vessel to bring her the power that he drew from the Magia. Like a diver returning to the surface out of deep water, she began instinctively to struggle toward awakening. The voluntary movement of her spirit was accompanied by a sudden violent surge of dark emotions. When he would have quieted her, she protested with such vehemence that he realized it would be dangerous to oppose her.

As soon as he withdrew his protective restraint, she shivered and opened her eyes. Blinking owlishly, still disoriented, she called out his name on a fearful note of uncertainty. "I'm right here," said Ulbrecht, gently reassuring. "You're quite safe. Everything's going to be all right now—"

"No! No it's not!" Tugging an arm free of the many folds of cloak wrapping, she clutched at his hand, her clarifying gaze seeking his face. "Ulbrecht, you must listen to me! There's a plot afoot to murder Arch Mage Baldwyn, along with a great number of other high-ranking Hospitallers. Earlis Ap Eadric is in on it—Earlis and a renegade named Borthen—"

"Borthen!" exclaimed Ulbrecht. Again that name— one he had come to associate with death and the powers of darkness! Feeling as if he had just stumbled into a waking nightmare, he said, "Kherryn, how do you know about this?"

Her brow darkened. "I learned it from Earlis himself," she said with a shudder. "He was trying to force some information out of me, but it went wrong somehow. Instead of his prying into my mind, I found myself looking into his. I don't know how, or when they're going to do it, but the plan involves the destruction of St. Alanin's Cathedral."

Pulling away from him, she went on with sharp insistence. "You've got to warn His Holiness that he's in terrible danger. Whatever he does, he mustn't set foot in the cathedral—not even to celebrate office or—"

"Or conduct a synod—merciful God!" said Ulbrecht. "If it's going to happen, it's going to be soon. Baldwyn's supposed to be holding a convocation of magisters, starting at noon today!"

They gazed at each other in horror. "Can you do anything to stop it?" asked Kherryn.

"I don't know," said Ulbrecht. He sprang to his feet and went to the door. "Lieutenant!" he called sharply. "Lieutenant Geston!"

The door opened. "Yes, Master Ordinaire, what is it?" asked the young officer.

"What's the time?"

"It must be getting on for twelve o'clock—I heard the bell tower chime out eleven a while back," said Geston. Seeing the look on Ulbrecht's face, his gaze sharpened. "Why? Is it important?"

"It could be," said Ulbrecht shortly. "Allow me to present Lady Kherryn Du Penfallon. Besides being the daughter of the late Seneschal of Gand, she happens to be a highly gifted seer—and what she's foreseen is a disaster about to befall the mages of St. Alanin's unless we can intervene."

He hurriedly recounted all that Kherryn had told him. "You don't have to believe us," he finished. "In fact, I don't really expect you to. But for heaven's sake, at least give me the loan of a horse to ride back to the abbey to warn His Holiness concerning our suspicions—"

"If speed's what you want, you'll be better going back by boat, the way you came," said Geston. "You had your boatman wait, didn't you? Good. One of my men can use our own launch to take a message to Sir Manfred Du Bourne at the commandery. In the meantime, I'd better come with you."

Striding over to his desk in the outer room, he caught up his sword belt and began to buckle it on. "Ever since you arrived, I've been trying to figure out where I'd seen you before," he told Ulbrecht with a thin smile. "Just this minute it came to me: you were with Arvech Du Penfallon at the Council of Kirkwell, weren't you?"

"That's right," said Ulbrecht.

"I recall you offered to testify against Gwynmira Du Bors on behalf of one of my colleagues, a man by the name of Cergil Ap Cymric," said Geston, his blue eyes hard as sapphires. "I was glad to see someone defend his honor and his right to justice. Cergil used to be a good friend of mine.

"Not knowing what he'd been involved in, there wasn't much I could do at the time," he continued, giving his belt a final hitch, "but I feel I owe you a favor. Unless something happens to prove you a liar, consider me at your service . . .."

Kherryn insisted on accompanying them, despite Geston's expressed opinion that she would be better off remaining behind under the protection of his sergeant-at-arms. Aware that she was still suffering some aftereffects of her recent ordeal, Ulbrecht appreciated the lieutenant's concern for her welfare. However, he was afraid of what might happen, should they get separated. And so on his recommendation she was included in the party.

Leaving Ulbrecht to assist her, Geston led the way to the barge. At the sight of an officer in the livery of the Farrowaithe Guards, the boatman Colby started up and groped for his oars. Geston sprang into the boat, then turned back to help Kherryn on board. As Ulbrecht followed, the lieutenant turned to Colby and said crisply, "St. Alanin's—as quickly as you can manage it!"

BOND OF FIRE

THE PALE NOVEMBER SUN CLIMBED toward its zenith in an otherwise empty sky. Ghost-pallid, its bleached disc shed no warmth within the walls of Farrowaithe Castle, where a bewildered crowd of servants, grooms, artisans, and groundskeepers were gathered outside on the brown grass beneath the northeast tower of the central Keep. Gazing down on the assembly from above, Earlis Ap Eadric counted over a hundred upturned faces. Like frightened sheep, they huddled together, waiting to be told why they were there, little guessing the truth.

Men-at-arms prowled like wolves along the fringes of the gathering, the steel of their weapons glinting like bared fangs in the wintery sunshine. Not Farrowaithe Guards, but creatures of Borthen Berigeld's choosing, bound by rites of gall and fire to serve the iron crown that the dark mage had seen fit to lay upon the brow of young Gythe Du Bors. Earlis could sense their mounting appetite for violence. It was as if these new-made hounds of war already smelled spilt blood.

The mercenaries were not alone in their feverish anticipation. Masked for the moment from general view behind the roving figures in armor were other forms more familiar to Earlis: apostate mages who had traded their Hospitallers' robes for the vestments of sorcery. They clung to the shadows, waiting for their acknowledged master to appear—a new priesthood poised to offer sacrifice to a new god.

Some herd instinct of uneasiness was beginning to spread throughout the men, women, and children penned within the courtyard. His own sensibilities raw-alert, Earlis might have allowed himself to savor the pungency of their fear, had he been able to banish Kherryn Du Penfallon from his mind.

It was impossible to do so, even though the thought of her made him writhe inwardly in mingled rage and mortification. When Arvech's young daughter had been committed to Kirkwell, Earlis had suspected that she might possess some latent affinity for the Magia. But nothing had prepared him for his shattering experience of the night before, when she had turned his inquisition against him, exposing not only his most ambitious intentions, but also his most intimate desires. That he should have been so humiliated by a woman was intolerable, and he had promised himself the satisfaction of crushing her, body and spirit.

Except that she had managed—somehow—to escape from the confines of Kirkwell Abbey even as he was contemplating his revenge.

The uninitiated brethren who had allowed her to slip through their fingers had since paid a heavy price for their negligence. But in the course of interrogating them, Earlis had learned enough to confirm his belief that the Du Penfallon girl had other gifts besides her spontaneous powers of discernment. He had ordered his subordinates to conduct an exhaustive search of the area downriver from the abbey, but they had found no trace of her anywhere. With so much now at stake, Earlis could only hope that she had not found any way to warn the mages of St. Alanin's of their impending danger.

The crucial moment was fast approaching. The

tension in the air was building. Earlis could sense the presence of deadly energies gathering like an invisible storm cloud above the southwest tower of the donjon where Gythe Du Bors was preparing, with the aid of Borthen Berigeld, to put on the armor of infernal darkness. The grand prior's gaze flashed across the grey water of the Castle Tarn toward the brittle spires of the Hospitallers' basilica. "Not long," he whispered to himself. "Not long now."

Even as he spoke, a door swept open at the opposite end of the east battlement. Earlis turned in time to see a slim, boyish figure step lightly across the threshold into the open air. Gythe seemed almost to shimmer in the sunlight, his dark male beauty enhanced to a soul-destroying pitch of virility. Scarcely able to tear his eyes away, Earlis unconsciously gave ground as Gythe advanced toward him along the rampart walk. Dazzled by the boy's dangerous glamour, the grand prior only belatedly noticed that the young demon-lord was accompanied by Borthen and Gwynmira.

Gythe strode forward to the edge of the parapet to address the people gathered below. His appearance was greeted by an awestruck murmur of confusion and uncertainty. Like an archangel stilling a stormy sea, he gestured for silence. At once the clamor died away, leaving the air supercharged with dread.

He spoke in an eerie choral blending of two voices, a boy's clear treble piercing thinly through the deep booming tones of the dominant bass. "Children of dust!" he called, "Mark well what you are about to hear! This is a day of reckoning, a day of reformation! Today, the old order shall be cast down, and a new order raised up in its place! Today we come into possession of this, our earthly kingdom, and you who are present shall bear witness to our ascendency!"

"Children of dust!" the voices continued. "Know that we are already your master—jealous of our rights of majesty. Serve us willingly, and you shall be allowed to keep your lives. Oppose us, and you shall surely perish.

The moment is even now upon you when we shall try your hearts and minds with fire. Those who are found wanting shall be struck down, and their bodies shall be given over for devouring!"

The last word rang out like a clash of brazen cymbals. Leaping up onto the parapet, the boy who had spoken flung wide his arms, fingers outspread like striking talons. Magnified out of all human proportion, his shadow darkened the ground beneath. All those on whom it fell cowered back, glassy-eyed with mute terror.

Flames burst forth from Gythe's extended fingertips, crackling like chain-lightning. Smiling cruelly, he lashed out with sudden venom at the crowd of people below. Crimson tentacles of wildfire ripped through the assembly, striking like serpents, searing and entangling. Some victims after a brief struggle surrendered to the embrace of the flames with moans of ecstasy. Others, trapped like moths in a web of fire, writhed voicelessly in agony.

Gythe curled a hand in a gesture of summoning. His mercenary cohorts rushed forward with drawn swords. Faces rapt with blind passion, they stormed through the holocaust, striking down all those whose torments marked them out for sacrifice. Spilled blood turned to vapor in the sulfurous air. Like a cloud, the red mist of slaughter rose toward the battlements where it hovered about the lissome figure of Gythe Du Bors.

The demon lodged within him was drawing fresh vigor from the issue of blood. Himself maddened almost to the point of abandon, Earlis felt the upsurge of power in his own veins. His body ached to discharge itself in some act of violence. Dimly, he sensed the stroke of noon. "Now!" he screamed. *"Now!"*

Under the powerful sweep of Colby Sims's oars, the canal boat carrying Ulbrecht, Kherryn, and Geston shot through the archway of Marischal Bridge, coursing downstream toward a crossway of intersecting channels. Beyond lay the cathedral, its grey walls glinting in the sunlight. "Almost there!" cried the lieutenant. "Thirty yards to the breakwater—"

Even as he spoke, above the crowded rooftops of the city, a brazen bell began sonorously to toll out the hour of twelve. As the barge made for the cathedral embankment, Kherryn's gaze was swept across the sullen waters of Castle Tarn to the topmost turret of Farrowaithe Castle. High up on its crenellated rampart, she glimpsed a soul-piercing flash of scarlet fire.

The mere sight of it seemed to burn, like a needle in the eye, but she could neither cry out nor rip her gaze away. The kernel of fire began to glow with infernal intensity. As she stared at it transfixed, she became aware of a rumbling coming from somewhere deep underground.

Ominous as the mutterings of a live volcano, the noise rolled up through the bedrock of the tarn like an unchained explosion. It surfaced with a boom that sent the waters of the lake leaping skyward in a fountain of mud and foam. The shock waves raced outward in all directions, rippling up the canals like the writhing arms of some monstrous sea creature. "We're going to get swamped!" shouted Geston. "Hang on!"

A black wall of water was converging on them like a tidal wave. Paralyzed with horror, Kherryn was unable to move. Ulbrecht flung an arm around her and dragged her to the floor of the boat. An instant later, the barge reared up on its stern and leaped like a wayward horse.

Water crashed over Kherryn in an icy wave. Pinned against the keel by the weight of Ulbrecht's body, she buried her face in his shoulder as the barge rebounded off the bank and spun crazily around. The air was full of thunder, as though the sky itself were falling. Deafened by the tumult, she choked on water as a second cataract raked the barge from stem to stern. Then all at once the noise and the movement shuddered into silence.

Breathing hard, Kherryn ventured to lift her head. She was relieved to see that both Geston and Colby were still with them. Clinging to the gunwales, they were staring around them in dumb disbelief. The look on their faces filled her with foreboding. She raised herself a little higher to peer over the side of the boat.

The buildings nearest the waterside lay in ruins. Inland, there were gaps among the houses, streets clogged with the broken stones of tumbled walls. Dazedly, she searched the skyline, looking for the spire of St. Alanin's as she had seen it only minutes before. It wasn't there anymore.

In its place was a mountainous heap of rubble. Beside her Ulbrecht whispered, "Dear God have mercy—" then stopped short, unable to say any more.

It was difficult to tell how far the destruction had spread. Near at hand, they could hear tentative outbursts of individual voices: the wails of children, the moans of the injured. Dust-coated figures were beginning to clamber up out of the confused tangle of collapsed houses. "Get me to shore!" rasped Geston. "I've got duties to perform on behalf of these people. We have to start getting them away from here!"

With a few lateral sweeps of his remaining oar, the boatman brought them in close enough to disembark on the west side of the canal, opposite the cathedral. First out of the boat, Geston caught Kherryn firmly by both hands and whisked her onto the muddy knoll beside him. Ulbrecht struggled after them, leaving Colby to bring up the rear.

They gained the street by scrambling through the remains of a cobbler's shop. The cobbler himself was lying half-buried in a bed of rubble with his skull broken in. Ulbrecht clasped Kherryn by the shoulders and turned her aside, hoping she wouldn't see. But then they almost tripped over the legs of a second corpse pinned under a fallen beam, and he realized that there was no shielding her from anything that had happened there.

With Geston bounding impatiently ahead, they emerged into a cobbled lane between two rows of buildings, to find themselves in the midst of chaos. Surviving townsfolk were staggering out of their tumbled houses, some leaning on each other, some on their own. Geston leaped to the top of a low heap of broken bricks. Raising his voice to a ringing pitch of command, he called out, "Attention, all of you! If you value your lives, listen to me!"

Heads turned. The dazed murmur of shock and confusion subsided as those present recognized his uniform and his air of grim purpose. "Now then," said Geston crisply, "we're going to have to clear this area in a hurry in case there's another upheaval. Here's what I want you to do . . ."

DEMON-SEED

THE NEIGHBORHOOD WAS HEMMED IN by three intersecting canals. The footbridge to the west had been swept away in the surge of high water, but the one to the north was still standing. While her companions fought to organize an orderly evacuation as quickly as possible, Kherryn clambered up to the top of an exposed flight of stairs and looked fearfully back toward the Keep. What she saw made her blood run cold.

A crowd of people had gathered at the northern point of the castle island, where a luxuriously appointed barge was putting out into the lake. The members of the crowd were cheering and dancing in wild veneration. The object of their worship was standing bareheaded on a canopy-covered dais in the stern of the barge. Even from a distance, Kherryn had no difficulty recognizing Evelake's half brother, Gythe Du Bors.

There were three other people with him aboard the sleek, silken barge. The beautiful hard-faced woman in scarlet and sable was Gwynmira Du Bors. The fair-haired cleric behind her was Earlis Ap Eadric. The tall

dark man who stood at Gythe's right hand was someone
Kherryn had never met face to face, but she knew who he
must be: the mysterious and sinister Borthen Berigeld.

The barge glided over the water like a black swan of
ill omen, making for the ruined cathedral. Its rich
draperies undulated with the surging speed of its movements. Kherryn felt the presence of those on board like
poison in her soul. She shuddered, but could not pull her
eyes away.

The barge slid effortlessly into a small backwater
below the tumbled wall of the abbey. Gythe was first to
go ashore, closely followed by his attendants. Together
they climbed the cathedral embankment and entered the
broken enclosure. Gythe paused briefly, one booted foot
planted with negligent contempt upon the face of a
smashed icon. Then he and his attendants moved on,
disappearing among the ruins.

For a long moment nothing appeared to happen.
Then, out of the dead mass of the tumbled cathedral, a
black pillar of cloud began to rise.

Dense as the smoke cast up by a funeral pyre, the
cloud thickened and spread. It billowed out over the
corpse-littered remains of the hospital and outbuildings,
then condensed like fog to the ground. As it settled,
individual motes of shadow abruptly separated and
began to take on independent form.

Like maggots swarming over carrion, the motes
crawled over the bodies of the dead, burrowing into the
eyes and ears, filling the slack, unresisting mouths. The
sight brought Kherryn to her knees, choking with nausea. Momentarily bereft of the strength to stand, she
clung weakly to the newel post of the stair and tried to
catch her breath. She was still struggling to get up when
she glimpsed something moving beneath the slimy infestation that covered the cathedral yard.

In spite of her revulsion, she was drawn to take a
second look. The black ground-pall heaved and cracked.
A man's head and shoulders broke through the mass of

slug shapes. Sloughing off a clinging shroud of black larvae, he rose jerkily to his feet.

Kherryn's first paralyzed thought was that someone still living had been caught in the smothering tide of darkness. Then she saw the sickly grey-white trickle of brain tissue spilling out through a gaping cleft in the man's skull and realized that the figure wading unsteadily toward the water was an animated corpse.

The sight of a dead man moving defied reason. Nerveless with shock, Kherryn watched in numb incomprehension as other man shapes began to come to hideous life among the ruins, lurching into whatever form of motion their shattered bones would allow. "This isn't really happening!" she protested desperately to herself. "Any minute now, I'm going to wake up—"

Not daring to believe otherwise, she clung to this conviction as the nightmare continued to unfold before her eyes. Once animated, the corpses gained speed and freedom of movement, as if the controlling power that had set them in motion was also capable of repairing their broken limbs. Like grisly marionettes, they shambled jerkily down the cathedral embankments, making for the water. The black cloud mass moved with them, like a plague of locusts.

A living hand tugged at Kherryn's wrist. "Come on!" cried Ulbrecht. "Time for us to join the retreat toward the bridge—" Then he caught sight of the array of walking corpses, and froze in horrified dismay. "My God!" he choked. *"Revenants!"*

The animated corpses were plunging into the canal with soulless abandon. Looking down into the water, Ulbrecht saw several ranks of submerged man shapes converging on the bank below his vantage point. His face blanched white, he dragged Kherryn to her feet. "Run!" he ordered, and bundled her precipitately down the stairs.

Motes of black shadow were already settling on the body of a man sprawled out in one of the doorways off to the right. As Ulbrecht hurried Kherryn past the threshold, he saw the cadaver begin to twitch. A sidelong glance at his pupil told him she was all but blind with shock. He caught her round the waist and sprinted after the main party.

They reached the footbridge just as Geston was shepherding the last of the stragglers across. "We've got to get out of here fast!" panted Ulbrecht. "In another few minutes, this whole area's going to be swarming with revenants."

Still half carrying Kherryn, he clattered out across the bridge. The lieutenant bounded after them. "Revenants? What are they?" he demanded. "What are you talking about?"

Eyes fixed grimly in front of him, Ulbrecht didn't slacken his pace. "I'm talking about necromancy," he said shortly. "The power to reanimate dead matter through demonic influences. That's what revenants are: sleepless dead . . . walking corpses. . . ."

He sounded wildly distracted. "That's impossible!" protested Geston. "No human being has power like that!"

This declaration seemed to penetrate Kherryn's numbed state of shock. "Gythe does," she announced.

"Gythe *Du Bors*?" Geston was incredulous.

Kherryn's gaze was abstracted. She seemed like a sleeper struggling to wake. "That's right," she said. "Necromancers taught him how to summon up a demon. It gives him power—destructive power." She paused to give herself a shake, her eyes wide and dark. "We need to make for the river," she asserted. "That's our best chance to escape."

The certainty in her voice convinced Ulbrecht that she wasn't merely expressing an opinion. "Listen to her," he told Geston. "She knows what she's talking about."

Geston's brows lifted. He might have argued the point, but something in Kherryn Du Penfallon's manner made him think better of it. "I don't pretend to understand your gift, Lady Kherryn," he said, "but I haven't got any better ideas. We'll do as you say."

He frowned. "It'll be quickest if we head for Marischal's Bridge from here. Once we're on the other side, it's only another half mile to the riverfront."

"You lead," said Ulbrecht. "We'll follow."

With Geston setting the pace, the group hurried on. They followed a zigzag course east through the broken streets, but they were clearly moving with direction and purpose. Consequently their ranks swelled as other refugees, lost and frightened, joined the moving fringes of the party. By the time Marischal Bridge loomed into view in front of them, their ranks numbered almost three score.

Geston was first onto the bridgehead. There he came to a sudden halt. "What is it?" asked Kherryn; then saw for herself. The midsection of the bridge had fallen in, leaving a nine-foot gap between two jagged shards.

Geston spun around to confront the throng of people at his back. "Part of the bridge is down, but we can compensate for that," he announced, and pointed to the flattened heap of a building to the left of the causeway. "There's plenty of loose timber in there. Some of you go fetch us a few good stout lengths."

A small knot of men broke away from the main party. Within a short space of time, they returned carrying two long beams which they laid side by side across the gap. Geston tested the makeshift catwalk, then beckoned the front ranks forward. "Once you're across, take the way to Corvisar's Landing," he told them. "We'll catch up with you once we're finished here."

The refugees made the crossing in pairs. Those at the end of the party gained the far side of the bridge just as the first wave of marching corpses emerged from among the tumbled houses at the bottom of the low bank. Some carried crude clubs, others clutched blood-smeared hand tools. "Ulbrecht!" cried Geston. "Help me with these planks!"

The mage sprang to his aid. Muscles straining, the

two men tumbled the two heavy beam ends into the water under the bridge. "From what you tell me, that won't hold these accursed creatures very long," panted Geston, "but it'll help slow them down. Come on!"

Three streets east of the bridge, they met up with a second party of refugees. At the sight of Geston, another figure in uniform detached itself from the head of the column he was leading and ran forward. "Geston!" exclaimed the newcomer. "Thank God! I was afraid the signal message might not have got through to you."

"I didn't receive any message, but never mind," said Geston. "Where are you and your people heading?"

"Corvisar's Landing. Allyn and some of the others are getting evacuation proceedings under way for the citizens of this borough. If you didn't get the message from the commandery," said his colleague, "how did you know to come this way?"

Geston glanced obliquely toward Kherryn and Ulbrecht. Ignoring the question, he said urgently, "Let's get our folk together and start them on the move again."

The two groups merged quickly. It was another quarter of a mile to the landing. The combined party arrived to find the water's edge lined with clumps of people waiting to embark under the organized direction of a number of Farrowaithe Guardsmen. The waters beyond the haven were already dotted with departing vessels of various shapes and sizes.

The withdrawal was proceeding quickly, but not quickly enough. Standing at the edge of the shore, Ulbrecht looked back in the direction from which they had come. He could see the deadly cloud of darkness hovering ominously above the broken skyline only a furlong distant. Blacker than any thunderhead, the shadow mass was bearing down on them like a wave of flesh-eating locusts. His ears picked up the heavy inexorable shuffle of nerveless feet over the cobblestones as the army of the dead closed in upon the outpost of the living. "Geston!" he called out. "They're coming!"

There were still a score of refugees waiting on the

quayside, half of them children. The shambling vanguard of walking corpses appeared between the houses
overlooking the waterfront. Geston reacted promptly.

"Vesterly!" he called. "Send the rest of those people
out to the end of the pier, while Martyn and Jerrold bring
the boat around! Colby, you go with them, and make
sure everyone gets aboard safely. He turned to his other
men. "The rest of you come with me." Armed with
swords and torches, the lieutenant and his fellow Guards
took their stand at the foot of the dock.

The forerunners of the revenant army reached the
beach as the Guards who were manning the last barge
brought their craft alongside the end of the pier. Huddled among those waiting to embark, Kherryn heard the
sudden onrush of feet and the clash of weaponry. Turning around, she saw the flash of blades and torchfires as
the thin line of Guardsmen fought to hold their position
against a surging crush of enemies who couldn't be
killed.

Other revenants plunged into the water and began
swarming toward the barge. The darkness moved with
them. At close range, Kherryn could see its individual
particles dancing thick as gnats in the air. As she faltered
in her tracks, urgent hands gave her a push from behind.
"Colby, get Lady Kherryn into the boat," called
Ulbrecht.

The ferryman caught her round the waist and swung
her bodily across the narrow gap onto the upper deck of
the barge. Struggling to maintain her balance, Kherryn
looked anxiously back along the pier. Geston and his
fellow Guards were being forced to yield ground. One
man fell screaming, chopped down by a lich wielding a
broken scythe. Another was dashed off the dock into the
water where other ravening corpses overwhelmed him.
Ulbrecht leaped to safety with the last of the townsmen.
"Come on, lieutenant!" bellowed Colby. "You're all
we're waiting on!"

At a barked command from Geston, the surviving
Guardsmen broke rank and bolted for the end of the

pier. A shambling hoard of revenants lumbered after them, dead eyes burning with infernal radiance. "Cut the rope!" shouted Geston as he ran. "We'll jump for it!"

Colby slashed a knife through the barge's mooring line and braced himself to shove off. The first two Guards cleared the edge of the dock with a bound and landed inboard in a clatter of accoutrements. Gripping the taffrail with both hands, Kherryn spotted a sudden black boil in the water next to the nearest piling. "Colby, look out!" she screamed, but before he could react, a pair of revenant hands broke the surface and seized hold of his ankle.

He fell with a startled cry, but managed to fling both arms around the bollard. More corpses clawed at him. Like a frenzied school of cannibal fish, they surrounded the boatman and began dragging him down into the midst of them. "Hang on!" yelled Geston and dived to reach the other man's sliding hands.

His fingers closed around Colby's wrists. Before he could pull back, a knot of revenants armed with knives bore down on him from behind. He took a gash across the shoulder that broke his grip. Colby vanished with a gurgling shriek, leaving Geston to fend off a battery of heavy slash blows from above.

Hands laid hold of his clothing, hauling him out from under the deadly rain of knife cuts. His two remaining companions drove back the encroaching revenants long enough to get him into the barge, then shoved off from the dock with all their strength. While the men at the oars were still trying to gain headway, a handful of corpses reached the back of the boat and began clambering up the tiller post. The Guards in the stern fended them off with boathooks, and beat them back into the water. No others rose to take their place.

The landing receded into the middle distance as the barge struck out for the main channel, forging downstream after the rest of the flotilla. The darkness pursued them for a little way, then fell back to hover like smoke over the stricken city astern. Ulbrecht knelt over Geston to examine his injuries. It was then that he discovered that the death-shadow had sown its spores in the young officer's open wounds.

The black slug shapes were weltering visibly in the lieutenant's blood. As Ulbrecht stared aghast at the pulsating motes of darkness, Geston gave a convulsive shudder and cried out on a wordless note of denial. His own gut muscles rigid with apprehension, Ulbrecht was forced to take an extra moment to prepare himself spiritually for what he knew he had to do. Then he took his magestone in his hands and invoked the Magia, praying for the grace to counteract the evil that had taken the lieutenant in its grip.

When he reached out to Geston from the threshold of Orison, he did so fearing the worst. Even so, he was ill-prepared to receive the blast of nightmare impressions that assaulted him as soon as he made contact with his patient. The initial instant of rapport communicated the revelation that these sluglike parasites were not mindless creatures of darkness, but rather the degenerate remains of individual human souls, reduced to the residue of their own irreconcilable evil.

The mastering force which drove them was hunger —an insatiable desire to consume what was not already a part of their collective voracity. Each single mote of hunger was an individual. At the same time, it was also a part of the demonic principality that knew itself by name simply as the Devourer.

And now Geston Du Maris was the Devourer's feeding ground.

If the evil could not be driven out, Geston himself would be swallowed up and lost. And it could only be driven out through direct contact. Ulbrecht's stomach lurched violently at the idea of having anything to do with these obscene black slugs, but he gathered to himself all the power his spirit was capable of containing. Then, like a man harvesting leeches, he reached out to rip away the parasites that had embedded themselves in Geston's body and soul.

The young soldier screamed in wordless agony as the creatures were torn free of his wounds. Like an infestation of ticks, the ravening motes relinquished their lamprey grip only to turn on Ulbrecht, swarming thirstily after his human vitality. Utterly revolted, the mage struck out at them with all his strength. The refining fire of the Magia hurled the teeming slug-souls back into the midst of the Devourer itself.

The demon's response was a tempestuous backlash of power. The black heat of its wrath smote Ulbrecht to his knees. His field of Orison collapsed around him like an imploding mineshaft, leaving him blind and choking in a whirlpool of darkness. He had just enough residual strength left to force open a doorway back into the physical world. He tumbled across the threshold and then lay still.

It was only after some indeterminate amount of time that he crawled painfully back to consciousness. The palms of his hands were burning, as though they had been branded with hot irons, but the rest of his body was quaking with chills, as though he had been stricken with plague. In spite of his shudders, he attempted to sit up. A small hand restrained him. "Please don't struggle," said a beseeching voice that he recognized as Kherryn's. "Just try to rest easy."

It was sound advice. All Ulbrecht's joints were aching as though he had been stretched on a rack. Settling back, he said huskily, "Where are we?"

"Somewhere out in Lake Damanvagr, making for Cheswythe," said Kherryn. "The Farrowaithe Guardsmen who organized the evacuation from Corviser's Landing say that's the best place for us to put ashore for a rendezvous."

Farrowaithe Guardsmen . . . "The lieutenant!" rasped Ulbrecht. "How is he?"

"Sleeping." Kherryn sounded relieved. "He's very weak," she continued. "But he's alive. And he's in his right mind."

Ulbrecht relaxed, his heart easing in weary thanksgiving. Kherryn's small fingers took his hand. "What about you?" she asked anxiously. "Are you going to be all right?"

"I'll be fine. All I need is a little more time to recover my strength," Ulbrecht assured her. "But," he added silently to himself, "we're far from out of the woods. Whatever that demon-thing is that our enemies have let loose in Farrowaithe, it's going to be coming after us. And when it does, the Mage Hospitallers are going to have to find a way to send the creature back to the hell it came from, or die themselves making the attempt. . . ."

SAILING TOWARD FALMYTH

ON THE EIGHTEENTH DAY OF November, Gudmar, Harlech, Evelake, and Caradoc assembled in the *Mermaid*'s state cabin to attend the formal exchange of betrothal vows between Serdor and Margoth. It was a very simple ceremony, unencumbered by the usual lengthy process of arranging a dowry and a marriage settlement. Having no earthly wealth to bestow on one another, the two parties in this instance had only to declare their intention to marry, in the hearing of witnesses, for the compact to stand confirmed.

That night the four witnesses repaired to the *Mermaid*'s chartroom to celebrate in honor of the newly plighted couple, who had been left to solemnize the occasion in their own way. Harlech paid a visit to the hold and returned with a wooden cask tucked like a piglet under his arm. He set it down with a bump on the chartroom table and gave it a loving pat. "What's that?" asked Evelake with interest.

Harlech showed a double row of gold-wired teeth. "This, milord, is *shirazhi*—what the janissaries call 'nectar of paradise.' Nothing like it tae raise the crest on a cockerel!"

"I've heard of it, but I've never tasted any," said Evelake.

"Have ye no'?" said Harlech, his grin broadening expansively. "Ye're in for a real treat then."

The *shirazhi* was a delicate shade of pink and savored headily of attar of roses. "Harlech, are you sure we're supposed to *drink* this stuff?" asked Caradoc. "It smells more like perfume."

"Dinnae let yourself be taken in, laddie," said the little mariner, with a sidelong glance at Gudmar. "It may smell dainty, but it's got a kick like a Mervainian mine mule."

Once the measures had been handed around, Gudmar raised his glass. "To Serdor and Margoth!" he said, then capped the declaration by reciting a traditional toast. "May they always be faithful in loving, fruitful in labor, hearty and hale all the days of their lives!"

All present saluted and tipped their cups. Evelake's first unsuspecting mouthful took his breath away so sharply that he choked. Gudmar thumped him on the back and said amusedly, "Steady on! That isn't small ale you've got there."

Evelake nodded, still momentarily bereft of speech. His eyes were watering and his tongue tingled. After a recuperative pause, he said hoarsely, "What do they make this from, anyway? Alchemical ether?"

"Best not to ask," said Gudmar with a chuckle. "Just enjoy the experience."

Caradoc eyed his tumbler with respect. "This is even stronger than Mervainian pine-mead."

"Aye, it is," agreed Harlech. "The only thing I've ever come across tae beat it is Nhuboran *ginkoa*. Your first drink o' *that* is something ye'll never forget—if your constitution's able tae stand the strain . . ."

This observation led to an exchange of drinking stories. Simultaneously listening and sipping, Evelake decided it was quite possible to develop an appreciation for *shirazhi*. In spite of its scent, it wasn't sweet in the least. On the contrary, thin as springwater, the liquor seemed to evaporate coldly in the mouth, leaving behind only a tart hint of flavor. After rolling the last few drops around on his tongue, he swallowed then announced, "I think I've just discovered what moonlight *ought* to taste like."

"That's the dandy," said Harlech approvingly, and raised an inquiring eyebrow in Gudmar's direction. Gudmar appraised Evelake with a long look, then, satisfied that the boy was taking no harm, gave Harlech a nod of assent. "So—that'll be another round for everyone," said the little mariner cheerily. "If you lot will oblige me, I'll do the honors."

The others tendered their glasses. After returning them replenished, Harlech rendered homage to his companions with an inelegant gesture, inhaled to the bottom of his lungs, and began to sing in a gravelly bass:

> "Oh, there's naught like a noggin
>   Tae gi' ye good cheer,
> Be it arrack or cider
> Or brandy or beer.
> It tickles the pleasure
> And cushions the pain,
> So let's have another
> And sing the refrain!"

Rising gamely to the occasion, Caradoc and Gudmar chimed in together in raucous harmony:

> "Come, fill up my cup
>   With wine that is sweet!
> Come sing me a tune
>   Tae quicken my feet!
> If I can't find a lady
>   Tae light me tae bed,
> Then gi' me a bottle
>   Tae kiss in her stead!"

Everyone paused to drink. "God, you sing flat!" said Gudmar to Caradoc. "Where's Serdor when you need him?" Then before the mage could summon an indignant rejoinder, he launched into the second verse:

> "There's naught like a maid
> That is winsome and spry,
> Unless it be claret
> And venison pie!
> Let's eat and be merry,
> Let's drink up again!
> Let's toast to our sweethearts
> And sing the refrain!"

Evelake added his voice to the choruses while his elders took the verses in turn. The song became progressively more ribald with each successive stanza. As he came to the end of the final refrain with competitive gusto, Caradoc suddenly realized that the tenor part of the quartet had abruptly dropped out. He turned toward Evelake and discovered that the youngest member of the party had dropped forward in his chair and was lying with one cheek resting flat on the tabletop.

Relaxed as a sleeping cat, he was breathing softly and evenly, the merest hint of a smile hovering about his mouth. Harlech reached over and gently shook the empty cup from Evelake's lightly curled fingers. "Well done, laddie," he told the sleeping boy, with a wry grin. "Ye've done fair justice tae your manhood."

Gudmar gathered himself unhurriedly to his feet. "I'd better go put him to bed," he said. "Hold the next song till I get back."

He hoisted Evelake's light body easily over his shoulder and made for the door. The boy murmured something drowsily under his breath, but didn't wake. Looking after the departing pair, Caradoc experienced a slight guilty qualm. He said, "Maybe we ought to have given him something less potent."

"Och, dinnae fret yourself on that account," said Harlech. "Gudmar kenned well what he was about, lettin' our eaglet test his flight feathers. It's the crowning beauty of *shirazhi* that however it takes ye of an evening, it leaves ye your self-respect on the morning after."

"Is that a fact?" said Caradoc. "In that case, I believe I'll help myself to some more."

Though he didn't admit as much to Harlech, he was trying to repel a mild attack of melancholy. At a loss to account for it, he was impatient with himself for being so temperamental. Embarking on his third measure of *shirazhi*, he made an iron resolution not to let his inconvenient mood get the better of him. By the time Gudmar came back from turning Evelake into his bunk, the mage had himself firmly enough in hand to challenge his two companions to a contest in competitive rhyming.

Throughout the rest of the evening, the three celebrants contrived to keep up a steady stream of songs, jokes, and apocryphal stories. As the hour of twelve approached, Harlech finished off the liquor in his cup and got to his feet. "Well, there goes the ship's bell," he said. "That's the signal for me tae take myself off."

"What for?" asked Caradoc. "Where are you going?"

"Up on deck tae take a spell at the helm," said Harlech. "The *Mermaid*'s no' so canny she can steer herself in the dead o' night."

"We threw dice for the privilege of standing the midnight watch," explained Gudmar, and grinned up at his fellow mariner. "Harlech fell out with his fortune."

"Next time," said Harlech without rancor, "we'll make it the best three throws out o' five."

He saluted them both, then made his exit. Left alone with Gudmar, Caradoc found himself suddenly at a loss for conversation. Seeing his companion looking thoughtful, Gudmar poured each of them another glassful of *shirazhi* and settled back in his chair, his golden eyes shrewdly discerning. When Caradoc continued to nurse his cup in silence, the *Mermaid*'s captain said, "Why so glum all at once?"

Caradoc gave a self-deprecating sigh. "I wish I knew."

"You wouldn't, by any chance, be harboring any reservations about Serdor and your sister's wanting to marry?" asked Gudmar.

"Reservations! You must be joking!" Caradoc gave a rueful chuckle. "Serdor's the best friend I have. There isn't anything I value that I wouldn't entrust to him with a clear conscience."

"Even your sister's honor?" said Gudmar.

"Especially that," said Caradoc. "Which is probably just as well," he added dryly, "since the nearest Hospitallers' enclave is still three days away."

"Why don't you administer the sacrament of marriage yourself?" asked Gudmar. "You're a mage, aren't you?"

"A mage, yes. A Hospitaller, no," said Caradoc. "I can't exercize an authority I haven't been granted."

He took another swallow from his cup. "You know," he continued, "a year ago I'd have raised more than an eyebrow at the idea of Margoth bedding down with a man—even Serdor!—without the benefit of the proper ceremony beforehand. Now . . ." He shook his head, then went on with sudden vehemence, "Damn it, we could all be dead by this time next month. Every day is precious! And so I say, let Serdor and Margoth drink deep of every solace they can find in one another's company, this day and every other. Whatever blessing I have to give to their union, I bestow it freely!"

A long silence followed this declaration. Peering down into his own glass, Gudmar said, "Caradoc, have you ever been in love yourself?"

"No," said Caradoc heavily. "No, I haven't."

A painful smile tugged at the corners of his mouth. "I don't think I've ever lain with a woman without wondering if she might turn out to be the one. But so far, that one has eluded me. Don't ask me what I'm looking for. I just know I haven't found it yet."

Gudmar reached over and clapped him on the shoulder. "Cheer up!" he said, not unkindly. "Has it ever occurred to you that maybe the lady is destined to find *you?*"

The suggestion drew a reluctant chuckle from his companion. "No, it hadn't," said Caradoc, "but I like the idea." He discovered that he was feeling better for having aired his troubled spirits. "Shall we drink to it?"

"With pleasure," said Gudmar. "Once you've poured us both another measure. . . ."

The following morning dawned chilly and overcast. All the celebrants of the night before who weren't involved in the running of the ship were slow to emerge from their berths. Entering the captain's cabin shortly before the noon meal, Serdor and Margoth found that the only face missing from around the table was Caradoc's. "Lord, is he *still* in his bed?" said Caradoc's sister. "It's almost twelve o'clock!"

"Take it as a compliment," advised Serdor with a grin. "Shall I go wake him up?"

"It's about time somebody did," said Margoth.

"Consider it done, then," said the minstrel. "If you people will excuse me . . . ?"

He ducked out into the companionway and rapped on the door to Caradoc's cubicle. When there was no immediate response, he knocked again more loudly. This time he heard above the creak and whine of the ship's timbers another noise, not unlike a groan. Frowning, he tried the door. When it opened to his hand, he pushed it wide and stepped inside.

Too tall for the bunk, Caradoc was visible as a cramped ball of long limbs. Serdor reached down and shook his friend gently by the shoulder. Caradoc caught his breath on an incoherent syllable of protest. He sounded acutely uncomfortable. "Caradoc?" called the minstrel softly. "It's me, Serdor. Are you all right?"

The mage shuddered and rolled onto his back. His green eyes were bleary, and there was a furrow of pain between his brows that deepened as he tried to focus his pupils. "Good God," said Serdor. "You really look ill!"

"I-it's the air," muttered Caradoc. "It's throbbing . . . makes my head feel like the inside of a drum—"

Wincing, he clutched at his temples. "Can't

see. . . ." he gasped. "Can't seem to catch my breath. . . ."

"I don't know what's wrong with you," said Serdor, "but I'm damned sure it isn't a hangover. Let me call Margoth—"

Before he could finish, Caradoc uttered a strangled cry and went rigid, his tall frame twisted into an inflexible spiral of tension. Bending over him in alarm, Serdor took a glancing blow across the cheek as the mage threw out both arms before his face in a desperate gesture of warding. Caradoc's body gave a series of convulsive jerks. It was as though he were being battered by a hail of invisible projectiles.

Serdor shouted for help and flung a bracing arm across his friend's writhing body. Physical contact brought with it a backlash of agonizing sensations. Dark thunder crashed over him. Vileness filled his mouth like the taste of week-old carrion.

Breathless and nauseated, Serdor almost let go. Instead, he held on. For an eternity of seconds, the black storm of destruction continued to rage around them both. Then all at once a deathly silence fell.

Serdor forced open his eyes and found he was kneeling on the floor beside his friend's disordered bunk. The mage was lying on his back, limbs sprawled wide as though he were too spent to control them. He was staring up at the ceiling, his face wrung with shock.

The doorway to Serdor's right was filled with anxiously peering faces. As Serdor turned his head to gaze at the rest of the party, Margoth pushed across the threshold and tumbled to her knees next to him. Looking wildly from the minstrel to her brother, she said, "My God, Caradoc, what happened?"

The mage drew a labored breath, as though his chest hurt. He said in a constricted voice, "There's been a terrible disaster in Farrowaithe. Arch Mage Baldwyn is dead. So is An'char Maeldrake, the Grand Master of Ambrothen, and thirty-eight other magisters with him. . . . I *felt* them die!"

His audience stared at him in horrified silence.
Collecting himself, Caradoc went on. "All the mages at
St. Alanin's are dead—their lives snuffed out like candles. Something *evil* killed them . . . buried them in the
ruins of their own hospice. . . ."

He broke off with a violent shudder. "I felt it, too,"
said Serdor. "The evil had purpose. And identity—"

"My brother!" said Evelake in a voice of chill
certainty. "Employing his demon-powers at Borthen
Berigeld's instigation!"

No one disputed his statement. After a moment's
stricken silence, Gudmar said thinly, "I think I begin to
see why we've been spared any further trouble of the
kind we encountered at Sherat Jeshuel. Apparently
Borthen Berigeld's unholy alliance has been building up
its strength to strike a major blow against the Hospitallers."

Margoth shivered. "Those were some of the most
gifted men in all the Order," she said protestingly.
"Surely they must have been aware of the danger hanging
over them."

"Even magisters can misinterpret what their senses
tell them," said her brother darkly. "If they already had
an explanation to account for any forebodings they may
have experienced—like evidence of necromancy being
practiced farther afield—they wouldn't necessarily have
thought to investigate closer to home."

"Where does this leave us?" asked Evelake.

"Better informed than the mages outside of
Farrowaithe," said Caradoc. "The backlash of what
happened just now will have been felt in all the Hospitaller communities that remain. But none of them will
know what caused it. Their members will certainly try to
communicate through Orison with their brethren in St.
Alanin's. But there may not be anyone left alive capable
of responding."

He paused, then continued, his tone bleak as winter.
"If we, and the Order, are to survive the assault that is
sure to follow, the provincial mages need to know what

we know. That means we need to press on toward Falmyth with all possible speed."

"Could ye no' make contact wi' them yourself through Orison?" wondered Harlech.

"You don't know what you're asking!" said Caradoc with a shake of his head. "I'm prepared to *try*, but the odds against my succeeding are practically astronomical. In the first place," he went on to explain, "I have nothing to use as a focus: no name, no face, nothing that would serve to establish a personal link between me and any other mage in the area. In the second place, in order for two mages to communicate effectively in the way you're suggesting, both have to be capable of achieving Higher Orison—something only mages with magister-class talent can do. And thirdly, both parties would have to *consent* to communicate—something which isn't likely to happen in this case. Even if I were able to make my presence felt to another mage, I doubt I'd get a response: no mage with any sense of self-preservation would agree to open up his mind to someone he didn't know."

"In other words," said Harlech sourly, "we may have a boat, but we havena got a paddle."

"No," agreed Gudmar. "It looks as if we'll have to do things the hard way. Let's hope the winds will be fair between here and Falmyth."

GRAVEYARD OF WHALES

FOR THE REST OF THAT afternoon and all through the next day, the *Mermaid* forged ahead due north under as much canvas as her yards could safely carry in the ever-changing winds. Shortly before nightfall of the party's sixth day out from Telphar, the masthead lookout sighted land off the port bow. Gudmar put the helm over

thirty degrees to port and sent the ship reaching for the
distant shoreline. As she settled into her new course, he
turned to Caradoc, who had come on deck for a breath of
air, and gave the younger man a mirthless smile.

"By my reckoning we should be coming up on
Falmyth by this time tomorrow," he told the mage.
"This is where we go in close and try to remain incon-
spicuous, just in case there are any Du Bors warships in
the area. I don't want the news to get out prematurely
that the *Mermaid* has changed her alignment."

That night the weather turned clear and cold. The
next day, monitoring their progress from the eminence
of the quarterdeck, Caradoc saw that Gudmar had not
exaggerated in describing the seashores as rugged. Here,
as in Gand farther north, the ceaseless fretting of wind
and wave had eaten away sections of the headlands to
leave isolated columns of rock standing free of the
mainland. Stark as cenotaphs, their sheer bases wreathed
in white foam, the sea pillars towered above the *Mermaid*'s mastheads as she wove a cautious path among
them. The chilly, steel-azure waters on either side of the
ship's prow showed occasional ominous shimmers of
amber to mark where submarine rocks lurked beneath
the surface of the rolling swells.

The pilot Jamie Greenham remained stationed at
the forecastle railing throughout most of the afternoon,
keeping a sharp eye out for dangerous shoals ahead of the
Mermaid's prow. Guided by the pilot's instructions,
Gudmar steered his ship in and out like a weaver's
shuttle among sentinel rocks half again the height of the
mainmast. The frosty winter twilight was gathering by
the time the *Mermaid* nosed her way into a deeply cloven
cove, bounded to the north by a long saw-toothed
promontory. To the east, the full moon was rising, cold
as the eye of a shark.

Its light glittered off the waves as they broke against
the pebble beach below the cliffs inshore. Standing next
to Margoth and Serdor on the quarterdeck, Harlech
drew their attention to a tall spindle of natural stone,

where it glimmered in moonlit relief against a dark backdrop of steeply sloping upland. "Yon's Thread-needle Rock," he told them. "Falmyth'll be just beyond that headland north of us."

It looked to be a distance of about a quarter of a mile. "It's a good thing we'll have the benefit of bright moonlight," said Margoth. "I understand Falmyth Harbor is a bit tricky to get in and out of."

"Och, it's no worse'n what we've already come through, getting here," said Harlech with a shrug. "Besides, Jamie Greenham kens every rock and reef in this vicinity like they was kin tae him. I've no doubt he could find our way into the haven in a night blind-dark wi' fog."

Caradoc was with Gudmar in the wheelhouse. As the *Mermaid* approached the rocky tip of the barrier-promontory, he remarked with a frown, "Funny: I didn't expect ours to be the only vessel in sight in these waters. As it is, I haven't seen so much as a lobster boat, let alone anything like a merchant ship."

Hands steady on the ship's wheel, Gudmar did not take his eyes off the pilot in the bow. "If you're wondering if Falmyth is normally this quiet," he said, "the answer is a resounding no. Something's unquestionably amiss."

Caradoc experienced a tightening in the pit of his stomach. "A Du Bors embargo?" he suggested.

"They'd need to use warships to enforce it," said Gudmar. "And—as you've just pointed out—we haven't seen any."

"What else would bring all shipping in the area to a standstill?" wondered Caradoc.

"I don't know," said Gudmar. "Unless for some reason, the Merchant-Adventurers themselves decided to close the harbor—"

He broke off short, his whole attitude stiffening. Casting a swift glance forward to see what had claimed the other man's attention, Caradoc saw that Jamie Greenham was waving his hands and gesticulating excitedly. The deckhands amidships were converging on the portside railing to peer over the side. "You men, get back to your stations!" ordered Gudmar sharply. "Dury! Come here and take the wheel."

Turning over the helm to one of the ship's steersmen, the *Mermaid*'s captain sprinted for the ladder leading up onto the foredeck. Caradoc followed one step behind him. They arrived to find Jamie standing shoulder to shoulder with Giles Penrith, the ship's sailing master. Both men were looking grim. "See there, Master Gudmar!" said the pilot, pointing toward the shore. "What d'you make of that?"

Lynx-eyed, the *Mermaid*'s captain gazed out across the water toward a massy jumble of boulders at the base of the cliff. Copying Gudmar's example, Caradoc realized that what he had casually taken to be an exposed flange of sea rock was in fact the hull of a foundered ship.

She was lying on her side on top of a submerged reef, a dismasted sea-sodden hulk. Floating upright, she would have rivaled the *Mermaid* for size. Staring at the other vessel, Gudmar swore under his breath, then stood back from the railing. "Master Penrith, give the men the order to let go the mainsheets," he said tersely. "And tell Dury to bring her in close. I want to give that wreck a good look in passing."

As the wind spilled from her slackened sails, the *Mermaid* slowed to a crawl. Jamie scrambled nimbly out along the portside cathead to watch the waters beneath. As the caravel edged cautiously inshore, Harlech and Margoth joined Caradoc and Gudmar. "Serdor's gone to fetch Evelake," said Margoth, then lapsed into sober silence as her gaze was drawn toward the ruined remains of the other ship.

The light of the rising moon picked out with surgical precision the lines of her waterlogged timbers. As the *Mermaid* skirted the other vessel's keel, Harlech squinted along the line of her exposed flank. "No sign of any shot holes that I can see," he said with a scowl. "I wonder what it was that took her down."

"She's got an almighty rent in her stern," said Gudmar. "The rudder must have been the first thing to go."

The sound of footbeats on the ladder heralded the arrival of Serdor and Evelake. "That looks bad," said the young Warden, surveying the wreck with grave brown eyes. "Do you think she might have been driven aground in a storm?"

"With Falmyth so close at hand, the port reeves would have made some attempt to salvage her," said Gudmar. "Or so I would have thought. . . ."

His voice trailed off. The *Mermaid* glided on past the grounded vessel in a shallow wake of silver ripples. Gazing back in the direction of the wreck, Margoth noticed something that gave her pause for thought. "That's odd!" she exclaimed. "Look at the shards of planking around the edges of that hole in the stern: doesn't it look as if the missing timbers were *torn out*, rather than *smashed in*?"

Gudmar took a second, closer look. "You know," he said, "I do believe you're right."

His golden eyes narrowed to the watchful slits of a hunting lion. "It's worth taking a few risks for the sake of some answers. But before we go so far as to enter Falmyth Harbor, I think we'll run out our guns."

In addition to her two stern-chasers, the *Mermaid* carried ten artillery pieces a side. Thanks to the military prudence of Lord Gervaise, her previous commander, she also carried her full complement of powder and shot. Moving with well-drilled efficiency, the men who made up the gun crews swarmed along the deck, wheeling sakers and culverins into position, before priming them for firing. By the time the ship cleared the headland, her weaponry was in a state of readiness.

Gudmar resumed control of the helm. An icy wind struck the ship headlong as she rounded the cape. The *Mermaid* jibed slightly, then recovered as her captain brought her around onto her starboard tack. "Steady as you go, princess," Gudmar silently told his ship. "I've a shrewd notion we're heading into trouble, but I'm trusting you to get us out of it again when the time comes."

The bite of the wind was sharp enough to drive the *Mermaid*'s five passengers down off the forecastle into the relative shelter of the ship's waist. Off to port, the inner wall of the promontory thrust out a rocky spur of high ground, gnarled like a tree root. The spit was surmounted by a circular watchtower, its uppermost story faceted with glazed windows. "Nobody at home tae mind the lighthouse," rumbled Harlech. "This whole situation is beginning tae stink like an open privy!"

The entrance to the harbor was flanked to the northeast by an enormous natural archway of stone, jutting out into the channel like some huge unfinished aqueduct. Churning foam flashed white beneath the moon as the outgoing tide rolled seaward between the two massive plinths of the arch. The sheer size of the rocks made Margoth feel uncomfortably small and insignificant. She moved closer to Serdor, glad of his nearness.

Gudmar steered the *Mermaid* toward the center of the narrow waterway. Marking their progress from the port railing, Caradoc curled his lip in sudden disgust. "The situation isn't the only thing stinking around here!" he declared. "Phew! What a stench! Just like a heap of rotten fish!"

Margoth inhaled, her nose twitching curiously. "I don't smell anything but tar and seawater," she said.

Her brother stared at her, then sniffed the air a second time. "I don't smell it anymore," he said in some surprise. "Whatever it was, it seems to be gone now."

"Never mind that. We've got worse things tae worry about than dead fishes," said Harlech. "Look up ahead."

His companions looked. Thrown into deep shadow by the massy bulk of the harbor's sheltering arch, the shoreline was visible only in jagged silhouette. "I don't see anything," said Caradoc.

"Aye, that's just it," growled Harlech. "From here we should be able tae see the lights from Falmyth. *Only there aren't any lights.*"

An appalled silence greeted this announcement. After a moment, Serdor said, "Oh well, we've come too far to back out now."

"Aye," agreed Harlech dourly. "May as well carry on till we find out what's at the bottom o' the tar barrel."

Laboring against the wind and the outbound tide, the *Mermaid* took another quarter of an hour to work her way the length of the channel. She emerged from under the shadow of the arch as the moon climbed above the clifftops. As the cold lunar light began to spread across the waters, the spotters in the forecastle sighted the upended foresection of a second scuttled ship.

The haven was awash with pieces of floating wreckage. Caradoc looked out across the sea of flotsam in numb dismay. "My God, what happened here?" he wondered aloud to his silenced companions. "Could there have been a battle?"

"I dinnae ken what else could ha' wreaked so much havoc," said Harlech, "except maybe a tidal wave." He shook his head dubiously. "And as tae that, it would ha' taken some floodtide tae get in past Horseshoe Spit back there."

"Whatever disaster overtook this place, it wasn't confined to the water," said Serdor.

He pointed toward the shore, where the harsh moonlight had laid bare the upper levels of the town. Even from a distance, they could see evidence of widespread destruction. Shops and houses had been reduced to heaps of darkened rubble. Public buildings had been gutted and defaced. The wind sweeping down through the deserted streets carried the faded odor of fire and smoke. "Judging by the look of things, Falmyth must have come under some form of attack only a few days ago," continued the minstrel. "Maybe Gudmar's Merchant-Adventurer colleagues decided to oppose Du Bors authority."

"Maybe. To their cost." Evelake eyed the ruins and shuddered.

"And ours," Harlech reflected soberly. "I cannae see any sign of survivors, but no doubt Gudmar'll want tae go ashore and check tae see there isna some poor bastard left stranded in all that ruin."

He proved right in this prediction. With Jamie Greenham posted again out over the bowsprit, the *Mermaid* crept forward through the litter of floating spars and broken timbers. Under her captain's direction, she gave wide berth to an exposed reef jutting up out of the water a bowshot's distance from shore. As she approached the shallows, she veered around to port to avoid a second submerged reef lurking off her starboard side.

Crossing over to the starboard railing, Caradoc stared at the dark shape lying a few feet below the surface of the sea. The fickle glitter of the moonlight picked out bars and blotches of white along the sides of the reef, pale as exposed bone. The wake of the *Mermaid*'s passing disturbed the water. As the ripples parted, Caradoc's nostrils caught again the sudden overpowering reek of rotten fish.

He recoiled in instinctive revulsion. At the same time, a hoarse cry went up from the bow. "Master Gudmar!" cried Jamie Greenham. "That's no rock a'starboard! I just saw it move!"

His cry sent Harlech and the other passengers darting across the deck to join Caradoc. "It looks like another ship turned turtle," called Harlech over his shoulder to Gudmar. "Ye'd better sheer off, in case we get rammed."

The deck shuddered underfoot as Gudmar put the helm over to send the *Mermaid* gliding around the inshore side of the adjacent reef to port. In the same instant, the waters off the starboard aft quarter were suffused with sudden churning phosphorescence.

Bubbles shot to the surface and detonated like marsh gas. The dark torpedo shape lying under the water humped and heaved. Its foresection broke the water in a streaming torrent of sea brine and putrefaction. Margoth uttered a choked cry as she discovered that she was looking into the gaping saber-toothed maw of a monstrous killer whale, fully half the length of the ship.

The creature had been dead for some time, its massive bones only partially covered with stinking flesh. But it was moving as though it were alive. Margoth's mind reeled at the nightmare realization that the thing was actually coming after the *Mermaid.* Serdor dragged her back from the railing as a fetid surge of contaminated seawater swept the caravel's deck. "Gudmar, give Giles the helm and *get out here!*" shouted Caradoc.

The corpse-whale's empty eye sockets blazed with a sickly, gristle-white luminescence. Jackknifing after the *Mermaid,* the creature butted the ship astern with force enough to hurl half the crew off their feet. Timbers cracked and crunched below the level of the maindeck before the corpse-whale sheered off, its rotting flukes tossing up sheets of discolored spume. It banked in the shallows and began to circle round again.

Evelake was among the many who had lost their footing in the first collision. Lying bruised and breathless at the base of the mainmast, he watched the corpse-whale's gleaming back cleave the water as it converged on the ship a second time. Strong hands caught him under the armpits and hauled him to his feet. "Here, hang on to this, my lord!" said Gudmar. He guided the boy's fingers to one of the mast's support cables, then bounded on, making for the starboard battery.

The ship was rocking and wallowing, fighting to regain lost headway. "Starboard gun crews, to your marks!" roared Gudmar. His deep voice boomed out above the din of dismay and confusion. There was a ragged scramble of movement as men leaped to obey his order.

The monster was closing fast. The stench of its decaying flesh was nauseating. "Sight your guns!" called Gudmar. "Prepare to open fire on my signal."

Wood and metal groaned in protest as the culverins swung into position on their trunnions. Matches flared into sputtering life. The corpse-whale bore down on the ship's flank in a flume of putrid radiance. "Ready!" shouted Gudmar. *"Fire!"*

There was a sizzling flash, followed by a deafening roar as the guns discharged in an explosion of smoke and stone shot. Gobbets of decaying flesh flew into the air as a series of nine-pound cannonballs ripped into the body of the oncoming monster. The waters off the ship's side boiled wildly. "Master Gudmar!" shrilled an anonymous voice. "We hit it, but it's still coming for us!"

Something heavy smashed up hard against the *Mermaid*'s flank. She heeled over onto her side, her decks canting crazily to port. A jagged ridge of fleshless vertebrae tore at her timbers from beneath, then vanished from view. The ship fell back in a welter of spray and foam. "Rhodri! Get a team below to check the hull!" barked Gudmar. "Giles! Take her over hard a'port!"

The *Mermaid* was slow to respond to the helm. Bucking mulishly, she rounded the point of the reef, then leveled out as the wind took her from behind. Her sails bellied out with a crack. Canvas straining, she lurched into forward motion and began to pull away from the shore.

"Look out, Cap'n!" shrieked a voice from the masthead. "Here it comes again!"

Gudmar had already marked the telltale track of gleaming bubbles, moving into line behind the ship as she sped for the channel mouth. His mouth tightened in an instant of calculated reflection. He turned abruptly on his heel and strode across to the railing overlooking the maindeck. With a glance he singled out two men who weren't involved in running the ship.

"Harlech! Caradoc!" he shouted down. "Get down to the hold and fetch me up two casks of *bashanti*! I'll also want an empty barrel to float them with!"

"Right ye are!" Harlech yelled back. He and the tall mage wheeled and made a dash for the hatchway. Left behind, Evelake exchanged swift glances with Margoth and Serdor. The three of them ran for the ladder leading up to the quarterdeck.

Under Gudmar's direction, the crews manning the stern chasers were doggedly preparing to open fire in the direction of the pursuing trail of sickly light. "What are you hoping to do? Disable that thing somehow?" asked Evelake anxiously.

"No," said Gudmar tersely. "We're just range-finding."

He gave the gunners a nod. The twin falconets belched shot. Three seconds later and some distance astern, two small jets of pale foam leaped skyward, thirty feet apart. Squinting through the dissipating smoke, one of the gunners said, "Just over two hundred and fifty yards, Cap'n."

A disturbance on the ladder signaled the arrival of Caradoc and Harlech with three small barrels, one empty, two full. "What the de'il are ye plannin' tae do wi' this *bashanti* stuff?" panted Harlech. "The bloody firin' tube's still in its crate—we cannae just pour it over the side like so much stink-house gin wi'out settin' *ourselves* alight along wi' yon fleyboggart—"

"We're not going to pour it over the side," said Gudmar, kneeling over the barrels with a stout rope in hand. "Once I get these kegs lashed together, we're going to turn them adrift in our wake and try to detonate them at a distance."

"Wi' what? A three-pound cannon-ball? That's going tae call for some pretty fancy shooting!" objected Harlech.

"Have you got a better notion?"

"No, but—"

"If precision's what you need," said Serdor, "let Margoth do the siting—"

"Me?" protested Margoth. "I don't know anything about ordnance—"

"You don't need knowledge," said her brother. "*You* have instincts. I think you ought to use them."

Margoth's heart was hammering against her chest.

"I—I don't know," she faltered. "But if you think it may save our lives, I'll damned sure give it a try."

"That's the spirit!" said Caradoc, and hustled her over to the starboard gun. The gun crews hastened to reload. "I'll site the portside chaser myself," said Gudmar. "We're probably only going to get these two shots at our target, so let's hope one of 'em tells!"

The distance between the ship and pursuing corpse-whale was rapidly decreasing. Caradoc and Harlech hoisted the bundle of kegs onto the taffrail. "If this doesna work," said Harlech, "it's been nice knowin' ye, laddie."

"If it does work," said Caradoc, "I'll stand you a pint at the next inn we come to. Ready? Go!"

They tipped the bundle over the railing. It struck the water with a splash and bobbed to the surface. Rolling over and over, it floated away astern in line with the ship's wake. The whale bore down upon it in a boiling surge of pallid light.

Standing behind the breech of the starboard falconet, Margoth felt her throat tighten. "Oh God," she thought, "please let me place a cannonball as accurately as I can throw a dagger!"

She laid hands on the barrel of the gun, exploring by touch the technicalities of its balance and power. Impressions surged up through her fingertips: range factors . . . variable angles for firing . . . poise and counterpoise. . . . "Bring the muzzle down a notch," she told the men standing ready on either side of the gun mount.

Grunting and heaving, they did as she instructed. Off to her left, Gudmar was bending low, peering along the line of the portside gun barrel. "Coming into range . . ." he muttered, *"now!"*

Flame whisked like a mouse down the powderhole. The falconet went off with a roar. Gudmar snapped upright to watch the ball strike the water six feet short of the intended target. "Damn!" he hissed. "Margoth?"

Evelake wordlessly passed her the linstock. She held her breath for three seconds, measuring the rise and fall of the deck. The corpse-whale's putrified head broke the surface just beyond the bundle of floating kegs. Margoth gulped air and touched off her measure of powder.

The gun detonated with a bang. Blinded by a backlash of smoke, Margoth heard the departing hiss of the cannonball as it swept low over the waves. There was a splash and a splintering crack. Suddenly the sky astern burst into sheets of dazzling blue flame.

It roared across the surface of the water like wildfire. Engulfed in the midst of a howling conflagration, the corpse-whale reared back on its tail, heaving its foresection upright out of the burning swells. Fire raced up its flanks, devouring rotting blubber and sinew. Blazing like a funeral pyre, the creature hung suspended for a moment against the desolate backdrop of the sky, then crashed back into the sea, where it sank, still burning, into the murky depths.

A hollow cheer went up from the men in the rigging. Serdor threw both arms around Margoth and kissed her resoundingly. Carried along in the teeth of the wind, the *Mermaid* burst free of the Horseshoe and sped for open water. As the sea fire continued to burn itself out in the distance, the other people of the ship's quarterdeck began to breathe again.

Gudmar was the first to break the silence born of shock and relief. "That was *quite* an impressive piece of marksmanship," he told Margoth. "It's a privilege to have you on board!"

Margoth gave a shaky laugh. "I wasn't at all sure I could make it work," she confessed. "What *was* that thing anyway?"

"What a demonologist would call a 'revenant,'" said her brother grimly. "Something no longer alive in its own right that has been animated by means of necromancy."

"If I recall correctly what the histories of the Order have to say about revenants," said Serdor, "there are only two ways of dealing with them. Either you drive out the animating power by means of exorcism. Or you destroy the host body—completely."

"Wonderful," growled Harlech. "D'ye suppose

there'll be any more o' these beasties floating around out there?"

Gudmar shrugged darkly. "I hope not—but I'll not lay any bets against it. We'll review the situation a bit later. Right now, I'd better go find out how badly we're in need of repairs. . . ."

EVENING OF THE WOLF

THE *MERMAID'S* HULL HAD BEEN breached just above the waterline astern. By the time Gudmar arrived to inspect the damage, Rhodri Blantyn, the ship's carpenter, was already taking measures to patch up a gaping rift to the right of the rudder shaft. "Any lower down, Captain, and we'd have found ourselves swimming for our lives," said the carpenter with a shake of his head. "As it is, we've taken in a fair bit of seawater. It'll take us the rest of the night to pump her dry."

"I'll have the men shift everything forward that isn't nailed down on this level," said Gudmar. "That should keep her beam end in the air till you can get that hole plugged. How's her keel holding up?"

Rhodri frowned. "Hard to say for sure without taking her into dry dock, but I think she's not much more than scarred. Still, don't go dragging her over any barnacle beds until I get a chance to check her out proper. . . ."

No one on board managed to get more than a few winks of sleep during the night, but the dark hours passed without further incident. The next day dawned bright and freezing cold. Pacing the deck beside Gudmar in the early light, Harlech blew on the chilled fingers of his right hand and growled, "This is more like Mervaine in January! If this is the kind of winter we're in for, I cannae say I relish the thought!"

Caradoc too was uneasy about the turn of the weather. His mage senses warned him that there was trouble in the air. The day wore on without bringing him any enlightenment. When the party gathered for supper at sunset, he was too restless to eat. Eventually he excused himself and went out on deck for a breath of fresh air.

The firmament to the east was dark. To the west, half a mile to port, the coastal cliffs of southern Gandia made a jagged black silhouette against the lingering light of sunset. But Caradoc's eyes were drawn northward. Directly athwart the *Mermaid*'s bow, a dark headland jutted out into the sea. Beyond it, the sky was strangely luminous, brighter than the western horizon.

It had an angry look, like the canopy of burning ash overhanging a forest fire. As Caradoc scanned the skyline in sudden apprehension, the dense black outline of the headland was thrown into stark relief by a blazing upsurge of red-gold flame. His own involuntary exclamation clashed with an outcry from the watchman in the crow's nest overhead. "Master Penrith!" shrilled the lookout. "I see fire on the other side of that headland! Yske's on fire! It's burning!"

The watchman's cry carried as far as the stern cabin. Arrested in the act of looking over a sea chart, Gudmar traded lightning glances with Harlech across the table. As one, they both thrust back their chairs and bounded for the door to the companionway. After a startled instant of delay, Serdor, Margoth, and Evelake sprang after them.

They found Caradoc standing next to the *Mermaid*'s sailing master at the forecastle railing. The sky in front of them was luridly aglow. As she watched the lights flicker sullenly from garnet to smoky topaz, Margoth felt her mouth go dry. Turning to Gudmar, she asked fearfully, "*Is* that the town on fire?"

The big merchant-adventurer didn't answer. His face was set like a casting in bronze. He watched the sky for a few heartbeats longer. Then he spun around and called out to his men to crowd on more sail.

Trimmed to achieve her best possible speed, the *Mermaid* raced through the black water in a trail of foam. Even so, it was half an hour before she cleared the point of the headland to give her crew their first unobstructed view of the blazing buildings and smoke-filled streets of what had once been a prosperous fishing town.

Golden eyes narrowed to fierce slits, Gudmar tersely requested the loan of his pilot's watchglass. Training the lens on the shore, he raked the waterfront from end to end. A moment later he announced grimly, "I don't see any signs of life. But we'll go ashore as soon as we can get the boats in the water. If there are any survivors, they'll be needing all the help we can give them."

The two remaining gigs stowed aboard the *Mermaid* could accommodate ten men apiece. Before leaving the ship, the men chosen to take part in the explorations ashore put on steel caps and mail shirts. Armed with broadaxes and shortswords, they took their places at the oars and waited for their captain to join them before pushing off for the beach.

They had no need for torches to light their way through the skeletal remains of gutted fishing boats. The air inshore was bright as day, its heat tainted with the greasy stench of liquifying metal. Catching an acrid whiff of scorched hair, Margoth choked and buried her nose in a fold of her cloak. "Are you all right?" asked Serdor.

"I will be, once I find something constructive to do," Margoth assured him. "I'd much rather be here, than sitting idle back at the ship, wondering what kind of trouble the rest of you might be getting yourselves into."

Even as she spoke, the boat's keel grated to a halt on the sand. The rowers shipped their oars inboard and began clambering over the gunnels. Once everyone had disembarked, the crew dragged the boat up onto the dry shingle above the tidemark. While they were waiting for the second boat to come aground, Gudmar turned to Evelake, who was standing at his side. "There's no telling what danger we may run into once we enter the town itself," he said gravely. "You know that as your liegeman,

I am responsible for your safety. Take no offense if I entreat you to stay close by me at all times."

This injunction won him a fleeting smile from the young Warden. "Don't worry—I know my place," said Evelake with arid humor. "Just think of me as your shadow."

The shops and houses lining the waterfront were little more than slagheaps of smoldering rubble. Bypassing these hopeless tangles of charred brick and glowing ash, the party pressed on toward the next tier of buildings. Here the damage was less extensive. Many of the structures had been left with their external walls still standing; some had kept their roofs partially intact. But here also the reek of cinders and smoke was overlaid with the stomach-turning odor of scorched flesh.

The air was full of sounds of shifting and breaking, as fire-gnawed boards and timbers gave way in the eviscerated interiors of the burned houses. Senses raw-alert, the members of the landing party scanned the street, looking for signs of movement amid the shadows. Smoke drifted in and out through the smashed and blackened cavities of windows and doors. But when no immediate danger presented itself, the group broke up into smaller detachments to begin the ugly task of searching the buildings.

Harlech's party was the first to stumble upon a partly burned corpse sprawled out in a sideroom of a chandler's shop. His loud hail summoned the rest of the group to the spot. Beckoning Gudmar over to join him, Harlech pointed to the body on the floor. An eight-inch blade, its handle burned away, protruded from between the corpse's blackened ribs.

"See that?" said the little mariner. "There must ha' been some fighting before the burning started."

Gudmar bent down to take a closer look. "Odd: that's no weapon. It's just an ordinary kitchen knife. Let's see what else we can find around here."

As the search continued, more corpses came to light, but no survivors. "This is worse than I imagined!" muttered Caradoc as he and Serdor emerged from the smoldering darkness of the last house on the street. "At least half these people—judging from the signs—died fighting *each other!*"

"And the rest were murdered outright—probably because they were either too young or too weak to defend themselves," agreed the minstrel with a shudder.

"It's almost as if some madness came over them, to turn even families against each other," mused Caradoc. He squared his shoulders with an effort, then added darkly, "I don't suppose anyone is harboring any doubts concerning who engineered this disaster. What we need to find out, if we can, is *how*. And *why*."

Hoping to uncover some clue to the mystery, the party moved on again, systematically exploring street by street until they came at last to the ruined gate of St. Merrow's hospice, on the northern edge of the town. As he gazed out across the array of broken buildings, still smoldering under a heavy pall of smoke, Caradoc experienced a sudden heart-stopping pang of desolation. He said softly, to no one in particular, "You know, this was one of the oldest priories in all East Garillon. St. Alanin himself consecrated the ground on which it was built—"

His voice jammed in his throat before he could finish the sentence. Words from the Lamentations of Caer Ellyn rose unbidden to the surface of his memory, echoing elegiacally in the silence of his own mind:

Thy pastures stand empty, Lord God of Hosts.
Silent and dark are the courts of thy praise.
Where was the sword of thy wrath in the morning
  of the jackal?
Where was the shield of thy love in the evening
  of the wolf?

A hand touched his shoulder. "Come on," said Serdor quietly. "There's no looking back now."

The party moved on through the gateway. The grass of the priory's forecourt was scorched with fire. There was nothing left of the chapel but a black mound of ashes. The infirmary, likewise, had been reduced to a heap of tumbled stones and cinders. The building beyond the infirmary, however, was still standing. Its walls were scarred with fire and all the doors and windows had been smashed in, but it was otherwise largely intact. "Ransacked, but no' set alight," said Harlech, gazing up at the upper floors from the ground outside. "Now why d'ye suppose they didnae torch this place along wi' all the rest?"

Gudmar plucked a still-glowing brand from among the remains of a nearby tree. Mounting the steps to the front entrance, he thrust his makeshift torch through the yawning doorway and shone the light around. "This must have been the library," he reported over his shoulder. "Maybe there was something stored here that was as likely to prove valuable to the enemies of the Order as to the members of the Order itself."

He turned to his men, who were waiting beyond. "Walther! Dunstan! Fitch! I want you three on guard patrol out here. The rest of you find yourselves torches and come with me. . . ."

The first room the party entered appeared to have been a general study area. Seen by firelight, the place was a shambles. All the reading desks and bookshelves had been overturned, then smashed. The books and writing materials had been hurled to the floor and trodden into pulp underfoot.

A doorway in the left-hand wall gave access to a corridor with a staircase at the far end of it. There were two smaller chambers on each side of the hall. The doors had been torn off their hinges and the rooms beyond turned upside down. Leaving five of his men to sift through the wreckage in the study hall, Gudmar dispatched the other six to investigate the cubicles on the left side of the passage. Taking Harlech with them, he and Evelake entered the first room on the right, while Caradoc, Serdor, and Margoth took the one at the far end, under the stairs.

As her companions began gingerly to clear away the broken furniture to get at the torn books and scattered papers underneath, Margoth was drawn to take a closer look at the fireplace, where a number of books and manuscripts had been thrown on the hearth and set alight. The white marble of the mantelpiece had been defaced with illuminator's paints; the carving had been chipped and cracked. Margoth ran her fingers lightly over the damaged stonework, sorry to see its artistry spoiled. As her hand moved across the marble frieze, the inborn gift that she shared with Caradoc told her that there was more to the fireplace than met the eye.

Guided by her own special instinct, her fingertips located a release mechanism hidden among the whorls of leaves and flowers. She tripped it with a dextrous turn of the wrist and heard the grinding whirr of small gears turning. A panel shifted aside in the wall of the fireplace. Beyond lay a dark opening.

Her cry of discovery brought her two companions running. "What is it?" demanded Caradoc, then stopped short as he caught sight of the narrow doorway she had found. Edging past Margoth, Serdor waved his torch across the threshold. "A stairway leading down!" he exclaimed.

"Gudmar will certainly want to take a look at this," said Caradoc. "I'll go fetch him."

Gudmar brought Evelake and Harlech with him, along with Jamie Greenham, the ship's pilot, and Rhodri Blantyn, the ship's carpenter. The big merchant-adventurer was keenly interested in Margoth's discovery. "Nobody builds a concealed stairway without a reason," he said. "It'll be instructive to find out what's at the bottom of this one."

"There's only room on the steps for one person at a time," said Serdor. "Shall I go first?"

Steel glinted blue as Gudmar drew his broadsword. "Better let me take the lead," said the *Mermaid*'s captain with a thin smile.

The stairs descended twenty feet before opening into a small square room with a door in each of the three remaining walls. Gudmar waited for Harlech and Caradoc to join him, then went over to the west door and tried the latch. The portal swung toward him with a

creak of rusty hinges. Peering through the gap, the
Mermaid's captain gave a grunt of surprise. "Here,
Caradoc," he said. "What do you make of this?"

Caradoc looked over the older man's shoulder. The
second room was identical in size and shape to the first
one, with the same number of doorways placed in the
same relationship to one another. The difference was
that the walls between the doorways had been fitted with
shelves full of dust-covered books. After a glance around
Gudmar's opposite shoulder, Harlech went to the door
to the left of the stairs and pulled it open. "This one's a
match for the other twa," he reported.

"A maze!" exclaimed Serdor from the bottommost
step. When the others turned to him inquiringly, he went
on to explain. "I've read about such things being built in
the days of the early Hospitallers, as a precaution against
Pernathan raiders. But I didn't know this particular
hospice had anything like that."

"It *is* a very old priory," said Caradoc. "With a lot
of ancient manuscripts and relics to protect."

"It may have afforded protection of another sort to
the residents of the priory today," said Gudmar. "Let's
look around."

Evelake consented to remain behind in the vestibule, with Margoth for company. "We'll be marking the
doorways as we go," said Gudmar, "but I'd still like to
have someone here to call up assistance if we need it.
This maze may have more tricks to it than a confusing
layout." He turned to Margoth and added, "If anyone
should fall afoul of a trap, I want to know where you are,
in case your special talents are called for."

Taking Rhodri Blantyn with him, the big merchant-
adventurer set out to investigate the rooms at the center
of the complex. Harlech and Jamie Greenham, for their
part, chose to explore the chambers to the south. "I guess
it's the north side for you and me," said Caradoc to
Serdor.

"Right," said the minstrel. "After you . . ."

Neither he nor Caradoc was surprised to discover

that the configuration of the adjoining room matched the one they had left behind. Serdor carefully removed a book from the shelf to the right of the doorway and set it on the floor by the threshold. He positioned it so that the top end of the spine was angled toward the cubicle they had just left. "If we do that for each room we enter," he explained to Caradoc, "we'll have a ready-made set of pointers to show us the route back to the stairs."

"We've got three other doors to choose from," said Caradoc. "Which way from here?"

"We'd better keep our sense of direction," said Serdor. "Let's carry on north and see how far that gets us."

They did as the minstrel proposed. Two rooms later, they met up with blank walls to the north and east. "That puts us three cubicles away from the vestibule," said Caradoc, looking around him with arms akimbo. "It looks as if we go west from this point."

The tall mage led the way through the doorway into the next chamber. The cell had three other doors beside the one through which they had entered. "What a rabbit warren this is turning out to be!" exclaimed Caradoc. "For God's sake, be careful with your markers."

"Don't worry: I don't want to get lost any more than you do," Serdor assured him. "Keep going west."

They passed quickly through the next three cubicles, pausing only to mark the way. Serdor was first to enter the fourth consecutive cell. As the little chamber came to life in the light of his torch, he uttered an exclamation of surprise and darted across to the doorway on his left. Bounding into the room behind his friend, Caradoc saw that the south door was standing open a few inches, as if there were something propping it ajar.

Serdor was kneeling down on the threshold. "Have you found something?" asked Caradoc.

The minstrel nodded vigorously. "It's a book—but *not* an old one, like the rest of these down here. Look!"

He rose to his feet and presented Caradoc with a small volume bound in brown leather. The cover, apart from some dust off the floor, was bright and new. Caradoc turned the book over in his hands. "It's a breviary," he announced.

"And it's been printed, not handwritten," said Serdor. "Judging by the signs, this was just dropped here by accident. And not very long ago."

Caradoc opened the flyleaf. The owner's name leaped out at him from the page, inscribed there in a scholar's elegant bookhand: "Caithmar Caerlyoch." As the mage stared at the name, he became all at once aware of a familiar tingling in his fingertips.

The influx of power carried with it a strong imperative. Without thinking, Caradoc stepped past Serdor into the south room. The tingling in his fingers grew stronger, spreading along his hands. He felt almost as if someone were tugging at him with pleading insistancy. All at once he realized what it meant: the owner of the book was alive, and not very far away!

Not far away, but in desperate need of help. The revelation drove every other consideration momentarily from Caradoc's mind. He closed his eyes, trying to focus on what the Magia was telling him. His mage senses impelled him toward the door to the west. He threw it open and kept moving, intent on following the call that was drawing him on.

Serdor heard the door creak open and swing back. Starting up from placing his most recent marker, he called, "Caradoc! Wait!" and sprang after his friend in alarm. He chased Caradoc through three more doorways, and eventually overtook him. "Caradoc, what are you doing?" he protested. "You're going to get us lost!" Then he saw the expression on the mage's face and abruptly fell silent.

Caradoc's green eyes held a look of intense concentration. He said tersely, "There's a mage lying badly injured somewhere off to the north and west of where we are at the moment. The Magia will guide me to him, but we've got to hurry. There isn't much time."

Serdor blinked in mute astonishment. Then he

nodded and fell into step behind his friend. Guided by senses subtler than either sight or hearing, Caradoc hurried onward. The fifth door he opened gave access not to another room, but to a rock-walled tunnel. "Do you think this might be some kind of secret exit from the priory?" murmured Serdor. Caradoc merely shrugged the question aside and strode on.

After forty feet the tunnel split three ways. Caradoc unerringly chose the central branch and quickened his pace. He led Serdor without hesitation along a series of twists in the passage until they arrived at a point where the corridor they were following made a goosenecked turn. A chill current of moving air tugged at their torchfires, carrying with it a charnel stench of fire and death. Caradoc swore under his breath and sprang forward. Hand on his sword hilt, Serdor darted after him.

The tunnel mouth was half choked with the charred remains of burned scrub brush. Heedless of himself, Caradoc forced a way through the smoldering barrier and stepped outside. Here he came to an abrupt halt. Hearing his friend's sharp intake of breath, Serdor hurried forward to join him. Then he too swallowed hard and turned his eyes away.

The earth outside the passage was littered with blackened corpses.

Surviving shreds of cloth and metal identified the dead men as mages. His stomach muscles knotted tight in sick horror, Serdor whispered, "My God, they must have run into some kind of ambush."

Caradoc nodded. But he was recovering his resolution. "Come on," he said, pulling at Serdor's arm. "We've still got a chance to save one man anyway."

Beyond the ring of burned bushes, the ground fell away, sloping downward toward a line of dark alder trees. A ribbon of running water glinted in the light of their torches. "That's where we want to go," said Caradoc, pointing, and set out down the hill.

At the stream's edge they came across a path. The

path ran parallel to the water for several hundred feet before it entered the fringes of a thick woods. Though it was dark under the trees, the Magia showed Caradoc a trampled trail through the underbrush leading away from the path itself. Turning aside, he followed it for thirty paces until he reached the edge of a drooping stand of elderberry bushes. There he knelt and pushed aside a screen of brown brittle leaves. A dark shape lay tumbled on the ground among the twisted roots, voiceless between shock and agony.

The other mage had been badly burned, but he was still breathing. "Here—take my torch," said Caradoc to Serdor. "I'll see what I can do for him."

The minstrel nodded. "I'll stand watch," he said.

Caradoc reached out with gentle hands to bestow on the injured man the healing power that reposed in his touch. Backing off several paces, Serdor found himself wishing there had been time to let someone else in the party know where they were going and why. Had the circumstances been any less urgent, it would have been sheer folly for them to strike off on their own into unfamiliar territory. Remembering the corpses scattered about the exit from the library vault, he decided it would be a good idea to keep his hands free for his weapons, if need be.

He bent down and planted both torches in the loose cold earth, then straightened up to listen to the surrounding night. He could hear nothing stirring but the wind among the frostbitten branches; even so, he could not rid himself of the sense that the shadows held secret movements, noiseless and subtle. To test his feelings, he turned away from the torchlight and ducked into the shadows to the right of the trail.

Stepping lightly over dry twigs, he pushed his way carefully through the underbrush. He had covered only a dozen paces before a murky flicker of motion, glimpsed out of the corner of his eye, made him stop short and look back. His darting glance picked out a shadowy shape among the leaves that hadn't been there a moment before. Before he could shout out a warning to Caradoc, another dark figure shot up out of the bushes beside him and aimed a hammering punch toward his jaw.

Agile though he was, Serdor wasn't quite quick enough to evade the blow. Gauntleted knuckles split open his lip and sent him tumbling back into the throttling grip of another pair of shadows. Heavy hands smothered his second attempted outcry. A cold voice hissed in his ear, "I'd come quietly if I were you."

The tone was menacing, but so far Serdor had seen no blades drawn. He drooped in his captors' grasp, as though in capitulation. Then, when they allowed their hard vigilance to relax a fraction, he hooked a sharp-pointed elbow backward to thump one of his captors squarely in the midriff.

It was a street urchin's trick, and it got the desired result. As soon as his mouth was free, Serdor uttered a breathless shout of alarm. It was all he had time for before his first assailant clipped him a second time across the face. This blow was hard enough to knock him senseless.

FOLLOW MY LEADER

HARLECH AND JAMIE GREENHAM RANGED south and west through a whole series of small cubicles until they finally fetched up against blank walls on two sides of a corner. Turning north, they made their way in a straight line through five more cells until the sound of voices ahead of them made them pause in their tracks.

One of the voices belonged unmistakably to the captain of the *Mermaid*. Two rooms later the two parties joined up. "We havenae found anything worth a thrip'ny nail," reported Harlech. "What about you?"

"Nothing particularly edifying," said Gudmar, "apart from the fact that the priory boasts a complete collection of the homilies of St. Merrow in the saint's own hand. Let's head back to the vestibule. Maybe Serdor and Caradoc will have turned up something of more immediate interest."

The four men retraced their steps to the cell at the foot of the stairs. Margoth and Evelake were crowded side by side on the bottommost step, poring over an illuminated bestiary they had borrowed from one of the adjacent rooms. They both scrambled to their feet at the sight of Gudmar and the others. "That's four out of six, anyway," said Margoth. "I gather you didn't cross paths with Serdor and my brother?"

"We were hoping to find them here ahead of us," said Gudmar. "Since they're not back, we'd better wait."

Minutes ticked by without the two absent members of the party reappearing. Margoth began to fidget. "Where *are* they?" she wondered out loud. "I hope the silly fools haven't got themselves lost."

Evelake turned to Gudmar. "What do you think? Should we go looking for them?"

Gudmar's golden eyes had hardened. "That's beginning to sound like a good idea. Jamie, go call down the rest of the men. We may need numbers. . . ."

The two missing men had laid down markers. Initially it proved easy enough for their companions to follow the route they had taken from cell to cell. Then all at once the markings came to an end. "That's gey queer," said Harlech with a scowl. "They've been careful enough up tae now, ye'd no' expect 'em tae lose their wits at this point."

"Whatever the case, they didn't just vanish into thin air," said Gudmar. "Check the adjoining rooms to see if we can pick up their trail from here."

A disturbance in the dust on the floor in the cubicle to the south suggested that someone had traversed the room not long before. The fuzzy tread marks wove in and out through a number of other cells. Following the faint signs of passing, the search party came at last to a door that opened out into a tunnel. Gudmar paused just inside the tunnel mouth to examine a sooty mark on the wall. When the soot came away on his fingers, he gave the residue an experimental sniff, then smiled thinly. "Wood ashes: somebody got a little careless with his torch," he announced. "I would say we're on the right track."

They followed the passage to a three-way fork. Gudmar sent splinter groups off to investigate the side branches while he and the rest of the party continued on down the middle corridor. "I smell something burning," said Margoth.

"Aye, me too," said Harlech.

"We're coming to the end of the tunnel. I can see the opening up ahead," said Gudmar. "The rest of you wait here. I'm going to take a look outside."

He was gone only a few minutes. When he came back, they saw that the expression on his face was grim. "Somebody else besides the mages who lived at the priory must have known about their so-called secret exit," he said bleakly. "Five of them were caught leaving the tunnel. They . . . didn't die easily."

A silence followed this ominous announcement. "What about Serdor and my brother?" faltered Margoth.

"There wasn't any sign of either of them to be seen at a glance," said Gudmar. "We'll have to examine the ground more closely." He added, "I suggest you leave the looking to us. . . ."

Exploring by torchfire, aided by the rheumy light of a pallid moon, the men from the *Mermaid* discovered two sets of footprints running away from the edge of the fire-blackened clearing toward the millstream at the bottom of the hill. "One set of prints demonstrably larger than the other," observed Gudmar, bending down to examine the evidence. "It certainly looks as if our two friends went this way." He straightened up and turned to his waiting men. "All right, lads, fall in and keep it quiet. We're in for an unscheduled game of follow-my-leader."

The party moved off in open formation behind their captain. "I don't know what possessed those two lunatics to go chundering off on their own in the dark," muttered

Margoth to Gudmar, above the padding rustle of
stealthy feet. "All I can say is, they'd better have a *good*
explanation ready!"

Gudmar wasn't deceived by her waspish tone. He
had not traveled for weeks in her company without
learning that in Margoth's case fear often manifested
itself as anger. And so he addressed himself to the
anxiety, not the temper. "Take it easy," he advised. "All
the signs indicate that they weren't in any trouble when
they left the priory. With any luck, we'll find them safe."

The bright sparkle in Margoth's blue eyes might
have been angry tears. "I hope so," she said.

The trail led them northward along the east bank of
the stream, where there was a path overhung by alder
trees. The party from the *Mermaid* followed the path
until they came to a point where the brush to the right of
the stream had been beaten down in a narrow swathe. It
was here, among the baffling interplay of moonlight and
shadows that Gudmar stumbled across the scene of a
struggle.

Motioning to his men to stay back, he searched the
area thoroughly and came back with a scrap of torn cloth
in his hand. He held out the scrap to Margoth, his face
sober. "That's a piece torn from Caradoc's cloak," he
said. "He and Serdor must have put up a fight." He
added, "For what it's worth, whoever jumped them
apparently wanted them alive. We'll do whatever we
must to get them back. I promise."

Margoth took the rag with trembling fingers. Her
initial horror and dismay was surmounted by a rising
tide of anger. She was suddenly furious with Caradoc for
being so willful, so impulsive, so thoughtless as to
blunder straight into danger, taking Serdor with him.
Her ire in that moment was almost blinding in its
intensity. She only dimly heard Gudmar's conversation
with Harlech: ". . . captors must have taken to the
water . . . no sign of tracks on either side of the bank . . .
virtually impossible to tell whether they went upstream
or down. . . ."

"Wonderful!" thought Margoth bitterly to herself. "We don't even know where to begin to look!" Her anger seethed in her nerve ends. Blistering words of recrimination boiled up in the bubbling cauldron of her outrage. "Caradoc, you *idiot!*" she cried mentally to her absent brother. "Where are you?"

The question flew up, not like words consciously directed by reason, but like a blazing spark shot impulsively from the depths of her being. She was caught wholly off guard when a series of images sprang spontaneously to mind:

. . . An ice-cold streambed with yellow moonlight slanting across the water from right to left . . . a naked willow tree trailing its skeletal branches in a dark, half-frozen pool . . . a muddy uphill path slippery with dead leaves . . . a great outcropping of stone, shaped like the prow of a ship . . . "There's another entrance around the back of the hill," Caradoc's voice informed her. "At the top of a rockfall. There are guards. . . ."

The transition from pictures to words was so smooth and instantaneous that Margoth accepted the information without hesitating. Then she realized what was happening!

Astonishment all but took her breath away. Unable to make any audible sound, she framed her brother's name in a single silent thought, piercing as a shriek. *"Caradoc!"*

His acknowledgment came not in words, but in a surge of emotion that told her he was profoundly relieved to find her capable of communicating by means of magecraft. Her own brain reeling under the impact of this momentous discovery, Margoth groped for the presence of mind to ask him one of several clamoring questions. "Are you hurt?"

His response was the mental equivalent of an impatient shake of the head. "What about Serdor?" queried Margoth.

This time his response was a scalding flare of anger and frustration. "I don't know. They separated us. . . ."

His temper was rising. Their rapport faltered as he struggled to keep his fury under control. "Who are *they*?" demanded Margoth.

Uncertainty. "Men in masks . . . at least a score . . . well armed. They took us by surprise—"

The fragile link between them abruptly dissolved. Left stranded on her own side of a suddenly unbridgeable gulf, Margoth gave an involuntary gasp of protest. "Caradoc!" she cried out in silent anguish. There was no response. "Caradoc!" she called again, unaware that she had spoken his name aloud this time. A pair of wiry hands clasped her arms above the elbow. She roused herself with a start to find Evelake gazing at her, his brown eyes intensely concerned. He said, "Margoth, what's the matter? Are you ill?"

Margoth shook her head, surprised to find herself weak at the knees. "Not ill—just a bit stunned," she said. She added distractedly, "I've always wondered what it would be like to experience Orison. Now I know."

"Orison!" Evelake stared at her.

"I don't know what else to call it," said Margoth. "I was thinking about Caradoc—and all of a sudden, he was . . . it was as if he were speaking to me, only in my mind! I could hear—feel—his thoughts. And he could hear mine!"

Evelake's brown eyes widened at this startling disclosure. "Are you sure—no, forget I asked that. Is he—are they all right?"

"Caradoc's not hurt," said Margoth, then bit her lip. "He didn't know about Serdor."

"Where are they?"

"He showed me some landmarks," said Margoth. "I'd recognize them if I saw them again. Their captors took them upstream—I could tell that from the angle of the moonlight."

Evelake caught her by the hand. "Come on!" he said. "You need to tell Gudmar all this!"

The captain of the *Mermaid* listened to Margoth's

revelation with interest. "We certainly have no better clues to go on at this point," he said. "Margoth, I know you share some measure of your brother's gift. If you're prepared to trust this vision of yours, I'm ready to trust your guidance."

When she affirmed her readiness with a nod, he put two fingers to his lips and whistled, signaling his men to regroup. Once the band had reassembled for marching, he informed them of the decision to pursue the chase upstream. The men traveled in single file along the east bank of the stream. Margoth went in front with Gudmar, Evelake and Harlech following close behind.

The moonlight was bright enough to allow them to extinguish their torches. The whole party maintained silence, speaking seldom, and then only in whispers. The frost in the air turned their breath to steam. Ice was forming among the reeds.

After twisting and turning for nearly half a mile through ever-thickening woodland, the millstream broadened out into a black rime-edged pond. On the far side of the pool, the trees crowded close to the water's brink. Margoth caught Gudmar by the sleeve and pointed: twenty yards farther up the opposite bank, a gnarled and naked willow tree leaned out over the surface of the pond, its branch tips touching the water in the moonlight.

The pool itself looked to be at least chest-deep. "I don't much fancy a full wetting in this temperature," said Gudmar, "and I don't suppose our friends up ahead of us will have wanted to risk it, either. We'll backtrack as far as the millcourse and make our crossing there."

It meant retracing their steps for twenty-five yards, but they were able to ford the stream more or less dry-shod with the help of a fallen tree. On the west bank, the soft mud showed signs of having been very recently disturbed. "This looks promising," said Gudmar with grim satisfaction. "Maybe we'll be lucky enough to find some tracks."

The party carried on, pushing through the shrubbery that bordered the water until they reached the willow tree. Just beyond it they came suddenly upon the beginnings of a path. "Well, I'll be hoist on a landsman's gibbet," rumbled Harlech with a shake of his head. When Margoth turned to look at him, he gave her a beetling grin through his beard. "I'll no' deny, lassie, I was thinkin' this could well turn out tae be a wild-goose chase," he told her. "But now I'm thinkin' we might just catch ourselves a whole flock at that!"

Closely hemmed in among the trees, the path at first was hardly more than a deer track, but here and there the ground cover had been displaced to show the imprint of a booted foot. Gudmar took the lead, shouldering the branches aside for the benefit of Margoth and Evelake, treading closely on his heels. A quarter of a mile farther along the zigzagging trail, Margoth found what she was looking for: a steep slope with naked hardwoods shading off into thickets of evergreen trees. Above and beyond the treetops, two or three furlongs distant still, the moonlight was glinting off a rising knoll of bare rock. The crown of the hillock took the shape of a ship's pointed prow.

"That's it!" she whispered excitedly to her companions. "That's where my vision ended. That must be the entrance to the enemies' lair!"

The party crept closer by careful degrees, taking every advantage of the tree cover on the slopes. Gazing up at the ship-rock from the shelter of a tall pine, Evelake saw something move against the moonlit sky. Metal flashed fleetingly in the shadows crowning the knoll itself. "Gudmar!" he breathed. "I've just seen a sentry posted on top of that great boulder!"

Gudmar looked where the young Warden pointed. "Yes, I see him, too," he told the boy, then surveyed the prospect through narrowed eyes. "Whoever chose that place for a base camp is no fool."

"Hard to get to," agreed Evelake soberly, "and easy to defend."

"Besides being high enough up tae gi' their lookouts

a corbie's eye view of the territory," growled Harlech.
"It's going tae be a tricksy piece o' work getting up yon
slope wi'out being spotted."

"Our chances will be better if we circle around to the
dark side of the hill," said Evelake. "Even if there are
extra pickets posted on the west slope, they won't be able
to see any better without lights than we will."

"What about leavin' a few of us behind here tae
create a diversion?" suggested Harlech. "Gi' our friends
a row at the front door, and mebbe they'll pay less
attention tae what's going on around the back. . . ."

CHOICE OF EVILS

CARADOC'S UNKNOWN CAPTORS TRUSSED HIM up hand
and foot before leaving him alone in a tiny chamber that
was more a cave than a room, but was, at least, warm.
Abandoned to his own bleak thoughts, he wrestled for a
time with his bonds to no good purpose. Firmly knotted,
the cords resisted the test of his strength. Eventually,
sweating profusely, and worn out by vain exertions, he
was forced to admit defeat.

Unable to escape from his bonds, he was similarly
unable to escape the dour conviction that he was largely
responsible for his own present predicament. In his
burning zeal to respond to the promptings of the Magia,
he had thrown all caution to the winds with criminal
fecklessness. Worse, he had dragged his best friend into
danger with him—not for the first time. "Fool that I
am," he thought savagely, "at least I should have had the
sense to send Serdor back to tell the rest of the party
where I was going and why." But, of course, he hadn't.
And now they were all three prisoners: Serdor and
himself, and the injured mage Caithmar. Caradoc re-

flected bitterly that in saving the Hospitaller's life, he had conveniently provided their captors with another victim to question.

He could make only guesses about the intentions and affinities of the masked raiders. With the aid of the Magia, he might have been able to learn more, but the sensible power that had guided him to the aid of a fellow mage had been all but exhausted through his labors of healing. Serdor's warning cry had roused him from Orison while he still had some small measure of the Magia's virtue remaining to him. That virtue he had poured out in his attempt to contact his sister, hoping that their shared aptitude for magecraft would bridge the separation between them.

He might, instead, have attempted to probe the mind of one of his masked captors. But for such an attempt to succeed, he knew he would have had to overcome the victim's innate resistance—a task demanding a considerable expenditure of strength. Lacking the reserves to force the issue, Caradoc had turned to Margoth, staking all he had left to give in trying to communicate with her, mind to mind.

Already tied to him by their bond of close kinship, she had felt his call; her own instincts had shaped her response. As a result of their brief moment of rapport, she knew enough—he hoped—to lead Gudmar and the rest of the party to this forest stronghold. But as Caradoc sat glowering in his torchlit cell, he began to wonder whether or not he had done the right thing. If the raiders he and Serdor had encountered were members of the same berserker force which had razed Yske to the ground, there might be individuals among them capable of arts other than fighting. Caradoc shuddered at the idea of his companions walking into what might turn out to be a necromancer's death trap.

Or torture chamber. His thoughts turned again to Serdor, whom he had not seen since they had first entered the cave warren under the hill. The possibility that his friend might at that very moment be writhing under some agonizing form of inquisition made Caradoc's blood run cold. He remembered only too vividly what had happened to Serdor back in Pernatha when the two of them had fallen afoul of one of Borthen Berigeld's lieutenants, the giant known as Muirtagh.

Muirtagh had wanted information concerning the whereabouts of Evelake Whitfauconer. When Caradoc had refused to disclose that information, he had been forced to watch helplessly while Muirtagh subjected the minstrel to a brutal ordeal of abuse. The sight of his friend in torment had broken Caradoc's resistance and loosened his tongue. It had been a terrible price to pay for an error in judgment.

All Caradoc's most harrowing recollections of that episode were coming back to haunt him now. He saw again, with the eyes of memory, Serdor lying unconscious on a bare stone floor, his face all but unrecognizable for the bruises, his body burned and broken. If the Magia had not imbued Caradoc with the grace to perform a miracle of healing, the minstrel would have died. The possibility that Serdor could end up facing a second excruciating ordeal turned Caradoc soul-sick with self-blame.

He tried to calm himself, to steady his spirit in humble petition, but his consuming need for direct action was not at that moment to be governed by reason or discipline. Too agitated to concentrate, too angry and distraught to pray, he resumed his struggles, writhing in his bonds till his joints groaned in protest. His contortions had turned him around and his eye fell upon a small firepit which had been dug out of the floor in the opposite corner of the rude cell and which was no doubt the source of its warmth.

The pit was covered by a crude iron grid. Caradoc bum-scraped his way across the room to take a closer look.

The stone encircling the pit felt warm beneath his haunches. Leaning down sideways with his face as close to the grid as he could get it, Caradoc felt a sullen wave of

heat against his cheeks. Sucking air, he blew lightly on
the embers. His breath scattered a blanketing layer of
ashes, exposing a cluster of live coals beneath.

Trying not to think too closely about what he was
about to do, Caradoc straightened up and glanced over
at the door. The fact that it had neither lock nor latch
meant that there was certain to be at least one guard
posted on the other side of it. Any betraying sound would
demand investigation. Caradoc could only hope that he
would be able to find within himself the fortitude to keep
silence.

Wriggling back from the edge of the firepit, Caradoc
set the heels of his boots cautiously against the edge of
the grid and gave it a careful nudge with his bound feet.
The metal covering shifted with a gravelly rasp. Caradoc
stopped pushing and held his breath to see if the noise
had attracted the attention of anyone outside the room.
He counted to thirty, slowly. When nothing happened,
he gave the grating another nudge.

It took him three more tries to work the grid away
from the mouth of the pit. Uncovered, the coals flared up
into fresh life. He gazed down at the pulsing embers and
felt cold sweat begin to break out between his shoulder
blades.

His pulse quickening, he slewed his body around so
that his back was to the fire. Feeling behind him with his
fingers, he groped for the edge of the pit. Warmth rippled
up off the ashes. Cocking his wrists, he leaned back and
lowered his bound hands toward the glowing coals
below.

Heat scored his knuckles, causing him to jerk away.
Clenching his teeth, Caradoc paused a moment to school
his reflexes. Then he forced his arms downward, planting
his hands palm up on top of the bed of embers.

Searing pain flashed up from the backs of his hands.
Biting back the sharp outcry that rose to his lips,
Caradoc struggled to keep his wrists in place long enough
for the cords to catch fire. Agony blurred his vision and
took his breath away, but he held on in choking silence
until he felt a sudden slackening of the ropes.

As his straining hands broke away from one another, he toppled forward in a gasping heap on the floor. Reaction turned him momentarily faint, but after lying prone for a minute or two, he mastered himself sufficiently to sit up. The skin of his wrists and the backs of his hands were scorched, but he could still move his fingers freely. Breathing hard, he reached down and went to work on the knots that bound his legs.

His ankles were stiff, but there was still feeling in his feet. He staggered upright, then stooped to retrieve the rope from the floor. It was a good stout bight, about six feet long. Folding it double, the mage took a firm grip on either end and padded over to the badly hung door.

The paneling was cracked and warped with age. Putting an eye to one of the crevices, Caradoc could see the flicker of torchlight, and a dark silhouette in the shape of a man's arm and shoulder. The guard was standing a few yards beyond the threshold in the middle of what Caradoc recalled was a narrow passageway. Smiling grimly to himself, despite the throbbing pain in his wrists, the mage set his shoulder to the planking and gave the door an experimental push.

Rusty hinges squawked in protest. Throwing care aside, Caradoc rammed the portal wide open and lunged like a wolf for the guard as the other man spun around. The mage took a passing cut along his right thigh as his opponent made an awkward swipe at him with a shortsword. Then he was inside the masked raider's guard, grappling for the other man's throat.

With strength and desperation on his side, Caradoc managed to get a grip on his opponent's windpipe in time to stifle an attempted cry for help. Whipping the rope around the raider's neck, he drew it tight with a jerk and hissed in the other man's ear, "One false move, and I'll crush your larynx. Now hand over your weapon."

The raider defied him with a glare, then gagged as Caradoc gave the rope a twist. "I know you're not deaf," growled the mage, "so do as I say, and do it quietly."

His captive's blade was looped to his wrist with a length of braided leather. His breath coming in shallow gasps, the raider detached it and proffered it hiltfirst to Caradoc. Caradoc adjusted his improvised noose, then plucked the sword from the other man's gauntleted hand. "Now," continued the mage through set teeth, "you are going to take me to where my two companions are being held. . . ."

After a brief discussion concerning strategy, the party from the *Mermaid* split up. Harlech took six men with him. It had been decided that his party would launch a feint attack on the cave's front entrance to draw as many enemies as possible out into the open. The rest of the landing force, including Evelake and Margoth, remained with Gudmar. With the *Mermaid*'s captain leading, the second group set out under cover, working their way by careful degrees around to the west side of the tall hill. The ground there was rough and broken. "Listen!" breathed Evelake. "I hear water running."

"So do I," said Gudmar. "It's coming from over there."

Guided by the sound, the party made their way stealthily through the underbrush until they came across a small ravine with a swift vein of water running along the bottom of it. "This must be the stream Caradoc was talking about," said Gudmar. "Right, lads: keep your eyes and ears open, and your mouths closed. It's dead silence from here on out."

They followed the ravine upward in a cautious series of starts and stops. The way was strewn with boulders and fallen trees. The crown of the knoll, eight hundred feet above them, was outlined in cold shimmery light. "The moon will be over the yardarm in less than another quarter of an hour," muttered Gudmar to Margoth and Evelake. "I want us inside the entrance by the time its light clears the hilltop."

He turned to his men. "Jamie! Geordie! You two come with me. The rest of you wait here."

Two shadows brushed past Evelake to join their captain. All three men faded noiselessly into the darkness farther up the brae. The young Warden edged closer to Margoth and offered her his hand. She gripped it tightly with nervous fingers. Neither of them spoke, but kept their eyes fixed on the shadows overhead.

A yellowish sliver of moon appeared above the ship-rock on the hilltop. Even as the surrounding gloom began to brighten, a broad-shouldered silhouette emerged from behind a large boulder. "All clear!" hissed Gudmar's voice. "Come on!"

The rest of the group sprang into motion, scrambling up through the scree and scrub. At the head of the ravine, they found their two scouts in the act of binding three unconscious prisoners together. "Leave them here for the moment," ordered Gudmar in an undertone. "The mouth of the tunnel is behind that screen of bushes."

The tunnel entrance itself was dark, but there was faint torchlight to be seen beyond the first turning. "You all know your-positions," said Gudmar. "Prisoners are more useful to us than corpses, but don't get yourselves killed over the issue. Now let's go."

There was a furtive rustle as the men readied their weapons. Once past the first bend, the passage slanted off to their left. The floor sloped upward at a noticeable incline. After thirty paces, the narrow corridor hooked back to the right. Gudmar spotted a lighted doorway farther up the tunnel. He beckoned two of his followers forward and signaled them to investigate.

On the threshold, the *Mermaid*'s advance guard came face to face with three masked men armed with cudgels. The dull thud of wood against metal was attended by a warning shout from one of the defenders. There was a startled clatter of roused activity from farther up the winding corridor. "That's done it," snapped Gudmar. "The rest of you with me, quickly!"

He sprinted toward the next turn in the passage. Leaving their embattled companions locked in combat, the rest of the *Mermaid*'s party sprang after their captain. Just beyond the bend, Gudmar and his close followers met up with four more resident defenders, naked swords in hand.

Lips drawn back in a snarl, Gudmar raked his own weapon along the leader's foible, so that the two blades locked hilt on hilt. A powerful twist of his wrist wrenched the defender's sword away. With a kick to the groin, Gudmar sent the other man reeling back into the midst of his companions. "Jamie! Piers! Hold the rear guard!" he rapped over his shoulder, then raced on.

Margoth had a dagger ready to hurl. Sword in hand, Evelake pelted along beside her, a few strides behind Geordie Glendowr, the ship's blacksmith, who was keeping pace with Gudmar. Two more turns of the corridor brought them to the foot of a wooden ladder leading up to a ledge three feet across. A wooden door had been set into the wall beyond the head of the ladder.

Gudmar was first up the ladder with Geordie right behind him. "Evelake! You and Margoth keep back!" hissed Gudmar over his shoulder. "We'll handle the door."

He and Geordie took up positions on either side of the threshold. On Gudmar's signal, they put their shoulders to the paneling and heaved. The aged hinges burst and the timbers gave way. Gudmar and Geordie plunged through the opening, then fetched up short, blade points upraised.

The chamber they had entered was not large: a rough-cut oval fifteen feet across. Three figures in masks were barring their way to a second doorway at the opposite end of the chamber. The figure in the middle was clearly the leader, a tall, supple figure who carried a finely balanced blade. "Clever of you to find your way in here," said the raider captain with icy clarity. "It would be even cleverer of you to surrender now, while you still have a life to preserve."

"You are holding prisoner two associates of mine," said Gudmar, his voice as sharp and level as his blade. "If you're so eager to preserve lives, I suggest you *surrender* them, because I have no intention of leaving unless I take them with me."

Light, cold eyes flashed at him from behind the anonymity of the mask. "You're free to try and take them," said the raider captain. "Only you'll have to get past me first."

The raider's declaration carried clearly as far as the passage outside. Evelake froze with his free hand on the upper rung of the ladder. He shot a lightning glance back at Margoth, his brown eyes wide and startled. "I know that voice!" he exclaimed. And before Margoth could forestall him, bounded up onto the ledge.

In the room beyond, steel clashed, shrieked, and clashed again. Evelake leaped for the open doorway, his cloak billowing behind him. "Wait for me!" cried Margoth. She scrambled up the ladder after him, but he was already past the threshold.

Inside the room, the masked raider traded ripostes with Gudmar in a ringing shower of sparks. "*Halt!* both of you!" shouted Evelake. And hurled himself toward them across the room.

His own sword shuddered as he rammed the blade forward, deflecting both their thrusts in a scream of skidding metal. Aghast, Gudmar called out sharply, "My lord, *stand back!*"

He made a move to seize the young Warden's arm, to wrench him out of harm's way. "Leave me! I know what I'm doing!" snapped Evelake.

His voice carried the incisive ring of steel. Turning, he raked back his hood so that the torchlight fell full upon his face. Chin held high, he challenged the masked raider captain with brown eyes ablaze. "Well, Tessa Ekhanghar?" he said. "Are you truly prepared to strike *me* down?"

The firm lips below the edge of the concealing mask parted with an audible gasp. Their owner's broadsword wavered, the weapon point sinking to the floor with a light clang. Left with his blade unopposed, Gudmar took a guarded step backward. Seeing that their leaders had separated, the other combatants in the room broke off the fight and fell back, glowering at one another in darkling uncertainty.

The leader of the raiders was staring hard at the boy who had so forcibly brought hostilities to a standstill.

Drawing breath, he spoke the young Warden's name aloud in blank astonishment. "Evelake!" Then repeated it with stunned conviction. *"Evelake Whitfauconer!"*

"Alive and well, as you can see," said Evelake shortly. "Now call off your men—both of you—before this misunderstanding gets somebody killed!"

THE FORESTERS OF GANDIA

ON THE EAST SIDE OF the hill, a hundred and twenty yards short of the entrance to the raiders' cave-lair, everything had been silent for several minutes. Harlech Hardrada warily poked a rumpled black head up from behind the boulder he had been using for cover. His brief appearance elicited a barrage of arrows from above. He ducked back behind the rock just in time to avoid being pincushioned by half a dozen clothyard shafts.

Beside him, Rhodri Blantyn, the *Mermaid's* carpenter, swore under his breath in mingled awe and frustration. "Who the hell *are* those buggers up there?" he muttered. "You'd think they were target-shooting in broad daylight!"

Harlech peered up at the sky with a jaundiced black eye. "Broad moonlight's all ye need if ye ken your business. It may be we're no' going tae get any farther ahead at this game till the moon goes behind the hill."

"It shouldn't take that long for the captain's party to find the back entrance to that warren," protested Rhodri. "They'll be expecting us to draw off some of the opposition."

"Aye," agreed Harlech sourly. He tapped his black-bristled upper lip with the steel hook that served him in place of his left hand. "We could do wi' setting up a smoke screen, if we only had the materials on hand," he mused, then added trenchantly, "We've got naught tae lose by lighting a fire: yon shrikes ken well enough where we are already—"

"Harlech!"

The cry, pitched to a youthful tenor, came floating down from the top of the hill. The little mariner started upright and pulled a face like a gargoyle's. "Harlech!" called the voice again. "Are you there?"

"Aye!" Harlech bellowed back. "Who wants tae know?"

"Harlech, it's me—Evelake," shouted the voice. "Look—just stay there. I'm coming down to you. And I'm bringing some friends with me."

He laid stress on the word "friends." Harlech and the men with him exchanged nonplussed glances. Harlech pronounced an epithet under his breath and got to his knees to peer over the top of the boulder in the direction of the hilltop. This time there was no deadly flurry of arrows. Instead, there was a string of torches moving down on their position from the top of the knoll.

Evelake was the first to emerge from among the trees. Harlech noted that the young Warden still carried his weapons at his side. He slowly stood up. "Over here, milord," he announced.

The people with Evelake all wore foresters' green. But they weren't all men. Indicating the tall young woman at his side, the young Warden said, "Harlech, this is Lady Tessa Ekhanghar, daughter of the Marshall of Gand. She and her followers are responsible for organizing the free companies of Gandia to oppose the Du Bors invaders. Tessa," he added, "this is Harlech Hardrada, a friend of Gudmar's—and a friend of mine."

Evelake's friend was short and squat, with a face like a bulldog's. Tessa plucked off her archer's gauntlet and extended her hand. As Harlech reached out to take it, she said, "I'm glad to make your acquaintance, Master Hardrada. And I regret the misunderstanding that has taken place between your party and my own. Are any of the men with you injured?"

The little mariner showed gold-capped teeth in a mirthless grin. "There'll be no scars tae show off tae our grandchildren."

Evelake breathed a visible sigh of relief. "In that case, we'd better rejoin the others," he said. "There's more than a little talking to be done on both sides."

Tessa led the way back up the hill to the clearing in front of the entrance to the cave complex. She had to fight to keep from glancing back at Evelake every few steps just to make sure he was really present in the flesh. Her mind was buzzing with questions, but she reserved them, knowing that inquiries would have to wait until all the principals were present. In the meantime, she would only wonder at the inscrutability of providence, that it could render up both a disaster and a miracle in a single place, in a single day.

A small group of mingled foresters and seamen was waiting just outside the cave mouth. Among them were the stalwart leonine captain of the *White Mermaid* and the lissome, copper-haired woman that Evelake had introduced as Margoth Penlluathe. Tessa couldn't help noticing the other girl's enviable good looks and vibrant air of vitality. It was easy to see that she must be closely related to the tall auburn-haired stranger that Tessa and her men had captured earlier in the evening.

He was not, after all, in league with the apostate lords-spiritual who had inspired a blood-crazed rabble to make Yske into a funeral pyre. Knowing that much about him gave Tessa one less cause for worry in a situation that was becoming worse day by day. She herself had enough experience as a leader to know that a man with that much personal charisma to draw on would be a formidable enemy. Such a man could, if he chose, use his own emotions like weapons, bending other men to his will by his sheer force of personality.

Having already encountered the daunting impact of the stranger's hostility, Tessa was not disposed to accept him without some reservations. But Evelake had vouched for him with warmth and confidence. Though the young Warden was several years her junior, Tessa reminded herself that he had been accurate in his understanding of both Kherryn and Devon Du Penfallon, despite the fact that neither of them had ever been easy to get to know. She hoped he was not mistaken in trusting Margoth Penlluathe's brother so completely.

At the cave's entrance, Tessa paused to assure the red-haired girl that her brother and her brother's friend were both unharmed. Then she led the way through the main hall to a doorway in the north wall. The doorway led into a narrow winding tunnel that branched out into two passages after twenty yards. Tessa turned into the right-hand corridor, then came to a halt, her blue eyes narrowed in puzzlement.

Evelake stopped a pace behind her. "What's wrong?" he asked.

"I posted a guard before the door at the far end of this passage," said Tessa. "He's not where he's supposed to be."

Not only was the guard gone, but his auburn-haired prisoner had likewise vanished. Surveying the charred fragments of rope lying by the firepit in the room Caradoc had occupied, Tessa experienced a queer pang of chagrin mingled with a certain reluctant admiration. "Your enterprising friend appears to have given us the slip," she told Evelake with a grimace. "Patience must not be one of his virtues."

"No, it isn't," agreed Evelake. "But loyalty is one of his strong points. I suggest we check the chamber where you put my other friend, Serdor. Caradoc wouldn't have made any attempt to leave this complex without taking Serdor with him."

They hastily retraced their steps to the intersection, then took the fork to the left. As they approached the doorless room at the end of the tunnel, Tessa could feel an element of bristling tension in the air. She suspected Evelake's missing associate couldn't be far away. Before she could volunteer her opinion, a shadow moved against the backdrop of dim light from the doorway.

Steel flashed in the light of the torches as a tall man carrying a broadsword stepped across the threshold.

The torches also caught the rich rutilant sheen of dark red hair. Evelake called out, "Caradoc!" and shot past Tessa to interpose himself between them.

The red-haired man checked sharply. His face lost some of its sternness in his first startled instant of surprise. His keen emerald gaze flashed past Evelake's slender figure, flickering like wildfire among the rest of the people present until it came to rest upon the face of his sister. Reading the expression in her eyes, he abruptly relaxed and lowered the point of his sword. "Don't tell me—let me guess," he said. "There's been an unfortunate mistake."

It wasn't often that Tessa found herself obliged to lift her eyes in order to look a man squarely in the face. Refusing to be diverted by the novelty, she said shortly, "Not as unfortunate as it could have been, considering that both your party and mine were expecting to meet up with an enemy. Some of my followers are from this area. After what we found at Yske, you're lucky I didn't let them execute you on principle."

"In that case, we're very grateful," said a well-modulated tenor voice from behind the man in the doorway.

When the owner of the voice stepped out into the corridor, his friends saw that he was sporting a cut lip and a black eye. The girl Margoth gave a small gasp of dismay. "My self-esteem hurts far worse," Serdor told her with a rueful grimace. "I've always prided myself on having good ears, but I didn't hear a thing until these people were right on top of us."

Caradoc Penlluathe's green eyes retained their inner fire, muted but present. He said to Tessa, "The mage you brought here along with us—how is he?"

"As comfortable as we could make him," said Tessa. "But he hasn't regained consciousness."

"A mage!" exclaimed Gudmar. "A survivor from St. Merrow's?"

Caradoc nodded. "We found a breviary that belongs

to him in the labyrinth. When I handled it, I sensed his presence, and so Serdor and I set out to find him—"

"Will he live?" Gudmar was keenly interested.

"He was badly burned," said Caradoc, "but he'll recover in due time."

Tessa wondered how he could be so sure of that. She said tartly, "I hope you haven't damaged my sergeant too badly?"

"I merely gave him a fright," said Caradoc, with a coolness that Tessa found nettling. "He was taken rather by surprise."

It occurred to her only belatedly to look at his hands. Strong, long-fingered, and shapely, they showed raw burns between wrist and knuckles. "Serves him right for his arrogance," thought Tessa. All the same, it had taken courage to do what he had done. Aware that he was looking down at her, she drew herself up sharply and turned to the young Warden. "My personal quarters—such as they are—are located on the opposite side of the main hall. They are at your disposal, if you would like some place private in which to talk."

Not knowing where the boy had been, or what he had been doing during the months he had been missing, she did not want to press for an explanation in public. She hoped, however, that he would not reject an opportunity to confide his story to her alone. Nor did he disappoint her. "By all means," said Evelake. "We have a lot of catching up to do."

SHADOWS OF MEMORY

THE OTHER MEMBERS OF THE party from the *Mermaid* dispersed, claiming other business to attend to. While Gudmar was arranging to send a message back to Giles Penrith, whom he had left in charge of the ship, Caradoc

departed with the others to look in on the injured mage
from St. Merrow's. Left alone with Tessa, Evelake held
his peace as he accompanied her to her quarters: two tiny
connecting cubicles separated from the main hall by a
short passage.

A curtain of hides had been hung across the doorway to keep in the warmth given off by a brazier set down
in the middle of the small room. Tessa moved the curtain
aside and held it, allowing Evelake to precede her.
Entering behind him, she said, "I suggest you sit on my
bedroll. It'll be softer and warmer than the floor."

The young Warden plumped himself down without
ceremony on one end of the heap of furs and blankets,
and began to pull off his gloves. "I'm afraid you'll have to
overlook the general lack of amenities," continued Tessa.
"My squire Owain does his best to look after my
comfort, but we're obliged to travel light."

Evelake crossed his ankles and wrapped his arms
around his knees. "Don't apologize," he said. "I've been
in worse places."

Looking at him more closely, Tessa didn't doubt
that for a minute. Though his movements were sure and
supple, his light bones might easily have carried more
flesh. And his hands, now that she could see them, were
marred with rough calluses, like a peasant-laborer's. He
said with a wry smile, "You've beaten me at swordplay
far too often in the past to stand on ceremony now.
Please sit down."

Disarmed of all would-be formality, Tessa took him
at his word. Once she was settled beside him, Evelake
continued. "I know I owe you an account of myself," he
said, "but before I begin, I'd be grateful if you could give
me news of the Du Penfallons."

Tessa drew a deep breath. "How much do you know
already?"

"Not a great deal. I know that Lord Arvech is dead,"
said Evelake. "And I know that Devon chose to defend
Gand Castle, rather than yield it over to my half brother's minions. But that's all."

"Gand Castle is still under siege," said Tessa baldly. "At last report, both Devon and my father were still alive. But the garrison is low on fuel and supplies. Their situation is growing more difficult with each passing day."

"Maybe together we can change that," said Evelake. Tessa had never before heard him speak with such grave resolution. He paused briefly, then asked, "What about Kherryn?"

Knowing something of Evelake's feelings toward Devon's sister, Tessa wished she could have reassured him that all was well. Painfully honest, she said, "All that I know for certain is that she entered Kirkwell Abbey as a supplicant right after her father's death. That was over two months ago."

"You've heard nothing from her since?"

Tessa shook her head. "Only rumors, I'm afraid." She hesitated a moment, then asked, "Are you aware that St. Alanin's Hospice in Farrowaithe was destroyed by an earthquake?"

He nodded. "Caradoc had immediate knowledge of the fact by a revelation from the Magia."

This came as a startling surprise. Tessa's men had searched Caradoc Penlluathe without finding anything like a magestone on his person. She said protestingly, "But . . . he's not a mage."

"Oh yes, he is," said Evelake, with a strange half smile that she found difficult to interpret. "Caradoc's story and mine are bound up together," he continued. "Suffice it to say, for now, that his gifts are unique. What are these rumors you mentioned?"

"I don't know how much truth—if any—there is in them," said Tessa cautiously. "A great many people fled Farrowaithe on the day of the earthquake. Among the refugees was a small group of mages who—for one reason or another—hadn't been present at St. Alanin's when the disaster struck. As near as I can make out, they made their way to Cheswythe and reported to the magister in charge of the hospice there. My principal contact—the ordinaire in charge of the infirmary at Tavistock—said he'd heard there was a little dark-haired girl traveling in the mages' company. But he didn't know her name."

"I see." Having accepted this meager information with a nod, Evelake lapsed into silence. After studying the boy for a moment, Tessa could contain her curiosity no longer. "It's seven months since we last had news of you," she said in a low voice, "Where have you been, this length of time, that neither your father nor all his men could find out what had become of you?"

Evelake was gazing down at his right hand, fingering a small puncture-shaped scar in the center of his palm. At her question, he raised his eyes to meet hers. "Why couldn't they find me? It's because Evelake Whitfauconer had ceased—for a time, anyway—to exist."

His words sent a chill down Tessa's spine. She said, "I don't understand."

"Nor do I, entirely. Caradoc, I think, is the only one who does," said Evelake. "But let me ask you this: how do you know who you are?"

The question caught Tessa somewhat off-guard. "I've never thought about it," she said, and frowned, trying to see what he might be aiming at. "There's my name, of course. That links me with my family. Then there are all the things I've done, the people I've known, the places I've visited—"

"In other words, the experiences you remember," said Evelake, with a nod. "What if someone came along and changed all your memories—gave you a new name and a new history?"

"I suppose," said Tessa dubiously, "it would amount to having a new identity."

"Precisely," agreed Evelake. "Now maybe you'll have some idea what happened to me."

He drew a deep breath. "The band of brigands who captured me was led by a man who calls himself Borthen Berigeld. He's a renegade mage who's since expanded his powers to include the practice of necromancy. He might have killed me, but he wanted me alive—for reasons of his own.

"To keep me under his control," he continued, "Borthen used his powers to tamper with my memory. He made me forget my own identity and believe I was someone else entirely: a person named Rhan Hallender, with a past to go with the name."

He hunched his shoulders slightly, as though he felt cold. "As Rhan, my past was complete enough to satisfy even me. As far as I knew—once Borthen was finished with me—I was the second son of a landowner whose elder son had ruined the family fortunes. Those 'facts' seemed to explain what was happening to me."

When Tessa remained silent, he went on with his story. "I spent a fortnight in some underground vault somewhere. The man who brought me food told me it was a cell in the local debtors' prison, though that was, of course, a lie. I don't recall either arriving or leaving—Borthen's flunkeys must have drugged me—but eventually I was packed off to a roadside inn not far from Rhylnie, where I spent the next three months doing scullery work for the proprietor, a fellow named Haskel—"

"Rhylnie!" exclaimed Tessa. "But agents from Gand visited every house in every village in that whole area!"

"Yes, I know," said Evelake with painful irony. "A troop of soldiers paid a call on the Manticore Inn, where I was staying. When they questioned me, all they got was the story Borthen had planted in my mind. And so they went away again none the wiser."

Feeling slightly breathless, Tessa took herself firmly in hand. "Did this Haskel have any idea who you really were?"

Evelake shrugged. "I'm sure he suspected that *something* was afoot. But I doubt he knew anything for certain: Borthen would never have allowed such a worthless underling to know what was really at stake. In any event, Haskel had only one set of orders: he was simply to make sure I didn't stray too far from the premises. Apart from that, he had a free hand to use me as he pleased."

Judging from the visible evidence, Haskel had not scrupled to use the boy hard. Tessa said, "But you managed to get away from him in the end."

Evelake gave her a wry smile. "That was largely Serdor's doing. He turned up at the inn one evening, leading a lame horse. I felt at once that he was different from most of the other travelers who came through the Manticore's front door. For one thing, he had a kind word for me, which was something I hadn't heard for a long time. And that prompted me to confide in him— my story, as I knew it. He promised to help me—"

A shadow crossed his face. Tessa had the feeling that he might have been repressing a shiver. She said quietly, "Then what happened?"

Evelake seemed quite composed, but his eyes were still haunted. He said with forced lightness, "The next night, one of Borthen Berigeld's lieutenants arrived at the inn. I didn't know, of course, who he was at the time, but I overheard him telling Haskel that he was going to take me away with him the following day. He didn't say where, but I knew it would mean losing the help Serdor had promised me. That didn't bear thinking about, so I decided to risk running away."

His face in the torchlight had lost some of its windblown color. "What I didn't realize," he continued, "was that Borthen had given Haskel an artifact of some kind—a necromancer's rod. It showed Haskel the way I had gone. He caught up with me—"

He abruptly fell silent. Gazing at his face, Tessa did not press him to explain his silence. After a moment, Evelake resumed his tale. "Serdor arrived in time to put a stop to things. But by then I was in no fit state to travel very far. A farmer from Rhylnie took us in—looked after me as though I'd been his own son. I'd dearly love to meet him again—to thank him for his kindness. I hope he and his family will be spared the horrors of this infernal conflict that Borthen and my half brother have unleashed on us."

"You make it sound as though there were a connection between this Borthen and Gythe," said Tessa.

"There *is* a connection," said Evelake. "As soon as the Du Bors found out that I was still alive, they realized they would have to fight to retain their preeminence. They had good reason to expect that the Mage Hospitallers would uphold any claim I might make against my half brother. So they had to look elsewhere for allies with power—and found Borthen Berigeld waiting to oblige them by initiating Gythe into the exercise of the black arts. Since then, Gythe has allowed himself to be drawn into union with a demon."

Tessa stared at him in blank dismay. "A demon!" she exclaimed. "I'm sorry, Evelake, but that's an extraordinary assertion to make."

"I'm well aware of that—but I promise you, I don't make the charge lightly," said Evelake. "The earthquake that destroyed St. Alanin's Cathedral was no natural phenomenon, but a supernatural attack directed against the mages who were gathered there. Caradoc was present in spirit when they died. He said something evil killed them. And I believe him."

"Why?" asked Tessa. "Who or what is Caradoc, that you are prepared to accept his word for truth?"

"Caradoc is something quite out of the ordinary," said Evelake. "He has the ability to call upon the Magia *without the aid of a magestone.*"

Tessa gazed at the young Warden in frank astonishment. Seeing her expression, Evelake went on to explain. "Caradoc's magecraft saved not only my life, but my sanity. He's the one who gave me back my memory. You've noticed the streaks of white in his hair?"

Tessa nodded.

"In order to free me," said Evelake, "he had to grapple with a demon-guardian Borthen had appointed to torment me in my dreams, whenever my past memories tried to intrude on my delusions. The dreams got so terrible and so persistent that they almost broke my mind before Caradoc stepped in to challenge the demon. It almost overwhelmed him, but in the end he managed to cast it out. Those white locks of hair are the scars of a hard-won victory."

He might have said more, but the sudden impetuous clatter of boots up the passageway outside forestalled him. Tessa left her seat with a bound as the footbeats slowed to a halt on the other side of the threshold. A voice that Tessa recognized as her squire's called through the curtain, "Lady Tessa! Lord Evelake! The mage from St. Merrow's is starting to come around. . . ."

Caradoc Penlluathe was sitting at the bedside of the injured mage when Tessa and Evelake arrived. Among those hovering discreetly in the background were Gudmar Ap Gorvald, Caradoc's friend Serdor, and his sister, Margoth. The tall mage warned everyone to silence with a gesture, then bent forward so that the man lying prone on the bed could see his face clearly. The injured man reached out a shaky hand to touch Caradoc's arm where it rested against the frame of the bed. "Who . . ." he whispered hoarsely, "who . . . are you?"

"My name is Caradoc," answered the tall mage. He added, "Don't be alarmed. You're among friends."

To Tessa's ears, it sounded as if his voice had taken on an extra element of resonance, deep and soft. The mere timbre of it seemed to communicate calm reassurance. The injured man did not quite relax, but the apprehension in his haggard face yielded to curiosity. Gazing up at Caradoc, he asked, "Are you a merchant-adventurer?"

Caradoc cast a glance over his shoulder at Gudmar before replying. "No, I'm not. But there is a member of the league present if you want a word with him."

When the other man nodded, Gudmar stepped forward. "I'm Gudmar Ap Gorvald," he said. "Can I be of service to you?"

The survivor from St. Merrow's glared at him

through hollow eyes. "You could have been," he said with weary bitterness, "if only you had arrived on time."

"Forgive me," said Gudmar, "but I'm afraid I don't understand. Whoever you were expecting, it certainly wasn't me."

The injured man's pain-clouded eyes turned bewildered. "Weren't you sent here by the Consortium of Falmyth?"

"No," said Gudmar. "My friends and I have been at sea since leaving Telphar ten days ago."

"If the consortium didn't send you," said the mage from St. Merrow's, "why are you here?"

"We saw fire on the horizon and came in close to investigate," said Gudmar quietly. "I'm sorry if we arrived too late to render material assistance. Can you tell us what happened?"

The survivor from St. Merrow's shuddered at the recollection. "Reivers came up from the south . . . several thousand of them, maybe more. They burned the outlying farms before attacking Yske itself. The town militia tried to hold them off, but they overran the walls like rats. A killing frenzy was on them—"

His chest rose and fell as his breathing quickened. "Some of the townsfolk were in league with the reivers. Even before the town gates fell, they were slaughtering their neighbors in the streets. And afterward . . . We mages tried to intervene—tried to put a stop to the madness. And that was when we discovered the worst."

He clutched at Caradoc's sleeve, his eyes feverishly alight. "The leaders among our attackers weren't just ordinary brigands. They had strange powers—powers of necromancy. Their followers seemed almost *possessed*. We called upon the Magia to help us, but there were only six of us. We did what we could, but our gifts of magecraft weren't equal to the task of casting out so much evil. Look!"

He groped for the pendant that hung from the chain about his neck, and held it up for his listeners to see. The bezel that should have held his magestone was empty. "Our magestones burned out in our hands!" he rasped.

"When there was nothing more we could do, we fled—only to find a band of reivers waiting for us outside on the mead."

Tears were standing out in the injured man's blood-shot eyes. Caradoc laid a gentle hand on the other mage's brow. "Rest easy," he told his patient quietly. "You and your companions made a noble effort. If the enemy proved beyond your strength, that was not your fault."

Tessa edged forward. "I'm sorry to intrude, reverend brother, when you so sorely need your rest," she said, "but there is one question I *must* ask. St. Merrow's never used to have any fewer than fifteen mages in residence at any given time. Why were there only six of you present here today?"

The injured Hospitaller's eyes were heavy with exhaustion, but he made the effort necessary to answer her. "By order of the Du Bors, a host of reivers and warlocks has invaded Gandia from the west. Grand Master Lliam Brynmorgan of Gand has ordered all mages above the rank of servitor to muster at Tavenern to meet the enemy. My colleagues and I were instructed to remain here to arrange for the contents of the library to be removed to Glyn Regis for safety. The Consortium of Falmyth was to send a ship—"

He broke off, his weak voice failing. "That's enough questions for now," said Caradoc firmly. "Any others can wait until Brother Caithmar is feeling stronger. . . ."

CALL TO ARMS

SOME TIME LATER, NINE PEOPLE gathered together around the fire in the main hall to discuss the import of what they had learned from the sole survivor from St. Merrow's. Besides Evelake and Gudmar, the party from the *Mermaid* included Harlech, Caradoc, Serdor, and

Margoth. The foresters of Gandia were represented by Tessa Ekhanghar, her esquire Owain Arillan, and her lieutenant, a grizzled old veteran with a peg leg whom she introduced as Duncan Drulaine.

"It doesn't surprise me to hear that a Du Bors army has crossed over Lake Damanvagr into Gandia," said Tessa grimly. "It was only a matter of time. What I don't understand is why Gythe and Gwynmira Du Bors should traffic in necromancy when they already have every advantage of military strength in their favor."

"The answer is simple, if brutal," said Gudmar. "The subjugation of Gandia is of secondary importance at the moment. The real objective behind this invasion is to advance the destruction of the Hospitallers' Order."

He shifted his weight, bringing one arm to rest across his upraised knee. "Evelake's told you something about this man Borthen Berigeld. All existing evidence suggests that he was at one time a member of the Order, before going his separate way to dabble in sorcery. He's since perfected his grasp of the black art, and has gone on to gather a following. Recruiting Gwynmira and Gythe Du Bors represents his crowning achievement, since an alliance with them has made him a master of armies as well as a master of necromancy."

Duncan Drulaine had been listening to the conversation in silence, but at this point he was moved to object. "Necromancy!" he exclaimed. "I'm sorry, but I don't find talk like that easy to swallow. I don't deny there's been plenty of evil committed round about here in the last few days. But *we* haven't seen anything that qualifies as black magic."

"We have," said Evelake. "At Falmyth."

He glanced around at his companions from the *Mermaid*. When none of them volunteered to speak, he continued the tale. "We put into Falmyth Harbor two nights ago, only to find the town a smoldering ruin—just like Yske. When we took the ship in closer to investigate, we were attacked by something out of a madman's nightmare: the carcass of a whale several days dead. It was animated by some malignant power, and it would have destroyed us if we hadn't used Pernathan seafire to destroy it first. You can't kill something that's already dead."

"Incredible as it may sound, we all saw the creature," said Gudmar, his deep voice calm and level. "My crew will testify to a man that it was no living thing."

Duncan Drulaine subsided, his weathered face puckered in serious consternation. "Speaking of necromancers and the like," growled Harlech, "I'd stake my last copper the reivers that did for Yske were the same ones tae make a knackersyard out o' Falmyth. Where d'ye suppose they'll be heading next?"

"My scouts report that they're heading west along the road to Hamyl," said Tessa. "I confess I was puzzled by that at first: there's nothing at Hamyl but a fording station across the Amberhyl. But if this band is on their way to rendezvous with the Du Bors forces, it makes sense they should be moving in that direction: Hamyl offers the only obvious river crossing east of Cambury."

Evelake frowned. "What about the Bridge of Ambre? That's only a few miles west of the city of Gand."

"It isn't there anymore," said Tessa with a thin smile. "It was just a bit too conveniently placed to serve the purposes of our enemies."

Her voice was as clear and cool as her eyes. Gazing at her across the flickering flames of the campfire, Caradoc found her worthy of respect. She was, demonstrably, an effective commander, able to inspire loyalty and obedience in her followers through her own resourcefulness and hardihood. But he sensed she had proven her capacity for leadership at the cost of sacrificing her more personal needs and desires.

He had not seen enough of her yet to do more than guess at what those needs and desires might be. But he was himself aware of the femininity that she had deliberately and consciously suppressed. She wore the role she had assumed as she wore her forester's mask—with intelligence and competence. But Caradoc found himself regretting the circumstances which had prompted her to adopt both forms of disguise.

The realization that Evelake was speaking roused him from his brief reverie. "Brother Caithmar said the mages of Gandia were gathering at Tavenern," mused the young Warden. "If Tavenern is where the Hospitallers expect to encounter the Du Bors army, might it not also be the place the reivers are making for?"

"I should think nothing is more likely," said Gudmar.

Tessa found the prospect far from encouraging. To Gudmar she said, "If you're right in your conjecture—if the Hospitallers *are* in fact the primary target in the coming assault—what are their chances for survival?"

It was Caradoc Penlluathe who answered her question. "Probably not very good," he said with bleak candor. "Borthen Berigeld possesses the most formidable affinity for power I've ever seen. My own teacher, a highly gifted magister, was killed trying to oppose him. As for Evelake's half brother and his demon-ally—we encountered a spectral projection of Gythe in his dual persona before we left Pernatha. If the spiritual bond between Gythe and the demon had not broken down when it did—through no doing of ours—the attack would have cost us some lives. Gythe and Borthen each represent a formidable threat individually. Put them together, with a host of followers at their heels, and I don't fancy anyone's chances of standing up against them in a head-on clash."

He spoke with a chill authority that seemed to belie his earlier display of impetuosity. Tessa marveled that the same individual should be capable of such extremes of passion and discernment. She said, "You seem very sure that both Gythe and Borthen will be traveling with the army from Farrowaithe."

Caradoc's green eyes flared into smoldering fire. "Borthen has been planning the downfall of the Order for a long time. He would not deny himself the exquisite pleasure of being in on the kill. About Gythe I am less

certain—but I doubt he would willingly part company
with his mentor at the point where a victory lay almost
within their grasp."

"Then you think the mages of Gandia really have no
hope at all of withstanding the assault?" said Tessa.

Caradoc grimaced. "The Hospitallers who are gathering at Tavenern are men who've been trained to heal,
not to fight. If they've made any plans at all, those plans
are likely to amount to nothing more strategic than
simply placing themselves squarely in the path of the
enemy, trusting Providence to do the rest. And that isn't
going to be good enough. The only way to deal effectively
with this unholy alliance is to divide its leadership. *We*
just might be able to manage that—but only if we can get
to Tavenern ahead of the enemy."

"We could almost certainly get there ahead of the
reivers from Yske," said Tessa. "It'll take them at least
five days to complete the journey to Tavenern by way of
Hamyl. But there is a quicker way. My people have set up
a crossing at the Falls of Linnock, half a day west of
Bryndalen. It won't accommodate horses, but the watchmen at the falls could arrange to have mounts waiting for
us on the other side of the river if we signal ahead."

She paused to study Caradoc's face in frank curiosity. "But how is our—your—presence at Tavenern likely
to make a significant difference? What's the plan you
have in mind?"

"Nothing very clever, or even original, I'm afraid,"
said the red-haired mage. "Borthen Berigeld has a
personal score to settle with me. The plan—once we get
to Tavenern—is for me to approach him through Orison
with a personal challenge, daring him to meet me
separately in a duel of power. If he takes me at my word,
I'll be in a position—hopefully—to draw him away from
the main army with whatever following he sees fit to
bring with him."

"And just to make sure Gythe isn't tempted to join
Borthen in the chase," said Evelake, "*I'll* remain with the
mages of Gandia, and let Gythe know that's where I
am."

"I think the pair of you have taken leave of your senses!" declared Margoth. "That sounds to me like a recipe for suicide."

"Maybe." Gudmar's golden eyes were glinting like molten metal. "But the plan also offers us what may be our one and only chance to strike a telling blow against this diabolical evil that has been unleashed on East Garillon. If we hold back now out of fear for our lives, leaving the Hospitallers of Gandia to face the assault alone, they will almost certainly be destroyed. And if they are destroyed, what in God's name have we left to hope for?"

His glowing gaze swept the faces of those present. Tessa looked too, to see how her companions were responding. Caradoc and Evelake, clearly, had already made their decision even before Gudmar had put the issue into words. Harlech Hardrada was now grinning fiercely, showing teeth like a wolverine squaring off for a fight. Serdor and Margoth exchanged glances, then turned to Gudmar and nodded their silent agreement to the proposal that had been previously put before them.

Tessa's own followers were waiting to see what she would say, but she sensed their rising commitment to the idea of taking decisive action. Her own heart soaring suddenly toward chilly heights of fear and exhilaration, Tessa thrust her lingering doubts aside. She said, "I vote we set out for Tavenern as soon as it's light."

ARRAY OF POWER

THE AIR WAS BITTERLY COLD, and the bleak ridges on either hand were the color of lead. Kherryn Du Penfallon braced herself against the chill wind that beat in gusts against her back and urged her small, rough-coated hill mare to keep pace with the gelding that Ulbrecht

Rathmuir was riding. The trail beneath the animals' hooves was slick with patches of hardening ice. Despite the fact that Kherryn was wearing fur-lined gloves, her fingers were so numb that she found it difficult even to keep hold of her reins.

It was five days since the party—fifty-four people in all—had set out on the road from Cheswythe to Tavenern. Their journey had taken them through the heart of the Grey Hill Country in freezing temperatures under menacing skies. Hot in summer, cheerless in winter, the Grey Hills were never hospitable. But all the travelers from Cheswythe—the men-at-arms as well as the Mage Hospitallers—knew that there was something unnatural and sinister in the gathering snowstorms that had followed them eastward, and were now threatening to overtake them.

The mages in the group numbered fifteen. Eight of these, including Ulbrecht, were from Farrowaithe—the fortunate few who had been pursuing duties elsewhere in the city when the disaster at the cathedral had claimed the lives of their colleagues. The other seven were from Cheswythe—the senior members of the Hospitallers' community there. The nine junior mages from Cheswythe—six servitors and three novices—had been sent off, along with a large train of civilian refugees, to seek the relative safety of Strathwellyn in the north. Where they would go from there would depend on the outcome of a battle that Kherryn sensed was now only a matter of hours away.

The evacuation of Cheswythe had gotten under way shortly after a final boatload of refugees from Farrowaithe arrived to report that the Du Bors and their necromancer allies were preparing to cross Lake Damanvagr with an army many thousands strong. The impending invasion of Gandia represented an overt declaration of war against the Hospitallers' Order. Grand Master Lliam Brynmorgan of Gand had decided against the Order's making any stand against their enemies at Cheswythe, where the open country offered little natural protection. Instead, he had decreed that the

Hospitallers should center their resistance at Tavenern, the eastern gateway of the Grey Hills, where the rugged terrain would favor a small but determined band of defenders against a force of superior numbers.

United with the Hospitallers in the face of their common danger, the townships loyal to Devon Du Penfallon, the young Seneschal of Gand, had pledged support for the mages. And so thirty-eight men-at-arms had accompanied Ulbrecht's party on the road to Tavenern. Twenty-six of these were volunteers from the ranks of Cheswythe's local militia. The other twelve were Farrowaithe Guardsmen—survivors, like the mages, of the ruin of their brotherhood. These had formally renounced their allegiance to Gythe Du Bors, and had placed their swords at the service of the Hospitallers' Order.

Lieutenant Geston Du Maris was not among them. The deadly wounds that he had taken at Corviser's Landing had left him too weak to sit a horse, and he had been sent north with the rest of the refugees, in the care of one of the servitors. Kherryn was glad, for his sake, to see him out of danger, if only for the moment. She wished her gift of prescience would show her reason to hope for success in the conflict to come. But her spirits remained chilled, her heart heavy as stone.

Glancing nervously back over her shoulder, she could see that the hills to the west were white with snow. The sky above the hills was an eerie shade of violet, opaque as a bruise. The slopes and ridges off to the south had disappeared under a spreading blanket of freezing fog. It would be dark, she sensed, long before the setting of the sun.

As the afternoon wore on, the cold grew sharper, the roadbed more treacherous. The horses skidded and floundered over ground that was slick with thickening ice. Eventually the whole party was forced to dismount and proceed on foot, leading their exhausted animals behind them. Flurries of snow spun past them on the blustery winter wind.

Trudging along in the rut trodden down by the men

in front of her, Kherryn found it hard to keep her feet. Ulbrecht saw that she was struggling, and caught her by the arm just in time to keep her from falling. "Here— give me your reins. I'll lead the horses," he told her. "You walk beside the mare holding on to your saddlebow. That should help you stay upright."

Kherryn did as he suggested. "How much farther is it to Tavenern?" she panted, trying not to let her anxiety show.

"Not far now—maybe another mile or two," said Ulbrecht. "The daylight should hold out at least long enough for us to reach the lower end of the Taven Valley—hullo, what's that?"

The men-at-arms at the head of the party had come to a bristling standstill. Listening, Kherryn heard the drumming tattoo of iron-shod hooves trotting briskly toward them down the trail from the east. The hoofbeats grew louder, bursting into sudden thunder. Three horse- men rounded the bend in the road up ahead of the mages' party, and brought their animals to a plunging halt. "Hoy, there!" called a deep voice. "I'm looking for Magister Ulbrecht Rathmuir. Is he with you?"

"Yes, he is. I'm Ulbrecht Rathmuir." Passing both sets of reins to one of the ordinaires from Cheswythe, Ulbrecht strode forward to meet the speaker. At close range, the leading horseman proved to be a burly blue- eyed man mounted on a heavily built roan stallion. Ulbrecht tilted his head. "You have the advantage of me. I don't believe we've met."

"No," agreed the rider, swinging himself down from the saddle. "My name's Vult Hemmling. I'm here on behalf of a kinsman of mine—Magister Corwyn Ap Culross of Gand. He says you're a friend of his."

"Corwyn and I were novices together in Farrowaithe," said Ulbrecht with a nod. "I consider myself privileged to know him. Are you from Gand yourself?"

Vult pulled a mirthless grin. "No, I'm from Rhylnie. Or rather, I *was*—till the Du Bors jackals ran me off my farm a few months back. Me, and a good many of my neighbors. Since then, we've been making royal nuisances of ourselves—as far as the jackals are concerned. When Corwyn let us know there was a scrap brewing, we came along to help out on the side of the angels."

He looked past Ulbrecht toward the rest of the party, strung out along the trail in the ominous twilight. "I'm bound to say I'm mightily glad we found you. Corwyn was expecting you to arrive earlier—around midday. As it is, the weather's made the low road into Taven Valley impassable. In order to win through, your people are going to have to go around by the other way."

"I didn't know there *was* another way," said Ulbrecht.

"It isn't much more than an upland sheep track," admitted Vult, "but it's the only route open, I'm afraid. Fortunately, the cutoff isn't for another quarter mile yet. We'll go in front and show you the way."

Ulbrecht was looking worried. "How difficult is this roundabout way?" he asked.

"The trail bed itself is solid enough," said Vult, "but it's steep and it's narrow. I'd advise you to continue leading your horses."

"Is riding completely out of the question?"

"I'd consider it a bit of a gamble," said Vult. "Unless you have some people with you who aren't likely to make it otherwise."

"Most of us are able enough," said Ulbrecht. "But there is one I'm concerned about."

Half turning, he pointed Kherryn out among the waiting company. She was leaning heavily against her mare's flank, her small face pinched with cold and weariness. "Aye, I understand," said Vult. He fingered the bridge of his prominent nose. "I don't see why we couldn't put her up on my horse. If I lead him, she should be all right, so long as she can keep herself awake enough to stay in the saddle."

"She certainly can't walk much farther," said Ulbrecht, "so I guess we'll have to try it."

"Whatever you think best," said Vult. "Though I'm bound to say," he added on a note of censure, "I don't know why you should have brought a little maid like that along on a venture like this. If you have any regard for her, I'd have thought Tavenern was the last place you'd want her to be just now."

Ulbrecht winced slightly. "As it happens, I have every regard for her. And you're right—Tavenern *is* the last place I want her to be. But this journey was her choice, and I had no authority to deny her the right to come. You see," he finished, "that 'little maid' is Lady Kherryn Du Penfallon."

Vult's blue eyes widened. "There's only one family in Gandia to bear that surname," he said, "and they're the seneschals of Gand itself. So she's our Lord Devon's sister?"

Ulbrecht noted the familiar expression, "*our* Lord Devon." In spite of his anxiety, he almost smiled. "So the people of Gandia have taken Kherryn's brother to their hearts," he thought. "That's a triumph no Du Bors could ever hope to emulate." To Vult he said aloud, "That's right, she is. She's come this way, hoping eventually to join him."

"That's not going to be easy to manage," said Vult, "but my men and I will certainly do our fighting best to give her every chance." He cast another glance in Kherryn's direction and gave his head a wondering shake. "Who'd have thought she'd turn out to be such a little bit of a thing? Well, no matter—we'd better get her mounted up and be on our way."

The trail which Vult had described as a sheep track cut off to the right from the main road at a point where two adjacent slopes dipped down to form a stony gap between twin ridges of high ground. The path led through the gap, then veered to the left. Within minutes, it had become little more than a climbing ledge, winding its way along the south face of a tall steep-sided hill. Snow lay heavy in the fissures and gullies lower down among the rocks.

The members of the party were obliged to travel single file. Coming next behind Vult, Ulbrecht kept an anxious eye on Kherryn, a small dark huddle perched on top of their guide's big horse. Vult had promised to keep close by her in case she should start to slip, but that assurance brought Ulbrecht little comfort. Even though he was certain he could trust the farmer from Rhylnie, he couldn't forget for a moment that there were windy chasms gaping only a few feet to the right of the path.

His anxiety increased as the darkness thickened around them. Bitter gusts of icy air swooped down off the heights, hissing and moaning like eldritch birds of prey. As the party continued to ascend, the buffeting of the wind grew stronger. Shielding his face with a fold of his cloak against a stinging bombardment of snowflakes, Ulbrecht was just beginning to wonder if they were going to be forced to turn back, when the path ahead of them abruptly leveled off.

After another thirty yards, the ledge broadened out into a tablelike shelf, protected from the main force of the wind by a bulwark of low bluffs. Here, at Vult's recommendation, the band stopped for a brief rest. "It's all downhill from here," he told Ulbrecht. "Once we get to the bottom, it's only another few furlongs up the valley to the gates of Tavenern."

"That sounds like good news to me," said Ulbrecht. Sidling past the guide, he leaned up against the stallion's flank to lay a hand on Kherryn's bowed shoulder. Her head lifted. He couldn't see her face, but he knew she was looking at him. "How are you holding up?" he asked.

"I'm all right," said Kherryn. Her voice sounded thin and drowsy. Vult drew Ulbrecht's attention with a tap on the arm and pressed a flask into the mage's gloved hand. "Give her a few sips of that," said the guide.

Ulbrecht uncorked the bottle and sniffed the contents. The spicy scent told him it was a restorative cordial. "Corwyn brewed that up himself," said Vult. "When you're done with it, I'll pass it on to anyone else who's flagging."

By the time the party was ready to move on again, Kherryn had managed to pull herself upright in the saddle. Seeing her take a tight grip on the stallion's mane, Ulbrecht knew she had waked up enough to be aware of her surroundings. "We haven't far to go now," he told her. "Just hang on for a little while longer." The nod she gave him had some conviction behind it. "We're ready now," Ulbrecht told Vult. "Let's go."

The track descended in a series of zigzags. The last downslope turned into a shallow snow-filled gully running north and south like a crooked seam between two sheer escarpments. Footing was treacherous, and the depth of the snow hampered their progress. Though they made the best speed they could, it was another quarter of an hour before they at last clambered up out of the white slough of drifts and pitfalls onto the level floor of the Taven Valley.

To the west the lower end of the valley was shrouded in darkness. But to the east Ulbrecht's straining gaze picked out a pallid scattering of lights, faint as will-o'-the-wisps. "We're practically on the doorstep," said Vult's voice in his ear. "Now that we're back on the roadway, I'll send one of my lads riding on ahead to make sure there'll be plenty of firing and hot food waiting for your people when they arrive."

With their destination in sight, the band from Cheswythe pressed on with renewed energy. Though he was as eager as any of his companions to get in out of the bone-freezing cold, Ulbrecht spared a moment to cast an eye over the natural layout of the area as they approached the walls of Tavenern. The vale at its eastern end, he saw, was hardly more than two hundred yards across, its span hemmed in on either side by frowning escarpments too sheer to afford easy climbing. The two sides of the valley came together at the top of a steep incline to form a natural gateway. "I can see why the Grand Master of Gand chose this place for our defense," he thought to himself.

The gap between the bluffs had been closed off by stone walls eight feet thick and twenty feet high, with only enough space left between to accommodate a fortified gatehouse. A dozen yards out from the base of the

wall a trench had been dug from one side of the narrow
vale to the other. The permanent wooden bridge, which a
previous generation of residents had built across the
trench, had been dismantled and replaced with a movable frame of timbers. There were sentries posted at the
bridgehead, and more watchmen strung out along the
wall-walks.

The late arrivals from Cheswythe crossed over the
trestle bridge and continued on through the gatehouse to
the accompaniment of cheers from the ramparts. A
welcoming party of soldiers, Hospitallers, and lay servants descended on the newcomers as soon as they were
inside the walls. While Ulbrecht was exchanging formal
greetings with the preceptor in charge of the hospice at
Tavenern, Vult handed his reins over to the younger of
his two companions, then turned to Kherryn. "Here we
are at long last, milady," he said kindly. "Shall I help you
down?"

The small figure nodded wearily, her eyelids drooping with exhaustion. When Vult reached up to lift her
from the saddle, she tumbled loosely into his arms, like a
doll made of rags. Seeing her collapse, Ulbrecht started
around in alarm, but Vult caught her easily, gathering her
up so that her head was cradled securely against his
shoulder. "She's all right—just worn out," he called over
to the mage. For the benefit of everyone else present, he
added, "I think we could all do with a hot drink and a bit
of a rest, so why don't we take ourselves off indoors and
save the talking for later?"

It was only a short walk up the High Street to the
gates of the Hospitaller's priory. Vult dismissed the
preceptor's suggestion that they send for a litter on
Kherryn's behalf. "She's not much of a burden—it'll be
quicker if I just carry her," he said. "Bricre, see that my
horse is taken care of, will you? I'll join you at the
commandery once I've had a word or two with Magister
Corwyn and the reverend brother here. . . ."

Ulbrecht raised no objections. Bone-weary as he was
himself, he suspected that Kherryn would be safer

entrusted to Vult's capable hands. When they arrived at the priory's guesthouse a few minutes later, an ordinaire ushered them inside and upstairs to a door at the far end of a long hall. Here they were warmly welcomed by Corwyn Ap Culross himself.

It had been three years since Ulbrecht had last seen his friend, and he was struck immediately by the other man's careworn appearance. Habitually cheerful and tough-minded, Corwyn had never been one to fret himself needlessly over trifles. Though his greeting now was hearty, he looked as though he had not found much time for either food or rest in the last few days. The realization gave Ulbrecht a qualm of foreboding.

Explanations, however, had to be deferred until more pressing matters had been dealt with. Beckoning his guests into a small firelit sitting room, Corwyn pointed to a door in the left-hand wall. "That leads to the bedchamber," he told Ulbrecht. "Lady Kherryn is welcome to the use of it. You'll find everything you need in there to make her comfortable. I'll have my ordinaire fetch some hot milk from the kitchen, if you think she'll feel up to drinking it. . . ."

The bedroom was small as well, but there was a fire burning brightly on the hearth, and the bed itself was well furnished with pillows and blankets. By the time Ulbrecht had Kherryn warmly ensconced under the coverlets, the ordinaire arrived with a steaming posset. Though she was more than half asleep, Kherryn allowed herself to be coaxed into drinking most of it. Satisfied that she was no longer in danger of taking seriously ill from cold and exposure, Ulbrecht moved the bedside candle to the table by the door, then paused briefly to look back at her where she lay asleep.

She was curled up like a bedraggled kitten, one small-boned hand clenched tightly around the little leather pouch she wore strung by a thong about her throat. Ulbrecht had noticed that she often slept like that—clinging to the pouch as a child might cling to a treasured toy she feared to lose. Nor was Ulbrecht surprised: the pouch contained the tiny crystal box that Evelake Whitfauconer had given her—the box she had wrested from Evelake's enemies in an impressive display of power.

It was this achievement that led Ulbrecht to suspect that Kherryn might be something very special indeed: a periegete. Periegesis—the ability to move through intervening planes of time and space—was the rarest of all mage-talents. Only three instances of it had ever been recorded in the Book of Caer Ellyn—so few that skeptics were inclined to dismiss the entries as legend rather than history. For this reason, Ulbrecht was reluctant to voice his suspicions, even to Corwyn. But he was becoming increasingly convinced in his own mind that the potential was there, waiting to be awakened.

Kherryn's knowledge of magecraft—perhaps fortunately—was too limited just now for her to see the momentous possibilities of her gifts. That awareness would have to come naturally, as she learned to control and direct her powers so as not to burn herself out through overexertion. She needed experience as well as knowledge. Ulbrecht hoped she would have time to acquire both. With a prayer on her behalf at the back of his mind, he bade her a silent, affectionate good night and left the room.

VEILS OF MYSTERY

ULBRECHT RETURNED TO THE SITTING room to find Vult warming the backs of his legs by the fire. Corwyn was sitting in a wing chair to the left of the hearth, his expression bleakly preoccupied. At the sound of Ulbrecht's footfalls, however, he roused himself from his reverie. Indicating the neighboring chair, the magister from Gand said with wry solicitude, "For God's sake, come and sit down before you fall down. I swear you look worse now than you did the morning before your acceptance examinations."

"I do recall times when I've felt better." Ulbrecht sank down in the cushioned seat with a grateful groan. "A reminder that I'm not getting any younger."

"Don't let it rankle—advancing old age is probably the very least of our worries just now," said Corwyn with a grimace. He added, "Considering what's in the wind, you were damned lucky to reach Tavenern in one piece."

"So were you. I don't imagine it was exactly child's play slipping out of Gand under the noses of an occupying army," said Ulbrecht.

"Fortunately we had help from a local band of insurrectionists," said Corwyn. "They smuggled us secretly out of the city. A detachment of Farrowaithe Guards made sure we made it the rest of the way."

"Farrowaithe Guards!" Ulbrecht sat up in some surprise. "What were *they* doing in Gand?"

"Lady Gwynmira dispatched four companies of them in association with the Black Baron and his army. It's pretty obvious that our Dowager-Regent wanted an excuse for sending some of the more influential captains out of Farrowaithe. What she failed to consider, however," said Corwyn with a thin smile, "was the fact that the Guards have their own code of honor. Baron Khevyn Ap Khorrasel gave the corps sufficient provocation to commit mutiny—much to the gratitude of those of us from St. Berengar's who got elected to go on this bloody suicide mission."

He picked up a poker from the hearthside and prodded the embers into fresh life. "Those of you who got *elected*?" said Ulbrecht. "Do you mean some stayed behind?"

Corwyn nodded. "Half the household. It was decided by majority vote by the Council of Magisters that there was good cause to hold back some measure of our strength—in case the Order should be forced into exile. The selection—go or stay—was determined by lottery. I can see the sense of the argument. As to whether it was the right decision to make or not . . ."

He left the end of the sentence hanging. "What about Lliam Brynmorgan himself?" asked Ulbrecht.

"Our Grand Master? Oh, he's here, of course. Having summoned virtually all the senior mages under his jurisdiction to this place, he was bound and determined to be here himself—God bless him," said Corwyn. "But then he took Arch Mage Baldwyn's death hard. They were lifelong friends."

Silence settled over the room, broken only by the crackle of the fire. After a minute, Ulbrecht asked, "Where is Lliam at the moment?"

"In the chapel, praying for our deliverance," said Corwyn. "I should be there too, I suppose—except that someone's got to be on hand to keep everything organized. Though frankly," he continued, "I don't see how we can organize anything unless and until we get some clear idea what we're going to be up against."

"At least here our enemies won't be able to turn the earth itself against us, like they did at Farrowaithe," said Ulbrecht.

"No," agreed Corwyn. "Thank God Tavenern's built on solid rock instead of shifty marshland. But I'm sure they'll have other dirty tricks to play. I only wish I knew enough even to make some educated guesses about what's likely to happen when the Du Bors forces get here."

He shook his head darkly. "You've seen this damnable weather moving in. There's something at the heart of it worse than anything the Order's encountered since the days of the Ninth Synod of Magisters. But just *what* that something is I don't know and I haven't been able to find out—either through normal methods of reconnaissance, or through Orison."

Ulbrecht merely stared at his friend in mute dismay. After a pause, Corwyn continued in a lower voice. "That storm out there—it's like a cloud of confusion. You simply can't get through it to investigate what lies beyond. One of my preceptors has inquisitor-class gifts for far-seeing, and even *he* hasn't been able to penetrate that fog. It's all a blank bloody veil of mystery—and I have a nasty suspicion it's going to roll in on top of us before morning."

Ulbrecht digested this with a sinking feeling in the pit of his stomach. He understood now the reason behind Corwyn's fraught air of grim anxiety. Before he could offer comment, the mage from Gand spoke again in sharp admonition. "It'll be up to you, of course, whether you want to stay here and face whatever lies in store for the rest of us. But whether you go or stay, I really think you should make sure that little girl—Lady Kherryn—is out of this town by midnight. For I'll tell you frankly, I don't much fancy our chances."

"Get her out? I'd like to," said Ulbrecht. "But I'm not sure it would be possible at this point, as exhausted as she is. You just said yourself this weather was damnable. It would be criminal to send her out again tonight, unless there really were no other choice. Unless the worst were to happen."

"Just what do you mean by 'the worst'?" asked Vult Hemmling, speaking up for the first time after a long period of thoughtful silence. "What is the *worst* that's likely to occur? I mean, if it's just a choice between freezing to death or getting spitted on some freebooter's sword—"

"It's worse than that," said Ulbrecht. "This force is commanded largely by necromancers. We may not know much about the infernal principles that give them their powers, but this much I can tell you: they can use even dead bodies to serve their purposes."

The farmer from Rhylnie gazed at him incredulously. "I know what I'm talking about," said Ulbrecht harshly. "The dead stood up and walked in Farrowaithe, and I assure you, they make formidable enemies. You can't hurt them, because they have no feelings. You can't kill them, because they're already dead."

"Sounds like you're saying they're invincible," said Vult.

"Not quite." Ulbrecht pulled a fleeting mirthless

smile. "But it does take magecraft to put a revenant down."

He went on to explain. "Mages, normally, have their own defenses against most forms of conventional attack: their heightened sensibilities allow them in many cases to anticipate a hostile move in time to evade it. And the same power that enables a mage to heal other people also enables him to put off an attacker—for instance, by disrupting his enemy's balance or perceptions. But it's not the same with revenants. They have no senses to disrupt. The only way to deal with a revenant is to drive out the dark power that is animating it—and that usually means taking on the necromancer who brought the revenant to life in the first place.

"Then," he continued, "it becomes largely a question of endurance. Both mages and necromancers have their limitations. A necromancer has only as much power as he has 'bought' from his demonic ally. A mage can sustain the flow of the Magia for only so long: when he reaches the limit of his strength, his magestone will simply burn out. Whichever party proves to have the greater resources will eventually find his weaker counterpart completely at his mercy."

At this point Corwyn interposed. "That's why it would be very useful if we knew how many necromancers are traveling with the Du Bors army," he said. "Also, if we had some notion of how powerful they are, both individually and collectively. As it is, we haven't any idea."

"And so if you ask me what 'the worst' might be," said Ulbrecht grimly, "it's what we have to expect."

"In other words," said Vult sourly, "hard luck, and nary a wishing well in sight."

He fingered the prominent bridge of his nose. "From the sound of things, the pair of you have enough on your plates already, without having to worry about Lady Kherryn's welfare. If it'll set your minds at ease, I'll arrange to have some of my men standing ready to spirit her away to safety if the fortunes of battle turn against us."

"I'd be better satisfied knowing you were personally in charge," said Ulbrecht with a wry grin. "But I daresay you have a deputy in mind."

Vult nodded. "Young Bricre—my son-in-law. He won't like the idea very much, but it gives me a good excuse to send him out of trouble. He's as trusty as they come, and no fool: if I can't join them on the trail, he'll make sure Lady Kherryn wins free to a secure hiding place."

Ulbrecht traded glances with Corwyn. "I believe you can manage it, if anyone can," he said to Vult. "I accept your proposal. And I thank you from the bottom of my heart!"

While her elders were discussing the issue of her safety, Kherryn slept, but not soundly. Restless and inquisitive, her dreaming self prowled the grey borderlands between slumber and waking, until at length she stepped through a misty veil of cloudy obscurity into a dim enclosure full of the sound of dogs barking.

She stopped to get her bearings. As the dream images sharpened, she saw that it was dusk. She was standing on a patch of twilit grass just inside a wooden gate wide enough to accommodate a cart. Ahead of her stood a stout half-timbered farmhouse with a thatched roof. To her left lay well-grown rows of summer vegetables, flanked by a neat free-stone wall.

The belligerent chorus of yelps and growls was coming from off to her right. Turning, she saw two large dogs and a half-grown puppy confronting a cloaked figure astride a sturdy bay mare. The bigger of the two adult dogs made a darting run at the mare's forelegs, dodging away at the last minute to avoid a bridling snap from a set of strong equine teeth. When the animals separated, Kherryn corrected her first impression: there were in fact two riders mounted double on the one horse.

Even as she arrived at this realization, a man with a lantern emerged from around the corner of the house. Seen by lamplight, he was middle-aged and strongly built, like a mature chestnut tree. Though he was wearing a farmer's serviceable smock and leggings instead of chain mail and leather, Kherryn knew him at a glance for the scout, Vult Hemmling.

Scowling, Vult called away his dogs and strode forward, brandishing the light in the face of the foremost rider, a lean, lightweight young man, brown as a sparrow. The second rider, muffled in a travel-stained hood and cloak, was only a boy. His downcast face was partly hidden, but Kherryn was seized by the sudden unshakable conviction that this second traveler was none other than Evelake Whitfauconer.

From the way he was sitting, loosely slumped against his companion, she feared he might be ill. Or hurt: when the first rider eased his hooded companion down into Vult's waiting arms, she noticed that they both handled him with care, avoiding contact with his back. Before she could react, the scene abruptly faded. In its place, a face materialized before her dreaming eyes.

A handsome, sneering countenance, with full, smiling lips and dark heavy-lidded eyes.

The face of Borthen Berigeld!

The shock of recognition jarred her wide awake with a start. Sitting bolt upright amid the scattered bedclothes, she pressed both hands to her pounding heart and tried to recover her wits. The sound of lowered voices filtered in from the adjoining room. Hearing Ulbrecht's comfortingly familiar tones, she scrambled off the bed and threw a shawl on over her nightgown. Then she made for the door.

As she stepped across the threshold, Ulbrecht turned in his chair. "Kherryn, what's the matter?" he asked, giving her a searching look. "Did we wake you?"

Kherryn shook her head. "No, it's all right. I woke myself." Her wide, dark gaze as she crossed the room was fixed not on Ulbrecht, but on Vult, standing by the fire. Appealing to him with her eyes, she said, "I seem to have an idea that . . . weren't you at one time a farmer?"

Vult's smile was kindly quizzical. "That's right, Lady Kherryn. I had some property a few miles north of Rhylnie."

"Then tell me—" Kherryn hesitated, then went on in a rush. "While you were still living on your farm, were you ever paid a visit by two people—a man and a boy—riding double on a bay mare?"

The twinkle faded from Vult's eyes, to be replaced by a look of surprise. "Yes, as a matter of fact, I was," he said wonderingly. "That was about four months ago. But how did you know about that?"

Kherryn didn't seem to hear his puzzled inquiry. "The boy," she said. "Please, did he happen to tell you his name?"

"He did indeed." Vult was looking more bemused than ever. "He said his name was Rhan Hallender."

"Rhan?" It was Kherryn's turn to look puzzled. "*That* was the name he gave you?"

"That's right," said Vult with a nod. "I suppose he and his friend might have been lying," he conceded. "But they didn't look like the lying sort to me—if they had, I wouldn't have taken them in. And anyway, they had no reason not to be truthful to me."

He eyed her more closely. "I hope you won't mind me asking, Lady Kherryn, but what's this all about?"

Kherryn's slight shoulders were drooping. "N-nothing, I suppose," she said haltingly. "Just a dream I was having. It made me wonder if . . . no, never mind. I must have been mistaken."

"That's all right, milady. No harm done," said Vult. His expression was still somewhat baffled.

"You're more than a little overtired, Lady Kherryn," said Corwyn gently. "Why don't you let Magister Ulbrecht put you back to bed?"

Ulbrecht was already on his feet. When Kherryn nodded dispiritedly, he wrapped a fatherly arm around her and steered her toward the bedroom door. Though the mage offered no comment on Kherryn's conversation with Vult, the name Rhan Hallender was striking a curiously familiar chord somewhere in his own memory. He found himself wondering if perhaps his late friend and colleague Forgoyle Finlevyn might have mentioned that name back in Ambrothen.

The precise connection, however, eluded him, and he filed the question away. For the moment, such considerations were of light importance compared with the more pressing problems he had on his mind.

Specifically, how he and his colleagues were going to deal with the storm that was gathering at the gates of Tavenern.

OBLATION OF LIGHTS

VULT REMAINED AT THE PRIORY long enough to share a measure of mulled wine with Ulbrecht and Corwyn. He declined an invitation to stay and eat with them. "I'll be taking my supper at the commandery with the rest of my lads from Rhylnie," he said. "As soon as we're finished there, I'll send Bricre along to you here, with four or five of his mates to fill out a reasonable escort."

"Where will you be?" asked Corwyn.

Vult shrugged. "Wherever I'm most needed, I expect. Which means we'll almost certainly be meeting up again before this night is out."

The three men exchanged handshakes all around. Then the burly farmer took his leave. As the door closed behind him, Corwyn cast a glance at the horologe on the mantelpiece. "Speaking of supper, it's time we took ourselves off to the refectory," he said to Ulbrecht.

"You go ahead," said Ulbrecht. "I'd better stay here to keep an eye on my fledgling."

"I'm afraid you have other responsibilities," said Corwyn. "Grand Master Lliam intends to make a special Oblation of Lights in the chapel immediately after the meal. As magisters, our presence is going to be required."

The Oblation of Lights was one of the most solemn rites of the Order; Ulbrecht was not surprised to hear that the Grand Master of Gand proposed to celebrate this particular sacrament in the face of mortal danger. "I understand," he said with a nod. "Nevertheless, I'd prefer not to leave Kherryn alone. Is there anyone who could remain here in my place?"

"My ordinaire, I'm sure, will be happy to oblige," said Corwyn. "Will that be acceptable? Good. In that case, we'd better get our cloaks. . . ."

It was only a short walk across the priory forecourt from the guesthouse to the entrance to the mages' hall of residence. As soon as he and Corwyn stepped outside, Ulbrecht was quick to feel the nerve-numbing bite of a killing frost in the black night air. The wind had subsided and the snow had stopped falling, but he took no reassurance from the creeping change in the weather. The quiet, deadly chill that was stealing over Tavenern and its environs was, to his way of thinking, more ominous than the howls of any honest winter blizzard.

Gritting his teeth, he glanced uneasily up at the sky. Heavily overcast, it seemed to be pressing down over the rooftops of the town, as if to crush the houses by its weight. At the same time, the darkness had an eerie life to it, as though it were charged with energies he couldn't see with his unaided eye. He had the feeling that if he were to call upon the Magia, his mage-sight would show him shooting patterns of force, like corposant slug trails flickering among the clouds.

The candlelit refectory was filled to capacity. The atmosphere in the crowded room was charged with grim expectancy. Following Corwyn along the right-hand side aisle toward the high table where the senior magisters were seated, Ulbrecht was aware of an unspoken sense of crisis overhanging the company. "We're almost like so many castaways packed into one frail lifeboat," he thought bleakly. "Each one of us wondering how we're going to survive the storm."

The Grand Master of Gand acknowledged their arrival with a grave nod. No sooner had Ulbrecht and Corwyn taken their chairs at the table than Lliam rose and gestured for silence. What low-voiced conversation

there was died instantly. The tall silver-haired grand
master bowed his head over his folded hands to offer up
the conventional prayer of thanksgiving. The choral
"amen" at the close of the prayer signaled the resident
serving brothers to begin setting out the food. Ulbrecht
ate the lamb stew that was laid before him more as a
matter of necessity than for the sake of enjoyment,
knowing that he was going to need his strength.

When supper was over, the Grand Master of Gand
again rose from his seat to address the company. "My
brothers-in-spirit," he said solemnly, "I think we are all
united in the realization that we—and perhaps the
whole of the Hospitallers' Order—may be standing on
the brink of dissolution. In a moment we will be repairing to the chapel to dedicate ourselves anew to our
Divine Master, and ask his blessing on all our endeavors.
Before we go, I would like to thank you for coming here
to Tavenern of your own free will—for consenting to be
bound in faith, perhaps even unto death, by the vows of
your vocation."

He raised his voice, its tones vibrant with deep
emotion. "Let the fires of that faith burn high in your
spirits tonight in this vale of shadows. And when the
time comes for us to go out to meet our enemies, let this
prayer be on our lips and in our hearts: that if we may not
ourselves be vouchsafed a decisive victory, we may at
least, by our unified and willing sacrifice, so wound and
divide the powers of darkness against themselves that
they shall not ultimately prevail!"

At these words, a swelling murmur of assent passed
over the crowded room, like a wind passing over a field
of green wheat. As its echoes died away, two preceptors
rose from their chairs and went to the doors at the
farther end of the refectory. At a nod from the grand
master, they threw the doors open, admitting a chill
influx of air from the cloister outside. All present stood
up as Lliam Brynmorgan left the high table and moved
toward the center aisle.

His fellow magisters fell into step behind him. They
were followed in turn by a gathering of preceptors. The

Grand Master of Gand led the formal procession along the cloister walk into the chancel of the Hospitallers' church. At the head of the short nave, he turned toward the altar and genuflected before mounting the three shallow steps leading up to the sanctuary.

The little chapel was hardly large enough to hold the combined number of Hospitallers present. It was dark, except for the frail glimmer of votive candles burning on the altar and in the ambries at the back of the apse. The magisters assembled in a row along the foot of the sanctuary steps. Last of these to arrive, Ulbrecht took up his station at the end, nearest the chancel door.

The Grand Master of Gand waited quietly at the altar with his back to the apse, while the preceptors filed in to take their places in the shadows toward the back of the chapel. Before him on the table of the altar stood a silver monstrance in the form of a six-rayed star, the hexagonal disc at its center set with a pure green emerald. The tip of each ray of the star was surmounted by a small silver dish holding lamp oil perfumed with myrrh. Each reservoir of oil held a floating wick.

An expectant silence settled over the congregation of mages. His face sternly composed in the dim light from the candles on either hand, the grand master lifted a thin wax taper from a silver tray at the back of the monstrance. He lit the taper from the right-hand altar candle. Holding it up before the raised eyes of the men assembled in the body of the chapel, he intoned the opening verse of the Oblation: "Illuminate our darkness, we beseech thee, oh Lord God of Hosts—"

From the ranks of his fellow mages rose the antiphonal response: "Enter into this place of shadows, and hallow it with the brightness of your presence!"

With a touch of the taper, the grand master set alight the uppermost point of the star. He continued with deepening resonance, "Daystar of Heaven, dawn upon our earthly night!"

"Source of the Magia," chanted the congregation, "lend us thine aid!"

The grand master kindled a second point of the Hospitallers' star. The aromatic fragrance of the burning oil reminded Ulbrecht sharply of the fact that three of the most significant events in his life as a mage had been commemorated by this particular rite: the commencement of his novitiate; his ordination as a full-fledged mage; his elevation to the Council of Magisters of Ambrothen. Always before, the Oblation of Lights had been for him an occasion of joy and celebration. But tonight the ritual savored not of sacramental perfume, but of funeral ashes.

When all six lights had been lit, the grand master lifted up his voice, to lead his flock in chanting the "Hymn of St. Berengar":

"Clothe thyself with radiance, as a warrior girding
     himself for battle.
Let thy purity shine forth, as a shield upon thine
arm.
Let thy virtue blaze like a sword in thy right hand.
Let hope be thy breastplate, and faith thy helm.
Though thine enemies surround thee in chariots of
     darkness,
The power that rules the heavens shall burn like
     the sun for thy salvation.
In the valley of shadows, thou shalt see thy way
     clearly.
The fire of the Most High shall be forever the
     light of thine eyes."

As the strong echoes died away, Lliam Brynmorgan lifted up the magestone pendant that he wore at his breast. Presenting it like an offering in the open cup of his two hands, he called out, "Join with me, reverend brothers, in renewing the commitments we made at our investiture!"

There was a ripple of movement as his fellow mages emulated his ritual gesture. His own smaragdus cradled in the palms of his upraised hands, Ulbrecht added his voice to the chorus that recited the Hospitallers' prayer of consecration:

"Lord of the Magia, take my eyes,
     That I may see and understand what makes the body suffer.
Take my ears, that I may hear
     The tongueless cry of the broken spirit.
Take my mouth, that I may speak comfort
     To the afflicted mind.
Take my hands, that I may rightly administer
     Your healing power."

The air came suddenly to life with tingling energy. As the Hospitallers' prayer soared to its culmination, the green stone at the heart of the altar-star began to glow with emerald fire. An answering shimmer of green lights shone out from the elevated hands of the mages gathered among the pillars in the chapel, brightening until the green light filled the little church like sunlight filtered through a screen of young leaves. The air within the chapel all at once seemed warm as a spring day.

The beauty of the Magia seemed both subtle and supernal, lifting the heart above its fears. Gazing at its loveliness with fresh strength of purpose, Ulbrecht became all at once aware of a small dark figure standing at his side. It had not been there only an instant before. Looking down sharply, he saw that the form was Kherryn's.

Her silent unlooked-for appearance gave him a start. He opened his mouth to reprove her for slipping out without shoes or a cloak; then he realized that the figure he was seeing was semitransparent in the glimmering light. She turned her head to gaze up at him in white-faced appeal. There were traces of what might have been tears on her cheeks.

There was no misreading the distress of mind that had driven her separable dream-self out of her body in search of him. Now, as before in Farrowaithe, Ulbrecht

opened his heart to her. The voice of her thoughts
carried the shrillness of a cry. "Ulbrecht, we must leave
this place at once! Your life is almost certainly forfeit if
we stay!"

Images poured through his mind like a cataract:
red-eyed shadows gliding over snow . . . a guard wall
crumbling . . . the contorted face of Earlis Ap Eadric,
teeth bared in vengeful glee. . . . "He'll kill you if you let
him anywhere near you," sobbed Kherryn. "Please,
please don't give him the chance! Run away! Run away
now!"

An hour earlier, Ulbrecht might have been tempted
to heed her urging. But since then, he had discovered his
own inviolable mission. "I can't flee," he told her gently.
"I'm afraid my place is here."

"That's not true. You can leave if you choose!"

"I'm not so free as that. My leaving would weaken
my brother Hospitallers—"

"I don't care!" she cried fiercely. "I don't want you
to die!"

"It need not come to that," he argued patiently.
"Not if all of us stand firm."

Her response was a choked sob of protest. Knowing
her gift of prescience, Ulbrecht experienced an icy prick
of dread. At the same time, however, he knew that the
decision had already been taken, by his own consent, out
of his hands. He groped for words with which to ease her
pain. "You mustn't cry on my account, dear heart," he
told her with quiet remonstrance. "It may well be that we
will be forced to part company, but—"

"No!" Stricken with grief, she refused to be com-
forted. Feeling her tremble, Ulbrecht knew that somehow he had to bring her to her senses. There was so much
she needed to know—so little time for him to tell her
what he could. "Listen to me, Kherryn!" he urged her.
"Maybe my death here and now *is* inevitable. But you of
all people should understand that death is merely a
transposition of essence and spirit. This material world
represents only one of many possible levels of existence.

There are countless others—shadowy pararealms that most of us glimpse only imperfectly in our dreams."

"But you—" he continued, "you are different. Special. For you the doorways to these pararealms are always open. You travel back and forth across their thresholds as easily and as naturally as I might step from room to room in any large house. Up to now, your explorations have been almost accidental. But the time will come when you will *choose* where you want to go—and when that happens, the Providence which gave you your gifts will show you the way."

She was steadier now. Though she was far from resigned, he sensed that she was making a sincere effort to take in what he was telling her. At the end of his disclosure, she had only one question. "How do you know all this?"

He almost smiled. "I have my own gifts—and one of them is deep sight. Trust me, dear heart: you have a remarkable talent. Whatever happens once we separate, remember what I've told you."

Another surge of grief threatened for a moment to overwhelm her, but this time she managed to control it. "I won't forget," she whispered. "I promise."

He held her close for a moment in his heart, before releasing her. "Go now," he told her. "Vult Hemmling's men will see to it that you win free to safety. If you find Evelake, give him my blessing on behalf of the Order."

"I will," she said. "Good-bye . . . Father. I love you. . . ."

And then she was gone.

A sudden impetuous burst of noise roused Ulbrecht from the thoughtful quiet of his own thoughts. As he resumed command of his outer senses, the chapel door flew open, admitting a disheveled figure in armor. "Your Eminence!" called the newcomer in hoarse excitement. "The enemy host has been sighted! They're moving into the Taven Valley. The vanguard could reach here within the next half hour!"

Standing at the altar, Lliam Brynmorgan drew himself up to his full height. "They will not find us unprepared!" he declared. "All that could be achieved through prayer we have accomplished. Now it is time to match force with force! My brothers, let us go. . . ."

LEGIONS OF SHADOW

IT HAD BEEN A WEEK since Earlis Ap Eadric had last felt any need to sleep. As one of Gythe Du Bors's closest attendants, he had become infused with a dark inexhaustible vitality that obviated all normal demands for either food or rest. Immune to cold, hunger, and fatigue, Earlis had made the journey from Farrowaithe in an explosive state of ever-mounting tension. As the vanguard of the Du Bors army approached the lower end of the Taven Valley, he could hardly contain the internal tempest of his own nervous excitement.

The force that was converging on Tavenern numbered more than six thousand. Roughly half of these were revenant corpses: gruesome puppet-warriors animated and controlled by the demonic principality that had taken up residence within the living body of the boy-king Gythe. The rest were recruits of various kinds —criminals and mercenaries who, for one reason or another, were prepared to serve a master even more rapacious than themselves. These marched in the grip of a murderous battle-frenzy induced and maintained by the black arts of over a hundred necromancers. Most of the latter were apostate mages, who, like Earlis, were feverishly hungry to test their strength against the Hospitallers whose fellowship they had forsaken.

Their own shadowy brotherhood had been shaped by Borthen Berigeld. Patiently, insidiously, over a period of fifteen long years, he had made it his business to seek out those individuals within the Hospitallers' Order whose restlessness or discontent had marked them out as likely initiates. Though he had frequently left the bargaining to an intermediary agent, Borthen was the one—always—who dictated the terms of the compact binding the new disciple to his fellows. A master of the art of temptation, the dark mage knew only too well how to stimulate a hidden desire without ever fully satisfying it.

First among Borthen's many conquests, Earlis comprehended his master's methods better than most. They had both been little more than boys when he had initially fallen under Borthen's magnetic spell. Recalling past encounters, Earlis felt his breath come and go. Even then, Borthen had known just what to give and what to withhold.

It had always given Earlis a shadowy thrill of mingled shame and pleasure to reflect that however Borthen might use him, the dark mage knew him, in all his complexities, as no one else did. In the past, Earlis had derived secret solace from the knowledge that even the punishments Borthen could inflict upon him were expressions of their unique intimacy. But the sanctity of that bond had been violated less than a fortnight ago by Kherryn Du Penfallon. Her unwitting intrusion into the inner sanctum of his soul had robbed him of his consolation, and for that theft he intended to have his revenge.

He knew she was at Tavenern. The exquisite acuity of perception that had made him a formidable inquisitor had rendered him conscious of her presence as soon as the demon-storm overreached the town. He knew also that she was not alone: with her was her self-appointed mentor and protector, the mage Ulbrecht Rathmuir. While Ulbrecht lived, he would certainly do his utmost to shield Kherryn from harm. But Earlis did not propose that his troublesome counterpart should be allowed to live long, once the fighting began.

A shadowy figure on horseback materialized at his side in a spray of displaced snow. "Hello, Narcissus," said a mocking inimitable voice. "A rose-noble for the maiden secrets of your blushing heart."

Earlis turned in the saddle to gaze at his questioner. Borthen had his hood flung back, and his black hair shone like moon-silvered water in the light thrown round them by the surrounding torches. The dark mage's heavy-lidded eyes were bright as a cobra's with veiled malice. The beginnings of a provocative smile played about the corners of his full mouth.

As always, Earlis was palpably aware of the lithe strength reposing in the other man's supple body. Meeting Borthen's sardonic gaze, he said resentfully, "What secrets could I possibly have that are not already common property?"

The look Borthen gave him was mildly admonishing. "You're not still bitter over that episode with the little Du Penfallon girl, are you? I doubt very much if an innocent like that would be capable of understanding very much about a man of your . . . sophistication."

This observation earned him a hot-eyed glare from Earlis. The former Prior of Kirkwell said hardly, "Innocent or not, she's going to pay dearly for trespassing."

"If you say so." Borthen was unimpressed. "You'll have to get past her watchdog first."

"The earnest Ulbrecht Rathmuir?" Earlis was waspishly scornful. "He's as good as dead." Seeing Borthen's expression, he snapped, "Perhaps you don't believe me?"

"You *have* been known," Borthen reminded him doucely, "to underestimate your opposition."

Earlis stiffened, pale eyes flashing. He said between set teeth, "I want one thing clearly understood: when we reach Tavenern, I want Kherryn Du Penfallon for myself. Alive."

"Really?" Borthen elevated an eyebrow. "How novel. Are you perhaps seeking to broaden your experience?"

Earlis recoiled as though he had been slapped across

the mouth. "Damn you!" he spat, and struck out for the other man's calmly mocking face.

Borthen intercepted the intended blow with contemptuous ease. Holding Earlis's wrist suspended in a practiced grip, he said reprovingly, "Save your strength, Narcissus. I rather imagine you're going to need it."

His gloved fingers made a small punitive adjustment. Earlis gasped and wrenched his arm away. Trembling between pain and indignation, he demanded, "Doesn't it mean anything to you that that *brat* should have taken advantage of me?"

Borthen shrugged negligently. "Why should it? If you want to play dangerous games with children, that's your own affair."

Earlis was still breathing hard. He said nastily, "And I suppose you haven't been playing games with Gythe?"

Borthen did not look like a man cut to the quick. "Gythe is a very interesting case," said the dark mage. "In his own right, he is merely an adolescent lordling with more pretensions than he has talents. But in the presence of Herech Thanatos he acquires some really remarkable powers."

Something in the other man's tone drew Earlis's attention momentarily away from his own grievance. He asked, "Is he more than you expected?"

Borthen's heavy-lidded eyes drifted. "He might well be," said the dark mage. "We shall see."

Earlis copied the direction of Borthen's gaze. The other man was studying the gracile figure of Gythe Du Bors. The young king was superbly mounted on a vicious black stallion, riding close beside the litter that carried his mother, Gwynmira, along in the midst of the army. Aware of the atramental aura of power emanating through the boy's human presence, the Prior of Kirkwell said, "Do you think you will be able to control him?"

Borthen's smile was thin and mirthless. "You had better hope that I can," said the dark mage. "Otherwise, we may all find ourselves in serious trouble."

The steep rock faces flanking the western entrance to the Taven Valley flared into yellow prominence as the reiver-vanguard of the Du Bors army surged through the gap in a swirling blaze of torches. Ogreish black shadows bounded over the snow ahead of the front lines of wild-eyed foot soldiers. Overhead, the turgid impenetrable cloud-roof crackled with sinister energies. Forks of dark lightning darted like dragon's tongues from one side of the narrow valley to the other, sweeping clear the road ahead of the advancing host.

Going mounted in the midst of the reivers, shadowy in their heavy hoods and cloaks, Earlis's fellow necromancers wore their mantles of power like battle armor. Like so many dark shepherds, they herded their charges up the winding course of the valley toward the gates of the town still half a mile distant. The freezing air throbbed with demented voices. The general rattle of weaponry became a rhythmical *clash—clash—clash* as the reivers began beating their blades against their shields as they marched along the frozen road.

Borthen dropped back so that he rode between Gythe Du Bors and the opulent litter in which Gwynmira lay curled like a leopardess amid a luxurious riot of sables and silk velvet. The wild staring eyes of the horses mirrored the antic flames of the torches going before them. In the darkness behind the moving circle of firelight the shuffle of nerveless feet announced the mindless following presence of legions of the revenant dead.

The nimbus of power projected by the Devourer obscured everything outside itself. Watching as the wings of the storm reached the upper end of the Taven Valley, Earlis became suddenly aware of a dim shimmer of lights ahead. Closer in, under the lowering canopy of cloud, the pallid strung-out course of lights became more clearly visible as a line of watch fires topping a high curtain-wall providing ground protection for the town. All along the allures, and above the crenellated arch of the fortified gatehouse, flame shone red on chain mail and weaponry to mark a grim assembly of armed defenders.

The air below the level of the gates carried an electrifying charge of impending violence. Mage-senses quickening, Earlis scanned the ramparts above him. Enhanced beyond the strength of normal vision, his mage-sight showed him an array of shimmering forms scattered throughout the dusky anonymous ranks of the men-at-arms. Glowing silver-green in the darkness, the luminous ghost-shapes proclaimed the presence of Mage Hospitallers gathered on the wall-walks overlooking the valley.

The spiritual emanation of a mage's power—his penumbra—was uniquely his own. Knowing well what he was looking for, Earlis set himself to single out the penumbra that belonged to Ulbrecht Rathmuir.

The magister from Ambrothen was standing out on one of the open-roofed turrets flanking the gatehouse. His penumbra glimmered more white than green against the ominous cover of storm. With a feline smile, Earlis turned to the members of his personal following. "Do you see that man there?" he hissed. "When it comes to duels of power, he's mine."

Even as he spoke, there was a roar from the ranks of the reiver battalions. Baying like warhounds, they surged forward up the slope toward the guard trench before the town gates. There was an answering ripple of movement among the defenders crouched behind the merlons. As the foremost reivers converged on the west bank of the foss, they ran straight into a whining rain of arrows.

Those who were hit tumbled to the ground to be trampled by those pounding up from behind. Heedless of self-preservation, the survivors plunged over the lip of the gaping ditch and began scrambling down its steep inside face. On the ramparts above, beads of flame broke out in crimson clusters as the defenders set fire to their arrowheads. Like a burning hail of comets, the second wave of missiles plunged over the walls into the trench below.

The ditch glowed with red light like a volcanic rift. Then the fire worked its way down to the gunpowder hidden under the bracken at the bottom of the foss. With a bellow, the dyke belched up sudden sheets of blinding flame.

The reivers caught in the womb of the explosion died instantly. More were driven back, hair and clothing ablaze. The ones behind gibbered and frothed in mindless battle-rage. The air was shrill with bedlamite yammering.

Above the clamor of screams there sounded three braying notes on a brazen trumpet. The advancing reivers halted in their tracks, eyes staring, tongues abruptly stricken dumb. Earlis spun around in his saddle to look back in the direction of Gythe Du Bors and his entourage. His youthful face aglow in the lurid firelight, the boy was standing up in his stirrups, cloak flung back, one arm upraised. A crimson ball of multifaceted flame blazed like an infernal star in the palm of his hand.

As Earlis watched in spellbound fascination, the fiery orb began to revolve. Moving slowly at first, it gathered speed as it turned, until it was only a coruscating blur in the darkness. The sound of its whirring was like the dissonant laughter of legion voices. As the pitch of the noise intensified, the surrounding air rose to create a whirling funnel of angry winds.

The winds lashed out at the drifted piles of snow, heaped twelve feet deep on either side of the pass. Snow crystals cascaded in sheets down the slopes, thickening into a whirling maelstrom of white. The tornado of snow swept along the fire trench in an angry cloud. Ice met flame in a howl of opposing elements.

Buffeted by blasts of shooting steam, Earlis buried his face in a fold of his cloak. The noise rolled over him like a crashing wave and carried on down the valley. When Earlis raised his head, he saw that the trench fires had been smothered under tons of melting snow. The twenty-foot gap had been bridged by a smooth and solid sheet of frozen water.

Gythe dropped his hand and uttered a guttural, deep-throated cry. The reivers came to life again with resurgent violence. Shrieking like dervishes, they lunged forward over the dark crystalline bridge to hurl themselves at the gatehouse.

As the first wave of crazed attackers reached the foot

of the portcullis, the shimmering figures on the walls
above moved forward in unison. Power poured in sparkling cataracts from their outstretched hands, the bright
streams interweaving in midair to form a shining net of
silver-green filaments. The reivers entangled in the seine
of light abruptly lost their will to move. Blank-eyed in
sudden confusion, they collapsed into enervated heaps
on the frozen ground.

To Earlis's augmented senses, the radiance of the
Magia was audible as well as visible. Struggling to close
his ears to its sidereal melody, he drew from the pouch at
his belt a spindlelike phial of blood-black glass. It
glittered balefully, a bared fang. Pale lips moving in
silent incantation, he broke the phial in half with a snap
of his wrists.

An inky tendril of foul-smelling vapor jetted up
from between the shards. Curling and writhing, the
vapor expanded in a gust of brimstone. Two malevolent
points of bloodred fire unhooded themselves in the
midst of a growing mass of darkness. Beneath the
glowing eyeslots, the shadow hardened into a horned
black beak armed with a double row of razor-teeth.

Above the forming head, the darkness unfolded into
a naked pair of membranous wings, each wingtip ending
in a taloned spread of bony fingers. Beating the air, the
creature heaved itself aloft. It hovered for a moment,
toothed bill clacking hungrily. Then at a gesture from
Earlis, it veered away with a cawing cry and made for the
top of the town's high ramparts.

Other shadow-kites flocked to join the first. Shrieking like lammergeiers, they swooped low over the wall-
walks, lashing out with murderous viciousness at anyone
who came within slashing distance of their teeth and
talons. Earlis's shadow-kite homed in on the silvery
penumbra of Ulbrecht Rathmuir. Guided by its master,
the creature plummeted like a thunderbolt, claws braced
to strike.

Ulbrecht sensed its coming and flung up both hands
before him in a gesture of warding. Emerald fire shot
from his fingertips, flowering into a scintillating shield of

force. Scorched by mage-power, the shadow-kite sheered off with an ear-splitting yowl. It banked and lifted, fanning its wings in angry indecision.

Summoning the full force of his will, Ulbrecht set himself to hurl the creature back. Sensing the mage's intention, Earlis poured out a measure of his own strength to heighten the shadow's resistance. Revitalized, the creature shrieked and dived. One taloned foot broke through Ulbrecht's shield of force to rend a string of gashes across the mage's unarmored chest.

Blood sprang up from the wounds. Reeling with pain, Ulbrecht stumbled to his knees. Leathery neck outstretched, the shadow-kite snapped at him with wicked daggerlike teeth. The mage lunged aside to evade its grasp and fetched up against the base of the parapet.

Urged on by its master, the kite darted in close. Ulbrecht dodged out of the way with only inches to spare as the creature's fangs and claws gouged into the masonry of the wall. Scrambling backward, the mage got his feet under him and hauled himself upright. His face blanched but determined, he raised his right hand high.

Green flame blazed up from the center of his palm, taking the shape of a fiery sword. As the shadow-kite lunged at him again, he lashed out with his blade of light. The edge of it sheared cleanly through the substance of the shadow. There was a sulphurous explosion as the creature's hideous head fell away from its body. A split instant later, the shadow-kite winked out.

On the ground below, Earlis doubled forward in his saddle, his bowels gripped with sudden wrenching agony. Paralyzed with anguish, he did not see a vast black shadow take flight from out of the darkness at his back.

The shadow-kites still aloft broke off their individual attacks and flew to meet the rising black cloud-form. The lesser shadows merged with the greater, forming a noisome mass, all wings and tentacles. A myriad crimson eyes flashed malevolently in the darkness. The air stank of carrion as the creature converged on the town's ramparts.

Leaning against the inner face of the curtain-wall,

Ulbrecht was breathing hard, his nerves on fire after his climactic exertion of power. Gazing numbly down at his magestone, he saw there was a crack at the heart of the jewel. Horror blinded him for a critical instant. In that moment, the shadowy nightmare swooped down on him from above.

The downstroke of one monstrous wing dashed him back against the parapet. As he hung there breathless, a pair of lashing, razor-taloned tentacles struck the wall itself. Stone and mortar gave way with a sickening crunch. Caught in the disruption of masonry, Ulbrecht tumbled backward off the crumbling edge of the rampart and plunged to the ground below.

Earlis marked the hospitaller's fall with a cry of mingled rage and glee. Jabbing his spurs to the flanks of his wild-eyed mount, he sent the animal bounding forward to the place where Ulbrecht Rathmuir had landed. The mage was lying face-up on top of a pile of rubble. Earlis's heightened perceptions told him that the other man's back had been broken.

His whole body tingling with dark power, the Prior of Kirkwell vaulted down out of the saddle. As he touched the ground, the critically injured mage stirred feebly and turned his head. When he saw Earlis, he tried to lift himself up. Failing, he watched with fey, unflinching eyes as his enemy drew a dagger and knelt, preparing to deliver the cruel disemboweling stroke that would mean the end of mortal life. . . .

THE PRICE OF CONQUEST

THE WINGED DEATH-SHADOW HOVERED above the gatehouse, battering the ramparts with great flailing sweeps of its octopoid limbs. Pounding blows reduced whole sections of the parapet to rubble. The screams of dying men mingled with the sickening crunch of breaking rock. The air rained red with blood and mortar dust.

There was a panic-stricken rush for the guard-stairs leading to the ground on the inside of the town wall. Some of the hardier men-at-arms held back, risking crushing death to cover their weaker companions' retreat. Trapped out on the gatehouse roof by the destruction of the flanking towers, a small knot of mages banded together for a last desperate defense. Shimmering like ghosts in the howling, blood-spattered darkness, they linked hands in a circle, pooling their individual powers to form a shining hedge of emerald spears.

Scintillating like a constellation of morning stars, the pointed shafts blazed skyward with sudden unified intent. The power of the Magia penetrated the pendulous underbelly of the nightmare and exploded into solastral flower. Noxious vapors boiled out of the wounds like black ichor. Roaring in a brute frenzy of rage, the death-shadow bore down on its fragile tormenters, burying their light beneath the crushing weight of its reeking darkness.

Thrashing tentacles laid hold of the portcullis, rending it from its bedding. The gatehouse imploded, leaving ragged peaks of rubble behind. The waiting reivers began swarming forward over the piles of broken stones. Behind them followed mute legion hoards of revenants.

Once Tavenern's west wall had fallen, a murderous manhunt ensued, as bands of reivers set out to round up and put to the sword any of the town's defenders who had escaped the mass destruction at the walls. Mounted necromancers, drunk with success, led their followers on a bloody chase from street to street. The clash of fighting became submerged in the clamor of wanton breakage. The night grew shrill with the sound of orgiastic looting and rioting.

The din promised to continue throughout the night. Two hours after the invading army had made its triumphal entry into Tavenern, Borthen Berigeld returned to the High Street after making a tour of the outskirts of the town. He rode at a leisurely pace down the rubbish-strewn thoroughfare until he came to the entrance to the priory of St. Blaine's. Here he turned aside.

The priory's gates had been hurled down and wrenched to pieces by an advance guard of crazed mercenaries. Guiding his mount past the corrugated wreckage, the black mage entered the priory forecourt. The halls of residence on either hand had been savagely gutted, their walls scrawled over with obscenities painted in blood. Borthen drew rein and paused to listen.

A strange silence prevailed within the confines of the priory. A chilly wind gusted through the courtyard, disturbing the trampled snow. The breeze carried in its teeth an odd, unexpected savor of some heavy narcotic perfume. Catching the scent of it, Borthen frowned and swung himself down out of the saddle.

Leaving his horse tethered at one of the crooked gateposts, he made his way on foot across the forecourt toward the chapel, visible only as a gabled roof overlooking the adjoining cloister. Bypassing the cloister itself, he halted at the front entrance to the little church, one eyebrow elevated in saturnine surprise. The chapel, to all appearances, was still intact.

Not only that, but the heady scent of opiate perfume was stronger here than anywhere else. Dark eyes narrowly glinting, Borthen mounted the steps to the doorway. He paused at the threshold, using his mage-senses to reach beyond it. The impressions he received made him smile thinly to himself in the chilly darkness. Seeing no need to knock, he opened the chapel door and stepped into a firelit interior thick with incense.

The aisle leading the way to the sanctuary was decked with lamps that cast a dreamlike carnelian glow over columns and carvings. On the dais beyond the chancel, wreathed in sinuous clouds of scented smoke, Lady Gwynmira Du Bors sat enthroned in profligate luxury on the ornamented chair that had once been reserved for the priors of St. Blaine's. Her sable robes lay discarded in a heap at her bare feet. In their place, with voluptuous derision, she had put on a mage's embroidered chasuble and stole.

As Borthen entered, she extended slender braceleted hands in seductive greeting. "Welcome to my tabernacle," she called out to him. "Come, adore on bended knee!"

Her words were slightly slurred, her voice thick and throaty, as though she were under the influence of some potent aphrodisiac. Gazing at her with cool knowledgeable detachment, Borthen could see that her dark eyes were heavy and bright with inner fever. Her posture was wantonly careless, back arched, thighs parted to yield a suggestive glimpse of bare flesh beneath her vestment. She radiated a sensual aura of fecund desire.

Recognizing her ripe fertility, Borthen found himself in a position to consider several intriguing possibilities he had not foreseen earlier. Not averse to taking full advantage of the present situation for reasons of his own, he closed the chapel door behind him and turned to face Gythe's mother. Allowing the changeable light to make the most of his masculinity, he said, "Don't you think that's perhaps a bit extravagant?"

"Not at all!" Gwynmira's laughter was skittishly unsteady. "My son has the power of a god. Surely that entitles me to be worshiped as a goddess?"

"That depends." Borthen began thoughtfully to draw off his gauntlets. "Some might be tempted to say that a goddess should be distant and untouchable."

"Some! Those paltry Hospitallers, perhaps, whose notions of worship are restricted to playing games with pretty lights?" Gwynmira tossed her head in vicious scorn. "Where was their precious god-of-gods when we were crushing them like so many spineless worms? Asleep? Hiding? Or simply powerless to intervene? Those who call upon *me* for favors shall find me a more . . . responsive mistress."

She cocked her head, lips primmed in voluptuous promise. She murmured, "Perhaps you are curious to find out how responsive I can be?"

"Perhaps." Borthen was in no hurry to commit himself. Sauntering forward up the aisle, he took his time divesting himself of his cloak. At the foot of the chancel dais he paused to remove his doublet as well. Her gaze fondling him like a moist, importunate hand, Gwynmira demanded breathlessly, "Well? What are you waiting for?"

Gracile hands poised to untie the lacing of his shirt, he arched a sardonic eyebrow. "Why do you ask? Surely a goddess must be omniscient?"

Gwynmira's breasts rose and fell sharply beneath their covering of thin silk. She said with husky vehemence, "Passion is more important than knowledge. That's all any goddess needs to know."

She dampened her lips with a touch of her tongue. Her respiration was halting and heavy. "Granted that passion surpasses knowledge," said Borthen doucely, "shouldn't a goddess be mistress of her passions?"

Gwynmira uttered a small jarring peal of panting laughter. "I *am* mistress of my passions!" she declared. "Let me show you."

She lifted the hem of the chasuble and thrust her pelvis forward to display her glistening womanhood. "Here is the fountainhead of my divinity," she whispered sibilantly. "I make you free of its mysteries . . ."

Kherryn Du Penfallon was nowhere to be found within the environs of Tavenern. After leading his men on an exhaustive search—house to house, and street to street—Earlis Ap Eadric was finally obliged to admit that the girl must have contrived to escape during the course of the battle at the gates. His victory mood soured by frustration, the Prior of Kirkwell eventually dismissed his followers from his presence. Once they had departed, he reined his mount viciously around in the opposite direction and set out to find a place where he could nurse his grievances in private.

His heartsore meanderings brought him out onto the town's High Street. Yanking his gelding to a halt, he cast an angry glance up at the sky above the rooftops. With the demon-storm still blanketing the town, Earlis could not even use his mage-senses to determine where Kherryn Du Penfallon might have gone. His bitterness deepening, he goaded his horse into motion again and rode on.

The priory of St. Blaine's loomed ahead to his right, its outbuildings showing a gloomy array of shattered windows and desecrated stonework. Drawn by its funereal darkness, Earlis made for the broken gateway. When he got there, he was surprised to find another horse tied up at the gatepost. He was even more surprised when a second glance confirmed that the animal belonged to Borthen Berigeld.

Curious as to why the black mage should have stopped here, Earlis entered the priory courtyard and dismounted to look around. The ground between the main hall and the guesthouse had been trampled hard with rough passage of many feet, but Earlis's deep-sight showed him a shimmering trail of footprints leading along the outer wall to the cloister. The ruddy penumbral glow told him that the prints belonged to Borthen. Frowning slightly, Earlis set out to follow them.

The trail of footprints ended at the entrance to the priory chapel. Earlis got as far as the doorway when his sharpened hearing picked up a sound that brought him to a shuddering halt.

The sound of a woman's voice, moaning hoarsely somewhere between pain and ecstacy.

And beneath it, in baritone counterpoint, the rhythmic driving sound of a man's deep breathing.

There was no mistaking the identity of the two participants. Assaulted by crude impressions of sensual violence, Earlis stood frozen on the threshold and listened in mingled jealousy and outrage as the vigorous duet of voices continued unabated. After a moment or two, the woman's cries soared to a sudden shrieking crescendo. His gorge rising in a paroxysm of nausea, Earlis spun about and made a blind dash for the priory gate.

His flight carried him out through the forecourt into the snow-filled High Street. Weeping and retching, he stumbled to a halt a little way beyond the gateposts and collapsed into a heap on the curb. Oblivious to the cold and the icy snow-damp seeping through the seat of his robe, he buried his head in his arms. Overcome by a sick sense of having been betrayed, he heard nothing outside himself until an eerily matched pair of voices broke through the tumult of his misery.

"How dare you make of our victory an occasion of mourning?" demanded the voices in choral unison.

Controlling himself with an effort, Earlis lifted his head to find himself at the center of a semicircle of black-clad figures. Directly in front of him, glowing with dangerous splendor, stood Gythe Du Bors. The penetrating fire of the demon-youth's piercing gaze seemed to sear into Earlis's very soul. Speaking, as he always did, with two voices, Gythe said, "Tell us why you have forsaken our festivities."

Earlis wiped his wet eyes with a savage sweep of one wrist. Summoning breath, he said bitterly, "Dread lord, how can I rejoice, knowing—as I do—that there are some who dare to make light of your godhood?"

The boy's fiery eyes brightened dangerously. "Do not riddle us, Prior. How is it possible for our omnipotence to be held in contempt?"

"By association," said Earlis. "Your person—are we not to regard it as sacred?"

"You are."

"Very well. Since that is so," continued Earlis on a rising note, "isn't the person of your mother, Gwynmira, to be regarded as sacred also, by virtue of blood-kinship?"

"It is," agreed Gythe.

"Then here, dread lord, you have the reason for my distress," said Earlis, his tone shrill with vindictive accusation. "For even as we speak, the Lady Gwynmira dishonors herself and you by entering into carnal union with one of your own servants!"

There was a perilous pause. Then the two voices, base and treble, hissed together, "Which one?"

Earlis's thin chest rose and fell sharply. "Borthen!" he spat. "Borthen Berigeld!"

The demon's burning gaze flamed up. "Do you know where they are, these miscreants?"

Earlis nodded tremulously. "Yes, dread lord."

"Then take us to them," ordered Gythe Du Bors, "so that we may see their presumption for ourselves, and take reprisals. . . ."

Sprawled on the floor among her own cast-off clothing, Gwynmira Du Bors was for a time wholly unmindful of her surroundings. Luxuriating in painful satiety, she did not come fully to her senses until a sudden breath of chilly air penetrated the sultry afterglow of gratified desire. She opened heavy eyes to find the chapel's sanctuary filled with shadowy forms. At her feet, glaring down at her with hot eyes, stood her son, Gythe.

A startled, angry flush flooded Gwynmira's cheeks. Catching up a cloak, she gathered it hastily around her before lifting her outraged, inquiring gaze to meet Gythe's. "What is the meaning of this intrusion, my lord?" she demanded waspishly. "I hope you have some good reason for making a spectacle of me before these gaping underlings."

The fire in Gythe's eyes was churning like magma. He said, "We have been told that you have been unfaithful to us."

Something palpably menacing in her son's manner and aspect warned Gwynmira to modify her tone. Bare arms stippled with a rash of gooseflesh, she said, "Unfaithful? Forgive me, my lord, but I don't understand."

Gythe's chest swelled. The voices that issued from his mouth were implacable as steel. He said, "Have you perhaps forgotten our first commandment: 'You shall have no other lords before us?'"

"I have not forgotten," said Gwynmira. Forcing a smile, she gazed up at him in fawning appeal. "*You* are my lord. And *you* are my master."

"Then why," demanded the Devourer, "have you seen fit to traffic with one of our human chattels?"

The atmosphere within the chapel was crackling

with perilous energies. In dawning fright, Gwynmira reached out a hand to stroke her son's thigh. "Forgive me, if I have somehow offended you, my lord," she murmured. "I—I only thought to honor you—"

"*Honor* us?" snarled the paired voices. "You have allowed the bed of our inception to be sullied by the seed of a thrall!"

His taloned fingers made a lightning move to snatch Gwynmira by her unbound hair. With contemptuous, inhuman ease, he yanked her up off the floor. Gwynmira uttered a shriek of fearful protest and made a vain attempt to recover her cloak as it slipped from her grasp. Gythe held her fast in an unbreakable grip and addressed her with seething venom. "Understand, Gwynmira," he told her, "you belong to us, body and soul. You exist solely to serve our pleasure. Since you have violated your covenant, you have forfeited all claim to our good will. It remains only for us to administer a fitting penalty—"

Gwynmira was shivering in his grip. She made a small supplicating gesture. Dry-lipped and disheveled, she panted, "Dread lord, have mercy—"

"Mercy?" The alien gleam in her son's eyes was implacable.

"Punish me, if you will," moaned Gwynmira, "but don't kill me!"

Gythe's handsome face showed no sign of softening. "Are you so frightened of dying? What will you do if we let you live?"

"Serve you—serve you in all things!" promised Gwynmira eagerly. "Your pleasure henceforth shall be my only joy!"

"Indeed? Very well, then you shall have your life," said the Devourer. "But we do not trust the frailty of your woman's nature. Therefore, we shall take measures to keep you chaste for our sole delight—"

He wrenched her head back with sudden violence. Gwynmira shrieked again and tried to twist away, but her son held her fast. "Be still!" hissed the cruel voices of the young king. "It is your master's will that no mortal man shall ever again look upon you with concupiscent desire!"

Gazing up into Gythe's burning eyes, Gwynmira was stricken dumb. He reached out with his free hand, as though to caress her upturned face. As his fingers touched her cheek, there was a sudden caustic hiss. Under the pressure of her son's fingertips, the flesh of Gwynmira's face began to dissolve.

For the first horror-stricken instant, shock took her breath away. Then, as the pain scorched its way into her facial nerves, she gave a strangled scream and began to struggle with desperate animal violence. Retaining his grip with no apparent effort, Gythe traced the delicate lines of her lips, nose, and brow. His passing fingers left behind seared tissue and charred bone.

Piercing as knife thrusts, Gwynmira's shrieks reverberated throughout the chapel. When Gythe at length released her, her features had been reduced to a mask of cauterized scars. Deaf to his mother's mindless mewling whimpers, the boy-king thrust her from him with contemptuous strength, then turned to the mute ranks of his attendants. "Now," said Gythe Du Bors with sibilant menace, "find Borthen Berigeld, and bring him to us."

Slavishly obedient, the robed votaries dispersed toward the exits. Badly shaken in spite of himself by the Devourer's grisly demonstration of strength, Earlis Ap Eadric realized only belatedly that this time the boy had spoken with only one voice.

The voice of Herech Thanatos!

The discovery robbed him of breath. Before he could consider the implications of this sinister development, there was a stir of shadows about the chancel entrance. Earlis turned in time to see a tall cloaked figure step through the doorway. "Did you want me, my lord?" inquired Borthen Berigeld. "As you see, I am here."

Sparing not a glance for the naked skull-faced woman gibbering in the far corner of the sanctuary, the dark mage strolled forward unhurriedly through the midst of the Devourer's acolytes. At the head of the chapel aisle, opposite the altar, he halted and turned to confront the person of Gythe Du Bors. Hissing darkly among themselves, the acolytes drew back, leaving him standing alone in a pool of torchlight. His gaze sardonic, Borthen said, "My lord, have you perhaps some grievance to declare against me?"

Red eyes flashed balefully in the half-light. "Base mortal," rumbled the deep voice of the Devourer, "we are told you have had the temerity to lie tonight with our mother, forgetting that she is also our consort."

Borthen's eyes held a deep glint of watchfulness. He said calmly, "It is true, my lord, that I have lain with her. For that you should be glad."

"Glad?" Ominous as an earth tremor, the Devourer's voice set the shadows trembling.

"Indeed, my lord. As your lady mother's womb was your cradle," said Borthen, "it is fitting that it should also be the cradle of a new Order. By entering into carnal union, we ensure that a new priesthood will be initiated, to serve you in fear and trembling."

"You are certain she will conceive?"

"As is the way of mortal women. The signs are all propitious," said Borthen, "that your dominion shall be enlarged."

There was a perilous pause, as the boy's searing eyes searched the dark mage's well-schooled face. "No, not enlarged," grated the voice of the Devourer. "Say, rather, *challenged*!"

The echo of this declaration set the lamps guttering. "The counsels of your heart, mortal, cannot be hidden from us," hissed the demon. "We see that you would father a son not to serve us, but to stand as our co-equal!"

"If you believe that, my lord," said Borthen, "I invite you to examine me more deeply—"

"No!" The syllable rang harshly off the rafters. "You are too clever at defending yourself with subtleties. Let us see how well you defend yourself with power!"

The boy-king sliced the air in front of him with a slashing gesture of the hand. There was a sudden tearing sound, and a gash appeared out of nowhere. Like a surgical incision, the cut deepened and split. From out of the wound boiled a sudden suppuration of darkness.

Stinking of corruption, it poured across the floor like an issue of blood. Borthen leaped back, clenched fists forming a cross before him. From the ring on the third finger of his right hand, green light blazed forth with sudden angry radiance. Extending his arm, he directed its power into the midst of the pustular darkness.

The shadow-tide boiled under the fiery ray of inimical light, but the waves of black poison continued to tumble out of the unsealed rift in the air. Surrounded by a noisome effusion of venom, Borthen aimed the Magia's cauterizing power at the gash Gythe had created. The demon-lord countered with a crimson backlash of energy that seared and crackled as it fell. Borthen staggered under the impact and flung out his right hand in the direction of the altar.

Among the litter of Gwynmira's discarded clothing, metal glittered with a sudden responsive gleam. Bent and broken, but still sharp-tongued as a morning-star, the Hospitallers' monstrance reared up among the wreckage of blasphemy. In response to the pull of Borthen's open hand, the six-rayed star spun in the air, quickening into a wheel-blur of green light. Out of the heart of the wheel burst a shaft of verdant fire.

The shaft struck Gythe between the shoulder blades, boring inward from back to breast. The demon-king went rigid with a bellow of fury and anguish. The raging heat of his black breath set fire to the spreading shadow-dark on the floor. Even as the Devourer clawed at the spear of mage-power, the pool surrounding Borthen Berigeld went up in a roar of sulphurous flames.

Engulfed in the midst of the conflagration, Borthen uttered a cry of raw agony. Outside the wall of fire, the demon spun and ranted. Black foam gushed in spurts from his gaping mouth. Fed by the Devourer's rage, the shadow-pool roared like a furnace.

Cowering on the floor behind the altar, Earlis Ap

Eadric heard Borthen's elongated scream. Aghast at the storm he himself had unleashed, the prior started up in time to see the black mage roll helplessly to the feet of the demon-lord. Wrapped in a winding-sheet of black flame, he was writhing in torment. Earlis saw with a heart-stopping pang of horror that the other man's magestone had been reduced to so much dust.

The Devourer showed teeth in a gleaming rictus of anticipation and lifted his hand above the prostrate mage. Infernal flame began to form a fiery blade within his grasp. Earlis's heart leaped into his mouth. As the demon reared back to strike, the prior from Kirkwell shrieked out in protest and lunged for the boy-king's arm.

The demon turned to confront him. Blindly committed to his action, Earlis ran onto the searing point of the Devourer's sword. A blast of interior fire rent the prior's bowels asunder. He collapsed howling to the floor in paroxysms of torture.

Blackness yawned over him. Even as he attempted to fend it off, it opened up into a fanged red gullet. Bottomless as an infernal abyss, it reached to engulf him. For one awful mortal moment, he gazed into the belly of the Devourer; then he fell over the edge . . .

SINISTER SNOWFALL

As guide and accepted leader of the combined band of foresters and mariners from Yske, Tessa Ekhanghar did not find it easy to sleep on the knowledge that she and her companions had almost certainly lost the race to Tavenern. Sitting muffled up in the heavy folds of her weather-stained cloak, she glowered into the low-burning embers of the fire at her feet, wondering if there was any way the party might yet salvage something out of their present situation.

The company—thirty-two people in all—was encamped in what remained of an abandoned hill fort several miles north of the town of Rhylnie. It was approaching two o'clock in the morning, and they had been stranded there since mid-afternoon of the day before. The weather, which had started out fair, had turned bitter and stormy on their first night out from the crossing at Linnock. After another day and a half spent fighting their way through ever-mounting gales of icy wind and flurrying snow, the party had finally been forced to seek shelter under the onslaught of a full-scale blizzard.

Under the circumstances, it might have been worse. The old fort—once a provincial guardpost—was one of several hideouts now used by the outlawed loyalists of Rhylnie. Vult Hemmling and his men, fortunately, had left behind them a reasonable store of fuel and horse fodder. Tessa reflected that even if her followers might be short on provisions, they were at least in no immediate danger of freezing to death.

On the other hand, they were no closer to reaching their goal than they had been eighteen hours before. And that period of delay might well prove disastrous.

If the disaster hadn't happened already.

"There's more to this foul weather than mere adverse coincidence," thought Tessa grimly to herself. "What I wouldn't give to know what's been happening at Tavenern while we've been bottled up here!"

But that was something that not even Caradoc Penlluathe—for all his gifts of magecraft—had been able to find out. Ever since the party had been driven under cover, he had been striving to reach into the heart of the storm by means of Orison, but all his efforts so far had ended in failure. At the center of the tempest lay an ominous darkness which the light of the Magia could not pierce.

As far as Tessa was concerned, the existence of such

a blind spot was a very bad sign. Her glower deepening to a scowl, she drew her knees in close and pulled her cloak more tightly around her. As she changed positions, the measured scuff of soft-treading feet over bare stone called her attention away from the sullen glow of the firepit. Turning to see who, besides herself, was unable to sleep, Tessa recognized the tall figure of Caradoc Penlluathe.

One glance at his expression told her his repeated attempts to break through the psychic barrier of the storm were taking a heavy toll of his strength. His face was drawn and his green eyes were underscored with smudges of shadow. Catching her look, he pulled a weary grimace. "Still nothing to report," he said, pitching his voice to a tone just above a whisper. "I'll try again in a little while, but right now my head's ringing like a belfry. Do you mind if I join you?"

"Please yourself." Tessa shuffled aside to make room for him. Caradoc folded his long limbs and settled down next to her with a long-drawn sigh of relief. Studying his features in profile, Tessa said, "Is there really any point in your continuing, while the storm holds?"

"I don't know. Perhaps not," he growled. "But I hate to give up, with so little to show for my pains. . . . Have you noticed the change in the wind?"

To Tessa's ears, the eldritch, almost human wailing of the tempest seemed completely chaotic. Colorless brows pulling together over her freckled nose, she said, "What kind of change? Do you mean it's showing signs of dying down?"

"Not dying down . . ." The mage seemed to be groping for words. "It's more as if the whole storm system were contracting—drawing in upon itself so as to concentrate its force all in one place. The one place," he finished darkly, "that I can't seem to penetrate."

The implications of this announcement were not lost on Tessa. "I don't like the sound of that," she said.

"No. I don't like the *feel* of it," said Caradoc with grim frankness. "It's like being on the edge of a whirlpool, hearing the waters roar, without being able to see the center of it all."

He ended the sentence abruptly. In the ensuing moment of silence, he gave his wide shoulders a hitch to ease his stiff muscles. Watching him, Tessa asked, "Have you spoken to Gudmar about this?"

"Not yet." Caradoc shook his head. "I didn't see much point in waking him up merely to hand him a pack of unpleasant inferences that can't be tested until either I get the break I've been hoping for, or the weather clears off enough to allow us to continue our journey."

"Then you think it would be worthwhile, pressing on to Tavenern even at this late date?"

"Yes, I do," said Caradoc. "We need to know what's going on inside that zone of darkness. If all else fails, it may be that the only way we're going to find out is to go there in person and take a look."

"And maybe get close enough to strike a blow while we're at it? God knows there's nothing I'd like better," said Tessa, "but to be honest, I'm not sure our thirty-two lives would buy us that privilege." Her eyes sought his. "You're our resident expert on demonology. If Borthen Berigeld and his demon-worshiping cohorts succeed in crushing the Hospitaller alliance at Tavenern, what good are *we* likely to accomplish?"

"Ask me again, when I have more information to go on." Caradoc sighed and rubbed a hand across the back of his neck. "Right now I simply couldn't say. Maybe when my head is clearer, I'll be able to produce a worthwhile answer."

In the dim light of the fire, his face showed its bones sharply. In spite of herself, Tessa's attitude softened. "Perhaps for now you should try and get some rest," she suggested.

"Rest!" It came out as a derisive groan. Tessa waited, expecting an acid rejoinder. Instead, he turned to give her a discerning look from under his winged brows. "You're right, of course," he said. And added with quiet candor, "If you don't mind my saying so, it wouldn't hurt you to take your own advice."

Tessa found the sudden directness of his gaze disconcerting. Her cheeks warming slightly, she said with deliberate hardihood, "Don't worry about me. Ever since my people and I were forced to take to the woods, keeping nightly vigils has become a matter of accepted necessity."

"It's hardly a necessity tonight," said Caradoc dryly. "Not while this blizzard's still raging on our doorstep. Tell you what: I'll stop fuming and go to sleep, if you'll agree to do the same."

Regarding him somewhat guardedly, Tessa said, "What kind of a proposition is that?"

"A practical one," said Caradoc. "If you're even half as tired as I am, you won't object to giving it a try."

After a glance over his shoulder to make sure there was a clear space behind him, he settled back until he was reclining full-length on the floor. When Tessa hesitated, he rolled over onto one elbow and said, "All right, so it isn't a feather bed. But with any luck, neither of us will stay awake long enough to notice."

A demurral at this point, Tessa realized, would seem like a clumsy attempt at coquetry. Repelled by the very idea, she edged back from the firepit and stretched out on her side, facing away from her companion. Drawing her cloak around her with a small jerk, she said, "See you in the morning."

"In the morning," agreed Caradoc's voice softly from the shadows at her back. "Pleasant dreams . . ."

Silence fell. Lying prone in the darkness, Tessa fully expected her mind to return to work on the worrisome issues at hand. Instead, she found herself listening with drowsy thoughtlessness to the light, scarcely audible rhythm of Caradoc's even breathing. Oddly soothed by the sound, she settled effortlessly into sleep.

She slept deeply and dreamlessly, untroubled for once by any nagging peripheral awareness of the cold. A sunny sensation of warmth and security enfolded her like an extra blanket, cushioning her protectively against the harsh chill of her surroundings. Under its influence, her taut body relaxed and shed its accumulated burden of tensions. Delightfully comfortable, she resisted waking up for as long as she could. It wasn't until she at last reluctantly opened her eyes that she discovered there was a long arm draped in a loose embrace around her shoulders.

The lax hand resting on her arm was lean and sinewy, with strong bones and long fingers. The surrounding chamber was still half-dark, but there was light enough to show her a newly healed lacing of scars encircling the exposed wrist. She stiffened involuntarily, realizing who had been keeping her warm during the small hours of the night. As she tried to shrug herself out from under the weight of his arm, it lifted of its own accord. Caradoc's voice murmured, "Hello. Sleep well?"

Tessa's thoughts felt as disheveled as her person. Not at all prepared to make conversation, she said disjointedly, "Fine. Yes. Thank you." And made an abrupt move to put some distance between herself and her companion.

Caradoc remained where he was. Aware that he was watching her, Tessa scrambled into a sitting position and straightened her rumpled tunic with a tug. She raked harried fingers through her short pale hair, wishing she could at least wash her hands and face. It was only then that it occurred to her that she couldn't remember the last time she had spared any thought to her appearance.

The reason behind this sudden change in her attitude was so obvious that only a blind man or a fool would fail to see it. And Caradoc Penlluathe most assuredly was neither. Tessa suspected that, given his gifts, there was probably very little she could do to prevent his perceiving the interest he was arousing in her. All at once it seemed imperative that she should escape from his company until she could get her feelings back under the control of her will.

She cast a swift glance around her. None of the other sleepers scattered throughout the hall were stirring. In another few hours, the survival of all of them might depend upon her ability to think clearly—judge coolly. Duty, no less than necessity, demanded that she regain her self-possession before she had to make any decisions on their behalf.

Behind her, Caradoc made a small movement. "Tessa?" he said on a note of soft inquiry. "Is anything wrong?"

A part of her yearned for the liberty to nestle down again, taking full and luxurious advantage of the pleasures of companionship. But responsibility outweighed inclination. "The wind's died," she told him, without turning to face him. "I'd better go take a look outside."

Before he could forestall her, she rose to her feet and reached for her sword belt. Strapping it about her waist as she moved, she made for the door leading out into the courtyard. Outside, the grey dawn air was very still and deathly cold. Drawing up her hood, she paused on the threshold to take stock of her surroundings.

The old fort had been constructed around a central quadrangle. Within the confines of its crumbling walls, the snow lay three feet deep. On the opposite side of the small enclosure, a set of stone steps led up out of a snowbank onto the top of the wall. A flicker of red light from inside the cylindrical guardtower marked where the men on watch had built a fire against the bitter frost of the night.

As she scanned the length of the eroded wall-walk, a muffled figure stepped out of the shelter of the turret into the open air. Catching sight of her on the ground, her subordinate raised a hand in salute before taking up his station facing north. Tessa went on alone, out through the ruins of the fort's narrow entryway to the head of the trail that had brought the party so far the afternoon before.

Below her, the ground plunged away steeply into a wide gully cleft by a shallow stream—hidden now under a freezing weight of snow. On the opposite side of the gully, the land rose again, forming a low ridge heavily wooded with evergreen trees. Spotting a flat-topped boulder protruding above the surface of the snow a few yards to the right of the gateway, Tessa waded over, brushed off its snowcap, and climbed up on top of it.

From where she stood, there was nothing moving as far as the eye could see. Chilled by her bleak surroundings, Tessa had to fight hard against a rebellious tendency toward wishful thinking. "What do you think you're doing? Have you taken leave of your senses?" she asked herself wonderingly. "You've eaten—slept—lived in the company of men for weeks and weeks on end without ever being tempted to take anything but a strictly professional interest in any of them. What's the matter with you?"

The explanation, actually, was simple: she had failed to reckon realistically with the strength of Caradoc Penlluathe's personal magnetism. Her awareness of his manhood was strong enough that it was threatening to undermine her principles of command.

"Most fighting men won't find it easy to take orders from a woman—however skilled she may be in the arts of war," her father, Jorvald, had warned her. "If you intend seriously to take up arms in this fight, you are going to have to take pains to think of yourself as a soldier and nothing else. If ever you allow yourself to forget, you may jeopardize your effectiveness as a leader."

"You can hardly complain that you didn't know what you were doing when you chose to take up arms as your father's proxy," she told herself sternly. "It's too late in the game now to start complaining that you don't like the rules—"

Sounds of movement came to her ears from the direction of the courtyard at her back. Turning, she saw Caradoc himself floundering purposefully toward her through the snow. Tessa awaited his arrival in motionless silence. After taking note of her unsmiling expression, he made a wry face. "I couldn't help noticing that you left in rather a hurry," he said. "If you're angry with me, I wish you'd come out and say so."

"I'm not angry," said Tessa. And stopped.

Caradoc elevated a winged eyebrow. "You're giving a fair imitation of someone who isn't very pleased," he said candidly. When she didn't offer comment, he went on with brutal directness. "Look—if you think I took too much of a liberty, getting close to you last night, then I'm sorry. But you were shivering in your sleep. I wasn't about to just lie there and watch you quake while I had the means to give you comfort."

Tessa was conscious of a sudden tightness in her throat. She said, "I appreciate the gesture. Don't think I'm ungrateful. But you should have left me alone."

"Really?" Caradoc's gaze became disconcertingly sharp. "Why?"

"Because," said Tessa bluntly, "I can't afford to let anyone indulge my weakness."

"*Indulge* your *weakness*?" He scowled at her choice of words. "For God's sake, anybody can take a chill. It's not as though being cold were a sign of moral degeneracy!"

"No—but the capacity to endure privation and discomfort is regarded as a sign of strength," said Tessa. "For that reason, it is a quality I'm obliged to cultivate."

"What for?"

"To demonstrate my fortitude," said Tessa. "My men trust me largely because I ask no quarter."

"I wonder." Caradoc's green eyes were bright and keen. "From what I've seen, they serve you because you inspire in them all the virtues that righteous warfare can inspire: courage, loyalty, honor . . . the strength to uphold all bonds of trust."

Tessa was startled. "How can you be so sure that you understand their feelings?" she asked.

"How can you be so sure that I don't?" he countered. "You have, believe me, all the inborn gifts of a natural leader. And much more besides." Seeing Tessa silent, he continued. "I appreciate why your men are prepared to follow you into battle. But that doesn't mean that *I* wouldn't rather walk *beside* you—talking not of strategy and tactics, but of ordinary trifles. If we survive the days that are to come, that's a pleasure I won't easily be denied."

There was a warmth in his voice that brought the

quick blood rushing to Tessa's freckled face. She said rather unsteadily, "That sounds almost like a threat."

"Take it as a promise," said Caradoc with a smile. "In the meantime, unfortunately, we've both got work to do—and we'd better go back now and get on with it."

A VOICE FROM THE WOOD

IN THE ABSENCE OF INFORMATION from Tavenern, both Tessa and Gudmar accepted Caradoc's recommendation that the party continue its journey north. Leaving their respective followers to finish eating and packing up, the leading members of the band went out to inspect the lie of the land. Standing next to Gudmar at the head of the bank, peering down in the direction of the now-invisible stream, Harlech shook his head and whistled through his teeth. "If ye were hopin' we could just mount up and be on our way, ye can kiss that notion good-bye," he observed. "That snow down there must be six feet deep, if it's a draftsman's inch."

Tessa overheard this remark. "It'll be lighter on the high ground," she assured him. "No more than two feet thick in the open, I should guess, and less under the trees. Once we get across the gully, we can pick up a woodsman's trail that I know of. It will take us in the direction we want to go."

"Fair enough," said Harlech dubiously. "But that doesnae change the fact that we've still got tae bridge the gap between here and there. Last I heard, horses were no' so apt at flying."

"We'll have to dig our way through the drifts," said Gudmar. "Unless someone else has a better suggestion?"

Nobody said anything. "Looks as if we do this the hard way," muttered Harlech. "Especially since I doubt anybody in this whole crew had the good sense tae bring a proper spade wi' him. . . ."

A short time later, armed with broken lengths of timber salvaged from the fort's decayed interior, the whole party assembled for work. Even with everyone helping, it took the better part of an hour to clear a pathway wide enough for the horses. Laboring shoulder to shoulder with Serdor, Evelake reflected that at least the exercise was helping to drive away the leaden chill from his hands and feet. Pursuing that thought, he found himself recalling another winter's day, nearly twelve months gone by.

He had been included as a member of the party that had accompanied the Du Penfallon family to their manor house in the country, some distance from the city of Gand. While the adults had gathered in the overheated, overscented air of the great hall to drink and converse above the discreet murmur of lute music, he had persuaded Kherryn and Devon to steal away to the gardens at the back of the house for a snowball fight. Kherryn at first had been diffident—until a square hit from Evelake had startled her into laughter and determined retaliation. After that, the battle had raged blithely over half an acre of terraced hedges and flower beds, despite Devon's bad leg, ending in a spirited chase through the sprawling maze at the bottom of the garden.

Thickly hedged, full of twists and turns, the maze had provided an excellent theater for combat. They had spent a glorious half hour dodging in and out among the tangled aisles and passages until the light began to fail. Separated from her two companions, Kherryn had been unable to find her way back to the entrance, and Evelake had been obliged to go back after her, guided by the sound of her voice. His memory of the incident was so vivid, he felt as though he were reliving it now. He could almost hear her calling him urgently by name. . . .

"Whew! That's more than enough hard labor for one day!" Serdor's voice, breathless with exertion, broke in upon Evelake's reverie. The young Warden roused himself with a blink and discovered that all around him the snow had ceased flying. "Gudmar and Geordie have just broken through onto Tessa's woodpath," said Serdor. "That doesn't leave much for the rest of us to do, so we might as well take a breather before going back for the horses."

The path, Evelake found, was uncomfortably narrow—little more than a hollow tunnel winding its way upward toward the top of the hill through dense stands of pine trees. Thanks to the thickness of the branch cover, the snow on the trail was relatively light, but the abundance of low-growing boughs forced the members of the party to proceed on foot, leading their mounts behind them. Trudging along in the trough trodden down by the people in front of him, Evelake caught himself listening to the surrounding woods—not with fear, but with a curious expectancy. After a moment, he realized he was listening for Kherryn's voice.

He made a resolute effort to put memory behind him. At first the roughness of the trail obliged him to pay attention to his footing. But after a while, he began to lose track of both time and distance among the close serpentine lanes of snow-burdened trees. Almost without his being aware of it, his thoughts drifted back again to the maze at Penfallon Manor. . . .

He was back among the trimmed jigsaw-work of yew hedges. The sky overhead was ominous with snow clouds. The biting air carried the sound of Kherryn's voice clearly to his ears. She was calling his name with frightened insistency.

"Evelake!"

The cry might almost have come from somewhere off to the left of the trail. Without thinking, he cast an involuntary glance in that direction, then chided himself for letting a daydream get the better of his common sense. "My ears must be playing tricks on me," he thought. "I've got to—"

"Evelake!"

This time it brought him to a complete standstill.

Following next in line behind the young Warden, Serdor also came to an abrupt halt. "What is it?" asked the minstrel.

"I don't know." Evelake frowned perplexedly. "Did you hear someone cry my name just now?"

It was Serdor's turn to look bemused. "No. Why?"

Evelake gave his head a shake. "I must be imagining things," he said. "Just now I could have sworn I heard someone calling for me. It sounded almost like Kherryn—"

"Evelake!"

Both of them stiffened. "You didn't imagine *that*!" exclaimed Serdor.

"It *was* Kherryn's voice! I'm sure of it!" cried Evelake. "Come on!"

Before Serdor could stop him, he dropped his reins and plunged off the trail into the midst of the snow-heavy trees. "Wait! Hold on a minute!" called the minstrel protestingly, then sprang after the boy.

Lithe as a ferret, Evelake was burrowing purposefully through the frozen undergrowth toward the source of the cry. Fending off backlashing branches and tumbling cascades of displaced snow, Serdor had all he could do not to lose sight of his quarry. Behind them he could hear the startled outcries of the other members of the party. Trusting Gudmar and the rest to follow their trail, the minstrel shouldered and elbowed his way through a series of briary thickets and at last overtook Evelake at the edge of a small clearing.

The boy had come to a halt, bristling with uncertainty. "For God's sake, Evelake, this is begging for trouble!" panted Serdor. "At least give the rest of the party a chance to catch up with us—"

Evelake wasn't listening to the minstrel. His straining ears were picking up an intermittent crackling in the icy bracken off to his left, like the sound an injured deer might make, staggering through thick undergrowth. Even as he tensed in apprehension, he glimpsed something slight and dark moving among the trees a dozen yards from where he was standing. *"Kherryn!"* he cried out sharply, and hurled himself toward her through the intervening brush.

She was reeling with weariness, but the sight of him brought the blood rushing to her cheeks in a wild flush of joyful recognition. She stumbled to a halt in her tracks, watching his impetuous approach with her heart in her eyes. With a choked exclamation that had no words to it, Evelake jerked free of the entangling brush and threw both arms around her in a fierce embrace.

He knew he wasn't still daydreaming when she nestled close to him, clinging to the front of his doublet with one small determined hand, as though to reassure herself that he wasn't going to fade away. The fingers of her other hand were clenched tightly around a small hard object concealed in the palm of her hand. Temporarily speechless, he tilted his face to rest one cheek lightly on the top of her bowed head. Then, half laughing at his own incoherence, he finally found his voice. "I can hardly believe my eyes!" he said wonderingly. "What are you doing here—*here*, of all places?"

Kherryn lifted her gaze to meet his. Her dark eyes, in spite of their weariness, were full of breathless laughter. "I was looking for you," she said simply.

Evelake stared down at her in mounting astonishment. "For *me*? But I don't have any clear idea myself where we are at the moment—"

Smiling a little, Kherryn lifted her closed hand and opened her fingers to show him a small comfit box carved from clear rock crystal. Evelake's eyes widened as he recognized it as the box he had given her before leaving Gand. "This is the key," Kherryn explained softly. "Since it used to be yours, it was drawn back to you—like steel to a magnet. All I had to do was follow its pull."

Before she could explain herself further, three tall figures crashed through the bracken at Evelake's back, weapons drawn and ready. As the young Warden half turned, the trio caught sight of his companion and fetched up short. The slightest of the three uttered an audible gasp and hastily sheathed her sword. Recognizing the daughter of the marshall of Gand, Kherryn abandoned the shelter of Evelake's cloak in order to greet her.

As much amazed as Evelake had been, Tessa hugged the younger girl warmly, then reared back to survey her friend in mystified inquiry. "God, Kherryn, I can't tell you how surprised and relieved I am to see you!" she exclaimed. "But how did you get here? Where have you come from?"

More members of Evelake's party were arriving, to gather in the background, murmuring among themselves in wonderment. Glad to find Evelake himself again close by her, Kherryn said, "We've just come from Tavenern."

"Tavenern!" The tall auburn-haired stranger at Tessa's side stiffened visibly. Green eyes brightly intent, he said, "Please—can you tell us what's been happening there?"

Kherryn gazed up at him. Though they looked nothing alike physically, something about Tessa's companion reminded her sharply of Ulbrecht. The shadowy resemblance was painful. Evelake felt her shiver slightly within the shelter of his arm and hugged her more tightly. "This is Caradoc Penlluathe, a good friend of mine," he explained. "He's a mage."

A mage! Knowing that much, Kherryn understood the nature of the kinship she had sensed between him and the much-loved teacher she had lost. Directing her words toward Caradoc, she said, "I can tell you only this: when we left Tavenern, the Hospitallers were preparing to meet a deadly assault from an enemy wielding demonic powers. I wasn't there to see the outcome of the battle, but I fear the worst. This dreadful weather . . ."

Fists clenched in anxiety, she turned back to Evelake. "That's why I had to find you! We were caught out in the midst of the storm. The captain of my escort is hurt—the rest suffering grievously from the cold."

"In that case, we'd better get to them as quickly as

possible," said the auburn-haired mage. "If you'll show us the way, Lady Kherryn—"

Tessa traded glances with the third member of the trio, a big man with the coloring of a lion. "What do you think, Gudmar? Shall I round up the rest of our party?"

He nodded. "Best if we all go the same route, horses and riders. We don't know who or what may be lurking out there in the trees. . . ."

Evelake went in front with Kherryn. "Are you sure you'll be all right?" he asked anxiously. "You look exhausted."

Kherryn's eyes were trained not on him, but on some distant point farther afield. "I can manage," she assured him. "I'll rest once this errand's done."

The whitened trees seemed to open ahead of them like a gateway, and close again behind them, a door shutting fast. Marching side by side with Tessa, Caradoc was aware of an odd tingling in his nerve ends that had nothing to do with the cold. His mage-senses spontaneously quickening, he cast a searching glance around him and noticed the suggestion of a glimmer in the air above the treetops on either hand. The evergreens themselves seemed to carry an elusive hint of iridescence among their needles.

Baffled by this curious phenomenon, he petitioned the Magia to open the eyes of his mind. As his perceptions sharpened, the ghostly iridescence around him blossomed into a shimmering aurora. The colorless light of day seemed broken by the air as by a prism. Everything around him—the trees, the snow, his fellow travelers—flickered and flashed in a dancing display of polychrome gleams.

Caradoc stumbled in his tracks. He shut his eyes to keep from losing his balance. Even as he drew back from the threshold of Orison, a firm hand caught his arm. Tessa's voice said, "Caradoc, what's the matter? Your face has gone white as chalk."

Caradoc shook the lingering clouds from his head like a wolf shaking water from its fur. "I'm not sure," he said bemusedly. "I thought there was something odd about the light. When I went to investigate through Orison, it was as if everything around us had suddenly gone crazy with color. . . ."

Tessa eyed their surroundings sharply. "Everything looks normal enough to me," she said, "but I'm not a mage. Did you sense danger?"

"Not as such."

"What do you think might have caused this effect you're describing?"

Caradoc's green eyes held a glint of dawning insight. "The question may not be *what*," he said, struck by the strangeness of his own revelation, "but rather, *who*. . . ."

FREEZING ENCAMPMENT

EVELAKE WAS TOO PREOCCUPIED TO take any notice of the low-voiced conversation going on behind him. His attention was all for Kherryn, stumbling along beside him in a growing daze of fatigue. She was breathing hard, like some small animal harried to the point of collapse. She seemed to be keeping herself upright by sheer willpower alone.

It wrung Evelake's heart to see her driving herself so relentlessly. "Kherryn, slow down!" he urged her. "For heaven's sake, stop a moment and catch your breath."

Her response was a vehement shake of the head. "I can't!" she panted. "If we stop moving, I may lose the way!"

Evelake could see no reason why haste should be a factor in simple way-finding, but it was plain that Kherryn was determined to keep going at all cost. He hooked a hand under her elbow barely in time to keep her from tumbling to her knees in the midst of a snowdrift. As he pulled her upright, he said, "If you won't slow down, at least let me help you. Here, take my arm—"

He paused because Kherryn was no longer looking at him. She was scanning the woods spread out in front of them with hollow dark eyes. Peering over her head, Evelake glimpsed through the trees fifty yards farther ahead of them the conical outline of a snow-covered mound the size of a house. Gazing at it, Kherryn uttered a choked sob of recognition. "That's it!" she gasped. "We're here!"

And crumpled against him in a dead faint.

Hearing the young Warden call out sharply for assistance, the rest of the party surged forward. First to reach the spot, Caradoc took Kherryn's slight weight on himself and knelt down to examine her. After a moment, he lifted his eyes to meet Evelake's stricken gaze. "Don't worry," he told the boy reassuringly. "She's suffering from nerves and exhaustion, but she hasn't done herself any lasting injury. Is that mound over there the place we're looking for? Good, then she can get some rest while we see what we can do for the rest of her party."

The symmetrical shape of the mound proclaimed it the work of human hands. It was flanked on four sides by as many squat dolmens hewn out of rose-grey granite. From the blind face of the mound, a thin trickle of smoke drifted feebly skyward. Evelake and his companions set out in the direction of the smoke.

Five horses were standing tethered in a dejected huddle about the west dolmen. Seven motionless hummocks lay half-buried in the snow around the smoldering remains of a small campfire. When no one responded to Gudmar's inquiring hail, he and Caradoc exchanged darkling looks. "The first thing we'd better do is get that dying fire going again," said the captain of the *Mermaid*. "We'll help Tessa's men gather firewood, while you see to those poor bastards."

At Caradoc's request, Serdor and Margoth stayed behind to assist him. Four of the mage's patients responded sluggishly at first, but eventually were roused to groggy awareness. Two others, suffering from bruises and frostbite, were more difficult to wake, but at last showed signs of coming around. The captain, however, was in far worse state than any of his younger subordinates.

Kneeling beside the body of the prostrate man, Caradoc saw traces of blood on the blankets covering him. "Give me a hand here, will you?" he called over to Serdor.

Working together, mage and minstrel carefully drew back the captain's coverings and shifted him onto his back. As their injured patient's face came to light, Serdor uttered a startled ejaculation. "Good God!" he exclaimed. "I know this man!"

"You do?" Caradoc looked up in surprise.

Serdor nodded. "Remember the farmer from Rhylnie that I told you about? The one who took us in and looked after Evelake until he was well enough to travel again? This is the very man! His name's Vult Hemmling."

He stared down at Vult with troubled grey eyes. "Evelake will be sorry to see him in such sore straits— though I guess neither of us should be surprised to discover he's been fighting as a partisan of the Du Penfallons. I hope his loyalty won't cost him his life."

"I'll do my best to see that it doesn't," said Caradoc. "Help me get him out of his arming doublet so that I can see what damage he's taken."

Vult Hemmling's injuries included a spattering of burns and a strange wound that had bored through his armor deep into the right shoulder. The puncture had a venomous appearance—as though the weapon that had inflicted it had been steeped in some corrosive poison. It cost Caradoc a struggle to cleanse the wound and induce the damaged tissue to regenerate itself. By the time he was finished, he felt drained and exhausted.

"That's the best I can do," he said breathlessly to Serdor. "Time will have to finish what I've started."

"That's good enough for anyone," said Serdor. "You sit back and rest a minute. I'll look after the bandaging."

Deft as he was with his hands, he made an efficient

job of applying a dressing to the wound. He was putting the finishing touches on the binding when Vult twitched and groaned. The older man made a floundering attempt to sit up. "Easy," said Serdor. "You're among friends. All the people in your party are alive and well cared for, so you can just relax and let your wits settle."

At the sound of the minstrel's voice, Vult's sun-seamed eyelids flickered. Twin chinks of bright blue showed between his sandy lashes. After a squinting look at Serdor's watchful face, the older man's eyes snapped wide. "Serdor Sulamith, as I live!" he exclaimed on a croaking note of dour amusement. "I thought you were safely away to Ambrothen. What brings you back to these dangerous parts?"

"Like you, this is where my loyalties landed me," said Serdor. "Judging by the look of you, you've encountered more than your share of the dangers."

Vult peered down at his bandaged shoulder. "Souvenirs of Tavenern," he said.

Margoth had drifted over to listen. Seeing Vult's gaze flicker in her direction, Serdor said, "This is Margoth Penlluathe and her brother, Caradoc. Caradoc's the mage who treated your injuries."

"A mage, eh?" Vult gave Caradoc a grim nod by way of acknowledgment. "I'm sorry to be the one to tell you this, but if you and your companions were on the way to Tavenern to lend support to the Hospitallers' defense, you can forget it and go back the way you came. Gythe Du Bors and his bloody warlocks will have made a slagheap of the place by now."

He paused and shuddered. "Incredible as it sounds, they've called up dead corpses to fight for them."

"We know about the revenants," said Caradoc. "We've had to deal with them ourselves. The source of their animating power is Gythe Du Bors himself."

"Well, you can probably guess how it was," said Vult darkly. "We were cripplingly outnumbered from the start. We managed to repulse the first attack, but then the black conjurers stepped in. Something hit me—I don't know what, and I suspect I'm as well not knowing. When I came to my senses, I was dangling facedown across my saddle, being led off into as black a night as any I've ever seen, with the sky behind us all in flames."

He shook his head wonderingly. "It was one of my own lads that got me away. Since there was nothing to be gained by turning back, we made a push to overtake Lady Kherryn and her party, following the route I'd mapped out for them."

An anxious scowl crossed his face. "Where is Lady Kherryn, anyway?" he asked. "She's safe, isn't she?"

"She is indeed, having summoned us to your rescue," said Caradoc. "She's resting over there by that rock."

Vult looked where the mage pointed. His blue eyes narrowed to sharp slits. "God bless my soul!" he muttered. "Surely that's not young Rhan Hallender with her?"

He looked to Serdor for confirmation. The minstrel's expression went owlish. "It is—and it isn't," said Serdor. "I'm afraid I've got rather a lot of explaining to do. . . ."

Kherryn Du Penfallon's rescuers had made a makeshift bed for her out of cut pine boughs overlaid with blankets. Relieved from taking any part in the duties that kept the rest of his party busy about the camp, Evelake sat down on a rock beside her and watched her while she slept. Gazing down at her still face, he found it difficult to believe they had been so lucky as to find one another again, after more than half a year of separation. He looked forward eagerly to the moment when she would waken and they would be able to talk, as there had been no opportunity to do while the lives of her escort still hung in the balance.

He was keenly interested to find out why she had never given him up for dead, despite the months he had spent in exile. And he was curious too to learn what she had meant by her cryptic remarks concerning the crystal box he had given her. But most of all, he wanted to know all about *her*—where she had been and what she had been doing. And he wanted to ask her about her brother, Devon.

Knowing that she was exhausted enough to sleep deeply, he was just resigning himself to a long vigil, when the brittle crunch of footsteps approaching through the snow drew his attention off to his left. Turning his head, he saw Serdor and Margoth making their way toward him. Catching the repressed gleam in the minstrel's grey eyes, Evelake rose swiftly to his feet. "What's up?" he asked.

Serdor and Margoth exchanged looks. "I've just been having a few words with the captain of Lady Kherryn's escort," said the minstrel. "You'll be interested to learn he's an old friend of ours."

"An old friend?" Evelake was baffled. "Who?"

"Why not come and see for yourself?" suggested Serdor. "I know he'll be glad of a word with you."

Evelake glanced back at Kherryn. She seemed to be sleeping soundly. "I'll stay here until you get back," said Margoth. "If she wakes, I'll call you."

The suggestion met with Evelake's approval. As he accompanied Serdor across the snowy campground, the young Warden saw that the whole area was bustling with activity. The men from his own party had the construction of temporary shelters well under way. In the shadow of the mound itself the dying embers of an earlier fire had been resurrected into a crackling blaze.

Muffled in extra blankets, the members of Kherryn's escort were huddled close around the fire, warming themselves by its glowing heat. As he scanned the array of haggard, unshaven faces, Evelake encountered a familiar pair of seamed blue eyes above a jutting blunt-ended beak of a nose. Astonishment brought him to a momentary standstill. *"Vult!"* he cried, delighted, and darted forward to clasp the knotty hand that the brawny farmer held out to him.

Vult Hemmling favored him with a mordant grin. "Hullo, lad! Or rather," he corrected himself, "Your Lordship! I thought Serdor must be having me on when he told me who it was I'd had sleeping under my roof a few months back. I can see now he wasn't just spinning me one of his tales—but I hope you won't take offense if I still seem a bit inclined to stare."

"Surely I can't have changed that much!" objected Evelake. "Although," he amended ruefully, "I suppose I *was* a pretty sorry sight when we first came knocking at your door."

"You're looking—if I may say so—much improved now," agreed Vult. "But to think I put you in the second-best bedroom! Maudelyn will probably box my ears when she finds out."

Maudelyn was Vult's redoubtable daughter, of whom he was inordinately fond. From the lightness of the farmer's tone, Evelake inferred that she must be safe somewhere, at least for the time being. "I sincerely hope she won't do that: your hospitality was above reproach," he said. "Though I rather imagine she'll be far too concerned over the fact that you've gotten yourself hurt to spare a thought for anything else."

Vult squinted down at his bandages. "Och, it could have been a lot worse," he said. "Your friend Caradoc's repaired the worst of the damage."

He lifted his gaze and grinned. "I promise you, my lord, that I'll be well mended before Maudy gets the chance to see me again. And though I'm glad to have seen you, I expect you'll be eager to get back to that little lass of yours."

Seeing Evelake's brown eyes widen, he gave a deep chuckle. "I'm not blind, lad. I saw the look on your face when you glanced her way just now. And I don't blame you a bit: she's a bonnie wee thing."

Evelake had the grace to blush. "Yes, she is," he said with a crooked smile. "I owe you and your men a debt of thanks for keeping her safe for me. . . ."

While his friends were still talking around the campfire, Caradoc went off in search of Gudmar to report on the condition of the men from Tavenern. He found the big merchant-adventurer sitting on a rock at the edge of the encampment, tracing thoughtful designs in the snow with a long stick. At the sound of Caradoc's approaching footsteps, the *Mermaid*'s captain looked up from his meditations and raised a tawny eyebrow. "Well?" he said. "How are your patients?"

Caradoc sat down on the other end of the rock. "Better than I dared hope. But not in any fit state to travel very far. Those least affected are going to need a day's rest before attempting to move on. Their captain won't be up to doing any hard riding for a good bit longer than that."

"That's all right." Gudmar was philosophical. "I'd much rather we were building shelters than digging graves. At the same time, though, I can't help wondering—"

He paused and scowled. "Wondering about what?" asked Caradoc.

Gudmar's scowl deepened. "The little Du Penfallon girl," he said. "She's hardly what you'd call robust. Taking appearances at face value, I would have predicted that she would have been the first to succumb to the rigors of the weather. Instead, as it turns out, she was the only one still capable of striking out to look for help on behalf of the rest of her party. I keep asking myself *where* did she get the strength?"

Making her way past them with a fresh armload of firewood, Tessa Ekhanghar overheard Gudmar's puzzled question. Pausing to toss down her burden of sticks, she said thinly, "If you're taking time out to delve into mysteries, here's another one: how in God's name did we manage to cover a distance of more than thirty miles in less than half an hour?"

Both men stared at her. Gudmar said, "I beg your pardon?"

"You heard me." Tessa dusted the snow from her gauntlets with dour efficiency. Inclining her head in the direction of the mound, she said, "That barrow—do either of you happen to know the name of it?"

Her two companions exchanged glances, then shook

their heads. "Well, I happen to be well acquainted with this place," said Tessa. "The mound is called Glaive's Hough. And it's every foot of thirty miles away from the hill fort where we camped last night."

Gudmar said flatly, "That's not possible."

"Possible or not," said Tessa, "we're here."

Caradoc was thinking hard. One mystery had just provided the solution to the other. "I think I've got the answer to both your questions," he said.

Turning to Gudmar, he continued. "You were just wondering where a seemingly frail girl like Kherryn Du Penfallon might have got the strength to do what she did. All the evidence there is suggests that she got it from the Magia."

"The Magia!" Gudmar gave Caradoc a startled look.

"Are you saying that Kherryn has mage-talent?" exclaimed Tessa.

Caradoc nodded in her direction. "Not only am I convinced that she has talent," he said, "but I strongly suspect that she might be what the Book of Caer Ellyn refers to as a 'periegete.'"

His voice carried a note of repressed excitement. "What's a periegete?" asked Tessa. "From your tone, it must be something special."

"*Extremely* special," said Caradoc. "And extremely rare. A periegete is a mage gifted with the power to enter physically into the pararealm."

He groped for words to explain further. "Given the limitations of our physical bodies, most people experience little beyond the material world that their bodies belong to. What meager knowledge they *do* have about the pararealm they obtain when their bodily senses are either asleep or benumbed—in dreams, visions, or hallucinations. A periegete, however, is not bound by those restrictions that hamper the rest of us. Once he attains full command of his powers, he can move *physically* in and out of the paraworld at will."

He stopped because both Gudmar and Tessa were

staring at him. "Look, I know this all probably sounds incredible. But weigh the evidence for yourself: Kherryn appears apparently out of nowhere, leaving no trace of footprints. She appears within mere yards of where we are, specifically searching for Evelake, with whom she has a particularly strong emotional bond. Having found him—against all conceivable odds—she proceeds to lead us back to her own party, thirty miles away, in almost no time!"

"What you're saying, then," mused Tessa, "is that Kherryn somehow took us on a shortcut through this . . . this pararealm?"

"That's a good way to put it," said Caradoc. "Time and space operate differently in the paraworld than they do in the here and now. That would account for the distortion in the light that I was aware of on the way here. I sensed that the phenomenon had something to do with Kherryn—but I was at a loss for an explanation, until just now.

"It was quite a feat," he continued. "I'm not surprised that she collapsed at the end of it. The miracle lies in the fact that her power lasted long enough to bring us here."

"You mean we might not necessarily have gotten this far?" Gudmar was frowning again.

"It's always a danger," said Caradoc.

"In that case, where might we have ended up?"

"I don't know." Caradoc was brutally candid.

Tessa shuddered. "I'm glad I didn't have any idea what was happening at the time. But how likely is it that a periegete would fail to reach his intended destination?"

"I don't know enough about periegesis to say." Caradoc gnawed his lip. "I imagine that—as with any other mage—a periegete can sense when he's drawing near the end of his strength. But that's assuming that he's previously tested his limitations and knows how to read the signs aright."

He cast a glance in Kherryn's direction. "I doubt that little girl is experienced enough to pace herself—if she even fully understands her talent! I want to have a talk with her when she recovers. We need to know how much—or how little—she's learned about her own skills."

"Can you guide her?" asked Tessa.

"I can probably help," said Caradoc. "But the best any teacher can do is simply to be a companion."

He drew a deep breath. "The greatest danger is that a novice like Kherryn could accidentally burn herself out completely by pushing herself too hard too soon. Given the unique nature of her talent, the temptation—the moral impetus—to spend herself to the limit will be great. She might even consider herself expendable in the midst of this conflict that has arisen."

"Do you mean she could actually *kill* herself through overstress in the way you describe?" asked Tessa.

"In her case, the risk is certainly present," said Caradoc grimly. "Most mages are safeguarded by the fact that their magestones will burn out—turn to ashes —before they can do themselves any mortal injury. But Kherryn's talent, like my own, is not dependent on the mediation of any talisman of power. The Magia comes to us directly—a great gift, but not without its perils. If we are not bound by any need to use a magestone," he concluded, "we are likewise unprotected from the danger of accidental self-immolation."

Tessa assimilated this revelation in sober silence. After a moment's thought, she said, "Do *you* know your limitations?"

"No," said Caradoc baldly. "No, I don't. I was severely tried at Sul Khabir, when I was forced to match strength with Evelake's demon-tormenter. I survived that test of power. Next time I may not be so lucky."

For a long moment no one spoke. Then Tessa murmured, "I don't suppose Evelake has any idea of Kherryn's potential as a mage. Should we warn him, do you think?"

Caradoc shook his head. "No. That's something he needs to hear first from Kherryn herself. . . ."

RIDER IN SHADOW

EVELAKE REMAINED CLOSE BY KHERRYN'S side throughout the day. Serdor kept the young Warden company during his self-appointed vigil. When they weren't talking, they amused themselves by playing games with sticks and stones. The afternoon was wearing away and the winter shadows lengthening when at last Kherryn roused from her sleep of exhaustion.

Hearing her stir, Evelake abruptly abandoned the most recent of several games of nine men's morris. Bending over Kherryn, he waited for her to open her eyes. To begin with, her gaze was dazed and bewildered. When she shrank back in momentary confusion, Evelake said, "It's all right. It's only me."

At the sound of his voice, Kherryn relaxed. Watching her face, Evelake continued, "I was beginning to think you were going to sleep through until dawn tomorrow. Are you feeling better? Would you like me to bring you something to eat or drink?"

"Margoth was threatening to make a stew out of the game Tessa's foresters brought in earlier this afternoon," said Serdor's voice behind him. "Why don't I go see if it's ready?"

He didn't wait for an answer. Kherryn's sharpening gaze followed the minstrel's light-footed departure. Evelake grinned crookedly. "Serdor's always like that—the soul of discretion. He knows I've got a thousand and one questions to ask you—provided that you feel up to answering."

He spoke lightly, hoping to allay some of the anxiety that was clouding her countenance. Kherryn said huskily, "What about the members of my escort?"

"You can rest easy on their account," said Evelake.

"Caradoc says they're all well on the way to recovery. Even the captain's safely out of danger now."

His expression turned owlish. "Talk about coincidences! How did you and Vult Hemmling come to be traveling in one another's company?"

Kherryn stiffened slightly at the question. "We met at Tavenern," she said. "Are you and Vult acquainted with each other?"

Her voice carried an odd inflection. Puzzled, Evelake said, "Yes, I once paid a visit to the farm he owns, just north of Rhylnie—"

"A big half-timbered house," murmured Kherryn thoughtfully, "with a thatched roof, and a freestone wall running all around it. . . ."

"That's the place," agreed Evelake, startled. "But if you only met Vult at Tavenern, how do you know what his house looks like?"

"I've *seen* it," said Kherryn.

"But—" Evelake stopped and stared at her. "You're beginning to worry me, Kherryn," he said. "Ever since this morning you've been talking in riddles. Is there something I ought to know that you haven't told me yet?"

Kherryn bit her lip, then nodded. "It isn't easy to explain," she said, "especially since I'm not sure I fully understand it all myself. But it appears that I've got an affinity for the power of the Magia. I can't heal people, like your friend Caradoc. But I can do other things. I can see events happening at a distance. And I can find things. . . ."

She struggled for words to continue. "The first time my gift manifested itself clearly was the night your father was murdered. I awoke from a sound sleep to the sensation of being stabbed to the heart with a dagger. It was as though I experienced his death through a vision. After that, there were more visions. I found myself witnessing events in the past and in the future, as well as in the present. It was as if some part of me were capable of stepping outside of normal time—without my wanting it to happen."

She shook her head. "If it hadn't been for a magister from Ambrothen—a man named Ulbrecht Rathmuir—I'm sure I would have gone mad. He's the one who explained that my visionary experiences were proof not of insanity, but of mage-talent. He also said it was vitally important that I learn to control my powers. When I asked if he himself would teach me, he agreed."

A painful smile touched her lips. "It was while I was under his tutelage that we discovered that my talent goes far beyond simple clairvoyance. Not only can I 'see' things—but sometimes I can actually reach out and *touch* them. That's how I found you this morning: by invoking the Magia to show me where you were so that I could meet you in person. I wasn't entirely sure it would work, but . . . well, here we both are, together."

She looked expectantly toward Evelake, as though inviting him to speak his thoughts. "I hardly know what to say," he told her. "From what you've just told me, this talent of yours isn't exactly an unmixed blessing. How I'll feel about your possessing such a talent is going to depend largely on how you feel about it yourself. Are you glad of your gift?"

"Whether I'm glad or not doesn't matter," said Kherryn seriously. "What matters is that I've been given this talent for a purpose—"

She clearly intended to say more, but a sudden disturbance at the northern end of the encampment interrupted her. Craning his neck, Evelake saw Harlech dart across the clearing, making for where Gudmar, Tessa, and Caradoc were gathered together around a map Tessa was sketching on the ground at their feet. "Something must be up!" said the young Warden to Kherryn. "You stay here—I'll go find out what it is."

On his way to join his elders, he met up with Serdor and Margoth. The three of them arrived on the scene just as Harlech finished delivering his report. "What's going on?" asked Evelake.

"One of our pickets has spotted a rider heading this way," said Gudmar. "The rider appears to be alone, but we're about to go investigate in order to make sure."

"Do you suppose it might be someone else from Tavenern?" inquired Margoth.

"We'll know soon enough," said Caradoc grimly.

His green eyes were hard as chips of emerald, and his mouth was thin and tight. "What's the matter?" asked his sister.

"I'm not sure—but I've got an alarm going off somewhere in the back of my mind," growled Caradoc. "Let me be the first to accost this rider. I have a feeling he may be more than he seems."

"In that case, you'd better have some backup," said Tessa firmly. "I'll go with you."

Caradoc looked as if he would have liked to protest, but after a look at her face, he acceded with a curt nod. "All right," said Gudmar. "Harlech and I will circle around through the trees to cover your flanks. Evelake, you and Serdor and Margoth had better hang back until we make sure it's safe. . . ."

The lone intruder was approaching the Hough from the north. Watching from cover farther up the slope of the hill, Tessa tried and failed to gain any impression of the newcomer's possible identity. Swathed head to foot in a voluminous dark riding cloak, the horseman slumped low over his mount's withers so that his face was hidden from view. Black gloved hands slack on the animal's trailing reins, he allowed his weary horse to pick its own stumbling path upward along the line of a shallow snow-filled ravine.

"Whoever he is, he looks sick or injured—or simply too exhausted to keep himself upright in the saddle," she observed in an undertone to the tall mage at her side.

Caradoc nodded without speaking. A chilly sense of premonition was raising the hairs at the nape of his neck. As he and Tessa began moving down the slope toward the intruder, one part of him was trembling with queasy apprehension, like a small boy going to present himself before a sadistic schoolmaster. Another part of him was bristling with icy hostility.

While he and Tessa were still a short way off, the intruder's horse faltered to an exhausted standstill.

Slumped facedown over his mount's drooping neck, the rider made no move; if he was aware of Caradoc's approaching footsteps, he gave no sign. His own inner turmoil mounting, Caradoc advanced until he was within arm's length of horse and rider. With one hand he reached out and seized the animal's cheekstrap; the other he laid with shrinking authority on the newcomer's bent shoulder.

A shudder passed through the rider's sinewy frame. His cowled head slowly lifted and began to turn. Caradoc caught a fleet foreshadowing glimpse of a cruelly sensual profile before the rider twisted around in the saddle to confront him. In that instant, the red-haired mage found himself gazing into a fathomless pair of black hooded eyes.

Standing a few feet back from horse and rider, Tessa saw Caradoc recoil as though he had been stung by some venomous reptile. She whipped her sword from its sheath and crouched, ready to lunge. Her defensive movement did not escape the attention of the haggard dark-eyed rider. Raising himself a few painful inches higher in his stirrups, he looked from Caradoc to Tessa, and back again, then burst incongruously into laughter.

His laugh swelled to a gasping peal of hectic mirth. Struggling for breath, he at last recovered voice enough to speak. "Hello, Caradoc—sweet briar of my soul," said the intruder with rasping cordiality. "How fares the wildest flower in all the garden of the Order?"

Fighting to keep his head amid a black maelstrom of hatred and loathing, Caradoc could find no words to frame a suitable response. "What, no well-chosen phrases of vituperation, carefully rehearsed?" chided the dark rider. "Surely you must have known that sooner or later, one of us was bound to come looking for the other?"

Looking askance toward her companion, Tessa saw that the mage's strong fingers were clenched into white-knuckled fists. His green eyes were murderous. She said sharply, "Caradoc, who is this man?"

Her voice pierced cleanly through the stormy chaos

of Caradoc's churning emotions. Taking a firm, inviolable grip on himself, he half turned toward her and smiled, white-toothed as a young wolf. Indicating the newcomer with his eyes, he said scathingly, "This creature? This is the archapostate . . . the prince of carrion. His name is Borthen Berigeld."

Caradoc's voice, ringing hard as steel, carried as far as the treeline farther back up the slope, where Evelake, Serdor, and Margoth were waiting in the shelter of a clump of young firs. Hearing the name spoken, Evelake went rigid with horror. A black pit seemed to open beneath him, plunging him into a whirlpool of ugly memories.

It all came back to him in a choking rush— recollections of how this one man had stripped him of every shred of self-respect, before beating him into submission, body and soul. Even as he struggled in a black fog to master the violence of his own reactions, hands gripped his shoulders with steadying strength— the same pair of thin, strong hands that had pulled him back many times before out of abysses of pain and terror. Serdor's voice said, "Evelake, it's behind you! You and Caradoc fought and conquered that evil at Sul Khabir. It can have no further power over you unless you let it!"

Wrenching himself back from the edge of the whirlpool, Evelake forcibly recalled the moment of his reawakening. His breathing eased. Summoning strength of heart, soul, and will, he drew himself up and opened his eyes. "Come on," he said sternly to his two companions. "Borthen Berigeld may offer to strike me dead where I stand. But I will never—*never*!—cower before him again!"

Farther down the slope, standing shoulder to shoulder with Caradoc, Tessa stared at the black-clad intruder that her companion had just identified as their archenemy. Hard-voiced, she said, "How did he find us, Caradoc? The same way Kherryn did?"

"In a manner of speaking." Caradoc's tone carried echoes of bitter self-recrimination. "Several months ago he robbed me of my magestone. Since then, all he's ever had to do in order to learn my whereabouts is call the stone to life and let it show him where I am."

"A useful bauble," agreed Borthen, meeting Tessa's glowering look with a malicious half smile. To Caradoc he said, "Would you like to have it back? Very well, here it is."

He lifted his clenched hand and opened his fingers. A thin trickle of silver-green powder spilled out. The dust settled to the ground, to lie like a scattering of ashes on the snow. "I'm sorry the stone is no longer intact," said Borthen. "But as you well know, no smaragdus can withstand long use by anyone other than its original master."

"Your influence would corrupt anything!" Caradoc regarded Borthen with steady, dreadful loathing, wondering how he could protect his friends from whatever this visitation threatened.

"Well, you should know," said Borthen, and elevated a winged eyebrow. "Aren't you curious to find out why I've gone to the trouble of hunting you down, when it would have been easier to wait for you to come to me?"

"I can only infer," said Caradoc coldly, "that you are impatient to complete the destruction of the Hospitallers' Order, and regard me as one of the few obstacles left in your way."

"The destruction of the Order, as you know it, is already history," said Borthen. "Whether or not you will survive to found a new order is immaterial right now. Strange as it may seem, the last thing I want at present is to see you dead."

Caradoc stared at his bitterest enemy in mute incredulity. He did not need to turn to the Magia to know that Borthen was speaking the simple truth. But no truth from Borthen Berigeld could ever actually be simple.

In all his past encounters with the dark mage, Caradoc had always allowed his emotions to precipitate his behavior. Now he knew he dared not act without thinking. Why was it so urgent to find him that Borthen had been willing to sacrifice the magestone he had stolen? It could only be that his own had been somehow destroyed. Suddenly Caradoc had the answer to the riddle. He said slowly, "So—your demon turned on you, didn't it? In spite of all your knowledge, all your cunning, the demon turned on *you*—and its power proved even greater than your own. So great, in fact, that your own magestone disintegrated under the strain of the contest. Now I'm beginning to understand. . . ."

His green eyes narrowed. "This must be the first time you've ever been driven to defeat. I don't imagine there could be any greater punishment than that for someone like you."

"There is one penalty greater," corrected Borthen with chill venom. "The penance of being obliged to seek sanctuary among one's enemies—"

"*Sanctuary!*" growled Harlech Hardrada's gravelly voice from off to their right. "The only sanctuary ye'll ever get from me, Borthen Berigeld, is six feet o' cold earth!"

As the three people in the clearing turned toward him, the former captain of the *Yusufa* stepped out of the trees and advanced slowly, drawn sword in hand. "Ye bloodsucking shrike!" hissed the little mariner. "I wish ye had one throat for every lad o' mine ye murdered through your cursed sorcery, so's I could slit your black weasand that many times over for the satisfaction of hearing you choke!"

"Harlech speaks for me as well," said Gudmar, emerging from the trees off to Tessa's left. Golden eyes regarding Borthen with glinting contempt, he raised his voice. "You owe *me* one life at least in recompense for the death of my friend Delsidor Whitfauconer. And for the unmerited torment you inflicted upon his son Evelake, I'd gladly exact another from you, if you had as many to give!"

Three more figures—two male and one female— appeared out of the evergreen thickets at the top of the ravine. "To extend any form of charity to you would be to dishonor the memories of those friends of ours who have died through your agency," declared Serdor in a crisp carrying voice. "I call you to account for the death of Forgoyle Finlevyn, Magister of Ambrothen."

"And I," said Margoth, "for the death of Arn Aldarshot, resident of the same city."

"Gudmar has already named you as principal agent in the killing of my father," said Evelake Whitfauconer. "As hereditary Lord Warden of East Garillon, I summon you to justice, Borthen Berigeld, on behalf of the hundreds of innocent men and women whose lives you have twisted, bent, or broken in your lust for power. I summon you to justice on behalf of the mages and citizens of Farrowaithe and Tavenern. I summon you to justice for the seduction and perversion of my brother, Gythe—for it was through you that he has become transformed into a monster of death and destruction."

"If justice were to be truly served," said Gudmar, "You would be required to die a thousand times over. As it is, you have only one life to lose. Show me what you intend to do to prevent me from taking it!"

Borthen Berigeld scanned the circle of his accusers with inscrutable eyes until his gaze came to rest once more upon the implacable face of his challenger. "What do I intend to do?" he asked. "The answer to your question, Guildmaster, is *nothing*. There is nothing I can do. I am completely at your mercy."

FORCED ALLIANCES

TESSA SURVEYED BORTHEN NARROWLY. "AFTER all I've heard about you," she said, "I don't believe for a moment that you are as helpless as you claim to be. Even if the demon has robbed you of your power, you must be holding something else in reserve—something you're sure will prevent us from touching you, despite all the evil you have caused."

Borthen gave her a smile that glittered like a sliver of broken glass. "You're more astute than your blustering companions. I may have lost my magestone, but I still retain my knowledge of necromancy. You need that knowledge if you hope to prevent this kingdom from being transformed into a fief of hell."

"A fief of hell?" Margoth did not trouble to hide her skepticism at his choice of words.

"The phrase is not merely cheap melodrama," said Borthen thinly. "The demon that calls itself the Devourer has succeeded in becoming fully incarnate. If we can't send it back where it came from, it *will*—ultimately—re-create hell on earth."

Seeing that he had effectively silenced his listeners, he went on to explain. "The Devourer comes from a region of the spirit-realm known as Herech Zhulzar—the Pit of Hunger. The Pit is both the demon's point of origin and the source of its power. When the Devourer assumed complete possession over the corporeal body of Gythe Du Bors, it forced the boy's disembodied soul to take its place in Zhulzar so that the void would have a vital source of spiritual energy to feed on. As long as the boy's spirit remains a prisoner there, the demon remains all-powerful.

"It follows logically," he continued, "that anyone hoping to defeat the Devourer would first have to find the lost soul of Gythe Du Bors and deliver it from its prisonhouse in the pararealm. That's why you need me: I'm the only man alive who can guide you to Herech Zhulzar."

"And doubtless do your level best tae maroon our folk in some convenient corner o' the de'il's kitchen," rumbled Harlech. "Dinnae listen tae him, Caradoc. There's no trustin' such a one as this!"

Caradoc had not taken his eyes from the dark mage's haggard face. It seemed to him that Borthen's self-possession was becoming increasingly strained—as though the other man were fighting to preserve a cool, unruffled exterior. "How do you propose we should enter the pararealm, Borthen?" he asked. "Have you some necromancer's trick that will gain us admittance?"

"No," said Borthen. "Periegesis is beyond my capabilities. But not—unless I'm much mistaken—beyond the capabilities of Lady Kherryn Du Penfallon—"

"Leave Kherryn out of this!" exclaimed Evelake with angry vehemence. "She's been through more than enough already!"

This heated declaration earned him a heavy-lidded glance from Borthen. "So I was right in thinking she would eventually make her way to join you," said the dark mage with an air of satisfaction. "Does she still have in her keeping a small crystal box with the image of a hawk on its lid?"

"Yes," said a small voice from behind the assembled company. "Yes, I've still got it," said Kherryn, coming forward to stand beside Evelake. "Why do you ask?"

Her face was pale and set, her eyes darkly challenging. "Professional curiosity, I suppose," said Borthen. "The fact that you have it is proof of your talent as a periegete. You have what Caradoc and I lack: the ability to pass freely in and out of the paraworld."

"Surely you're not seriously suggesting that Lady Kherryn should take part in this venture you've described?" said Caradoc. "She's far too young—far too inexperienced to withstand the strain of such a journey."

"She is also indispensable," said Borthen. He turned to Kherryn. "You've been listening to all we've been saying. What are *your* thoughts on the subject?"

A small pleat creased Kherryn's smooth brow. "My teacher, Ulbrecht Rathmuir, was fond of saying that great talents carry great responsibilities with them. If this gift of mine can help save East Garillon, then it would be irresponsible of me not to use it—"

"Stop! This is crazy!" The protest came from Evelake. "Kherryn, I won't hear of you risking destroying yourself at the instigation of this—this *vampire*—"

"If I don't go," said Kherryn quietly, "we may *all* be destroyed."

An irresolute silence fell. "There *is* a way to put the girl's talent to the test," said Borthen.

Evelake stiffened, but said nothing more. "What is that?" asked Caradoc.

"It would involve taking a shorter journey—to Gand," said Borthen. "It's no secret that Gand is the Devourer's next target. If this party could reach the city ahead of the demon and its army, it would be to our advantage."

"How?" asked Tessa bluntly.

"By strengthening the defense of Gand Castle, we would be forcing the demon to spend valuable strength," said Borthen. "The more power it is obliged to use in attacking, the less it will have in reserve to use for self-defense."

He paused to let the import of his statement sink in before pursuing his point. "Don't forget: I would be a member of the party. If I am willing to stake my life on Lady Kherryn's ability, why should you hesitate to do the same? If she can take us to Gand, she will have proven that she is sufficiently mistress of her talent to take us to Zhulzar."

"You make it all sound very plausible," said Caradoc. "The only thing you haven't mentioned yet is the cost. I want to know what you expect to gain for yourself in exchange for the assistance you claim to be offering us. What have we got that you want?"

"What do I want?" Borthen made a slight move that might almost have been a shudder. "I want you to heal me of my wounds."

He eased himself upright. Supporting himself with one gloved hand braced against the front of his saddle, he used the other to draw aside the folds of his enveloping riding cloak. Following the other man's studied movements with chill foreboding, Caradoc was the first to catch sight of the devastation that his enemy had been nursing all the way from Tavenern.

The fine, rich cloth of his doublet, shirt, and hose had been reduced to a ragged network of blood-sodden tatters. The flesh exposed to view had been flayed as though by acid, its rawness left to fester. Like tissues infected by gangrene, the wounds were oozing with rampant corruption. Borthen was watching the younger man closely. "The damage is spreading, even as we stand here," said the dark mage, his voice rough as a file. "If you decline to use the power vested in you, I will be dead in a matter of a few more hours. And the fate of East Garillon will be sealed."

Caradoc's face was set like stone. "You know full well that I can't make that decision on my own."

"By all means, take counsel among yourselves," said Borthen. "But don't deliberate too long. Time is running short for all of us. . . ."

Borthen Berigeld was taken to one of the temporary shelters that the party from Yske had constructed in the shadow of the Hough. After posting a guard to keep watch over him, the five men and three women who had witnessed the dark mage's arrival withdrew to the relative seclusion of the south side of the mound to debate their response to Borthen's disquieting proposal.

Harlech Hardrada, grim and glowering, had no doubts at all. "I cannae believe we're even botherin' tae discuss this!" he declared roundly. "Yon clarty bastard's been the death o' more folk than I care tae imagine, and the plague of twice as many more. Ye cannae seriously think about givin' him back his filthy life so's he can turn around and slit our throats!"

"I agree," said Margoth, her blue eyes showing sparks of cold fire. "The man's utterly without conscience, and it would be nothing short of madness to place any faith in anything he says! I vote to let poetic justice take its course. We'll find some other way to deal with this demon."

"I don't think there *is* another way," said Caradoc, his brow deeply lined. "When it comes to demonology, Borthen is the supreme authority. If he says that the only way to fight the Devourer is to do as he's described, we can be pretty certain he knows what he's talking about."

"Is there any alternative to fighting it?" asked Serdor.

"Oh yes," said Caradoc thinly. "We could always attempt to run away. With a bit of luck, we could probably get back to where we left the *Mermaid*. With a bit more luck, we could probably find some conveniently distant port where we could settle down—at least for a time. But all the while, the evil that has been unleashed here in East Garillon would be spreading. And all the while, we'd be watching the skies, praying that the evil wouldn't reach so far in our own lifetimes."

There was a bleak pause. "We can't run away," said Kherryn's small voice. "Whatever we *can* do, that's what we *must* do."

She lifted her eyes to meet Caradoc's. "If you're convinced that Borthen's plan offers us our only chance to save East Garillon, don't let any fear on my behalf stop you from committing yourself. Besides, what about Devon? He's at Gand. None of them there know what now threatens them. If you are prepared to follow Borthen into the pararealm, surely the least I can do is be present to open the doors."

"I'm not sure I merit that kind of trust, Lady Kherryn," said Caradoc. "Before you decide, perhaps you should listen to what the other members of our party have to say."

He directed his gaze toward Tessa. She lifted her chin, her freckled face sternly composed. "Whatever the rest of you may elect to do," she said, "I will *not* flee East Garillon. As the daughter of the Marshall of Gand, I know where my duty lies. I shall stay as long as there is anything left to defend, and fight as long as there is breath in my body.

"But if I am going to lay down my life," she continued, "I would prefer to do it in support of a cause that is not already lost. If Borthen's plan can give me a hope worth dying for, then I am prepared to give it my endorsement."

"I wish I shared your singleness of purpose," said Evelake. "I feel like a house divided against itself."

He looked around at his companions, his brown eyes undershadowed with worry. "All of you are my friends: I hate to think what may happen to you if I agree to let you put yourselves in Borthen's hands. But the people of East Garillon are equally my responsibility. And try as I will, I can't see any other hope for them than the one Borthen's held out to us."

He lapsed into silence. "It sounds to me," said Gudmar quietly, "as though you've already made up your mind."

"Yes," said Evelake heavily. "I suppose I have."

Gudmar nodded and turned to the others. "As matters stand at the moment," he said, "we've heard two opposing voices, two voices conditional, and three voices in favor of accepting Borthen Berigeld's plan."

"What about you, Gudmar?" asked Evelake. "What do *you* think we should do?"

"I agree with the majority," said Gudmar. "It's the only way."

"I hope ye're right," grumbled Harlech. "If this thing blows up in our faces, it'll gi' me no pleasure at all tae say I told ye so."

"Does this mean you'll be staying in with us?" asked Gudmar. There was a glint of mordant amusement in his golden eyes.

Catching the glint, Harlech made a rude noise at the back of his nose. "Och, aye," he growled. "Win or lose, at least it ought tae be a good fight."

Caradoc turned to his sister. "What about you, Margoth?"

"What do you think?" said Margoth sourly. "Come hellfire or high water, you're still my brother. I'm not backing out now."

"I guess that means I can stop trying to be diplomatic," said Serdor. "You can officially count me in."

"And me," said Tessa. "All the more willingly, since it means taking a shorter route to Gand, where I know I shall be needed."

"Good," said Gudmar with a nod. "If Lady Kherryn feels ready, we'll set out early tomorrow on the first stage of this venture. Assuming, of course, that Borthen is in any fit state to accompany us."

"That's going to depend very much on the Magia," said Caradoc. "But for my own part, I'll do my best not to let my animosity get in the way of my performance as a healer."

He turned to Evelake. "With your permission, my lord, if our decision is final, I had better go and attend to Borthen now—before his condition gets any worse."

"Of course," said Evelake gravely. As Caradoc moved to leave, the young Warden transferred his gaze to Gudmar and Tessa. "In the meantime, I'd appreciate it if you'd call all your men together. I think it's time we let them in on what our plans are, and give them the opportunity to decide if they want to take part. . . ."

Ten minutes later, standing on top of a smooth rock at the edge of the encampment, he addressed himself without preamble to a combined company of mariners and foresters. "You all know what has happened," he told them. "A deserter from my half brother's army has found his way into our midst. From him we have received confirmation that the Hospitallers' attempt to defeat the enemy has failed. From him we have also learned of a way to rob my half brother of his demon-powers. We have discussed the plan, and we have come to the conclusion that it offers us our only hope for victory.

"To that end," he went on, "we are going to Gand, but not by way of any earthly road. Instead, Lady Kherryn is going to attempt to lead us on a shortcut through the pararealm—the realm of the spirit. That's the only way we can hope to reach our destination in time.

"Apart from Lady Kherryn, myself, and our informant from Tavenern," he continued, "the party so far includes Captain Gudmar Ap Gorvald, Lady Tessa Ekhanghar, Harlech Hardrada, and my friends from Ambrothen. The decision that each of them has made individually is not a decision that anyone should make arbitrarily on behalf of another. Therefore I am offering you the same choice that they were offered: to ride with me to Gand—or to remain behind and seek what safety you can. If you elect to come with us, I cannot promise you either success or survival—but what we hope to obtain through our self-sacrifice is nothing less than the salvation of this kingdom.

"The danger being what it is," he concluded, "I would not blame any man here who feels himself in all honesty unequal to the challenge. To that man I say this: if you cannot aid us with your presence, then give us at least the aid of your prayers. For we will be fighting—perhaps dying—in your name, and in your place, to save that which you love. We leave at dawn tomorrow. You have till then to consider your response."

A moment's grave silence followed. After lingering long enough to scan the faces of his audience, Evelake withdrew his gaze and made a move to step down off the rock he had been using as a platform. As he did so, there was a stir from the back of the assembled company. "You can have my answer right now, my lord!" called the voice of Jamie Greenham. "I'm tired of these devil-worshiping scabsters having everything their own way. If you're riding to Gand to spike their guns for 'em, I'm ready to go, too!"

The pilot's declaration drew a rumble of strong agreement from the men around him. The rising wave of assent swelled throughout the ranks. "Hands up, everybody who wants a chance to rub a necromancer's nose in the midden!" shouted an anonymous voice from off to the right.

Hands rose like a hedgehog of spears. Standing a pace to the left of Evelake's rock, Gudmar counted the waving arms and smiled with grim pride. "I make that twenty-five out of twenty-five," he told the young Warden. "I think you've got yourself a full party!"

The vocal storm of affirmation carried as far as the makeshift tent where Borthen was lying stretched out on a bed of bracken. Turning hollow eyes on Caradoc, the dark mage gave a malicious white-lipped smile. "Your young protégé appears to have roused the masses," he rasped. "Who would have thought he had it in him?"

Caradoc said nothing. Curbing his temper along with his shrinking disgust, he leaned forward and began to peel away the other man's moist, stinking rags. Borthen submitted to Caradoc's preliminary ministrations with rigid endurance. He uttered no outcry, but by the time the younger man was finished, the dark mage's blanched face was bathed in perspiration. Catching Caradoc's eye, he whispered huskily, "You're unusually quiet. Are you enjoying the spectacle?"

"Not especially." Caradoc was curt.

"How very superior of you." Borthen's chest rose and fell with labored constraint. "But then, I keep forgetting you're a reformed creature."

Caradoc paused in the act of wetting a linen swab from the pan of steaming water at his side. "Have you got some useful reason for baiting me, Borthen?" he asked. "If not, I suggest you keep quiet. Because the harder you make this for me, the more difficult it's going to be for you. . . ."

None of the noises about the camp could completely cancel out the sounds coming from the inside of Borthen's tent. Even fortified as she was with some knowledge of the renegade mage's manifold crimes, Tessa Ekhanghar winced to hear a voice she knew must be his muttering and groaning in anguish. A less disciplined person than Borthen would have been shrieking or collapsed long since. She wondered how much of the black mage's agony Caradoc was being forced to endure as a consequence of his healing rapport. Powerless as she was to do anything that could help him, she decided she had better take herself out of earshot.

The summit of the Hough seemed to offer both solitude and a good vantage point from which to keep watch over the surrounding woodland. Braving the cold wind, she climbed to the top of the mound and sat down on a bare outcropping of stone. By then the light was beginning to fade. As she looked east toward Gand over the shadowy trees, she tried to imagine what might lie in store for them on the strange journey they were to attempt on the morrow.

The balance of powers and talents was critically delicate. If Borthen failed to recover—if Kherryn failed to find a route through the paraworld—all would be lost, before it even began. So much depended on Caradoc Penlluathe's strength as a mage. The burden of responsibility rested most heavily on his shoulders.

Lost in thought, she was roused by a flicker of movement among the trees below. The light was all but gone, but there was no mistaking the auburn sheen of Caradoc's dark red hair. Tessa realized that he must have done all he could for the enemy who had bargained so effectively for his services. Pulse quickening anxiously, she rose to her feet and plunged down the snowy flank of the mound to overtake the mage.

She found him leaning heavily against a tree, his shoulders bowed with exhaustion, his breathing audible in the frosty air. At the sound of her footsteps, he turned to gaze at her with deep-shadowed eyes. Tessa checked in her tracks, her mouth gone dry. "Well?" she asked huskily.

He straightened up and knuckled his eyebrows. "What are you asking? If Borthen Berigeld will live? The answer is yes. He's still weak, but he'll be able to travel in the morning."

He sighed, his expression one of weary revulsion. "God!" he exclaimed. "To think performing my sacred duty as a healer should leave me with such a vile taste in my mouth. The terrible thing, Tessa, is that I share—*I share*—the feelings of this creature. You cannot enter to heal without *sharing*!"

He looked broken and spent. Tessa shuddered to think what the past few hours' experience had cost him. She said, "Is there anything I can do?"

He gave her a sickly smile. "Just stay here and talk with me a bit, if you don't mind. It's a relief just to be in the presence of someone who isn't tainted, body and soul, with the stench of brimstone."

"Would you be better off sitting down?" asked Tessa.

He shook his head. "No. If I stop moving altogether, I may start being sick. And frankly, I'm too tired to face the threat of that."

"Then walk with me," said Tessa, and gave him a wry smile. "I seem to recall your telling me this morning that it would give you pleasure."

She held out her hand. Caradoc reached out and took it. Even though she was wearing gloves, he could feel the graceful strength of her fingers. Weary from his besmirching rapport with Borthen, he was overwhelmed all at once by a realization of her integrity.

She was straight and clean-limbed as a young fir tree, and the scent of her was the scent of the pines, and the sea, and the stainless wind—a sharp clean savor, like the scent of virgin snow. As he stared at her with aching eyes, Caradoc experienced a sudden passionate longing to bury his feverish face in her hair, to drink in the freshness of her presence like a draught of pure water.

Something of his desire must have manifested itself in his eyes, for she drew back slightly and looked at him with the curiosity of a startled doe. But she did not pull away. Too tired to veil his yearning, he closed the gap between them and lifted light fingers to touch her face, reverently, as though it were the face of an icon.

Her lips were cold as a spring freshet. But her warm breath bloomed on the frosty air like a white rose, vital and fragrant. Like a thirsty pilgrim bowing to drink at a sacred well, he bent his head to take a kiss from her mouth.

In that moment he could not have concealed his desire, even if he had wanted to. But he had no wish to dissemble. Disarmed as much by his honesty as by the potency of her own feelings, Tessa yielded to the courteous importunity of his embrace.

Like a tree parched by drought, he drank in her presence as though it were rain from heaven. Locked in his arms, she felt his strength begin to come back to him, as though he were finding in her a source of renewed vigor. In return he allowed her to see herself through his eyes—not as a sexless figure of purpose, but as a creature of untarnished wonder.

The extravagance of his admiration threw her into sudden confusion. Seeing the red in her cheeks and the doubt in her eyes, Caradoc gave her a one-sided smile. "I can't help my feelings," he said, "any more than I can hide them as long as we are touching like this. Do you want me to let you go?"

"You know full well that I don't," said Tessa. "But you also know as well as I do that desire and duty are two different masters, each of them jealous enough to brook no rivals. I cannot enter into the service of the one until I am first released from the service of the other. It would give me too much I was afraid to lose."

"And you would rather have nothing?"

Tessa's breath caught in her throat. Her fingers reached yearningly to touch the deep shadows under his eyes.

"I would rather have hope," she said, fiercely gentle. "Something worth trying to stay alive for."

"What would give you that kind of hope?" asked Caradoc.

"A promise," said Tessa. "The promise of things to come in the fullness of a happier time."

"Then take this promise from me," said Caradoc. "If there should ever be a happier time, I won't be far away. . . ."

THE PATHS OF PERIL

THE NIGHT PASSED UNEVENTFULLY. AFTER a hasty breakfast under cold dawn skies, the party bound for Gand made ready to set out on their unprecedented journey.

Kherryn and Caradoc were to ride together on one

horse, maintaining psychic rapport through physical
contact so that she might draw upon his strength at need.
Vult Hemmling, too weak from his injuries to accompany the group, had made the red-haired mage a present of
his own horse, a big roan stallion. "You and Lady
Kherryn are going to need him far more than I am," he
told Caradoc firmly. "If there's any animal alive that can
get the pair of you where you aim to go today, he's the
one to do it."

Caradoc had accepted the gift with gratitude. After
bidding Vult and his remaining companions farewell, the
larger party rode down off the Hough and set out north
through the snow-covered trees. Tessa accompanied Caradoc and Kherryn as guide at the head of the group
until they reached a forest trail running east-west across
their path. After directing the company eastward on
their way, she fell back to join her foresters, who were
keeping the rear guard.

Evelake and Gudmar came next after Caradoc and
Kherryn. Behind them, a horse-length in front of Serdor,
Margoth, and Harlech, rode Borthen Berigeld, alone and
aloof. Bandages and borrowed clothes concealed beneath the enveloping folds of his heavy black riding
cloak, he appeared sardonic and self-contained as ever.
Earlier, he had laughed aside with contempt a suggestion
that he should be obliged to ride bound, as a prisoner.
Even Harlech had been grudgingly forced to admit that,
for the moment, he and they were united by a common
purpose.

Perched in front of Caradoc, who was astride Vult's
roan stallion, Kherryn carefully rehearsed the instructions the red-haired mage had given her the evening
before. "Once we set out, don't think about finding just
any door," Caradoc had told her. "Think about finding a
particular door associated with the place you want to get
to—say, one of the outside ports in Gand Castle. . . ."

Reassured by the steadfast strength of Caradoc's
presence now, Kherryn closed her eyes and put her
memory to work. Thinking back over all the entrances
and exits inside her family's stronghold, she focused her

attention on the one known as the Swan Port, on the west side of the donjon overlooking the gatehouse. Concentrating, she began to build up a picture of the port in her mind.

· First, there was a recessed archway. A heavy yett, wrought from interlocking bars of black iron, secured the archway against forced entry. A corbeled gallery projected out from the wall above the arch, showing a row of lead-lined murder-holes. Beneath the gallery and above the arch lay a rectangular panel on which was carved the coat of arms of the Du Penfallons: three swans, argent, above a wave, vert. . . .

She could see it all clearly in her mind's eye: the grey-gold ashlars . . . the mortared crevices between stone and stone . . . the stylized design of the swans' plumage. . . . She tried to imagine the iron yett shifting open. . . .

Peering ahead in eager anticipation, Evelake noticed a blurring in the outline of the trees in front of them. As they drew nearer, he saw that a diaphanous mist seemed to be gathering over the wood. More subtle than sea fog, it had a curious sheen to it, as though it carried infinitesimal motes of metal in its midst. "Look, Gudmar," he said in an undertone. "What is that?"

The answer came not from Gudmar, but from Borthen. "That, my lord, is the effect known as the chromata," said the dark mage. "Its presence means we are entering the borders of the pararealm."

The opalescent shimmer of the fog was plainly visible to Caradoc. As the mists reached out to encompass them, he called upon the Magia to link his perceptions with Kherryn's. "I can see what you see," he told her, "but you'll have to give the directions. Which way do we go?"

Kherryn pointed unhesitatingly toward a gap in the trees to their left. "There," she said. "The threshold is there."

Caradoc kneed the stallion forward. The rest of the company followed, murmuring uneasily among themselves. Beyond the gap, the ground fell steeply away into a fog-filled hollow. At the bottom of the hollow, wreathed in sinuous tendrils of moving mist, were two tall standing stones.

Twice the height of a tall man, the stones were ornamented with running scrolls of interlocking runes. As the party descended into the dell, the rune patterns seemed to shift and change. There was a pulsing vibration in the air that grew stronger as Kherryn and Caradoc approached the feet of the dolmens. Without warning, twin bolts of light shot up from the ground, whipping in coils around the stone columns to meet overhead in a prismatic arc of shimmering energy.

The big roan gave a stiff-legged start, but held its ground. There was a flurry of grunts and curses as the men and women behind fought to hold their own frightened mounts in check. Controlling his black gelding with vicious efficiency, Borthen wheeled around to confront the rest of the party. As the disorder subsided, he raised his voice in cold exhortation.

"This is the point of no return. Once we pass through the gateway, there is no predicting what you may see or hear. Pay no heed to anything that belongs to the paraworld. Turn aside, even for a moment, and you risk getting lost in its toils forever."

"We understand ye," grunted Harlech. "If ye're done makin' speeches, let's get on wi' it."

Above them the archway was flickering. "Kherryn and I will go first," said Caradoc. "We'll wait for you on the other side."

He turned back to face the gateway. The tingle of arcane energies was like the crawling of ants over his skin. "Ready?" he asked Kherryn. When she nodded, he drew a deep breath and clapped his heels smartly to the stallion's taut flanks.

The big animal sprang forward. Its leap carried them through the arch in a shimmering ripple of broken light. The instant of transition conveyed a chill shock to the nerves, like a plunge into icy water. Then the stallion brought them to earth with a jolt.

Still gasping slightly, Caradoc drew rein and looked

back in time to see Gudmar and Evelake pass together through the scintillating horseshoe of the gate. Borthen followed after, with Harlech, Serdor, and Margoth hard on his gelding's heels. More horsemen spilled in behind them to swell the ranks. As they set about regrouping, Tessa's lean, bad-tempered mare charged through the gap and fetched up short, all teeth and eyes and flying hooves.

"That's everyone," she reported.

"Good," said Gudmar. "Let's be off."

Caradoc looked around them. Iridescent mists enveloped them on all sides. There were no visible landmarks to be seen through the density of the fog. "It's entirely up to you," he said to Kherryn. "Which direction do we take from here?"

The image of the Swan Port was firmly fixed in Kherryn's mind. Constant as the pole star amid the polychrome flux and shift of the fog, it exerted a magnetic pull upon her senses. Like a mariner setting sail with the aid of a harbor-beacon, she allowed the image to be her guide. "That way," she told Caradoc, pointing ahead and to the right.

Caradoc wordlessly laid the reins to the stallion's neck. The big roan started forward, ears pricked, nostrils flaring. The rest of the party fell into double ranks behind them. In tense silence they moved off after their guides into the dreamlike swirl of the mist.

Opalescent as a soap bubble, the surrounding vapors coiled and shifted in ever-changing patterns. Streams of color flowed in and out of one another, alternately blending and separating. As the company pressed deeper into the cloud, the kaleidoscopic dance of hue and shade grew more frenzied and bewildering. "I can't see straight!" gasped Margoth. "The colors—they're making me dizzy!"

She swayed in the saddle. "Don't look at the mist, look at something solid!" ordered Serdor.

Margoth gulped and nodded. Gudmar was riding half a horse-length in front of her. She fixed her attention to a point between his broad shoulders and kept it there.

Behind her, other members of the party were floundering about in growing confusion. Tessa caught hold of one man's shoulder just in time to keep him from tumbling off his horse. "Gudmar, this is crazy!" she shouted forward. "We've got to do something!"

"I know!" he shouted back. "I've got a length of rope here. Let's see if we can rig up a guideline."

Margoth found herself suddenly with a length of hemp in her hand. "Take hold of that and pass the slack along," instructed Gudmar.

Margoth did as she was told. Within seconds, a taut stretch of rope had sprung up between opposite ends of the party. "Everybody keep a grip on the line!" called Gudmar. "If you find the light is getting to you, close your eyes and follow the rope."

The party struggled on through the whirling aurora of colors. Peering ahead between narrowed eyelids, Serdor became aware of a humming sensation in his ears. As the humming grew louder, a variety of strains and pitches began to emerge from the undifferentiated chaos of noise. The air seemed all at once to explode into manifold paeans of sound.

Out of the pandemonium of many tones rose snatches of eerie melody that faded away as soon as he tried to capture them. Harmonies alternately combined and dissolved without achieving resolution. Themes caught his attention, only to degenerate into cacophany. Conflicting rhythms formed and broke, crashing over him in opposing waves.

His head rang with tumult. Pain stabbed viciously at his eardrums. He doubled forward, wrapping one arm around his head in an ineffectual attempt to block out the reverberating noise. Then, just when he thought he could bear it no longer, the cataclysmic tide of sound turned back on itself and rolled away from him like departing thunder.

He straightened up unsteadily to find the other members of the party shaking their heads and rubbing their ears. The tempest of color, like the storm of noise, had subsided. The company was grouped at the center of a tall circle of standing stones, rising up like a barren atoll out of a sea of nothingness. The air was grey and still, broken only by the sound of panting breath as the members of the company recovered themselves.

Serdor turned toward Margoth. She gave him a ghastly smile. "Don't ask me where we are, or how we got here," said Caradoc's sister. "All I did was follow the pull of the rope. I hope Kherryn knows where to go from here."

Surveying the ring of stones, Kherryn had already found the gateway she was seeking. "Over there," she told Caradoc, speaking to him directly, mind to mind.

Caradoc was aware of more than her conscious thoughts. United with her in Orison, he realized that her strength was beginning to give out. Too inexperienced to recognize the danger signals for herself, Kherryn was chafing to press on. Subtly, so as not to interfere with her concentration, he brought his own power to her support.

She accepted his aid confidingly, without reservation. As their rapport deepened, Caradoc found he no longer needed her verbal instructions. Orienting himself according to her interior vision, he prompted the stallion toward one of the gaps in the circle, beckoning the rest of the company to follow.

Caradoc's eyesight told him there was nothing beyond the gateway but boundless chasms of emptiness. His insight told him that the only way to reach their intended destination was to entrust themselves to the ineluctable force that was guiding them. The power of choice rested with him, not with Kherryn. Muscles tensing, he steeled himself and gave the stallion the signal to jump.

The big horse left the ground with a bound. Half expecting to plummet headlong into an abyss, Caradoc caught his breath in wondering astonishment. The nothingness he had contemplated from the inside of the circle had resolved itself beyond into a wide and rocky plain.

The other members of the company arrived and gathered together, staring at the land around them. Bleached and barren as a lunar plateau, the plain seemed to sweep away in all directions toward impossible distances. The sky overhead was an eerie shade of violetgrey. The air was parched and dry.

Seeing the rest of the party wavering in indecision, Borthen turned to Caradoc and Kherryn. "What are you waiting for? Ride on!" he snapped. "Every moment we stand still here increases our danger."

"Danger?" said Margoth. "I don't see anything to be afraid of—"

Her words ended in a startled cry as the clump of stones off to her right began to move.

Her horse shied to the side, cannoning into Serdor's. The rockpile heaved convulsively and broke open, spitting up a dry geyser of earth and pebbles. While the dirt was still flying, another cairn of rocks a short distance away began to shudder. Underfoot the ground was starting to tremble.

"*Go*, you fool!" snarled Borthen to Caradoc.

Kherryn had already given him their heading. "Come on!" he shouted, and gave the roan its head.

The big animal reared off its haunches into a charging canter. Needing no urging, the other horses broke away and bolted after their leader. Fighting to hold the stallion back to a pace the rest of the party could match, Caradoc saw a jagged crack appear in the dry ground directly in front of them. "Jump for it!" he yelled back to the riders following behind him.

The crack was widening even as he looked. He gave the roan a shrewd kick. Hooves slashing the earth, the big horse pounded up to the fissure's edge and leaped for the other side.

The desert dissolved around them. For an instant they seemed to hang suspended over a void. When the stallion's forefeet touched the ground, the rocky plateau had become a teeming jungle.

Lush foliage was everywhere. The verdant air rippled with vaporous heat. Torn leaves and flowers showered down on them as the roan ploughed a determined path through the dense greenery. Holding their mount

firmly on course, Caradoc bent low over Kherryn to
shield her from wave after wave of lashing branches.

Drumming hoofbeats closed in behind them. Casting a fleeting glance over his shoulder, Caradoc spotted
the vanguard of his company surging after him through
the still-quaking shrubbery. He caught a glimpse of
Margoth's red head three ranks back. The others were an
anonymous blur of motion.

Javelins of sunlight were shooting through the gaps
in the trees ahead of the party. As they cantered on
through the forest, the angle of the light shifted before
their very eyes. Swiftly rising, the sun passed directly
over their heads in a catherine wheel of flashing beams
and tumbled toward the horizon at their backs. Evening
shadows sprang out of the grass to greet them.

A driving sense of urgency laid hold of Caradoc, so
that he pressed their mount to a gallop. The sky before
them went dark. White stars careened across the firmament above in a whirl of scintillating lights. The warm
wind of speed in their faces began to blow cold.

The company drew together behind their leaders.
All around them, flowers withered at a glance and
dropped to the ground. The full moon went up like a
silver rocket, trailing a tail across the sky like a comet.
The blighted trees shriveled and crumbled into dust.

An arctic wasteland opened up before them under a
night sky brightened by the eerie flash of northern lights.
The company galloped out across glimmering blue-white
snowfields toward the mouth of a valley hedged with ice
cliffs that glittered like mirrors in the flickering darkness.
Ahead of them, at the far end of the valley, glowed a
sullen point of dark-red fire.

"That's it!" cried Kherryn shrilly. "That's the *other*
door!"

"Run for it!" shouted Borthen. "Speed's our only
hope!"

He spurred his gelding forward. Closing ranks, the
party thundered down the valley in a storm of lifted
snow. Green eyes fixed on the fluctuating nebula of

flame, Caradoc felt Kherryn stiffen in sudden dismay. "Hurry!" she implored him. "I—I don't think I can hold on to the image much longer!"

The horses were blowing hard, their coats splashed with foam despite the cold. Whooping desperate encouragement, their riders urged them on. "We're never going to make it!" gasped Margoth. "Yes we are!" called Evelake over his shoulder. *"Follow me!"*

His gelding was running flat out, neck outstretched, hooves wildly flying. Drumming her heels against her mare's heaving flanks, Margoth tensely willed the animal to keep the pace. The pinpoint of flame before them broadened out into a seething oblong, like the gaping mouth of a furnace. As they swept toward the threshold, the doorway seemed to grow, rising up to a blazing height.

Heat lashed Caradoc in the face. *"Go!"* choked Kherryn. Staking all on her word, Caradoc gave the stallion a last command.

Deep chest heaving in the final stages of exhaustion, the big horse responded blindly. Too weary to jump, it lumbered into the teeth of the flames, with Borthen's mount following close behind. The fire shot up with a bellow as they vanished into its withering embrace.

Coming up hard on the gateway behind them, Evelake and his mount were caught in the fiery backlash. The gelding reared back, pawing the air in white-eyed panic. Charging up behind the boy, Gudmar snatched at the gelding's bridle and missed. Before Evelake could bring the animal safely down off its haunches, it lost its balance and toppled sideways.

Evelake hurled himself from the saddle to avoid being crushed under the gelding's rolling flank. As the boy staggered to his feet, Gudmar plucked him one-handed off the ground and hauled him bodily across his own mount's withers. "Hang on, my lord!" he gritted, and sent the horse hurtling into the fiery gateway.

Serdor, Margoth, and Harlech reached the threshold a racing stride behind their leader. Horses and riders vanished together in a blazing upsurge of bloodred light.

The horsemen following were momentarily dazzled. Like animals caught in a burning barn, their mounts blindly held to their course, rushing into the grasp of the flames.

For most of the members of the party there was no time to think. Holding her mare in dancing check, Tessa hung back and watched the numbers dwindle on her side of the gate. The flames flickered and thinned. She realized with a cold qualm of apprehension that the gateway itself was starting to fade out.

The last of the stragglers disappeared with a shimmer. Tessa turned to Owain, her esquire. "Go for it!" she ordered.

To her dismay, Owain hung back, his face blanched and set. "I—I can't!" he choked.

"Don't give me that!" snapped Tessa. "I said *go!*"

He gave her a blank look of frozen panic. With a curse, Tessa kicked her feet free of her stirrups and made a flying leap from her horse to his.

His mount staggered as she landed astride behind him. Reaching around him, she snatched the reins out of his nerveless grip and gave the doubly laden horse a vicious jab with her spurs. The animal lurched forward, eyes wildly staring. Too exhausted to fight her, it blundered across the threshold just as the last of the flames winked out.

EVE OF BATTLE

THERE WAS SMOKE EVERYWHERE. CHOKING on fumes, his eyes streaming tears, Caradoc reined in hard and brought the stallion to a jarring standstill. Behind him, Borthen's foundered horse stumbled brokenly to its knees.

They had halted at the edge of a deep trench in the

ground. All around them, fissures in the smoke yielded fleeting glimpses of high stone walls and frowning parapets. Up on the battlements, voices were clamoring in sudden confusion.

Mouth to Kherryn's ear, Caradoc demanded urgently, "Is this it? *Is* this Gand Castle?"

Kherryn nodded vehemently. Before she could elaborate, a third horse carrying Gudmar and Evelake burst out of the swirling chaos of fire and cloud. The young Warden jackknifed to the ground as more riders materialized behind them. Gudmar leaned over and yanked Caradoc by the sleeve. "Get down!" hissed the merchant-adventurer.

All along the encircling parapets, anonymous figures were lining up with crossbows cocked and ready. "Don't shoot!" shrieked Kherryn, as Caradoc swung her out of the saddle into Evelake's waiting arms. "We're not enemies!"

Her thin cry was drowned out in the growing tumult of alarm. A crossbow bolt whizzed past Gudmar's left ear to embed itself in the snowy earth a few yards away. "Goddammit, hold your fire!" he bellowed up at the bowmen on the allures. "We've got Devon Du Penfallon's sister with us!"

Full-throated as the roar of an angry lion, his voice resonated off the surrounding walls. Before his words could take effect, there was a hollow crash from the direction of the gateway, and the harsh flare of unearthly fire abruptly winked out.

The sudden darkness precipitated a fresh upsurge of panic. There was a random series of whining thuds, and a horse screamed in mortal agony. "God Almighty, we're going to get cut to pieces by our own allies!" thought Caradoc.

He looked around for Kherryn and Evelake. As he did so, a deep voice heavily weighted with authority rang out from above. "Cease your firing! The next man to shoot without orders gets one from me through the heart!"

The confusion abruptly subsided. Caradoc looked

up through wreaths of smoke. A tall, spare figure in helmet and chain mail stepped out onto the high parapet directly above him. The feeble flicker of the castle's watchlights picked up the menacing glint of mail gauntlets and a well-balanced arbalest. "Now then," said the newcomer coldly, "suppose you people identify yourselves."

Kherryn pulled away from Evelake and stepped out into the open. "Jorvald, it's me—Kherryn!" she called out with fluting clarity. "The folk with me are friends! We've come to help you hold the castle against Gythe and his armies!"

This announcement drew a rumbling murmur of surprise and incredulity from the ranks of the defenders on the walls above. "Silence, there!" ordered the tall commander. As the mutterings died away, he leaned over the parapet. "All right, I'm coming down," he informed the party gathered in the courtyard. "If this turns out to be some kind of sorcerer's trick, you will very speedily regret it."

A few moments later, a blossoming of torches on the far side of the trench signaled the approach of the Marshall of Gand, accompanied by a sizable escort. They came to a disciplined halt at the edge of the fosse. "We are going to run a footbridge across the ditch," called a voice from the center of the group. "In earnest demonstration of your good faith, send Lady Kherryn across first. Whoever is in charge of your party may follow her."

The voice, bright and hard, was not Jorvald's, but one that both Evelake and Kherryn recognized instantly as belonging to Devon Du Penfallon. Turning to Gudmar, Evelake said softly, "If it's all the same to you, I'd like to be the one to accompany Kherryn." When Gudmar nodded his assent, the young Warden drew a deep breath and called back across the gap, "We accept your terms. Extend the bridge, and we'll cross over."

Standing shoulder to shoulder with his young overlord on the north side of the trench, Jorvald Ekhanghar scowled in darkling surprise. "That sounded almost like Evelake Whitfauconer's voice!" he muttered in an undertone to Devon. "If I didn't know better, I'd almost swear . . ." Leaving the sentence unfinished, he drew his broadsword, then signaled his men to lower a narrow wooden catwalk across the span of the ditch. "Better safe than sorry," he said to Devon, and craned his neck to get a clearer view of the two shadowy forms waiting on the opposite embankment.

The plank ends of the bridge thudded to earth. "Let's go," Evelake said to Kherryn.

Kherryn was trembling between weariness and excitement as she started across the walkway a few paces ahead of Evelake. Anxiously scanning the ranks of men assembled on the other side, she caught sight of a slender upright figure in chain mail. Dark eyes gazed back at her out of a gaunt young face that showed the wearing influence of experience. *"Devon!"* she exclaimed. And rushed forward to hurl herself into her brother's waiting arms.

Devon hugged his younger sister tightly, hardly able to believe his eyes. But the sight of a smear of dirt on her cheek convinced him that she wasn't a spirit of the twilight. Gently rubbing the smudge away with his thumb, he said huskily, "If this isn't sorcery, it must be a miracle!"

"You might say it's a little bit of both," said her companion from the bridge end a few steps away.

Devon pricked up his ears in mute astonishment. After a heartbeat's pause, he turned his head to stare at the stripling individual who had spoken. His eyes went wide, then a fraction wider. He said, *"Evelake?"*

The other boy grinned. "I'd have announced myself sooner, but I was sure no one would believe me in the middle of all the confusion. Are you surprised?"

"Surprised? God!" Torn between shock and laughter, Devon leaned forward to clasp the wiry hand that Evelake held out to him. "I'm so thunderstruck, I hardly know where to *begin* asking questions. Where did you and your people come from? What's going on?"

"We'll explain everything in good time," Evelake

assured him. "Right now, with your permission, I'd like to get my people indoors. . . ."

Knowing that Gudmar and Harlech were keeping close watch on Borthen, Caradoc strained his ears to catch the tone of the conversation going on across the ditch. A hand touched his arm. He looked around to find Serdor beside him. "There's been an accident," whispered the minstrel. "Tessa took a fall coming through the gateway. You'd better come take a look at her."

The news sent a chill racing down Caradoc's spine. "Where is she?" he demanded.

"Come on," said Serdor. "I'll show you."

Tessa was lying flat on her back in the snow a short distance inside the Swan Port. There was a dead horse stretched out in a broken heap not far away. Tessa's esquire was kneeling beside her, but rose to his feet as soon as he caught sight of Serdor and Caradoc. "We ran straight into a volley of crossbolts," he said, his voice constricted. "The gelding took two shafts in the chest and went down under us."

Caradoc stepped past the other man and hunkered down to examine Tessa. Her breathing was ragged and her eyes clenched tight, but he sensed with relief that she was conscious. "Don't move until I tell you," he said. "I need to find out if you've broken any bones."

Tessa heard Caradoc's voice through a blur of pain. Too winded to speak, she managed a wordless nod of acquiescence. Her right lung felt as though it were on fire. "Just relax," said Caradoc quietly. "This won't hurt."

He bent forward, running light hands over her from head to foot. His fingers returned to linger over the fourth and fifth ribs below her right armpit. The touch of his fingertips seemed to draw the heat and soreness from her side. The sharp stabbing pain subsided to a dull but bearable ache.

Seeing the strain leave her face, Caradoc reached down and gave her cheek a friendly rub. "Just a bad bruise," he told her with a smile. "In another hour, you'll hardly be able to feel it."

Before Tessa could thank him, Margoth appeared out of the shadows to join them. "The bowmen on the walls are going back to their posts," she reported. "Now that we know we're welcome, we can all breathe easy."

"That's all very well for some," said Tessa, feeling her ribs with a grimace. Turning to Caradoc, who was still on his knees next to her, she said, "Do you mind if I get up now? The snow's melting through my breeches."

Caradoc nodded without speaking. His vision all at once seemed fuzzy. Gathering her long legs under her, Tessa righted herself gingerly. When Caradoc made no move to join her, she took a closer look at his face. "Are *you* all right?" she asked.

Caradoc knuckled his forehead, aware of a sudden sharp ache in his temples. "Just tired," he said. "It's been a long day."

"In that case, I suggest you come into the hall," said a crisp voice from behind him. "There's a lot of talking to be done, and we may as well do it sitting in chairs by a fireside."

To Tessa's ears the voice was keenly familiar. Her startled gaze flew past Caradoc's bowed shoulder to the face of a lean, grizzled man dressed for fighting. Her own face brightened in glad recognition. "Father!" she cried, and darted forward to embrace him.

His returning hug was cautious. "I'm relieved to see you on your feet," said Jorvald. "That simpleton Owain said you'd taken a tumble. Are you at all hurt?"

"I'll mend," said Tessa hardily. She glanced around at the battlements. "What's your situation here?"

"Too complicated to explain in a sentence or two," said her father shortly. "Aren't you going to introduce me to your companions?"

Caradoc was just getting to his feet. To her chagrin, Tessa found herself blushing. "I beg your pardon," she said with dignity. "This is Serdor Sulamith and Margoth Penlluathe. And this is Margoth's brother, Caradoc."

Trading handclasps with the Marshall of Gand, Caradoc found himself under close scrutiny. "Caradoc Penlluathe?" said Jorvald with a frown. "You must be the mage that Kherryn and Evelake were speaking about." He added thoughtfully, "Evelake seems to have a very high opinion of your abilities. I shall be interested to hear more about your past exploits. And your future aspirations."

"Any future aspirations I may have are likely to stand or fall by this citadel," said Caradoc, with a side glance at Tessa. "If my use of mage-power in our present circumstances seems unorthodox, I can only hope that I will be excused on account of the gravity of the danger hanging over all of us. . . ."

After handing over their exhausted horses into the care of the Keep's stablehands, the equally weary riders from Glaive's Hough were ushered into the Great Hall of the donjon. Gratefully shedding the weight of their weapons and other gear, they gathered around the hearth to warm themselves while members of the household staff bustled out to fetch bread and mulled ale from the kitchens.

The members of the company were soon busy refreshing themselves, while carefully ignoring Borthen Berigeld and staying as far from him as possible. Meanwhile the leaders of the group retired with Devon and Jorvald to the seclusion of a small presence chamber opening off the northeast corner of the hall. Here, seated around a circular wooden table, Evelake and his close companions exchanged information with their hosts.

At Evelake's invitation, Gudmar described the events following the *Mermaid*'s landing at Yske, with Tessa now and then furnishing further details. The *Mermaid*'s captain broke off his narrative after describing his party's meeting with Kherryn in the forest north of Rhylnie. "How your sister came to be there is something you should hear from her own lips, my lord seneschal," he told Devon. "She will be able to give you a clearer account of her achievements than I could hope to do."

Thus prompted, Kherryn diffidently took up her part in the story. Devon listened in growing consternation as she recounted all that had befallen her since their father's death at Kirkwell. The revelation that her gifts of vision had since given rise to the rare and dangerous power of periegesis made him fear for her safety. When at length she disclosed the ominous nature of the mission still to come, he found himself painfully torn between a strong desire to argue against her taking any part in it, and the disquieting realization that her participation was a matter of vital necessity.

Kherryn was quick to sense his warring reactions. "I know what I'm doing, Devon," she told him firmly. "You *must* believe that."

A sharp knock from outside prevented Devon from voicing a response. Tessa sprang to her feet and went to open the door. A disheveled yeoman entered, cradling a white pigeon against his chest. "It's the last of Delfrey's birds returned to the roost, my lord," he said to Devon. "Here's the message it was carrying."

He tendered a tiny scroll of paper to his young overlord. Devon accepted it and turned to read it by the light of the candles on the table before him. His face remained composed, but his mouth and eyes hardened. Looking up, he surveyed his assembled companions with grim reserve. "The forces of Gythe Du Bors have been sighted just west of the village of Lindismorne," he said. "All the signs indicate that the enemy will reach the gates of Gand by midnight tonight."

There was a fateful pause as all present took this news and its import to heart. "That gives us a little less than eight hours to make our preparations," said Jorvald.

"That's time enough to get our fighters and our conventional defenses in order," said Devon grimly. He turned his dark gaze on Kherryn and Caradoc. "Is there anything *you* need to do, before attempting to put this mad plan of yours into execution?"

Kherryn breathed an inward sigh of relief to see that her brother had apparently accepted what she knew she had to do. Caradoc said, "Kherryn and I both should try to get as much rest as we can in the next few hours. If you could arrange sleeping quarters for us—and for the man Borthen Berigeld—we will retire and leave you to your work. . . ."

THE CITY OF MONOLITHS

DEVON SUGGESTED THAT KHERRYN SHOULD make use of his own apartments on the upper floor of the donjon. Another chamber was prepared for Caradoc on the same hall. Borthen was shown to a smaller room in the adjoining wing. "I have instructed my men on the battlements outside to go about their business as quietly as possible," said Jorvald Ekhanghar blandly. "I trust their movements will not interfere with your meditations?"

"I shouldn't think your men will pose any difficulty," said Borthen silkily. "In the meantime, there are some properties I am going to require if I am to perform my part in the mission at hand. Perhaps you could arrange to let me have a word with the castle steward . . . ?"

While Caradoc and Kherryn were settling down to take their rest, Evelake and his other friends remained behind with Devon to find out all they could about the citadel's state of readiness. "All in all, I suppose it could be worse," said the young seneschal with a wry grimace. "Before your party arrived, we counted our full fighting strength at a hundred and twenty-four. Fewer than a third of them are professional soldiers, but we've had time to train up our auxiliaries to a fair level of proficiency. They'll know what to do when the time comes.

"As for ordnance," he continued, "we've got thirty-eight pieces still operational out of an original forty-nine. In terms of actual firepower, that's seven great basilisks, eleven culverins, and twenty drakonets. We haven't got enough powder and shot left to maintain a full-scale bombardment for more than an hour or two. But then," he concluded bleakly, "I imagine ordinary cannon won't be a great deal of use against balefire, once Gythe and his necromancers close in for the kill."

"How much do you know about my half brother's familiar demon and his cohorts?" asked Evelake.

"More now than we did a fortnight ago," said Devon. "Food supplies being as limited as munitions, we were starting to get desperate for news from outside. One of Jorvald's sergeants volunteered to make a break for the mainland if an opportunity arose. Two nights later a fog rolled in. We lowered a small dinghy on cables from the east rampart. The sergeant went down after it, carrying a crate full of homing pigeons with him."

A weary smile touched his lips. "Delfrey made it past the shore patrols—God knows how! We guess he got help once he reached the other side. Anyway, the pigeons started coming back to us, bringing Delfrey's reports with them, in his own hand.

"At first the news was better than anything we could have hoped for," he went on. "The day the Hospitallers of St. Berengar's left Gand for Tavenern, the Farrowaithe Guards that your stepmother posted here staged a mutiny against Khevyn Ap Khorrasel, her appointed governor. The Guards were joined by several partisan groups operating at large in the city, and together, they managed to drive Khevyn's troops back behind the Merkward Embankment into the Old Burgh on the other side of the causeway gap from us. Jorvald and I were seriously thinking of mounting an attack on Khevyn's rear guard, in the hope of pressuring him into surrendering. Then yesterday we got the news that the mages had been annihilated at Tavenern, and that Gythe and his reiver hoards were on their way here."

He shook his head. "That news changed everything, of course. Since then, the partisan groups have had their hands full, trying to evacuate the outer regions of the city before the arrival of the enemy. As for those of us walled up here in the castle—with Khevyn Ap Khorrasel's troops on one side of us and the harbor blockade on the other, it was only too clear that we were trapped. We haven't dared to hope that any help would come from Glyn Regis."

"Did you request any?" asked Evelake.

"Not personally," said Devon. "I understand that two separate messages—one from the mayor of Gand, and the other from Commander Clannach of the Farrowaithe Guards—were sent to your grandfather, begging his aid on behalf of this city. But what Dorian Du Ghelleryn's response was, I don't know."

Evelake shrugged, his brown eyes somberly determined. "Even if a whole fleet of warships were to arrive from Glyn Regis within the hour, we would still be committed to the course of action we have chosen," he said. "That being so, tell us how we can best serve you in upholding the defenses of the Keep."

Caradoc awoke with a start from unquiet dreams full of rushing winds and the distant cackling of demented voices. A glance at the horologe on the table beside the bed told him that it was approaching midnight. The air in the room was throbbing with pulsations irritatingly out of the range of normal hearing. The vibrations set his teeth on edge, like the sound of fingernails being drawn across a piece of slate.

Wincing, he threw off the blankets and stood up. His mage-senses quickening, he scrambled into his breeches and reached for his jerkin. Even as he drew it over his head, he heard a door hastily open and close farther down the hall.

Light footbeats pattered up the corridor toward the threshold of his room. As he moved to the doorway, knuckles rapped peremptorily on the paneling outside. Kherryn's voice called anxiously, "Caradoc? Are you awake?"

Caradoc opened the door. "Awake and dressed," he said. "I know: it's time."

They went down together to the Great Hall. Borthen
Berigeld was waiting for them on the threshold, flanked
by Gudmar and Harlech. "The rest of our combined
forces have taken up their positions on the battlements,"
said Gudmar. "We'll be joining them as soon as you're
on your way."

Inside the Great Hall, all the tables and benches had
been cleared to the walls, leaving a wide open area in the
middle of the floor. On the dais at the eastern end of the
hall stood a small tripod supporting a smoking brazier of
coals. An alembic full of dark red fluid had been set out
on a brass trivet over the embers. Caradoc caught the hot
charnel odor of blood in the air and curled his lip in
disgust.

Gudmar and Harlech stopped just inside the doorway. Signaling Caradoc and Kherryn to accompany him
to the foot of the dais, Borthen mounted the steps and
approached the tripod. He bent his head to inspect the
bubbling contents of the alembic.

There was a greyish-white stick protruding from the
neck of the retort. Looking more closely, Caradoc saw
that it was a length of bone taken from the leg of a sheep.
Borthen used the bone to stir the fluid inside the vessel.
As steam rose up in a reddish plume, the dark mage
inhaled deeply and closed his eyes.

His lips moved. Caradoc could not hear what the
other man was saying, but he felt the rhythm of a dark
incantation. The hairs rose along the back of his neck.
But before he could demand an explanation from
Borthen, the dark mage straightened up and opened his
eyes.

Directing a sardonic smile toward Caradoc, Borthen
lifted the alembic away from the heat with one gloved
hand and stepped down off the dais. He moved to the
center of the room and knelt down on the flagstones.
Using the bone as a drawing tool, he began with great
care to trace a pattern on the floor.

Vapor boiled up off the lines on the pavement with
an angry ongoing hiss. When Kherryn shrank back,

Caradoc put a steadying hand on her shoulder. Borthen continued to expand the design he was painting until it took the form of a pentagram. Closing the last point with a ritual flourish, he beckoned Caradoc and Kherryn over to join him. "There," he announced. "I've done all I can to ensure that the Devourer will be drawn to this place. Now we must be on our way."

He pointed to the device at the center of the pentagram. "See that symbol, Lady Kherryn? That's the key to the door through which we must pass if we are to find Herech Zhulzar."

Kherryn shivered slightly. Looking down at the hieroglyphic Borthen had inscribed, she saw that it took the form of an inverted triangle with an eye in the middle of it. "The Eye-tooth is the sign of the Devourer," said Borthen softly. "Focus your mind on that, and the door will open."

He turned to Gudmar and Harlech. "Defend this hall with all your lives," he advised grimly. "If anything should happen to disrupt the pentagram before we have accomplished what we are setting out to do, the gateway will collapse, leaving the demon incarnate on this side of the threshold and us stranded on the other."

After seeking reassurance from Caradoc with a look, Kherryn stepped inside the pentagram. As Caradoc and Borthen entered behind her, she fixed her gaze upon the sign of the Eye-tooth, concentrating until it filled her whole field of vision. The triangle shape seemed to rise off the floor, to hang suspended in the air before her. The ghost of a doorway began to materialize around it.

Aware of Caradoc's supporting presence beside her, Kherryn increased her concentration. The outline of the doorway grew more distinct, shimmering with prismatic radiance. As the portal brightened, the symbol of the Eye-tooth abruptly receded. Like a pebble tossed into a pool, it disappeared into the iridescent mists of the chromata.

Kherryn moved to follow it. Moving with her, Caradoc experienced again the chill shock of transition as they passed through the gateway between two worlds. They emerged onto what appeared to be a flat table of black rock. All around them lay gulfs of opalescent fog.

Borthen joined them in a shimmer of shifting hues. "Now the real journey begins," said the dark mage thinly. "This way . . ."

He stepped out with apparent confidence. His two companions hurried after him. The cloud opened up before them, yielding eerie views of a sky the color of tarnished bronze. As they advanced, the trio began to catch partial, disquieting glimpses of geometric structures rising up on all sides of them in the mist.

"What is this place, Borthen?" demanded Caradoc in an undertone. "Some kind of city?"

Borthen turned back with a fleeting smile, like the flash of a drawn dagger. "Yes—but not just any city," said the dark mage. "This is Gurshak Ghuladech—the City of Monoliths."

The name was unfamiliar to Caradoc, but it resonated with menace. He was about to request more information, when the fog lifted like a curtain, unmasking the place to which Borthen was taking them. Gazing out across the plain of Gurshak Ghuladech in mute horror, Caradoc felt all at once like a worm that had strayed into a graveyard of dragons.

He and his two companions were standing in the midst of a roadway built for giants. Fully forty yards across, the avenue cut a straight, undeviating line across a vast landscape crowded from horizon to horizon with towering edifices raised up in stone. The City of Monoliths had no boundaries that he could see. Sterile as a cinderyard, complex as the entrails of some enormous infernal machine, it sprawled away on all sides toward distances that confounded the eye and staggered the mind.

Huge mausoleums cowered sullenly in the shadow of colossal pyramids. Monstrous dark obelisks reared up rank on rank above a labyrinthine tangle of ziggurats. Kherryn shuddered and closed her eyes to the dread

sepulchral grandeur of the city. "Come on," said
Borthen. "The tomb of Herech Zhulzar lies near the
heart of this maze."

The course he marked out for them took them away
from the cyclopean highway into a wide peribolus enclosed by massive upright blocks of seamless grey stone.
Creeping like ants along the feet of the frowning men-
hirs, the three travelers entered a forest of pillars. Some
low and broad as tumuli, others soaring to dizzy heights
overhead, the pillars were joined together by ponderous
lengths of brazen chain. Around the base of each column
was incised a ring of hieroglyphics.

Once in the midst of the wilderness of columns,
Borthen veered off at a diagonal to the right. Working
their way from pillar to pillar, the party emerged from
the tortuous congregation of standing stones into a vast
courtyard bordered with monoliths. Surveying the
surrounding array of stark, inscrutable cromlechs, Caradoc felt his blood run cold. "Why does this place seem
somehow familiar to me?" he wondered out loud.

Borthen turned his head. A deep glint was in his
heavy-lidded eyes. "This is the breeding ground of
nightmares," he said. "No human soul is ever completely
a stranger here."

An oppressive silence brooded over the monoliths.
As the party advanced across the immense sweep of the
courtyard, the furtive whisper of their own footfalls
seemed to reverberate among the tall monuments that
hemmed them in on all sides. Once awakened, the
vibrations did not die away. Instead, they lingered
phantasmally in the air, rasping the ear with elusive
tooth-setting dissonance.

Borthen appeared to be following a needlessly complicated course toward the center of the courtyard.
Caradoc was beginning to wonder if the dark mage were
playing some kind of sinister game with them when the
other man halted abruptly in his tracks. Beckoning
Caradoc and Kherryn forward, he pointed out an area of
shadow on the ground some distance yet in front of

them. "There it is," he said with brittle satisfaction. "The entrance to Herech Zhulzar."

Opaque as a sheet of slate, the zone of darkness dominated the surrounding pavements. As the party approached, the shadow assumed the shape of a great slab of rock. Dense as lodestone, dark as iron, it looked like an entablature above a tomb. Gazing down upon it from above, Caradoc and Kherryn saw that the stone was inscribed with the triangular sign of the Eyetooth.

The symbol glowed red against its background of black rock. The fiery lines seemed to ripple sinuously before the eye, as though they had a life of their own. Studying the device in fascinated horror, Kherryn said tremulously, "If this is the entrance, how do we get in?"

Borthen turned his head to look at her. His dark eyes mirrored the volcanic glare of the rock's internal fire. "I think you already know the answer to that question," he said.

Kherryn swallowed hard. "I—I'll do my best," she said. "But where do I begin?"

Caradoc's strong hands came to rest lightly on her shoulders. His touch conveyed reassurance. "Stop thinking of the stone as a stone," he said. "Think of it as something else—something movable—"

He stopped when Kherryn nodded her understanding. Her mind was already racing ahead. She examined the stone more closely. It was four-sided, square . . . like a window. Or, better, a trapdoor.

The analogy gave her the focus she was looking for. She closed her eyes, beseeching the Magia to translate image into action. As energy quickened responsively in her nerve ends, she knelt down to lay hands on the stone slab.

It was deathly cold to the touch. Contact sent a bone-numbing shock throughout her body, but Caradoc's hands on her shoulders lent her the strength of will to resist pulling back. Concentrating hard, she envisioned a trapdoor swinging upright on its hinges.

The slab quivered beneath her fingers. Feeling it

move, Kherryn threw wide the floodgates of power within her own spirit, willing the stone to obey her command. Something inimical in the essence of the stone itself defied her. When Caradoc added his strength to hers, she felt it suddenly give way.

There was a momentous grinding sound, followed by a sonorous crash that shivered the ground beneath her feet. A backlash of caustic dust stung her hands and face so that she flinched aside. "That's it!" cried Caradoc. "That's done it!"

Feeling drained and weak, Kherryn shakily drew herself up. She opened her eyes, and caught her breath. The dark stone slab had been uprooted and overturned, so that it lay facedown on the pavement. Where the slab had lain, a black cavity now yawned.

Motioning Kherryn to keep back, Caradoc edged closer and peered down into the depths below. He could see nothing but a jagged flight of steps leading down into absolute darkness. "You will find Herech Zhulzar at the bottom of the shaft," said Borthen. "For what it's worth, I wish you success."

Caradoc turned to Kherryn. "This is where we part company," he said.

"No," protested Kherryn. "I want to come with you."

"I wouldn't advise it. Caradoc is the only one among us with the strength to resist the hunger of the void," said Borthen. "You would be seized and devoured—as would I. As for remaining here with me: I am hardly in any position to threaten you."

Kherryn nodded, realizing the dark mage was speaking the bald truth. "Don't be afraid," said Caradoc. "I'll come back for you. I promise."

Turning away, he hunkered down and lowered himself gingerly into the mouth of the shaft. The atmosphere inside was thick and black as tar, tainted with a throat-clogging miasma of ancient decay. When he put his weight on the topmost step, it yielded flaccidly beneath him, like the flesh of a corpse. Taking a tight grip on his nerves, he turned inward in spirit, beseeching the help and guidance of the Magia before attempting to venture deeper into the abyss that gaped beneath him.

The answering kiss of power roused his sensibilities to preternatural acuity. Unable to see, he found he could feel his way with surety from step to step. At the same time, however, he became aware of a source of insatiable hunger emanating upward out of the infernal depths below.

That hunger began to gnaw at him as he descended into the impenetrable darkness. The deeper he progressed, the more keenly he felt the drain on his strength. Like a vampire, the surrounding darkness sucked away his living vitality. Fighting to stay upright, he could only hope that the Magia would somehow sustain him.

The steps continued to draw him downward in an ever-descending spiral. Depleted of warmth and energy, Caradoc struggled on under a growing burden of leaden fatigue. His limbs felt numb, his heart like ice. Holding himself together by sheer force of will, he began casting around him in the void for any faint clue that might lead him to Gythe Du Bors.

At first there was nothing. The chill nullity of the surrounding darkness yawned before him, terrible and absolute. But even as his heart sank, his wavering mage-senses picked up an elusive glimmering of human life.

The discovery fired Caradoc with resurgent hope. Never doubting that he had located Gythe Du Bors, he probed eagerly into the abyss. Faint and fragmentary, the presence he had sensed seemed to have no center. The soul he was seeking seemed both everywhere and nowhere at the same time.

The truth struck Caradoc like a fist in the gut. Too weak to hold together, the boy's spirit had been pulled apart by the voracious hunger of the Pit.

The elements of Gythe's personality had been scattered abroad in the darkness, like a handful of dust cast adrift in an infinity of seawater. The only way to reclaim

the boy from the grip of the void was to find a way to call
those scattered elements together, and reintegrate them
as a human soul. The crushing magnitude of such a task
was beyond anything Caradoc could have imagined. But
he knew that somewhere he had to find the strength to
try.

THUNDER AT MIDNIGHT

HEAVY WITH THUNDER AND SMOKE, the sky over Gand
seethed like a cauldron of boiling pitch. Lightning
throbbed red among the clouds, like the pulsing of
exposed arteries. Lit from above by bursts of sheet-fire,
the pattern of streets and buildings showed up against
the night like a fresco painted in blood. The winds that
beat about the walls of Gand Castle reeked of burning
brimstone.

From the west rampart, the Merkward Embankment was visible as a broad serpentine of fortification
work dividing the Old Burgh from the new. Inside the
Merkward, the opulent houses surrounding the city's
great guild hall were feverishly ablaze with lights, marking the presence of Baron Khevyn Ap Khorrasel and his
adjutants. The embankment itself had been abandoned
in the course of the past half hour. A stone's throw inside
the old wall, strangely silent companies of red-coated
mercenaries were starting to assemble in the Oldmerkat
Square.

Outside the embankment, the streets were dotted
with isolated glimmers of torchlight, flitting with furtive
haste in the direction of St. Berengar's Cathedral on the
north side of the city. The cathedral's tall spires stood
out against the turbulent sky like the masts of a ship
foundering at sea. Lit from within, the great rose window

of the chancel flickered, a lighthouse beacon under a pall
of gathering storm.

Standing out on the west battlement of the castle,
bracing themselves against the swooping downdrafts of
sulphurous air, Serdor, Margoth, and Evelake surveyed
the fugitive procession of will-o'-the-wisps toward the
cathedral, where pallid gleams of light showed behind
the casements of residence hall and infirmary. Margoth
muttered, "I didn't realize there were any Hospitallers
still left in Gand. Why haven't they fled?"

"They're offering sanctuary to those who have no
other place of refuge in this eleventh hour," said Evelake.
"As to how effective their protection may prove . . ."

He left the sentence unfinished. "'Trust in God, but
look all the same to the strength of your walls,'" quoted
Serdor. "We're in a strong position here. That should
help—for a while, anyway."

Margoth appreciated what the minstrel meant. The
curtain walls of the castle's west rampart were thirty feet
high and twelve feet thick. At the height of twenty feet
above the ground, the stonework underlying the wall-
walks housed a running chain of mural chambers connected to one another by means of narrow wormhole
passages only wide enough for one man. Fitted with
boltholes and spy-squints, the mural chambers provided
effective protection for defending bowmen against
counterfire at close range. They also represented a second line of defense against any invaders who might
succeed in gaining the allures above.

The west rampart was strengthened in four places by
the presence of additional fortification works. The
southwest corner of the wall was defended by the beetling mass of the Peacock Tower, while the corresponding corner to the north was presided over by the Rooke, a
steep-roofed bartizan jutting out beyond the flanking
sections of parapet. Midway between the two lay the
Rouelle, a circular gun bastion supporting the Keep's
heaviest concentration of artillery pieces: two great
basilisks, three culverins, and twice that number of

drakonets. In the shadow of the Rouelle Bastion stood the Swan Port, surmounted by its own defenses in the form of a box turret which housed the workings of the portcullis.

As lord of the castle, Devon Du Penfallon had assumed command of the Rouelle and its arsenal, arranged in two stepped tiers, one above the other, on the roof of the bastion. Tessa Ekhanghar was directing the defense of the Peacock Tower, where a mixed complement of archers and crossbowmen had taken up firing positions all along the crenellated wall. Evelake and his followers were stationed in the Rooke, mounting guard over the stretch of wall on the north side of the Rouelle. Outside on the cliffs to either side of the ruin of the gatehouse, Jorvald Ekhanghar and a band of volunteers were preparing a special welcome for anyone attempting to scale the rocks from the shingle below.

Evelake, Serdor, and Margoth reentered the Rooke by the south door. Behind them, out on the parapet, the gun crews were fighting to lash down flapping sheets of tarpaulin over the boxes containing their powder reserves. Inside the Rooke, some of the men from the *Mermaid* were keeping watch over a pair of iron pots slung over a makeshift firepit in the middle of the floor. The air already stank of hot oil.

The trapdoor at the southeast end of the tower room was standing open. A clatter from the access chamber below was followed by the appearance of Harlech Hardrada. Catching sight of his three friends, the little mariner paused at the top of the ladder. "That's it," he reported. "They're on their way."

No one had to ask who "they" were—everyone present knew he meant the trio of mages. After trading glances with Serdor and Margoth, Evelake accepted the report with a nod, then squared his shoulders. "Where's Gudmar?" he asked.

"He's gone out tae the cliff-side tae gi' Marshall Jorvald and his lads a hand," said Harlech. "Have the Black Baron and his men made any move?"

"Not yet," said Evelake. "It's strange, too: they're all gathering in the market square of the Old Burgh without making any outcry. It's almost as if they were waiting for some sort of sign—"

He was interrupted by a sonorous boom from the direction of the Merkward. "Quick! Back outside!" cried Serdor.

The upper floors of the buildings flanking the High Street were flashing like mirrors in the light of an advancing wave of torches. Evelake groped within the folds of his cloak for the watchglass Devon had lent him. Snapping the eyepiece into viewing position, he trained the lens on the source of the activity. "There's a veritable hoard of people pouring into the Old Burgh through the Merkward Gate!" he reported. "From the look of them, they must be reivers."

The torchlit procession from the Merkward reached the western end of the marketplace where Lord Khevyn Ap Khorrasel and his troops stood mesmerized in regimental assembly. As their wild-eyed allies spilled into the plaza, the mercenaries started up out of their trance-like silence and began fumbling for their weapons.

The sullen mutter of voices was carried on the wind. The mutter swelled to a baying chorus. Waving swords and axes aloft, the enemy troops made a concerted, undisciplined rush for the eastern end of the marketplace. Like water flooding along the bed of a ravine, they surged down the causeway toward the head of the cliffs opposite the castle.

Standing out on the lower level of the Rouelle, Devon Du Penfallon watched the rabble advance on the cliffs. Behind him, the gun crews of the Rouelle shifted expectantly. "Upper battery reports all ordnance primed and ready, my lord," one of his sergeants informed him. "Lower battery is also standing by," called out another.

Mouth set hard, Devon turned to his men. "Gun captains to your marks!" he called. "On my signal—*fire!*"

Fifteen guns blazed out in unison with a roar that

shook the stones underfoot. An acrid wave of thick black smoke billowed back over the battlements. When it cleared, there was a collective mutter of consternation as the gun crews realized that their first volley had fallen short. "*Damn* this wind!" growled an anonymous voice from the ranks. "It's stolen ten yards off our firing range—"

"That's enough!" rapped Devon. "Reload!"

Stationed out on the cliff face below the castle walls, Jorvald Ekhanghar winced involuntarily as the Keep's west battery belched off a second round. But beside him, peering out from under the canopy of smoke, Gudmar uttered an exclamation of grim satisfaction. "They've got the distance right now," he said. "Even if we can't stop those reivers, we should be able to thin the ranks a bit."

The firing continued in rippling salvos, peppering the shoreline opposite with murderous spatters of stoneshot. Many reivers were dashed off the face of the inshore cliff as they scrambled down the steep incline toward the beach below. More clumps fell as the disorderly body struggled across the mudflats separating the mainland from the base of the castle rock. But despite heavy losses, the enemy fighters continued to multiply. For every man who fell, two more seemed to arrive to take his place.

Shielded from the Keep's batteries by the angle of the cliff, those reivers who survived the crossing began to clamber up both sides of the raw escarpment left by the destruction of the castle barbican many weeks before. As the guns on the battlements continued to pound the shore, Jorvald leaned out over the edge of the cliff head. The steep rock walls below were black with climbing shapes.

"Our time's almost up," he told Gudmar. "Let's go."

A stringcourse of barrels had been arranged end to end all along the crest of the bluff. Each barrel was held in place on its side by a sling of stout rope. Behind each

barrel stood a man poised with knife blade in hand.
Gudmar took up his station on the far right, opposite
Jorvald. He drew his dagger with a flourish and grinned
wolfishly over at the marshall before setting one booted
foot on the barrel lying in front of him.

The din from below was rising. Jorvald stole a
second swift glance over the edge of the escarpment, then
lifted one gauntleted hand above his head. "Ready—"
he gritted, *"now!"*

As the marshall's hand chopped down, men stooped
to slash through the ropes restraining the barrels. Assisted from behind with kicks and shoves, the kegs
lumbered over the lip of the gatehouse ledge. They hit
the slopes rolling, and rumbled off down the steep
incline below toward the climbers bunched up among
the rocks.

Weighted with rubble salvaged from the gatehouse
itself, the barrels smashed into the vanguard of the
enemy with the crushing impact of juggernauts. The men
highest up on the escarpment were hurled back into the
midst of those following behind. Within seconds, whole
streams of climbers were swept away and carried on
down the cliffside in a bone-shattering avalanche of lost
weapons and flailing limbs.

A cheer went up from the defenders ranged on either
side of the ruined gatehouse. "Don't be too quick to
crow," warned Gudmar. "Jorvald, look there!"

The marshall looked. On the lower levels of the cliff
wall, the enemy fighters were already scrambling to
regroup. Even as Jorvald watched, a second swarm of
reivers formed up to make another assault on the cliff. A
third wave of attackers was gathering, ready to follow.

The speed of the reivers' uphill progress was unlike
anything Jorvald had ever seen before. Weathered face
tightening, he turned to his men. "Clear out, and make it
quick!" he barked. "This place is going to look like a hive
of ants in another minute or two!"

The pathway that led up to the Swan Port doubled
back on itself three times before reaching the top of the

mound. While the rest of the detachment raced on ahead, Gudmar remained behind with Jorvald to hold the rear guard. The last of their subordinates had just reached the first bend in the trail when a score of crimson-clad reivers hauled themselves up over the embankment twenty yards from the foot of the path.

Mouthing wild abuse, the attackers picked themselves up and bounded through the rubble in a headlong charge. Gudmar and Jorvald wheeled and bolted up the footpath after the rest of their retreating company. More red-cloaked figures were pouring over the ruined walls of the gatehouse. Within seconds, the ledge was packed with enemy soldiers, all pressing forward in a lawless scramble to take part in the pursuit.

As the party from the Keep struggled to regain the safety of the castle, the archers ranged along the battlements unloosed a hissing rain of arrows. Crimson-liveried figures went down in mid-stride to be hurled aside and trampled down by others coming up from behind. A second volley of arrows from the castle ramparts was countered by a barrage of throwing spears from the ruins of the gatehouse. Four of the fleeing defenders, exposed on the high ground, were cut down as they ran for the postern gate at the base of the Peacock Tower.

Crowds of reivers were forsaking the path to scramble up through the rocks and crevices of the embankment. With pursuers closing in from behind, Jorvald took the next bend in the trail at a bound. As Gudmar vaulted after the marshall, the foremost of their harriers hurled himself forward in a flying tackle.

The reiver crashed into Gudmar at knee level. The force of the rush sent them both sailing off the pathbed into the rough ground beyond. Tumbling end over end through a bruising maze of outcroppings, they fetched up in a tangled heap among a nest of boulders several yards to the left of the trail. Gudmar had just breath enough to croak out, "Leave me, Jorvald!" before the reiver went for his throat with steel-gauntleted hands.

Gudmar's sword had torn loose from its wrist thong. His dagger was back in its sheath. Mail-clad fingers raked the left side of his face as his opponent tried to get a throttling grasp on his windpipe. Blocking the attempt with his right forearm, Gudmar dealt the other man a ringing clout over the ear with his left fist.

The reiver reeled to one side with an animal snarl of pain and reached for the shortsword at his belt. Gudmar rolled clear and got a grip on the hilt of his poniard. He wrested it free as his opponent closed in with a sword thrust aimed for his heart. Twisting out of the downward path of the blade point, he buried his dagger to the crossguard at the base of the reiver's neck.

More red-cloaked figures were converging on the spot, coursing through the rocks like weasels. Wrenching his dagger from the dead man's throat, Gudmar bounded to his feet and looked around him in search of a defensible covert. As he did so, a voice called out from above, "Gudmar! To me!"

Piercing clear, the voice belonged to Evelake. Gudmar wheeled around and looked up. Out on the rampart adjoining the Rooke, someone was energetically waving a lantern. Gudmar threw himself at the embankment and began to climb toward the light.

The sound of heavy breathing behind him grew closer yard by yard as a pursuing band of reivers clambered after him up the precipitous incline. Gudmar was within ten feet of the top of the hill when a clutching hand laid hold of his ankle from below. Hugging the rock scarp with arms outspread, he kicked himself loose with his free foot. But before he could heave himself out of reach, two more pairs of hands seized his legs and began to drag him back.

There was a swift stir of movement along the parapet overhead. A bristling array of crossbows appeared at the gaps between the merlons. *"Fire!"* shouted Evelake.

Steel quarrels clove the air at point-blank range. The imprisoning grip on Gudmar's legs slackened abruptly.

He broke loose with a twist of the hips and threshed his way to the base of the castle wall.

A length of rope unfurled within reach of his hands. He seized hold of it and yanked himself upright. "Hang on!" called Margoth.

The rope sprang taut. Gudmar's feet left the ground. He rode the cable upward in a series of swings and bounds. Hands caught him at the top and bundled him bodily over the battlement as a spray of javelins clattered off the masonry behind him.

Gudmar righted himself with a grimace and came face to face with Harlech. "Ye glaikit fire eater!" growled the little mariner testily, "I'll allow ye've all the makin's of a hero, but what gave ye the daft notion tae take on half Black Khevyn's army single-handed . . . ?"

WINGS OF MURDER

THE REIVERS SWARMED UP THE steep sides of the gatehouse embankment like a plague of locusts. Watching the retreating defenders stumble up the path toward the postern gate at the base of the Peacock Tower, Tessa Ekhanghar muttered an oath between her teeth as she realized that the party from the Keep was being overtaken with frightening rapidity. "Fire at will!" she called sharply to the bowmen under her command. "We've got to buy our people some time!"

Clothyard shafts slit the air in a whistling stream. Tessa nocked an arrow to her own bowstring and darted out from behind a merlon to shoot into the midst of the enemy ranks converging from below. Her victim dropped in his tracks, but scores more were on their way.

Strung out along the length of the open parapet, her fellow archers launched an ongoing stream of fire. Despite mounting losses, the enemy soldiers continued to press forward with suicidal abandon. "Bloody hell!" gasped one of the sergeants. "What's keeping those bastards going?"

Tessa didn't respond. Missing her father's tall, spare figure among the last of the retreating defenders, she cast a swift searching glance farther down the path and spotted his crested helmet approaching the highest bend in the trail.

Jorvald was not alone. His companion, leaning heavily on the marshall's braced arm, was limping badly, his right leg torn and bleeding. A pack of enemy fighters was closing the gap behind them, baying like so many wolves half crazed with hunger. "God, they're never going to make it!" gasped someone in dismay.

"We can't afford to lose them, either!" snapped Tessa. "Owain! Gather a dozen of our men and meet me at the postern door. Duncan! Keep the rest of our archers firing till I get back—"

The postern door in question was a narrow slot deeply recessed into the heavy masonry at the foot of the tower. The double yett defending the postern had been left open to receive the gatehouse party upon their return. Tessa and her auxiliaries shouldered their way out past the incoming stragglers. Even as they burst free from the entryway, Tessa heard the telltale clangor of swordplay break out below.

Jorvald and his wounded companion had veered off the path into the midst of a clutch of low boulders. Lightning flashed crimson off whirling broadswords as the marshall traded parries with a pair of snarling redcloaks. Racing down the slope at a hammering run, Tessa saw several more reivers vault up over the edge of the embankment.

She hauled her sword free of its sheath in a blur of fire and steel. *"For Gandia!"* she cried fiercely, and led her followers charging into the attack.

The two parties met in a clash of weaponry. Sparks

skated shrieking off bare metal. Tessa gutted one opponent with a sweeping slash of her blade, and whirled to
bring her blade edge scything down across the chest of a
second. The force of her downstroke sheared through
chain mail and cartilage to cleave him to the heart.

Blood jetted over her mail shirt as she ripped her
weapon loose. "Tessa! Watch your back!" shouted a
voice she recognized as her father's. She spun around
and narrowly avoided being skewered by a reiver armed
with a punch-dagger.

A heavy broadsword crashed down across the
reiver's armored knuckles, slicing through to the bone.
The man dropped to one knee with a scream of anguish
that ended in a fit of coughing as Jorvald ran him
through the lungs. Unlocking his blade with a skilled
twist of his sword hand, the marshall dropped his buckler
and caught his daughter by the arm with his free hand.
"Go!" he ordered, and thrust her ahead of him out of the
rocks into the pathbed.

A lightning glance up the trail showed Tessa a
scattered array of figures in Du Penfallon livery pelting
for the shelter of the Peacock Tower. "That's everyone,"
snapped her father. "Now run for it!"

Tessa did as she was told. Long legs flying, she
matched strides with her sire as the pair of them raced
for the postern door with a stream of reivers hot on their
heels. Cutting away from the trail as it hooked in toward
the Swan Port, father and daughter dashed along the
base of the Peacock and dived into the narrow shelter of
the postern archway. There was a hollow clang as the yett
slammed shut behind them in the faces of their harriers.

Bellowing in frustration, the enemy fighters hurled
themselves at the castle's west battlements with no
apparent regard for the ongoing hail of arrows raining
down on them from every embrasure. Some reivers,
armed with grappling hooks, went for the rampart above
the port. Others charged forward to plant steel-spiked
climbing poles against the walls of the two flanking

bastions. More gathered on the ground in the shadow of the Rooke and began gouging hand- and footholds into the supporting vallum with picks and mattocks.

The latter were temporarily driven back by blistering sprays of boiling oil and melted lead poured down on them from guttered sluice holes in the floor of the turret. On the crenellated rooftops of the Peacock and the Rouelle, defenders used billhooks to dislodge the pole ladders being thrown up against the walls below. Out on the Swan Port guardwalk, the castle yeomen waged war with hatchets against a burgeoning vine-growth of grappling lines.

The reivers continued to press their attack with single-minded fury. Before long, the members of the castle garrison were compelled to abandon their bows and arbalests in favor of swords and axes. Hand-to-hand combat raged up and down the parapets as the enemy soldiers tried repeatedly to force their way in over the walls. Fighting back with grim determination, the defenders managed to retain control of the battlement walks, but the repeated assaults were taking a toll of their strength.

The upper level of the Rouelle's rooftop battery afforded Devon Du Penfallon with a panoramic view of the whole west rampart from the Rooke to the Peacock. So far casualties among his own men and their allies had been relatively light, but given their limited resources of manpower, all losses were costly. The young Seneschal of Gand was just wondering how long it would be before fatigue and sheer weight of numbers would begin to tell against them, when the thick sulfur-tainted air reverberated with the sound of an explosion.

The noise came from the direction of the Peacock Tower. Turning sharply, Devon saw plumes of smoke rising skyward from somewhere below the level of the wall-walk. Even as he craned his neck to see what had happened, a figure that he recognized as Tessa Ekhanghar's esquire darted out across the Swan Port allure in the direction of the Rouelle.

Owain Arillan's footbeats echoed hollowly off the walls of the stairwell leading up to the Rouelle's upper gun balcony. He clattered to a panting halt on the uppermost step. "My lord!" he gasped. "Those maniacs down there are planting mine charges by hand and detonating them at point-blank range—"

He was interrupted by a second rumbling boom from the Peacock's outer wall. "It's sheer suicide, but they don't seem to care. And any minute now, they're going to break through into the lower guardroom," continued Owain breathlessly. "Lady Tessa requests permission to pull reinforcements off the northeast tower—"

Before the young seneschal could respond, there was a warning shout from the rampart below. Both Devon and Owain looked up to see a pulsating mass of darkness streaking toward them out of the west. Traveling swifter than any cloud, but fully as large, the mass of darkness swept low over the city, filling the air with croaking cries and a carrion stench. Darkening the sky overhead, the cloud descended on the castle ramparts—a cyclone of ravens.

The stinking blast of wind knocked Devon off balance and spun him around. Even as he pulled himself up short, something dark and heavy struck him a glancing blow across the back of the head. He flinched away from the impact with a startled grunt. In the same instant, two large V-shaped shadows swooped down on Owain out of the sky and sent him hurtling toward the parapet.

The forester struck the crenellated wall and tumbled backward over the edge toward the courtyard below. His vanishing cry was drowned out in a rushing gale of dark wings. Before Devon could react, he was engulfed in a screeching vortex of great black birds that converged on him in a storm of outstretched claws and gaping beaks. Shielding his face with one mail-gauntleted hand, the young seneschal groped frantically for his sword with the other. Razor-sharp talons raked across his back, tearing his surcoat to ribbons. His mail shirt protected his shoulders, but he took a deep set of gouges along the back of his upraised arm as his attackers veered off to strike again.

Pain all but took his breath away, but he kept his head. Briefly abandoning any attempt to draw his weapon, he dropped flat and rolled toward the nearest cannon. Wickedly hooked beaks thrust at his legs as he dragged himself under the sheltering framework of the gun carriage, but once there, he had a few heartbeats' grace in which to work his rapier loose from its sheath.

The birds circled in the air overhead, squawking in cacophanous frustration. He could hear other cries from below—human screams full of pain and panic. Not daring to think about what must be happening out on the wall-walks, he concentrated on doing what he could to save his own life.

To reach the safety of the tower room directly beneath him, he first had to get to the head of the newel stair. To reach the head of the stair, he was going to have to risk facing the fury of the birds. Difficult enough for a man with two sound legs. For a lame youth . . .

The distance to the topmost step was about fifteen feet—three running strides, for someone capable of running. Devon gripped the hilt of his weapon more tightly, drew a deep breath, and heaved himself into the open.

Birds swooped down on him from all sides. Flashing talons laid open his right cheek as he staggered to his feet. He fended off a second frontal attack with a hissing sweep of his rapier, and made a halting lunge for the head of the stair.

A weight like a falling stone struck him hard between the shoulder blades as he reached the wall flanking the stairwell. Knocked into the wall, Devon pivoted on his good leg to protect his back as he confronted a teeming array of snapping beaks and grasping claws. Bleeding face set hard, he struck the fencer's stance he had taught himself and straight-armed his rapier point into the breast of the leading gorecrow as it plunged to attack.

Devon let the bird's plummeting bulk carry his weapon downward. Dodging from the waist to evade a second gorecrow's talons, he freed his blade with a jerk and whipped it upright in time to spit another with a lightning thrust. His other attackers scattered briefly and regrouped in the air. Withdrawing his rapier point from the second carcass, Devon turned to bolt down the stairs.

A wave of gorecrows dived after him down the curve of the stairwell. With only one arm free to steady himself, Devon used the wall as a prop, hopping on his sound leg from step to step. His airborne attackers surged down behind him, buffeting him about the head and shoulders with their wings. He lost his balance and pitched head over heels down the six remaining stairs.

His sword hilt flew from his fingers. He landed at the bottom, battered and disarmed. Cawing and hissing, the gorecrows closed in to rip the flesh from his bones. He caught a half-stunned impression of gaping beaks and alien blood-lusting eyes, before a purposeful swirl of dark motion interposed between him and his attackers.

Jorvald Ekhanghar had traded his broadsword for a two-handed longsword. He swung it over his head in a whistling arc and sent it cleaving through the air. Blood and feathers went flying as the weapon's razor-sharp edge sliced through everything in its path. Jorvald reversed the blade with a sweeping backhand flourish and charged forward to drive back the gorecrows still on the wing.

Hands laid hold of Devon from behind and hauled him upright. "Quick, my lord! This way!" cried one of the Keep's sergeants, and steered him with a push toward the doorway of the Rouelle's tower guardroom.

Together Devon and his subordinate stumbled across the threshold. Jorvald bounded in behind them. Two auxiliaries, waiting on the inside, heaved the door shut and rammed home the bolt.

Shrieking, the birds assaulted the other side of the

portal with claws and beaks. Disregarding the din, Jorvald handed over his bloodstained sword to one of his adjutants before turning to Devon. The young seneschal inhaled deeply. "Trust me to be in the wrong place at the wrong time," he said wanly. "Thanks for coming to the rescue."

Jorvald bent down to examine the rips on Devon's cheek. "These will need tending," he said soberly. "Are you hurt otherwise?"

Devon grimaced. "I'm afraid so. I can't move my left arm."

"No mystery there: it's broken," said the marshall, after a swift downward glance. "I'll rig up a sling for you until you can get the bone set. The first chance we get, we'd better pull back to the donjon."

"What about our men?" asked Devon anxiously.

"We've taken some fairly heavy losses—too soon to tell exactly how many," said Jorvald grimly. "Tessa was supposed to be taking her people out of the Peacock by way of the souterrain under the south wall, but obviously we've had no report yet from that quarter."

"And Evelake?"

"We've had no word from the Rooke, either," said the marshall. "We'll just have to hope for the best."

But by now they all knew that the mindless fury of the assault was literally unhuman. . . .

ARMIES OF THE DEAD

THE ROOKE'S INTERIOR REVERBERATED LIKE the inside of a drum. Barricaded within, Evelake and his companions hugged the walls as flocks of gorecrows battered at the doors and clawed at the shutters covering the gun ports. Crouched on the floor next to Serdor, Margoth winced to see the heavy guard door to her right shudder violently on its hinges. Mouth close to his ear, she cried, "If this goes on much longer, they're going to break in. Isn't there *something* we can do?"

A loud crash against the gun port above their heads made them both flinch. Glancing up, Serdor saw that the shutter was split and sprung. "Get ready!" he called sharply to Margoth. "One more blow, and it's going to give way!"

Drawing her dagger, Margoth sprang to her feet and positioned herself to the right of the port. Serdor unsheathed his sword and stationed himself to the left. Weapons poised to strike, they waited for the next splintering attack. To their mutual surprise, it didn't come.

Instead, the raucous din from outside abruptly subsided. After a few sporadic thumps and bumps, an eerie silence fell. The people gathered inside the Rooke traded darkling glances around the room. Gudmar eased himself upright from bracing the east door. "Now what, I wonder?" he growled.

Harlech joined him, glowering. "Nothin' good, that's for sure," said the little mariner. "Crack the door a wee bit, and I'll have a peek outside."

Keeping his shoulder pressed against the door panels, the *Mermaid*'s captain carefully drew back the bolt. When nothing happened, he shifted the door inward a few inches. A breath of foul air filtered in through the gap, but no sound of rushing wings. Harlech sidled past Gudmar and stuck his long nose outside.

After a moment he pulled back with a grunt. "No sign o' those hellkites that I can see. They seem tae ha' taken themselves off, but God only kens why."

Gudmar frowned. Catching Serdor's attention from across the room, he said, "You've got sharp eyes. Take a look out the south door along the rampart and tell me if you see any of our people moving on the roof of the Rouelle."

The minstrel nodded and moved to comply. Watching his back, Margoth experienced a sudden icy chill at the base of her skull, like the dank clutch of dead man's fingers. The sickening cold turned her stomach. It also gave her a split second's premonition. "Serdor!" she cried. *"Don't open that door!"*

Her warning came a heartbeat too late. One foot already across the threshold, Serdor found himself confronting a grisly array of death's-head faces, all bulging eyes and grinning lipless mouths.

He leaped back with a yell and tried to slam the door. The foremost of the creatures on the outside thrust a leprous arm in the way and gave an inhumanly powerful shove. Serdor flew backward and tumbled to the floor. "Gudmar!" he gasped. *"Revenants!"*

The captain of the *Mermaid* was already on the move. Rearmed with a falchion, he lunged past Serdor and made a racing dive for the south door. A sweep of his heavy blade took the revenant's arm off at the elbow. Throwing the full weight of his body against the door, he forced the port shut and slammed the bar back into place with a clang.

"Get out of here!" he gritted over his shoulder to Evelake. "Take the north rampart and fall back to the donjon! The Great Hall must be defended, as planned."

An axehead struck home with a thud on the outside of the guardport. "What about you?" protested Evelake.

"I'll catch up!" Gudmar planted his feet and leaned into the door with all his strength.

More axe blades began to chop away at the exterior of the port. The door jumped on its hinges. After a last glance at Gudmar, the young Warden turned on his heel. "Jamie! Geordi!" he called crisply. "You stay with Gudmar and cover our backs. The rest of you, bring ropes and torches and follow me!"

The air outside reeked of corruption. As Evelake led his party out onto the north battlement, they could all see dark shambling forms crowding the courtyard below. An embattled cluster of torches gathered before the main entrance to the donjon hurled shadows all around the castle forecourt. Thrashing sword blades beat out a desperate tattoo in the fire-shot darkness.

Evelake glanced out across the yard. His searching gaze located the lean, long-limbed figure of Jorvald Ekhanghar among the men mounting guard over the entryway to the Keep. Under the marshall's direction, the defenders were fighting hard to hold their ground.

More revenants were assaulting the outbuildings that lined the courtyard's interior. Animated corpses had already overrun the smithy in the northwest corner of the compound below the entrance to the Rooke. Crowds of skeletal figures were struggling to clamber out through the smithy's half-dismantled roof in a bid to reach the allure above. "Hurry!" Evelake called back to the company following behind him. "This is going to be close!"

The north parapet came to an end at the base of a tall roundtower overlooking the sea. A stout oaken guardport, the mate to the doors in the Rooke, gave access in and out of the tower's lower guardroom. A small band of Devon's household retainers had been posted there to stand watch. Finding the port locked and barred, Harlech hammered out the signal pattern and shouted, "Open up, ye dozy barnacles, and make it quick!"

There was no response. "Something's wrong," muttered Evelake to Serdor. "Never mind—we'll just have to go around by the masons' gallery."

The gallery in question was a wooden brattice running around the inside curve of the tower wall between the north battlement and the guardwalk on the upper level of the donjon. To Margoth's eye, the wooden walk looked little better than a mere scaffold. "Are you sure this is safe?" she asked dubiously.

"No," said Evelake, "but it's the only route open to us. I'll go first."

He hoisted himself over the stone wall of the parapet and tested the boards underfoot. As the young Warden began working his way out across the makeshift bridge, Serdor cast a sidelong glance over at Margoth.

"I'm going with him," he told her. "You and the others wait here until we give you the all clear."

Before Margoth could argue otherwise, he slipped over the edge of the parapet and set off, light-footed, after Evelake's receding figure. Margoth looked after them with her heart in her mouth until a sudden upsurge of frenzied activity in the vicinity of the Swan Port dragged her attention away.

A hoarse howl of adulation went up from the ranks of the reiver-soldiery. In the same instant, a searing bolt of bloodred flame shot up in a blazing arc from the direction of the Swan Port arch. Like a gout of magma spewed up by a volcano, the fireball soared across the courtyard and struck the wall above the main port to the donjon. There was an explosive boom, and the stone-work above the architrave caved in, burying half of the port's defenders under a pile of smoking rubble.

Scarlet balefire splashed like a tide of blood over all the ramparts encircling the forecourt. Exposed in the wild glare of the demon light, Serdor and Evelake stood out against the pallid stone of the tower wall like moths splayed against a windowpane. A second globe of flame began to take shape in the shadow of the Swan Port. Margoth sensed its shapers' next target.

"*Run,* you two!" she screamed to the two people on the catwalk. "Run *now!*"

Her outcry penetrated the din from below. Taking Caradoc's sister at her word, Serdor and Evelake leaped together for the farther end of the brattice as the second burning orb catapulted into the air and hurtled toward them.

The firebolt struck the gallery midway. Wooden planking flew to splinters in a burst of seething flames. Serdor and Evelake lunged for the guardwalk parapet as the understructure of the brattice collapsed under them.

One stride ahead of the minstrel, Evelake made it over the wall with inches to spare. Picking himself up smartly, he looked around for Serdor without finding him. For one stricken moment he thought his friend had been dashed to his death in the courtyard below. Then he saw two hands gripping the outside edge of the parapet.

Serdor was dangling precariously by his arms. "Hang on!" cried Evelake, and bent to haul his friend up by the collar. Righting himself, Serdor said breathlessly, "That's left Margoth and the others trapped on the north wall."

"Hopefully not for long," said Evelake. "We'll have to try to go around and unbar that tower door, whatever we may meet on the way. Come on!"

The wall overlooking the guardwalk was broken by windows. "Living quarters for the seneschal and his family," explained Evelake tersely. "We'll force our way in through one of the bedrooms."

They found an unbarred casement at the north end of the guardwalk. After breaking out the glass and mullions, the pair slipped through the gap into the chamber beyond. The lurid glare from outside showed them a spacious open-beamed room with a tall four-poster bed in the center of the left-hand wall. "Quickly! This way!" hissed Evelake, and darted for the inside door.

He reached for the latch. In the same instant, something heavy rammed the door from the other side with force enough to hurl it open. The door struck Evelake head-on, knocking him back toward the bed. Several hulking half-rotted shapes lurched across the threshold, brandishing blades and cudgels in decaying hands. The stench was appalling.

Before Evelake could recover, the revenant nearest him took a heavy swipe at him with a notched shortsword. He rolled desperately but the weapon's jagged edge caught one leg. Evelake choked out a cry as the blade ripped along the outside of his thigh from hip to knee. Half paralyzed with pain, he only just managed to jerk himself out of the way as another revenant's broadaxe thudded home a hairbreadth from his right shoulder.

Serdor wheeled aside from the two creatures who

had attacked him and threw himself bodily at the nearest
of the two threatening Evelake. Flattening into a flying
tackle, the minstrel collided with the revenant at knee
level. Knocked off balance, the walking corpse tottered
into his charnel-house partner, giving Evelake a precious
second in which to scramble out of danger.

Tumbling away from the entanglement, Serdor
caught a fleeting pinwheel glimpse of the painted ceiling
before he bumped into the wall in the northwest corner
of the room. As he hastily pulled himself together, the
two revenants he had eluded originally converged on
him again, together with the pair who now abandoned
Evelake as "dead." Serdor vaulted to his feet and faced
the four creatures as they closed in.

Sprawled weak and breathless beside the bed,
Evelake started up at the clash of weaponry. To his
horror, he saw his friend with his back to the wall,
feverishly trying to parry attacks from two sides at once.
One revenant dashed Serdor's blade from his hand with
a sweep of its club, while another drove the point of a
rusty broadsword home beneath the short ribs on the
minstrel's right side.

With a gasping cry of agony, Serdor folded toward
the floor. Aghast, Evelake uttered a shrill exclamation of
denial. In the same instant, there was a resounding
clatter outside the window, and Gudmar Ap Gorvald
burst into the room, drawn sword in hand.

His golden eyes swept the scene, taking in at a
lightning glance Evelake lying bleeding by the bed,
Serdor holding himself slumped against the wall. Blade
blazing like copper in the glare from the courtyard, the
big merchant-adventurer lunged for the death's head
looming over the minstrel's fallen body. Gripping the
hilt of his falchion with both hands, he swung it from the
shoulder in a hissing sidesweep aimed for the revenant's
shriveled neck.

The blow connected with a crunch. Dead flesh
gaped at the base of the corpse's throat. There was a
crack as the cervical vertebrae broke apart. As the

revenant's head went flying, the body sagged devitalized to the floor.

More men from the *Mermaid* were spilling into the room. Foremost among them, Harlech Hardrada gave a hoarse battle yell and joined Gudmar in launching himself headlong at the revenants that still remained. "Aim for their heads!" shouted the *Mermaid's* captain. "That's the only way to put them down—"

Entering behind her male companions, Margoth at first could see nothing but the confusion of melee. Then her eyes lighted on Evelake as he struggled up from beside the bed where he had apparently fallen.

His forced movements lacked grace and control. A second, closer look revealed that he was hurt. "Evelake, be careful!" she cried. "Wait—let me help you!"

Darting through the midst of the subsiding conflict, she ran to his support. When she caught his arm, he sagged against her, his brown eyes cloudy with pain and shock. Focusing with difficulty on her face, he said thickly, "H-how did you get across the gap?"

"Gudmar rejoined us a moment or two after you'd disappeared. He swung across on a grappling line and set up a rope bridge for the rest of us," said Margoth. "You'd better sit down a moment. By the look of things, you've lost a lot of blood."

Gudmar and his men had driven the remaining revenants back into the corridor. Instead of relaxing, Evelake shook his head vehemently. "Can't rest," he said haltingly. "Serdor . . . he's over there. Maybe dying—"

The breath left Margoth's lungs as a suffocating fear gripped her. Evelake pulled loose from her nerveless clasp and dragged himself toward the dim corner of the room adjoining the bed. He dropped down next to a limp form that Margoth had missed seeing in the chaos of the fight. Feeling suddenly weak at the knees, Margoth went to join him.

Serdor was doubled over on his side, one arm loosely outflung, the quilted cloth of his gambeson soaked with blood along his right flank. His eyes were

closed, his breathing shallow and labored. Joining
Evelake on the floor, Margoth reached out and touched
the minstrel's upturned cheek with quaking fingers.
When she called him by name, he did not stir.

"He was trying to protect me when the death's head
struck him down," said Evelake.

Hearing the stricken note in the boy's voice,
Margoth took a firmer grip on herself. "It wasn't your
fault," she said flatly.

Shadows fell across their touching shoulders.
"We've got to get down to the Great Hall as quickly as we
can," said Gudmar. "Time's running out."

He turned to the men with him. "Jamie! Rhodri!
You take up Serdor between you. I'll see to Lord Evelake
myself—"

"No, you won't—you may be needed elsewhere,"
said Evelake. "I can manage all right if Margoth will just
give me a hand."

After taking a look at the young Warden's face,
Gudmar acquiesced with a nod. After assigning a detail
to hold the rear guard, the *Mermaid*'s captain led the
main party out into the passage and down the hall to a
side corridor leading to the east stairs. As the company
started down the steps, the harsh uproar of a disturbance
filtered up to them from the floor below.

At the foot of the stairs, a narrow passageway
running back west brought the party to the threshold of a
heavy iron-clad door barring off the newer north wing of
the Keep from the older wing to the south. Gudmar
wrenched back the bolts and flung the port open. The
general din of fighting was instantly and brutally sharpened, the ringing clash of swords punctuated by grunts
and choked outcries. One voice, uplifted above the
others, was tersely giving orders. "That's Tessa!" exclaimed Evelake.

Jorvald's daughter and her auxiliaries were gathered
outside the chamber guarding the main entrance to the
Keep. The door between the guardroom and the passage
had been reduced to a skeletal frame of burst timbers.

Blades clattered and flashed among the broken planks as the attackers inside the guardroom tried to force their way in across the threshold. The defenders fought back with grim fury born of necessity.

The floor of the corridor was strewn with the bodies of those who had already fallen. The thick air reeked of blood and decay. Tessa was directing her dwindling forces from the left of the doorway. When the party from the Rooke appeared at the east end of the passage, she disengaged and fell back to exchange swift reports with Gudmar and Evelake.

She had lost her helmet, and the short fair hair along her right temple was matted with blood from a broken contusion high on her brow. Her face was white and grim in its iron composure. "I'm glad to see you alive," she said. "We were wondering if you'd managed to make your withdrawal before the death's heads overran the outer walls."

"It was touch and go," said Evelake, with an oblique glance at Gudmar. "Where's Devon?"

"Downstairs, getting his injuries seen to," said Tessa. "He got caught out on the parapet when those infernal butcher birds swooped down on us. He was able to fight his way clear of them, but not before he took some nasty gashes and a broken arm."

"And Jorvald?"

Tessa's mouth twitched. "He's also downstairs. Did you see the firebolt that hit the entryport? Well, Father was one of the ones caught in the blast. He was still breathing when the orderlies carried him from the field," she concluded, "but I haven't been able to spare anybody to go asking for news of his condition."

"How many men have you got left?" asked Gudmar.

"What you see there," said Tessa thinly. "Plus another score or so on the ground floor, held in reserve to defend the Great Hall."

There was an appalled pause. Evelake turned to Gudmar. "Is it worth trying to hold this doorway as long as possible?" he asked.

Gudmar nodded. "The longer we can prevent the enemy from penetrating the building, the better."

"How many men can we spare to reinforce Lady Tessa's fighting strength?"

"Half our number. With your permission, my lord," said Gudmar. "I ought to be among those who remain."

Evelake made no argument. "I accept your recommendation," he said. "Choose those men you want to remain with you."

Gudmar lowered a hand to clasp the boy's taut shoulder. "Once we've divided our company, take your detachment down to the Great Hall and start setting up our last line of defense. We'll fight our way back to you. . . ."

HALL OF FIRE

WHEN EVELAKE AND THE REMAINDER of his company reached the foot of the west stair, they were met by one of Devon's sergeants-at-arms. From him they learned that the corridor outside the north entrance to the Great Hall had been blocked with rubble as a defense against forced entry from that quarter. The only other entrance to the hall was a set of service doors leading in from the kitchens to the south.

The passage running from the west stair to the kitchens had been partially blocked by makeshift breast-works constructed from meal bags. The handful of Keep yeomen who were left were grimly digging themselves in for a last stand. One or two of them saluted Evelake in passing. The rest were keeping their eyes fixed on the north doorway.

The party from the Rooke reached the Great Hall to

find that the two small presence chambers at the hall's
eastern end had been converted into casualty wards.
When Margoth pressed Evelake to have his leg wound
seen to, the young Warden shook his head. "There's not
going to be any time for that," he told her. "By all means,
do whatever you can for Serdor. But my place is here."

Devon came forward to meet them, his left arm in a
sling. On his advice, Jamie and Rhodri carried Serdor
into the south wardroom and laid him down on a blanket
one of the Keep's orderlies laid out for him. The two
mariners withdrew to rejoin their companions who were
receiving their last orders. Margoth remained at Serdor's
side.

One of the women from the castle brought water and
bandages. Using her dagger, Margoth cut the minstrel
free of his clothes so that she could bathe and dress the
wound. The revenant's sword had penetrated an inch
above Serdor's right hipbone. Even to her inexperienced
eye, the puncture looked ugly and dangerous.

Suppressing a vain yearning thought for Caradoc
and his healing powers, she set her teeth and prepared to
do her poor best. As she bent over Serdor's unresisting
form, a sudden feeling of breathlessness came over her.

The breathlessness was accompanied by a resur-
gence of the nausea she had experienced out in the
Rooke just before the onset of the revenant attack. Only
this time the sensation was infinitely worse. As she
fought to control her illness, the chamber around her was
rocked by the force of an explosion.

The blast had come from the west, strong enough to
blow open the door leading to the Great Hall. Closing
her ears to the panicky babble of civilian voices around
her, Margoth sprang to her feet and darted to the
threshold. She saw at a glance that the blast had torn a
hole in the wall opposite the dais. Only the strength of
the upright columns supporting the rafters had prevented the roof at that end of the room from caving in.
All around the hall men were picking themselves up

off the floor. Near at hand, Harlech was stooping to help
Devon to his feet. Looking around for Evelake, Margoth
spotted him as he dragged himself out of a bed of fallen
plaster. Even as she ran forward to assist him, a straggling handful of dust-covered figures staggered into the
hall through the smoky cavity left by the explosion.

The tall, slight figure in front was Tessa Ekhanghar,
her sword notched, her surcoat singed and smoldering.
The two men behind her were bearing a third between
them. The angry glare of fire from outside the hall picked
out a random glint of gold through the dust and ashes
that silted the unconscious man's hair and beard.
Margoth's heart plummeted as she realized the fallen
fighter was Gudmar.

Evelake shrugged off her supporting hand. "Never
mind me," he told her. "Find someplace where those
men can lay Gudmar down. Then go warn those people
in the wardrooms to take whatever shelter they can
find."

His face was bloodless in the mounting glare of the
firelight. He had about him a fey air of desperate resolve.
Motioning Gudmar's bearers on past them, Margoth
cast a fearful glance at the pentagram Borthen had drawn
on the floor. To her relief, it was still intact.

"Promise me you won't do anything rash!" she said
to Evelake. "Borthen's sign is unbroken—that means
there's still hope."

Evelake paused in the act of drawing his sword.
"Don't worry," he said. "The best any of us can hope to
do now is simply play for time."

A sudden upsurge in the fire out in the passageway
sent a sulfurous wave of smoke and flame rolling through
the gap torn by the blast. A volcanic shimmer of blistering heat rippled off the floor. The surrounding walls
turned red. As the blaze mounted toward the beams
overhead, out of the cloud of mingled fire and brimstone
appeared a graceful figure limned in radiant flame.

Its form was that of a boy on the threshold of sexual
maturity. Its face belonged to the beautiful demon-child

of Sherat Jeshuel. "Oh hell," breathed Harlech. "Oh *bloody* hell . . ."

As one, the defenders who were still on their feet drew together and arranged themselves in a semicircle in front of the symbol Borthen Berigeld had advised them to protect at all cost. Evelake positioned himself at the center of the group, with Tessa and Devon on his right hand and Harlech to his left. Joining Harlech on the left flank, Margoth found herself with her back to an upright beam. She braced herself against it and waited with grim fatalism to see what would happen.

Holding a large fiery jewel like a kingly orb in one clawed hand, the entity that wore the semblance of Evelake's young half brother strode naked through the inferno of its own kindling. The flames played caressingly about the boy's bare legs like lascivious hands. He came to a halt just beyond the circle of rubble and raked his opponents with eyes like molten rubies. Rigid and trembling, Evelake raised his voice. "That's far enough, Herech Thanatos!" he declared. "You have no business here!"

The demon's response was a hissing laugh that set the surrounding flames dancing. Burning eyes bent their alien regard on the slender, tattered figure of the young Warden. A deep voice, harsh as a brazen bell, issued from the mouth of Gythe Du Bors. "Foolissh mortal, you have no sstrength to opposse uss. You have only a choice to make: ssurrender, or perissh."

That much was true. The end seemed so near that for an instant Evelake was tempted to hasten it by an act of blind unreasoning defiance. Then he caught Margoth's eye, and took hold of himself. "Time!" he reminded himself. "We've got to play for time!"

Hoping that his companions would understand what he was about, he lowered his sword a few conciliatory inches. "I have no desire to die," he said. "What are the conditions for surrender?"

The demon's eyes were inscrutable. "That you sshould cursse the name of the Creator," intoned the

sonorous voice of the Devourer. "That you reject all
hope of ssalvation, and yield yoursselves to uss,
unresservedly—body and ssoul."

Tessa had pricked up her ears. Devon was thinking
furiously. Reinforced by their unspoken collaboration,
Evelake persisted. "To what end?" he asked the Devourer.

"That you sshould worsship only uss ass lord-
eternal," lisped the Devourer. "That you render uss
obedience, and sserve uss in all thingss."

Margoth cast a covert glance aside at the pentagram.
Her heart leaped into her mouth. In the pupil of the
symbol's painted eye, the ghost of a small emerald
whirlwind was forming.

Praying that the Devourer would not notice it, she
found her tongue. "But are you not yourself perfect and
complete?" she asked the fire-child.

"We are." The demon's response echoed sibilantly
off the rafters.

"Then what use," argued Margoth, "would our
worship and service be to you?"

A cruel smile touched the lips of Evelake's half
brother. "The exercisse of power iss the essence of
pleassure," said the Devourer. "Behold one who hass
tassted our power and our pleassure."

He swept out one bare glowing arm in a gesture of
summoning. A second shadowy figure appeared in the
midst of the flames behind him, moving forward through
curling waves of balefire. It took the shape of a naked
black-haired woman. Emerging from the blaze, she sank
to her knees before the demon and bent her head to kiss
the fiery jewel of power in an attitude of abject servitude.

The demon-child stroked her bowed head. "Go to
our brother," said the Devourer. "Ravissh him with your
beauty."

The woman rose and turned. Gazing at her, Evelake
found himself bereft of speech. Her face had been
devastated beyond all recognition—reduced to the semblance of a skull.

The woman advanced toward the young Warden, lipless mouth framing a hideous parody of a coquettish smile. Extending her hands, she whispered hoarsely, "See how he that is mighty has dealt graciously by me, his handmaiden? Join with me, Evelake Whitfauconer, in magnifying the dread name of Herech Thanatos."

She reached out as though to cup the boy's blanched face between her hands. Balefire flickered up from her palms. With a sharp cry of warning, Tessa lunged for the woman and yanked her back by the hair. With a shrewd, hard-knuckled blow of her fist she sent the demon's minion tumbling to the floor at her master's feet.

Infernal fury blazed up in the Devourer's crimson eyes. It raised taloned hands, arms spread wide like mantling wings. The firestone it bore crackled with sudden baleful energy. "The choice hass been made," hissed the inhuman voice of the demon. "Now learn what it meanss to be the food of Herech Thanatoss—"

Fire shot out from the heart of the firestone directed straight at Tessa. Half blinded, Margoth reeled back and tumbled to the floor at the foot of the beam. As she tried to pull herself up, a flying sheet of flame enveloped Tessa, Evelake, and his closest companions in a searing storm of power.

Whirling widdershins, the flames gnawed hungrily at fabric and flesh. The people caught in the blazing cyclone writhed and screamed in mortal agony. A wave of intense heat slapped Margoth in the face as she struggled to her feet. In that instant she exploded into incandescent fury.

"God damn you!" she shrieked. And dashed both clenched fists against the beam in ungovernable outrage at her helplessness.

To her utter astonishment, the impact of her blows sent a rumbling shockwave rippling toward the roof. Arrested, the demon-child cast a startled look upward. In the same instant, green light erupted from the masonry overhead like water bursting through a dam.

The flash flood of Margoth's undisciplined power

ripped the rafters loose from their mountings. Like logs going over a waterfall, they crashed down on the fire-child below, burying it under several hundredweight of wood and stone.

The firestorm flickered and winked out. Its victims crumpled to the floor, skins blackened, clothes smoldering. Half-dazed with shock, Margoth found herself without the strength to reach them. Clinging dizzily to the support of the beam, she could not tell if any of them were still breathing. Time moved slowly, slowly, as she dazedly watched vagrant tendrils of smoke drift to the open sky.

Then, as she continued to stare numbly at the wreckage, it heaved and shuddered. Stones and splintered planks rolled away. Random gleams of crimson fire glinted like eyes among the shifting rubble. With a sudden rumble, a fiery figure shook itself free of the surrounding ruin and pulled itself erect.

Margoth discovered she could neither move nor speak. Glowing eyes bright with malice, the fire-child smiled to see her horror and confusion. "Foolissh mortal," chided the voice of the Devourer. "We are not sso eassily desstroyed ass that. Come to uss and we sshall teach you the meaning of true power."

The fire-child beckoned lazily with a shapely hand. Aghast, Margoth found herself leaning forward against her will. She stumbled, almost fell. The naked boy's body before her was quivering with erotic energy. Averting her gaze in sick revulsion, she glimpsed a sudden shimmer of emerald radiance out of the corner of her eye.

The pentagram, she realized, was still unbroken!

Intent upon its prey, the demon lifted its stone of fire to summon the infernal power at its command. Through terror and exhaustion, Margoth sensed, clean and sharp, something of her brother's unmistakable presence. "*Now*, Caradoc!" she prayed in her own mind. "For God's sake, *now!*"

THE PIT OF HUNGER

In the devouring cold of the abyss, Caradoc felt his sister's scream of blazing rage reverberating through the deep chill of his own body. A window of vision burst open in his mind, showing him the Great Hall in Gand Castle—not as he had left it, but devastated now, its broken walls crawling with wormtongues of flame, its floor strewn with bodies. His heart contracted as he recognized friends among the fallen: Evelake and Devon, Harlech and Tessa. *Tessa!*

But two figures stood. One was Margoth, crouched, her clothes in tatters, her face white and desperate. She was staring at the other figure, mesmerized. It wore the aspect of Gythe Du Bors.

The boy was standing naked at the center of a rippling corolla of fire, and at some distance from Margoth. His eyes glowed like live coals, his smiling mouth was slick and red, as though he had been drinking blood. The lazy hand beckoned, confident. Margoth leaned forward, stumbled. Caradoc felt time stretch, knew the icy sharpness of his sister's terror like a dagger point tracing a line with infinite slowness through his every screaming nerve.

And in that time he reached out, sending a clear call to the Magia to use his own agonized, resonating being as a focus, an instrument to heal, to bring together the pathetic shards of a boy's lost personality. With self-torturing exactitude, he set himself to reconstruct a mirror image of Gythe in his own mind.

Like motes of cosmic dust drifting toward the center of a newborn nebula, the floating fragments of Gythe's shattered spirit began to come together, gathering like particles of cloud around the image Caradoc had made. Like an embryo forming in its mother's womb, the boy's spirit began to assume coherent identity. Under the influence of Caradoc's refining power, that identity reclothed itself by degrees in all the properties of consciousness: reason, imagination, will, and memory.

Memory—and conscience.

Linked to Gythe in Orison, Caradoc stiffened as a dark tide of images washed over them both: a dead deerhound . . . a courtyard full of screaming people . . . the charred and gutted shell of a Hospitallers' chapel. Sensory impressions accompanied the last image: the cloying odor of incense . . . the sound of a woman's seductive laughter. At that point, Evelake's half brother shied away from any further remembrance with a violence that nearly broke Caradoc's fragile sphere of rapport.

Faced with something too terrible to contemplate, the boy's spirit-self began to crumble. With a ruthlessness born of sheer desperation, Caradoc used the power of the Magia like a flaming sword to slash Evelake's brother free from his soul-destroying memories. Gythe's spirit quieted. But before Caradoc could turn the boy's passivity to any advantage, the surrounding darkness spawned another presence.

The presence demanded power. Before Caradoc could resist, he had a measure of his own faltering vitality ripped away from him with a brutality that wrenched a cry from his lips. Shaken to the root of his spirit, he lost his precarious grip on the boy Gythe. Even as he found himself alone in the void, a black wind came howling down the shaft to engulf him in a storm of sound and fury.

Shadows whipped around him like rags in a cyclone. Floating clusters of lidless eyes appeared out of nowhere and gathered to stare at him with bestial greed before whirling away. Red slavering mouths yawned wide to show carious tushes glistening wet with saliva. A chorus of lisping voices snarled, "Did you think to deprive uss of our food, Caradoc Penlluathe? Thiss iss Zhulzar, the banquet hall of Herech Thanatoss. Here you will remain to be our sservant and our ssustenance. . . ."

Moist lips brushed the nape of Caradoc's neck, quivering with avid anticipation. He started violently away, every nerve trembling in soulsick revulsion. His reaction drew rich, lubricious chuckles from the malignant presence surrounding him. "Come, little mage—tasste and ssee how ssustaining iss the power of Aeshma," breathed the manifold voices of the Devourer. "Join with uss in our unending feasst of dessolation. . . ."

The disembodied mouths drew in from all sides, cackling and drooling. Somehow, Caradoc found his tongue. "Get back!" he grated hoarsely. "The Keeper of the Magia is my master. While I am in his service, you can have no dominion over me!"

Antic laughter passed like a shudder through the encompassing darkness. The red sea of eyes glinted at him with seething mirth. "Your masster cannot aid you here. He iss lord of light—but we are hunger immortal, and thiss iss our domain!"

Mouths and eyes went up together in a shrieking blast of balefire. Caught in the heart of the explosion, Caradoc screamed in mortal agony. Fire whirled round him like a whirlpool in a lake of lava. At the bottom of the lake, a void gaped wide, expanding until it filled his field of vision.

The jaws of the Pit reached out to seize him. Struggling, he was swallowed and sucked down into the churning gut of the infernal maelstrom. The blackness burned like acid. Choking on fire, deafened and blinded, Caradoc clung to his frail, desperate hope in the Magia, like a drowning man clutching a twig in the midst of a tidal wave, holding to a lifeline in his mind's eye, a line as thin as a spider's thread.

The consuming blackness ate away skin and soft tissue, searing down to the bone. The agony soared to thresholds beyond mortality. But even as Caradoc felt his marrow turning into ashes, the spider thread opened a chink of pure green light in the scorched cinderyard of his mind.

The chink broadened to a cleft. Like a spring of clear water, the Magia poured power into the burning cavern of the inferno. Like a rippling cascade off a mountain crag, it raced in a torrent through the blasted shell of Caradoc's body and soul. In the pit of hell, he tasted the paradisical wonder of new life.

Cool air filled his charred lungs, restoring in a single breath tissues incinerated by fire. The coolness radiated outward from the center of his body, flashing like emerald lightning along networks of nerves and blood vessels, rebuilding as it shot toward his extremities. Glowing with internal radiance, his bones reclad themselves in flesh scoured clean of every wound and scar.

Power swelled up in Caradoc like an exultant chord of music. It blazed out against the darkness with verdant intensity. Invested with the Magia's supernal light, Caradoc became a living magestone charged with glory. Transformed, he turned on the Devourer.

The demon recoiled before his presence, howling and yammering with many voices. Wounded by the terrible purity of the Magia's light, the red eyes shriveled up and went dark. The gaping mouths tore at one another in the madness of frustrated appetite. As Caradoc's power expanded to fill the void, the Devourer began to disintegrate, its parts breaking free to savage each other.

The fabric of the Pit itself heaved and groaned. The darkness on the edges of the light roared with the noise of cataclysmic breakage. As the destruction spread, the demon Herech Thanatos tore itself away from its infernal fastness and dissipated, wailing, into its own endless night. . . .

Standing over the entrance to Herech Zhulzar, Kherryn Du Penfallon heard a sudden rumbling deep in the infernal bowels of chasms she only guessed at below. The pavement heaved beneath her, like a rock breaking loose in a landslide. There was a deafening crack, and a jagged seam shot across the face of the surrounding courtyard to lose itself among the monoliths in the distance.

Sudden terror rooted Kherryn to the spot. A hard hand seized her bruisingly by the arm and dragged her backward. "Come on!" snarled Borthen Berigeld. "We've got to get out of here. The city is starting to break up."

Too frightened and bewildered to resist, Kherryn allowed herself to be hustled away from the entrance to the Pit mere seconds before the sides began to cave in. The monuments enclosing the courtyard were shuddering. The air was loud with the grinding tumult of breaking stone. Everywhere Kherryn looked, she could see pillars and obelisks teetering on the brink of collapse.

Borthen dragged Kherryn up onto a fallen menhir. "If you value your life," he told her sharply, "you had better find us a door out of this place."

"M-me?" faltered Kherryn.

Borthen's grip took her breath away. "Who else but you, you little idiot?" he snapped. "You're the periegete. If we can't escape this plane, we're doomed."

The earth underfoot was writhing and roaring like a wounded dragon. All along the skyline, ziggurats were toppling in ruin. Building stones crumbled, forming grinding avalanches down tottering walls. The air was thick with rock dust and sulfur.

Heart hammering, Kherryn clasped her hands tightly in front of her and tried desperately to think in the midst of the rumble of rock and the howl of shifting earth. "A door . . . we need a door!" she told herself. "The Swan Port . . . it's as good as any—"

A sudden shift in the stones under her feet tumbled her to her knees. Grazed and bruised, sobbing with fright, she struggled up and tried to clear her mind. The image of the port took shape before her inner eyes.

Clinging hard to that image with every nerve, she willed herself to give it substance on her side of the paraworld.

The tingle of the Magia was like a feeble sputtering of sparks in her fingertips. Her heart and lungs labored as she fought to call up more power. Her mouth went dry and her head swam. A ghostly outline of a doorway began to materialize in front of her.

The drain on her strength was sickening, but she struggled to hold out against her growing exhaustion. Off to her left, a great stone column twisted off its pediment and broke free with a boom. The crash as it struck the earth threw her flat. A burning sensation shot like acid through all her straining body, and the image of the door winked out.

Borthen leaned over her. He was mouthing words in a cutting tone of anger, but Kherryn's ringing ears could make no sense of what he was saying. She attempted, sluggishly, to resume her task. But it was as though every nerve had gone suddenly dead.

She turned to stare up at Borthen with eyes that seemed to be losing their ability to focus. He met her mute, bewildered gaze with a snarl, then looked into her face more closely. His long mouth twitched in a bitter grimace. He straightened up abruptly and strode away from her.

His image blurred before her cloudy eyes. She could still hear his voice indistinctly. What he was saying had rhythm—as though he were uttering some kind of incantation. There was a shadowy flash in the air, and a flicker of rising movement. When she looked again, the dark mage was nowhere to be seen.

The cloud lifted briefly from her sight. High overhead, winging toward the safety of the sky, was a night-black raven.

Like a ragged bolt of shadow, it shot between the pinnacles of two collapsing towers and vanished from view. Abandoned in the midst of a spreading upheaval, Kherryn buried her face in her arms and gave herself up for lost.

The slab of stone on which she was lying jerked and spun. Heat flared up in a burning wave against her right side. Whimpering, she curled herself blindly into a small knot of quaking limbs. But as the fire rose to engulf her, a pair of hands reached down to pluck her bodily out of the black swirl of destruction and chaos.

Silence fell around her. Feeling the support of strong arms under her, she forced her still-burning eyes to open. Soft green light filled her vision—cool as water, clear as crystal. A face looked down into hers out of the shimmering glow of a power she knew for the Magia.

The face of Caradoc Penlluathe.

He smiled down at her and gathered her closer to him, so that she lay with her head resting against his shoulder like a child. Staring up at him in blank wonder, Kherryn realized that the glow that surrounded him was actually emanating from his living flesh—as though he himself were a living magestone. Summoning breath, she said hesitantly, "You're so—so *bright*. Is the demon gone then?"

Caradoc's smile deepened. "It's gone," he said. "Now let's go home. . . ."

Stretched out on the icy flagstones of Gand Castle, Tessa Ekhanghar roused from a black swoon full of nightmares to a waking nightmare full of pain. Every nerve in her body held fire like a dying coal. Her last waking memory was of a firestorm that had overwhelmed her party at the command of the demon Herech Thanatos. The storm had burned itself out, but the agony remained, eating like a canker into her very bones.

She tried to move, and found that she could not. It was as though all her joints had been melted and fused by the heat of the flames. Her face felt seared beyond recognition. Remembering the demon's featureless black-haired mistress, she shuddered deep in her soul. Then reminded herself that she was almost certainly dying anyway.

It was that thought that made her attempt to open her eyes to catch some glimpse—however fleeting—of the world she and her companions had hoped to save. Forcing her raw eyelids apart, she saw, dimly, that the roof of the Great Hall had fallen in, leaving it open to a sky pallidly flushed with dawn. The grey light showed her a handful of other ash-covered forms scattered across the broken flagstones before her. Despite the disfiguring brandings of fire, she recognized Devon, Harlech, and Evelake nearby—Margoth a little farther off.

And beyond Margoth's tumbled form, a pale blur that resolved itself upon closer scrutiny into the naked nerveless body of Gythe Du Bors.

Evelake's half brother was sprawled out on his belly on the cold ground. His bare skin was blanched white as marble in the frosty air, his half-averted face as still as the face of a corpse. Seeing him thus, with all the infernal fire gone out of him, Tessa experienced an aching surge of triumph in the midst of her pain. "They did it!" she thought dizzily. "Caradoc and Kherryn—they did it!"

Knowing that much, there was no further point in fighting to remain conscious. Yielding to pain and exhaustion, Tessa closed her eyes and slipped back into the sanctuary of delirious sleep. But the dreams that came to her now were no longer stormy visions of a dread apocalypse, but gentle recollections of pleasures she had known and loved—pleasures that East Garillon would now see again: the dewy freshness of a spring morning . . . the green light of summer filtering through canopies of flowering trees. . . .

Achingly lovely, the green light seemed to expand to fill the windows of her soul. She could almost smell the winsome lightness of mayflower warmed by the sun . . . could almost feel the soft flicker of forest lights against her closed eyelids. The agonizing pain of the demon's burning receded before the touch of the light. Her face felt cool, as though she had bathed it in a mountain stream. . . .

She drew a deep contented breath and stretched.

Only a belated instant later she realized she could move again!

Surprise jolted her into full wakefulness. She sat up with a start and opened her eyes.

She was still in Gand Castle, amid the ruins of the Great Hall. But now the hall was full of light. Silver-green radiance sparkled over the stones like the dance of summer sunshine over rocks in a shallow pool. It lingered gently over the bodies of Tessa's fallen companions, washing away ashes and injury in a healing tide. She could see now that they were breathing softly, as though peacefully asleep.

Heart beating high, Jorvald's daughter looked around for the source of the light. It seemed to be pouring out of a wellspring in the middle of the hall. Eyes fixed upon the flowing spring, she saw a human form take shape in the heart of the cataract. As it moved toward her, she recognized Caradoc Penlluathe, approaching with Kherryn in his arms, her body folded in the coruscating light emanating from his.

He stepped lightly over the flagstones, as though his limbs had no weight. Mantled in the verdant glow of the Magia, he halted and knelt to lay Kherryn gently on the floor at his feet. She was smiling a little, her eyes closed in sleep. There was about her now no sign of conflict.

The green light was now fading. As its radiance subsided around him, Caradoc looked up from Kherryn's still face. His eyes met Tessa's. Seeing joy leap into her unmarred face, he straightened up and moved slowly toward her.

Their hands touched, and then their lips. His mouth still close to hers, Caradoc murmured softly, "You have your promise now of things to come—in the fullness of a happier time."

As he spoke, the green light flickered out, leaving his face revealed in all its weariness. He swayed on his feet. Tessa felt the weight of his exhaustion briefly, before his long limbs folded under him and he slumped unconscious to the stone floor.

EPILOGUE

CARADOC AWOKE UNDER THE WARM weight of several coverlets. He was lying on his back in a bed that was not quite long enough for his height. Rosy light played across his closed eyelids; he could hear the soft crackle of a fire burning tamely on the hearth beyond the foot of the bed. Caradoc's last waking memory was of the ruined Great Hall of Gand Castle, his friends' last battleground. Wondering where he was now, he shook off a lingering lassitude and opened his eyes.

The whitewashed dark-beamed ceiling hanging over him was not one he recognized. Staring up at it with a crease between his brows, he murmured, "What is this place?"

"The infirmary at Maeldune Priory," said a familiar voice.

The voice belonged to Serdor. Coming fully alert, Caradoc struggled up on his elbows to survey his friend and his surroundings.

The room itself had been sparsely but comfortably furnished to accommodate two people. The minstrel was sitting in a chair at his bedside. The weatherstained clothes he had worn to the siege of Gand had been replaced by elegant garments fashioned from fine blue-grey wool. Seeing the question in Caradoc's still-haggard gaze, he gave a wry grin and opened his arms to display his newfound finery.

"I'm not sure I'm cut out for this sort of grandeur," he said, a shade ruefully. "I feel like a bird in borrowed plumage. You, on the other hand, look as though you just moulted—but that's easily rectified, once the Master of

Maeldune determines that you're well-rested enough to get up and get dressed."

Caradoc peered down at himself and discovered he was clad in nothing but a loose cambric shirt. He frowned, struggling to remember what had happened during the moments immediately following his return from the paraworld. "How long have I been here?" he demanded. "What's been happening outside?" And more urgently still, "Where are the others?"

Before Serdor could answer any of his questions, the door in the righthand wall swung open and a burnished copper-red head appeared around the doorframe. "If you'd give the man a chance to get a word in edgewise, you might find out what you want to know," said Margoth.

She had evidently just come in from outdoors; her skin was glowingly flushed, and her hair carried the fragrance of evergreens. Caradoc gave a wordless exclamation of joy and would have leaped from his bed if she hadn't restrained him with a laughing reproof. "For heaven's sake, do show a little propriety! I've brought another visitor to see you."

Serdor slipped from his chair and crossed the room to join her. The lurking twinkle in his grey eyes suggested that he already knew who the visitor might be. Before Caradoc could request enlightenment, Margoth turned and beckoned to someone waiting outside.

A willowy figure stepped lightly across the threshold. Caradoc caught his breath as he recognised Tessa Ekhanghar.

She was wearing not the forester's green he remembered, but a gown of dark blue velvet. Small sapphires sparkled along the close-fitting lines of her collar and cuffs. Her short thick hair shone like spun platinum in the wintery sunlight that streamed in through the window on the far side of the room. Caradoc's look of surprise yielded to an expression of wordless admiration.

A chuckle from Serdor roused him to his senses a moment later. "Margoth and I are going for a walk in the priory garden," said the minstrel. He added with emphasis, "We don't intend to come back any time soon."

The door closed behind them with a light click. Left alone with Tessa, Caradoc found his tongue. He shook his head wonderingly and said, "I'm sorry. It's just that you look so different in a dress."

Tessa smiled. "Were you expecting the frieze and leather? I've put those aside for another time." She crossed the room and seated herself gracefully in the chair that Serdor had vacated. After taking a closer look at Caradoc's face, she asked, "How do you feel?"

"Well enough," said Caradoc. "But very much out of touch."

"Don't worry: you'll soon catch up," said Tessa. "The important thing to bear in mind is that the demon is gone, and East Garillon is free. Yuletide this year is going to be a specially festive occasion."

She spoke lightly, but Caradoc was quick to hear the underlying note of constraint in her voice. He studied her more closely, noting the subtle traces of strain that he had overlooked in his initial delight at seeing her. There were faint smudges of shadow beneath her bright blue eyes and her face was pale beneath its fading overlay of windburn. The smile left his lips. Shifting his weight, he reached out and gently took her hand.

Here again, as at Glaive's Hough, touch proved merely the prelude to a deeper rapport. As Tessa wordlessly opened up her heart and soul to him, Caradoc received a sudden grievous impression of sadness and loss. Even as he came to share her pain, he learned its cause: her father Jorvald was dead.

He saw through the eyes of her memory the blast of balefire that had struck the marshall down as he fought to defend the main port of Gand Castle. Behind that single agonizing image lay a jumbled host of other impressions: a small girl's adoring view of a father who was both her dearest playmate and her greatest hero; a gawky adolescent, convinced she would never be beautiful, consoling herself with the reflection that she would always be loved and valued by this man whom so many other people admired; a young woman taking fierce pride in the knowledge that she was her father's most talented pupil as well as his closest confidant. The measure of Tessa's affection for her father was the measure of her sorrow now that he was gone.

No mage could heal the anguish of bereavement. Caradoc's heart ached with grief on Tessa's behalf. He could only hope that she would take consolation from the knowledge that he loved her and longed to comfort her. Trusting his emotions to speak for themselves, he said aloud, "Your father must have been a remarkable man. I regret very much that I never got to know him well."

Tessa lifted her face. Despite the hurt she had sustained, the spirit that showed in her eyes was as brave as ever. She said sadly but firmly, "The price of victory is never cheap. My father would be glad to know he did not give his life in vain. Indeed," she continued, "if he feared anything at all in this life, it was the infirmity that comes with old age. He would have considered it far more fitting to die as he did: in battle, with a sword in his hand."

"That doesn't change the fact that you miss him," said Caradoc. "I'm sorry that victory should have cost you so dearly."

Tessa managed a difficult smile. "Defeat," she said, "would have been far more costly—and not only to me. That is why I am not dressed in mourning: because the deadly evil we feared so much now lies behind us, and we have a future to look forward to."

Stirred by her courage, Caradoc clasped her fingers more tightly. For a while there was silence between them, more eloquent than any words. At length Caradoc sensed a brightening in Tessa's spirits, and knew she was ready to return to normal conversation. "It seems strange to be lying idle," he said with a crooked grin. "I'm finding it hard to get used to the idea that all the running and hiding and fighting are over."

Tessa nodded. "That's hardly surprising, considering what you went through while you were in the paraworld," she said. "Do you remember much right after you got back?"

Caradoc thought back. "It's a bit hazy," he said. "I must have been in a kind of ecstatic trance. I remember entering the ruined hall—and the healing virtue of the Magia going out of me to touch all of you. I remember how the power faded. Then it all goes blank."

Tessa nodded. "You collapsed. I've never seen anyone so exhausted in my life. I was afraid you and Kherryn had spent yourselves beyond recovery."

"In Kherryn's case, I'm afraid that might be true—at least as far as her mage-powers are concerned," said Caradoc. "When I got to her, she was very nearly finished. I was barely in time to save her life. It was already too late to prevent her from exhausting her gifts."

"Then you think she's lost her powers forever?" asked Tessa.

"She's lost them for the moment. Whether or not she will ever recover them, only time will tell," said Caradoc gravely. "She's all right otherwise?"

"Physically? Oh yes," said Tessa, "though the ordinaire in charge here says she still needs rest. With both her brother and Evelake safe and well, I don't think—somehow—she'll be too dismayed to learn that her mage-powers may have abandoned her. In fact, quite the contrary. Rumor has it that she and Evelake are to be formally betrothed, once the work of setting this kingdom to rights is well begun. This way she is free to follow the counsels of her heart."

That much, at least, was true. Even though she had come to accept her gifts as a mage, Kherryn had never found those gifts an easy burden to bear. Caradoc's own feelings were mixed. Aloud he said, "Where's Evelake now?"

"He and Devon both returned to Gand following my father's funeral," said Tessa. "With the aid of Dorian Du Ghelleryn, they're attempting to sort out all the damage that has been done there."

"Dorian Du Ghelleryn? The Seneschal of Glyn Regis?" Caradoc was mildly astonished. "I thought he's washed his hands of the conflict."

"Apparently when it came down to it, his conscience—or maybe his pride—wouldn't let him sit back and do nothing," said Tessa. "It's to his credit that when the people of Gand begged his help, he put together a fleet of ships and set sail to relieve the city.

"They arrived on the eve of the battle," she continued. "Seven ships from Glyn Regis, and another nine supplied by a surviving contingent of Merchant-Adventurers. While the Devourer was still present in the flesh the demon-storm prevented them from entering the harbor. But once the storm dissipated, they moved in and set out to deal with the enemy force that still remained."

"I gather, then, that Dorian and Evelake have made peace within the family," said Caradoc wryly.

"Indeed," said Tessa. "The old man would never admit as much, but it's obvious to anyone with eyes that he's glad to find he has a living grandson after all."

She paused, her brow furrowed in thought. "Speaking of family, what are they going to do about Gythe? What ought they to do?"

"What's been done so far?" asked Caradoc.

"Nothing. The mages here at Maeldune have taken him into their care, along with what's left of the men and women who were in closest affinity with the demon. None of them," said Tessa, "have much sense left them. Gythe has the wits of a three-year-old child."

Caradoc grimaced. "I rather expected that might be the case. In order to wrest him from the grip of the Devourer, I had to use extreme force. It was bound to have a catastrophic effect."

"If you ask me, I'd say it was probably a mercy,"

said Tessa. She shrugged. "How do you summon to justice someone who's little better than a simpleton? Even Harlech allowed as much before he and Gudmar left Gand."

"Where have they gone?" asked Caradoc.

"North to Briekirk," said Tessa. "All the Merchant-Adventurers who remain are assembling there to take stock of their numbers and their assets. Gudmar tells me that it will be their first step on the way toward rebuilding the League."

"They're not the only ones with a lot of rebuilding to do," said Caradoc. He sank back on his elbows, his green eyes momentarily dark and far-seeking. "How much is left of the Hospitallers' Order, I wonder?" he murmured softly. "When I think of Ambrothen—of Farrowaithe—of Tavenern, there seem to be so many dead, so much light gone out of the world. The Order is like a house in ruins. It would take a miracle to raise it up again."

"Either a miracle," said Tessa, "or a worker of miracles."

Her tone startled Caradoc out of his darkling reverie. Seeing that she had his attention, Tessa continued. "It's true that nearly all the members of the full College of Magisters are dead. But a far greater number of others have survived: novices, servitors, ordinaires. They are the foundations of the Order. And they're not asking for a miracle, they're asking only for a leader."

Her blue eyes held a flash of expectancy. Caradoc said, "You make it sound as though they already had someone in mind."

"It's more definite than that," said Tessa. She drew a deep breath. "All the existing members of the Order who could be found have gathered here at Maeldune to discuss their future. The feeling appears to be almost unanimous that you, and you alone, have the necessary strength and spiritual vision to reforge the Order—as its new Arch-Mage."

Caradoc assimiliated this announcement in silence. "I know what you're thinking," said Tessa. "You're wondering if your would-be subordinates aren't simply letting themselves get carried away in the heat of the moment, mistaking gratitude for good judgment. But let me remind you: you have already been singled out by the Magia. You may have no choice but to accept the role that your colleagues demand of you."

"We'll see," said Caradoc. He shook his head in some doubt. "What they may not realize—yet—is that the Order cannot simply be revived. If it is to continue to serve as a vessel for divine power, it may have to be changed—as I was changed. The talents of individuals like Margoth and Kherryn, not less than the capabilities of someone like Borthen, must be examined and questioned. What is good must be carefully nurtured, while what is evil must be vigorously combated—wherever it occurs, in men and women alike."

He sighed. "As Arch-Mage, I would be bound to uphold the spiritual enlargement of the Order. And who knows where that may lead? In the event of a conflict arising over schooling or membership, I couldn't promise to uphold tradition at the cost of the physical and spiritual welfare of the people committed to our care. Anyone who thinks he wants to risk giving me authority had better understand this."

"You will have your chance to give them fair warning—when the synod meets again tomorrow," said Tessa. "But I don't think you will make anyone change his mind who has already committed it to your election."

She was smiling, but a small betraying throb had crept into her voice. Hearing it, Caradoc caught her free hand and drew her closer to him. "What are you afraid of?" he asked softly. "That the Order will prove too demanding a mistress for me to desire a human bride?"

Tessa resisted the strong pull of his eyes and his arms. "What do you think?" she asked.

Caradoc's smile was very tender. "That nothing—not power, not eminence, not the expectations of other men—*nothing* will alter the fact that I love you.

"Don't you realize how essential you are to me?" he went on. "At Glaive's Hough, you saw into my heart of hearts. You know that I am telling you the truth when I say that I need you as much as I want you. What I want to know in return is, are you brave enough to accept me on those terms?"

Tessa's eyes were brighter than the sapphires at her throat. "My soul, too, is an open book," she said with a melting laugh. "Look there, and read the answer."

Then said nothing more, for Caradoc had silenced her lips with his own, as a seal and a pledge.

THE BEST IN FANTASY

THE BEST IN HORROR